Caroline Graham was bo educated at Nuneaton High the Open University. She was for the Theatre, and has written several plays for both radio and theatre, as well as the hugely popular and critically acclaimed Chief Inspector Barnaby novels.

Caroline Graham lives in Suffolk.

A Place of Safety

Caroline Graham

headline

First published in 1999
by HEADLINE BOOK PUBLISHING

First published in paperback in 1999
by HEADLINE BOOK PUBLISHING

2

ISBN 978-0-7553-3495-7

Typeset by Avon Dataset Ltd, Bidford-on-Avon, Warks

Printed and bound in Great Britain by
Clays Ltd, St Ives plc

HEADLINE BOOK PUBLISHING
A division of the Hodder Headline Group
338 Euston Road
London NW1 3BH

For my friend

PATRICIA HOULIHAN

*without whom none of it
would have happened*

CHAPTER ONE

Every night, at exactly the same time and whatever the weather, Charlie Leathers took the dog for a walk. When Mrs Leathers heard the gate of their breeze block council bungalow click to, she would peep through a gap in the net curtains to check he was on his way then switch the television back on.

Mr Leathers was usually out about half an hour but his wife would set her kitchen timer for twenty minutes then switch the set off just to be on the safe side. Once he had come back early, stared suspiciously at the newly blank screen and laid the back of his hand against the glass. It was still warm. Hetty had to listen to a droning lecture on how it stood to reason that nothing worth watching was on after ten and it was a known fact that valves wore out more quickly during the hours of darkness. Once she had had the temerity to ask him who paid the licence fee out of their wages and he hadn't spoken for three days.

Anyway this night – or the night in question as the police were to call it once its significance was appreciated – he was out rather longer than usual. Hetty could have watched every moment of *Absolutely Fabulous*. It was only a repeat but was still her favourite programme, being as far removed from her everyday life of domestic drudgery as it was possible to imagine.

★ ★ ★

Bright moonlight washed over the village green, illuminating the Best Kept Village notice and Ferne Basset's amateurishly painted coat of arms. This was a made-up, folkloric affair showing a badger rampant, several sheaves of wheat, crossed cricket bats and an unnaturally vivid lime green chrysanthemum.

Charlie Leathers strode across the shorn grass and onto the pavement opposite. He directed an angry stare at the dark mass of half-finished new homes and builder's equipment next to the pub and kicked a pile of bricks as he went by. He passed several Victorian cottages and a remarkable modern house made almost entirely of glass, over which the moonlight ran like silver rain. A few yards further and he was entering the churchyard behind which lay the beginnings of Carter's Wood. He walked quickly with the angry, vehement energy that drove all his movements. Charlie never relaxed and even slept twitching, sometimes flailing at the air with clenched fists.

The Jack Russell kept up as best she could, trotting along with many an anxious, upward glance. Tiredness or hard stones along the way were no excuse for faltering. A savage hoik on the collar or an even sharper flick of leather on her tender nose kept her up to scratch. She was only allowed to pause once to do what she had been brought out to do. A wee was accomplished hopping on three legs. And the wonderfully rich and varied scents that thickened the night air remained for ever unexplored.

After being half dragged through a tangle of thick brambles and undergrowth, Candy was relieved to find herself padding on soft leaf mould before a sideways yank on the lead pulled her round in an awkward half-circle as they turned to go home.

This involved approaching Tall Trees Lane, where Charlie lived, in the opposite direction from which they had left. This way they would pass some semi-detached bungalows, several almshouses, the village shop and the church of St Timothy in Torment. And then, before the money started to show itself again, there was the river.

The Misbourne was fast-running and deep. A shallow weir a few hundred yards downstream made a soft swishing sound which mingled with the rustle of leaves in the still night air. Over the river was a stone bridge with a carved parapet barely three feet high.

Charlie had just walked across this when he heard shouting. He stood very still and listened. Noises are hard to place at night and at first he thought the shrill, angry voices were coming from the council houses where people couldn't care less who heard them rowing. But then they suddenly became louder – perhaps because someone had opened a door – and he realised the source was the building close by the church: the Old Rectory.

Charlie hurried into the churchyard, stood on tiptoe and peered eagerly over the yew hedge. He wound Candy's lead round and round his hand until she was almost choking. Warning her to be quiet.

Light from the hallway spilled out, flooding the front steps. A girl ran out calling something over her shoulder, the sense of it distorted by gulping sobs. There was an anguished cry from inside the house. 'Carlotta, Carlotta! Wait!'

As the girl hared off down the drive, Charlie quickly

backed round the corner of the hedge. Not that she would have noticed him. Her face as she ran by, just a few feet away, was blind with tears.

'Come back!'

More running. A regular pounding on the gravel and a second woman, some years older but no less distressed, flew across his line of vision.

'Leave me alone.'

Reaching the bridge, the girl had turned. Although the way behind her was perfectly clear, Charlie had the most vivid impression of a wild creature at bay.

'I didn't mean any harm!'

'I know, Carlotta.' The woman approached cautiously. 'It's all right. You mustn't—'

'It was my last chance – coming to you.'

'There's no need for all this.' Her voice was soothing. 'Try and calm down.'

The girl climbed onto the parapet.

'For God's sake—'

'They'll send me to prison.'

'You don't have to—'

'I thought I'd be safe here.'

'You were – are. I've just said—'

'Where else can I go?' She hung her head, exhausted by her tears, swaying precariously backwards then jerking upright again with a little cry of fear. 'Ahh . . . what will happen to me?'

'Now don't be silly.' The woman moved forward, her face and hair ghostly in the moonlight. 'Nothing's going to happen to you.'

'I might as well be dead.' The girl on the bridge became considerably more agitated, covering her face with her hands and once more starting to cry, rocking wretchedly back and forth.

Momentarily unobserved, the woman approached quickly. Softly. She was level with the girl. Had her arms wrapped round the slender legs.

'Get down, Carlotta. Look – I'll hold your hand.'

'Don't touch me!'

Charlie Leathers had been easing forward, a breath at a time, while all this was going on. Tugged into the drama, not caring, such was his excitement, that he might be seen.

The moon slid behind a cloud. Detail was lost but there was still light enough to outline a dark agitated shape, grotesquely tall, as if one woman was balanced on the other's shoulders. For a few seconds they wrestled backwards and forwards, grunting.

The girl cried again, 'Don't . . . don't push—'

Then there was a terrible cry and a splash as something heavy hit the water. Then silence.

Charlie stepped back into the shelter of the hedge. He was trembling, his nerve ends jumping like fleas on a hot plate. It was some time before he could start to make his way home. And when he did, more than one person noted his progress, for an English country village, despite all appearances to the contrary, is never quite asleep.

For instance, in the beautiful glass house Valentine Fainlight and his sister Louise were enjoying a ferocious game of chess. Valentine played with savage vigour and a determination to win. He would swoop over the board, snatch up pieces and wave them in the air triumphantly. Louise, more detached but equally resolute, remained very still. She would smile, a cool parting of the lips, after a successful move but showed neither disappointment nor displeasure in the face of failure.

'Checkmate!' The board was tipped over and the figures, dark blue resin styled in the manner of mythical beasts and warriors, clattered and fell. Immediately Louise got up and walked away.

'Don't sulk, Lou. Fair and square. Wasn't it?'

'As much as anything ever is with you.'

'I wouldn't mind a glass of something.'

There was no denying that, so far, it had been good having Louise around. Valentine had been edgily uncertain when she had first asked if she might come and stay. He was sorry for her, of course. The break-up of her marriage had caused real damage. For the first time in her life she had been dealt wounds deeper that those she had inflicted. But it had worked out very well. On the whole.

To allay his anxiety and emphasise the transitory nature of her visit, Louise brought only two small suitcases. A month later she collected the rest of her clothes. Then her books and a tea chest full of stuff that had what is described as only sentimental value. Packing these things had hurt so much (why do people say 'only?') that the crate remained in the garage, unopened.

'A spot of Casa Porta would be nice.'

Louise started to pull the curtains. These were immensely long and full yet almost weightless, being made of gossamer-fine fabric scattered with pale stars. There was a gap between the upper floor, suspended from a huge loft by steel cables, and the external wall and the curtains fell through this, tumbling from the top of the house to the bottom, over a hundred feet to the ground. When Louise walked along, pulling them behind her, she always felt like someone in a theatre at the beginning of a play. Halfway across she stopped.

'There's Charlie Leathers with that poor little dog.'

'Aahh . . .'

'Why do you have to mock everything?'

'Not quite everything.'

No, thought Louise. If only.

'You're turning into a village drab, woman. Peering through the acrylics. You'll be joining the WI next.'

Louise stood for a moment staring at the dark, shifting silhouettes of trees. And the houses, solid black building blocks. She pictured people asleep, dreaming. Or awake, overcome by night-time fears of illness and their own eventual decay. As she moved again, the muslin soft against her arm, her brother called, 'Hang on.'

Louise stood still. She knew what was coming and kept her thoughts deliberately even and colourless. There really was nothing more to be said. They had exhausted all the arguments. In a way, having been through the same fire, she could sympathise.

'Is the blue door open?'

'It's too dark to see.'

'What about a light in the flat?'

The Old Rectory was shrouded by trees but the garage, over which the flat was built, stood some way from the house and was clearly visible.

'No.'

'Let's have a look.'

'Val, there's nothing to look at.'

'Humour me, darling.'

They stood together staring into the night. Louise averted her eyes from the sensual hunger and raging tenderness that consumed her brother's features. They waited for a few moments then she lifted Val's hand and pressed it sadly against her cheek. As she did this the powerful headlights of a car swept down the village street and turned into the Old Rectory drive.

Ann Lawrence was not asleep. But when she heard the front door slam and her husband climb the stairs, she jumped into bed, shut her eyes and lay very still thanking God they slept in separate rooms. Lionel opened the door of her room, spoke her name without lowering his voice, waited a while, gave an irritated sigh and briskly closed it.

Ann got up again and started once more to pace about, padding up and down softly on the faded yellow Aubusson carpet. She could not be still for a minute. Had not been still since that terrifying moment on the bridge when Carlotta had slipped from her grasp and drowned. For surely, by now, she must have drowned.

Ann had run along the side of the river calling, crying her name, staring into the dark, rapidly swirling water. Ran until she was exhausted. Eventually she reached the weir, a narrow strip of foam, curling and hissing in the moonlight. Nothing. Not the slightest sign of life, animal or human.

She trudged back to the village sick with emotion and fear. What could she do? Her watch showed that nearly half an hour had gone by since the accident had happened. What would be the point of telling anyone now? On the other hand, how could she not? Suppose, by some miracle, Carlotta had not drowned but was caught up somewhere beyond the weir. Perhaps she had managed to grab an overhanging branch and was hanging frantically on, cold, soaking wet and desperate for help.

Ann saw now that she had made a dreadful mistake in racing along the river bank, searching and calling. It had been instinctive, a natural human impulse. What she should have done was run to the nearest telephone and dial the emergency services. Surely they would not have taken half an hour. And they would be properly equipped with lights and ropes. And divers.

There was a telephone box next to the Red Lion now quietly shuttered against the night, all revellers departed. Ann stabbed at the figure nine three times, the receiver slipping and twirling in her sweaty hand. Asked what service she required she hesitated then said the police. They would notify the ambulance service surely, should one be necessary.

She described the situation somewhat incoherently while still managing to make it plain that a person had fallen into a river and been swiftly carried away. A search immediately afterwards had proved fruitless. She gave the exact locations but then, asked what time the accident happened, stared at her watch, struggling to make sense of the figures on the dial. She said she didn't know. Perhaps half an hour ago. Maybe less. And then the person on the other end of the line wanted her name.

Ann dropped the receiver which swung and clattered against the glass. Her throat constricted suddenly as if a hand had gripped it tight. She stood rigidly, swamped by horror. *Her name*. How could she possibly give her name? Her mind leapt ahead and saw it printed in large letters across the front page of the local newspaper – maybe even the nationals. She pictured the repercussions. Her husband's distress and its possible effect on his reputation. His sorrowful disappointment not only at her failure to provide the secure environment that Carlotta had so urgently needed but that she had actually driven the girl from the house. At least that was how it would appear.

Ann slid into a maelstrom of miserable reflection. When she emerged moments later, wretched and on the verge of tears, it was to realise she had put the phone back on the hook.

Fortunately there was no one to see her return home. Ann was horrified at the sight of herself in the hall mirror. Face streaked with dirt. Shoes and stockings soaked through. She was shivering as the sweat generated by her mad dash along the river bank dried coldly on her skin.

She started to run a bath before she had even taken off her coat. Bypassing her husband's Radox which promised to 'soothe away aches and pains, easing tension and tiredness', she reached for Molton Brown's Sensual Foaming Bath. A Christmas present from Louise Fainlight, ravishingly scented, wonderfully effervescent and surely much more likely to ease tension and soothe pain. Tiredness was not a problem. She had never felt so wide awake. Was inclined to believe she would never sleep again. Unscrewing the cap, she noticed without surprise that the bottle, which she had used only once, was nearly empty.

She dropped her clothes on the floor, put on a robe and went downstairs to pour herself a drink. There wasn't much choice. Harvey's Bristol Cream. Some dregs of Dubonnet which her husband would drown in soda and sip rather daringly. Rose's Lime Juice.

Ann sighed, terribly tempted in her present frame of mind to empty the lot into a giant tumbler and swig herself to oblivion. She opened the huge carved sideboard and discovered, right at the back, a single bottle of Sainsbury's claret. Five minutes later, lying in perfumed water and knocking back the fruity stuff, she replayed the dreadful events of the past two hours a frame at a time. She could still hardly believe that the ground could have been so violently snatched from under her. Or that events had whirled out of control at such a speed. Surely there must have been some point at which she could have avoided being sucked into the eye of the storm?

It had all started with the disappearance of her mother's earrings. Delicate exquisite things: rose diamonds and emeralds on an amethyst clip. They had been given to Ann on her eighteenth birthday, together with a fob watch on a watered silk strap, a garnet and turquoise necklace and several beautiful rings, too small for all but her littlest finger.

She had been looking for a handkerchief when she noticed that the tortoiseshell silk scarf under which she kept her carved jewel box had been moved. She opened the box. The earrings had gone.

Ann rarely used any of the jewellery. The life she led gave little opportunity for wearing such lovely things – or showing them off, as her husband would have put it. We mustn't flaunt our wealth, he would frequently say in his bland, determinedly non-critical way. And Ann always agreed, never ever pointing out that it was in fact her wealth.

She sifted through the other items in the box, her fingers shaking. She counted the rings, held the necklace briefly to her heart then put everything back. Nothing else was missing. She stared at her pale face in the glass, at her sandy lashes already fluttering and blinking with apprehension. But she couldn't, she *wouldn't* let it pass.

The fact that she knew who had taken the earrings made things worse rather than better. It meant a confrontation. Something from which her very private soul shrank. But the only alternative was telling Lionel and that would mean a deeply embarrassing meeting between the three of them. Herself struggling to appear non-accusatory. Lionel twisting himself into compassionate knots trying to understand and excuse and forgive Carlotta. Carlotta either denying she had taken them, in which case what could they do? Or playing her deprived, unhappy background card, whining that she never meant any harm. All she had wanted was to try them on, having never owned anything worthwhile or beautiful in her whole wretched unloved young life.

Ann was pretty certain that Carlotta occasionally wore some of her clothes. She had noticed a rather sour smell on one or two shirts and dresses. And various items had disappeared before. Some rather expensive diamond-patterned tights. A pair of fur gloves left in her coat pocket in the hall. Small amounts of money from her purse. Pretty much what she had come to expect from Lionel's succession of lame ducks.

Lifting her head, Ann stared upwards in the general direction of Carlotta's room from which came the relentless thud, thud, thud of rock music. It was played from the moment the girl got up until eleven at night: a curfew Lionel had imposed as, by then, even his patience was wearing thin.

She would have to tread carefully. Carlotta was supposed to have a history of instability. When she had first arrived, Lionel had urged caution, assuring his wife that the slightest criticism or pressure to embrace petty, bourgeois restrictions could well tip Carlotta over the edge. So far Ann had seen little sign of this. In fact she was starting to think the boot could well be on the other foot.

She felt queasy, as she always did when faced by the compulsion to demonstrate aggression. Feeling it, no problem. Showing it, well, maybe tomorrow. But perhaps – Ann started to backtrack – it might not after all be necessary. For instance, shouldn't she first make sure the jewellery was really missing?

Relieved at the possibility of postponement, Ann removed the top drawer, tipped the contents out on the bed and started to sort carefully through her tights and underwear. No earrings. She checked the other two drawers. Same result.

She recalled clearly the last time she wore them. It was the anniversary of her mother's death. Ann had taken fresh flowers to the grave. While her grown-up self had poured water into the stone urn and carefully arranged yellow roses with buds like candle flames, her six-year-old self, aching with grief and loss, had longed for her mother to appear, just for a moment. Just long enough to see that she was wearing the earrings. That she had not forgotten. That she would never forget.

The music suddenly became very loud. Whether it was this ugly intrusion into her painful reflections or the renewed conviction that the girl had indeed stolen one of her most precious possessions, Ann suddenly found the courage to move. She strode along the landing, half ran, half stumbled up the attic steps and banged on the door.

The volume increased again, hugely this time. The pounding bass battered her eardrums, burst through, invaded the inside of her head. The wooden panels of the door and the boards beneath her feet danced and shuddered. Consumed by anger – *this is my house, my house!* – Ann thundered on the door with her fists until the knuckles grazed.

The music stopped. A few moments later Carlotta appeared, standing square in the doorway in her dusty black jeans and T-shirt. Split sneakers on her feet. Long matted dark hair tugged through a purple scrunch band. She wore the expression so frequently present when they were alone together. One of amused contempt. Then she ducked under the Mind Your Head notice, crossed the threshold and stood, blocking Ann's way.

'Got a problem, Mrs Lawrence?'

'I'm afraid I have.'

Ann stepped boldly forward and, surprised by the sudden movement, Carlotta stood aside. She did not follow Ann into the room which was very untidy and reeked of cigarette smoke.

'What's that then?'

'I can't seem to find my mother's earrings.'

'So?'

Ann took a deep breath. 'I was wondering if you'd . . .'

'Thieved 'em?'

'Borrowed. Perhaps.'

'I don't wear old lady's stuff. Thanks all the same.'

'They were in my jewellery box the other day—'

'You calling me a liar?' Spittle flew as the words twisted thin scarlet lips.

'Of course not, Carlotta.'

'Search the place then. Go on.'

She knows I never would, thought Ann. Especially with her standing there watching. She imagined calling Carlotta's bluff but couldn't bear the humiliation of not finding the earrings. Or the awful scene that could ensue if she did.

She wondered if the jewellery had already been pawned or sold and felt quite ill at the idea. She pictured her precious things being handled by knowing, dirty fingers. Money, a fraction of what they were worth, changing hands. It was this that prompted her fatally rash next words.

'If you do know anything about this I'd like them returned by tomorrow. Otherwise I shall have to tell my—'

The girl ran forward then, pushing past Ann with so much force she nearly fell backwards. Carlotta hurtled around the room, pulling out drawers and tipping the contents over the bed – make-up, tights, underwear, hair spray. A box of powder burst: tawny dust flew everywhere. She ripped down posters, pulled old clothes out of the wardrobe and cushions from chairs, shook open magazines, tearing savagely at the pages.

'Don't seem to be here, do they! Or fucking here! Or here neither!'

'No! Carlotta – *please*.' It was a cry of horror. Ann realised Carlotta was weeping as she stumbled blindly about. 'Look, it doesn't matter. I must have made a mistake.'

'You'll still tell him though, I know you. Any chance to get rid of me.'

'That's not true.' Ann, facing the fact, protested too much.

'You don't know what it's like out there, do you? You spoiled bitch! You ain't got a sodding clue.'

Ann hung her head. What could she say? It was true. She didn't know what it was like out there. She didn't have a clue. The savage snarling raged on.

'You any idea what it's meant to me, this place? People want to harm you where I come from, you know?' She dragged her sleeve roughly across her face, grossly swollen with tears. 'They want to do you damage. Now he'll send me back!'

It was then she ran away. One second she was screaming in Ann's face and throwing books about. The next, gone. Down the stairs. Across the hall. Out into the night.

At this point Ann, by now lying in nearly cold water, struggled to put a clamp on these wretched reminiscences. She wrapped herself in her robe and took the claret and her glass into the bedroom. She drank a little wine but it made her feel sick so she simply lay down on the bed and prayed for oblivion. But it was nearly dawn before she fell asleep.

CHAPTER TWO

There was a certain amount of talk the next day in and around the village touching on the possibility that someone might have fallen in the river over Swan Myrren way. The Wren Davis milkman, whose cousin lived nearer the spot, said the police were there round about midnight. And an ambulance. He, his wife and the neighbours went out to see what was going on but the police were not very forthcoming. Asked a few questions but didn't give much in the way of answers. After a while they worked their way down river and that was the last the milkman's cousin saw of them.

But although the excitement was over almost before it had begun that did not stop Ferne Basset making something of a meal of it. Drama had been in short supply since the church fete when the pig, whose weight everyone was trying to guess, had broken out of its pen and ran amok, laying waste several stalls and making a mess in the refreshment tent.

In Monday's pension queue at the post office it was generally agreed that there was no smoke without fire. The police would not turn out for nothing and were no doubt concealing the true state of things for reasons of their own. It would all turn up, sooner or later, on *Crime Watch*. Disappointment that no one in their own village seemed to have disappeared was well concealed.

17

The conversation in Brian's Emporium, the single tiny self-service shop, had a harder edge. A bloody hoaxer, was Brian's opinion. Nothing better to do than waste police time with daft phone calls. If he could get his hands on them. Someone in the lottery line-up suggested it might be the old lady who lived near Penfold's Mill and was sometimes to be found wandering and reciting poetry. The poetry clinched it. People dispersed to await the news that she had been found floating downstream supported only by a brace of rhyming couplets.

Lunchtime in the Red Lion saw a more crude, even heartless response. Many customers suggested well-known personalities who could well be spared and were more than welcome to a watery grave. These included politicians, sportsmen and television personalities. The conversation then got more personal and several relatives, neighbours, a spouse or two and, inevitably, someone's mother-in-law were thrown into the ring.

Louise Fainlight heard the rumour from their postman. She strolled into the huge steel garage where Val was racing through his daily twenty miles, today on a dazzling Chaz Butler. The bike was balanced on rollers which made a powerful humming noise, like a tremendous swarm of bees. Speed transformed the wheels to a blur of flashing light.

Louise loved to watch her brother exercise though she knew he didn't really like this. Val rode like a man possessed, his face a grimacing mask of concentrated effort, eyes invisible behind screwed-up lids, lips clamped together over gritted teeth. Perspiration flew from his body in a constant glittering spray. Every now and again, when his legs would not, *could* not go any faster he cursed, using imaginative and profane language.

When he did this Louise laughed, relishing the contrast between this demonic display and the ironically detached persona Val liked to present to the workaday world.

She heard the computer attached to the frame click off. The humming gradually became less powerful, the outline of the wheels more distinct. Then the spokes. The hubs. The delicate but immensely strong chain. And finally the bike was still. Val climbed down, the powerful muscles in his legs and shoulders still quivering. Louise handed him a towel.

'You'll be back in the Tour de France yet.'

'Too old,' Valentine grunted and mopped his streaming face. He took the machine off the runners and placed it carefully at the back of the garage where there were already almost a dozen others. 'Got the coffee on?'

'Of course.'

'Good.' They made their way across a covered walkway leading to a verandah at the back of the house. 'Any mail?'

'Only junk. And some gossip from Postman Pat.'

'I was promised the proofs for *Barley Roscoe and the Hopscotch Kid*.'

'Don't you want to know what it is?'

'What what is?'

'The gossip.'

'For God's sake, woman.'

'Someone's jumped into the river down by the weir.'

'It's Lavazza, the coffee – right?'

'Right.'

'Good. I didn't like that chocolatey stuff we had last week.'

It was the cruellest type of day imaginable in which to wake to anguish and remorse. Ann, curled up tight, arms straitjacketed round her body, agonising cramp in every limb, squinted at the lovely pattern of greyish leaves floating and shifting on her bedroom ceiling. Through the window she could see a rectangle of brilliant blue sky. The whole room was flooded with autumn sunshine.

Already the torture had begun. The whole dreadful business of the previous evening, powerfully animated and brilliantly lit as if on a cinema screen, running and re-running through her mind. Herself climbing the attic stairs full of apprehension. Carlotta howling and throwing books and clothes around the room, her flight into the darkness. The quickly flowing water.

Today Ann would have to tell Lionel. She *must* tell him. He would want to know where Carlotta was. But, without knowing why, Ann knew she couldn't reveal the whole truth.

Not that he wasn't the most understanding of men. And to understand all, as she had so often been told, was to forgive all. He made endless and sometimes, she thought, foolish allowances for all the young people taken temporarily under his wing. Those to whom society had shown only a cruel indifference. The distraught and abandoned, the criminal and near criminal. She had always (with one exception) tried to welcome them into her home.

Ann hesitated because she knew Lionel would be bitterly disappointed in her. Even ashamed. And rightly so. What excuse could there possibly be for a woman in her late thirties, coming from a secure family background, comfortably off and living in a large, beautiful house to turn on a wretched creature who had taken refuge there and drive her into the night? Only the disappearance of a pair of earrings which she may or may not have taken. Which was no excuse at all.

Ann got out of bed, painfully straightening her bruised limbs. She put on her rose brocade slippers, stretched her arms to the ceiling then touched her toes, wincing.

Lionel would sleep for a while yet. He was home quite late last night. Ann decided to make herself some tea, take it to the library and work out just what she was going to say to him.

She was putting on her dressing gown when she heard the front door open and her daily help call out, 'Mrs Lawrence? Hello? A lovely day.'

Ann hurried onto the landing, forcing a smile and some semblance of warmth into her voice. She leaned over the stairwell and called a greeting back. 'Good morning, Hetty.'

Evadne Pleat, of Mulberry Cottage, the Green, had just concluded the most important business of her day, namely the loving care and maintenance of her six Pekinese dogs. Brushing, washing, clipping, feeding, worming and walking. Their temperatures had to be taken, their collars checked for cleanliness and comfort, their beautiful creamy fur closely investigated lest any foreign body should have dared to trespass.

Once this elaborate routine was over, Evadne had

her breakfast (usually some porridge and an Arbroath Smokie) then placed a white Kashmir geranium in the kitchen window. This signalled that she was 'at home' and from then on her day was so crammed with incident she had hardly a moment to breathe. The reason for her popularity was simple. Evadne was a miraculously good listener.

It is rare to come across someone more interested in others than in themselves and the inhabitants of Ferne Basset were quick to appreciate Evadne's remarkable qualities. She always seemed to have the time to give people her absolute attention. Her eyes never strayed towards the face of her pretty grandmother clock nor did its sweet chimes ever distract. Whatever the subject under discussion, she would always appear sympathetic. And totally discreet.

Inevitably people started to seek her out. The most comfortable chair in her cluttered little sitting room was always occupied by some troubled or excited soul getting it all off their chest while being sustained by shortbread tails and Earl Grey. Or, after 6 p.m., Noilly Prat and Epicure cheese footballs.

Evadne never gave advice, which, if they'd thought about it, would have surprised her visitors for they always left feeling comforted, occasionally going as far as to say they could now see their way clear. Sometimes they even regarded the people they had come to complain bitterly about in an entirely different light.

This day, of course, they talked about nothing but supposed events on the river bank. Lack of any solid evidence did not hold back a flood of almost Gothic extravagance. Not that there was anything to go on, she must understand. The vaguest of stories, my dear.

Apparently no one actually *heard* anything. Even so – no smoke without fire. By the time Evadne's lunch break arrived she was rather regretting that she had no writing talent for she had enough melodramatic narrative to keep a soap opera going for the next ten years.

At lunchtime she removed her geranium and called Piers, the oldest and most sensible of the Pekes, to her. Gave it a basket with a note and some money in an envelope and sent it round to Brian's Emporium for her *Times*, some Winalot and a few iced fancies. She was out of tonic water too but felt it wasn't right to expect a dog to struggle with heavy bottles.

When Piers came back with the wrong change (not for the first time), Evadne put the Yale down and started to prepare lunch. She sweated a couple of shallots and some chopped celery in unsalted butter, threw in a bay leaf, added fresh chicken stock and left the pan bubbling quietly. Then she poured out a small glass of elderflower wine and laid the table. Beautiful silver cutlery – a retirement present from the library staff at Swiss Cottage – a spray of hothouse mimosa, warm granary rolls.

As she stirred the soup and sipped her homemade pick-me-up, Evadne could not help her thoughts straying to the matter that had so concerned all her morning visitors. She wondered if anyone really had fallen into the water. And if they had, where were they now? Could they already have floated miles away? Or become caught up in weeds? Maybe they were stuck in the muddy river bed.

Evadne's hand trembled as she found a packet of cardamoms and took down her mortar and pestle, and her heart swelled with pity for this perhaps mythical person. Drowning was the one thing Evadne was afraid of. Once at school, asked to read from *Richard III*, she had been given the scene describing the death of Clarence and had nearly choked on the horror of it. Suddenly feeling less adventurous, she replaced the cardamoms on the shelf and served up the soup straight.

She was sitting down to eat it – indeed the spoon was halfway to her lips – when she suddenly remembered something that had happened the previous night. She had been in her bedroom under the eaves and preparing to retire. Having changed into a long winceyette nightie and sponged her face with rainwater and Pears soap, as she had done since she was a child, Evadne said her prayers. As always she brought various names to God's attention, even suggesting the odd course of action whilst allowing that, naturally, the final choice must be His. Then she climbed into bed.

Evadne always slept on her back, her hands crossed on her breast like an effigy in an old country church. She liked to think that, should her soul slip its moorings while she was unconscious, her remains would be discovered in a state of worshipful neatness. Invariably she fell straightaway into composed and dreamless sleep but last night, on the point of drifting off, she had been shocked into wakefulness by a strange cry, loud and rather fearful, almost a scream. At the time she had assumed it was a vixen or perhaps a small mammal caught in some predator's grip. But now, sitting in a bright, sunlit kitchen and staring into her rapidly cooling soup, Evadne was not so sure.

She gave herself a shake and told herself firmly that,

even if she had been mistaken and the cries turned out to be human, there could surely be no connection. Everyone said that whoever had fallen into the Misbourne had done so near Swan Myrren. And these sounds came from much nearer home. Even so . . .

Evadne finished her soup quickly, placed the dishes in the sink and her geranium back in the window. When the knocker was almost immediately lifted, she hurried to open the door. For this was one of the rare occasions when Evadne needed human company almost as much as it needed her.

Round about four o'clock that same afternoon Louise Fainlight called to see Ann Lawrence. They had become casual friends in a rather hit and miss way for, apart from a love of gardening, they had little in common. Certainly Louise was aware that, were she still living and working in London, they would have been ships that passed in the night hardly recognising, let alone acknowledging, each other's existence.

But in a small village choice is limited and, finding someone at least halfway compatible, an effort is nearly always made. And it was true that both women had come to find each other intriguing. Neither could understand how the other could possibly live the way they did.

Ann admired and was slightly afraid of Louise's glamour, her tough, ironical attitude to life in general and the joking, seemingly detached relationship she had with her brother. The younger woman's willingness to fight her corner was a source of envy. Some of the situations she had had to deal with as an analyst in the stocks and shares department of a merchant bank where she had previously worked would have had Ann running to the nearest loo in terror.

For her part, Louise simply could not believe that a potentially extremely attractive woman of Ann's age and intelligence could spend her time day after day, month after month, year after year doing nothing. Or at least what Louise regarded as nothing. Dreary preoccupations such as pottering in the greenhouse, chairing the WI, editing and printing the parish magazine, organising the church flower and cleaning rota. Unbelievable.

Curiosity as to why her friend came to be married to such a dry stick of a man was easily satisfied, for everyone in the village knew the story. Ann had lived with her father, Ferne Basset's resident vicar and over fifty when she was born, until he died some twenty-two years later. His curate, Lionel Lawrence, a timid, pleasant man then in his forties, gradually took over the Reverend Byford's clerical duties and also helped Ann to care for him in his old age.

When he suggested to the unhappy, bereaved girl that they should continue to care for each other, Ann, unused to anything but life in a village parsonage and of a painfully shy disposition, agreed. A couple of years after they were married Lionel, though still ordained, gave up the curacy. This, he explained, was to give him time to do the Lord's work where the need was greatest. Fortunately there was no question of losing the house which had belonged to Ann's mother and not the diocese. Services were now taken, one Sunday in three, by a vicar who also covered two other villages. On the single occasion Louise broached the matter of Ann's marriage, her friend just said, 'It seemed the simplest thing to do,' and quickly changed the subject.

This seemed a sorry state of affairs to Louise. She was sure Ann was unhappy – who wouldn't be, married to such a boring old wimp? As for the series of delinquent layabouts he was constantly bringing into the house, well. Louise had made the mistake, early on in their relationship, of advising Ann to put her foot down. To her amazement she discovered that, far from being resentful of this invasion, Ann felt ashamed that she was not able to welcome and care for these 'sad youngsters' more wholeheartedly. She felt she had let her husband down.

After she had got her breath back, Louise launched into some serious backbone stiffening, trying to convince Ann that this point of view was seriously skew-whiff. That the majority of people would think even accepting such a situation showed remarkable tolerance. And that throwing oneself into it heart and soul would surely argue, at the very least, a few screws loose.

A waste of time. Ann tried to listen but soon showed signs of impatience and some distress. Louise gave up but, in one small respect, there was a positive outcome. Not too long after this conversation a young man arrived at the Old Rectory. The moment Ann saw him she felt her skin crawl and coldness drench her flesh and bones. Though he stood patiently on the doorstep and his voice was low and civil, Ann sensed a prodigious unkindness. He only looked at her once but this glance had gleamed like a knife searching for a point where it could force an entry.

Afraid, she sought out her husband and told him

she would not have the man in the house. Lionel had been annoyed of course, especially when she could give no sensible reason for such an attitude, but, somewhat alarmed at the vehemence with which she spoke, eventually gave way.

Louise had praised her afterwards for standing firm but Ann said there was nothing to praise. She had simply been driven. At the time Louise had thought it was all a bit pathetic. Now she understood. Now, when it was too late.

The newcomer was put in the flat above the garage which had a connecting phone to the house. He offered to look after and drive the ancient Humber Hawk, inherited from Ann's father and costing more than she could afford to maintain. Lionel, who did not drive, was delighted, seizing on this single courtesy as the first inkling of long-term reformation.

The car was standing in the drive now as Louise walked towards the house. Of the chauffeur she was glad to see there was no sign. She passed the tall dining-room windows and saw Lionel Lawrence using the telephone. He seemed agitated, his grey-white hair standing up like Struwelpeter's, waving his free arm in the air.

Louise was about to go up the front steps when she caught sight of Ann. She was sitting absolutely still on a canvas chair near the great cedar in the middle of the lawn. Louise went over.

'Hi. I've brought you some viola seedlings. White ones.' She put the damp package on the grass and sat down. 'Ann?'

Louise realised then that Ann was not in fact sitting absolutely still. Her whole body was trembling. Her lips opened and closed and quivered. She was screwing up her eyes and blinking.

'What on earth's the matter?'

'Ah, Louise . . . I've done something so . . . terrible . . . I can't tell you.' And she burst into tears. Louise put her arm round her friend's slim shoulders and Ann cried and cried, slowly realising just how much she had needed to.

'Tell me.'

'It's too awful.'

Louise reflected that what she and Ann would consider awful were two vastly different things. 'You haven't left old Mother Craven off the flower rota again?'

'I had a . . . row. With Carlotta.'

'Good for you.'

'She ran away.'

'I'll bet she did.' Louise had her own ideas about Carlotta.

'Lionel can't find her. He's tried everywhere.'

'Is that all?'

After a long pause, Ann whispered, 'Yes.' She had stopped shivering but had become intensely pale. Her eyes slid away, she gazed over Louise's shoulder, into the air, examined the ground.

Louise thought Ann was the worst liar she had ever come across. The first bit had been convincing. She believed there probably had been a row with Carlotta. The girl might even have run away. But that was not all there was to it. Not by a long chalk.

'When was this?'

'Last night.'

'Have you told the police?'

'No!' A small scream.

'All right, love.' Louise stroked Ann's hair. Slow, calming movements. 'All right . . .'

'Sorry.' Ann produced a crumpled ball of tissue from her skirt pocket and blew her nose. 'Lionel said she'd hate that. Bringing the . . . the pigs into it.'

Pigs indeed. Louise had no patience. If Lionel thought aping the young would make him one of them, he was well up the wrong tree. Next thing it'd be a baseball cap the wrong way round and a Radiohead T-shirt.

'I'm not leaving you out here.' She got up, holding Ann's hand, hoiking her up too. 'Come home and have some tea.'

'I can't.'

'Course you can.' She tucked Ann's arm through her own and marched her off down the drive. 'I've got a gorgeous coffee cake from M & S.'

'I should let Lionel know—'

'Rubbish. He won't even notice you've gone.'

'No,' agreed Ann sadly. 'I don't suppose he will.'

Candy always regarded herself as Mrs Leathers' dog and knew that Mrs Leathers felt the same. Neither of them made a thing about it, especially when Charlie was around. This evening he was in the front room where they usually ate and watched television and had been there so long and was so quiet, Mrs Leathers thought he must have fallen asleep. So she patted her lap. Candy hesitated then, after an anxious glance towards the closed connecting door, sprang up.

Mrs Leathers fondled her golden-brown ears, like little triangles of warm toast. She scratched the dog's stomach and Candy gave an ecstatic whine. Mrs Leathers wondered what her husband could possibly be doing. He had disappeared nearly an hour ago with yesterday's *People*, some scissors and a tube of Super Glue.

We shouldn't grumble, should we? Mrs Leathers said to Candy and they smiled at each other, snug as two bugs in the shabby old rocking chair next to the Raeburn. But when another twenty minutes had gone by and no sound or movement had been heard, Mrs Leathers reluctantly put the dog in her cheap plastic washing basket and went to see if everything was all right.

On the rackety gateleg table Charlie, wearing a pair of his wife's washing-up gloves, was cutting out large pieces from the newspaper. Old football coupons and loser's lottery tickets had all been pushed aside to make plenty of space.

Charlie cut smaller. And smaller still. Selecting a paragraph, a sentence, a final word, a letter. He released a rattling sigh of satisfaction. That hadn't been too difficult. Only six words needed and all what you might call common or garden.

Charlie removed his gloves and picked up a Rizla packet to make himself a smoke. Laid the pungent ginger threads of Samson tobacco in an untidy pile, rolled up, ran the grey, corrugated tip of his tongue along the width of the paper and lit the end.

A click of the latch and his wife stood on the threshold. Charlie sprang to his feet, scarlet with rage.

'Get out!'

'I wondered if you were—'

31

'Can't a man read the papers in peace?'

'I'm sorry.'

Charlie Leathers glared at his wife as she backed away. At her meek scrawniness and straggly grey hair and sorrowful hunched shoulders. God, she was a whingeing pain in the arse. In normal circumstances he would have followed her out into the kitchen and given her what for.

But not tonight. Because tonight, for Charlie, was far from normal. Tonight you might say the writing was on the wall. In front of him were six wallet-cramming hieroglyphs that could spell freedom. He looked around the tiny room, treating himself to a good snigger at the pockmarked vinyl suite, cheap veneer sideboard and old-fashioned cabinet television. Because soon he would be saying goodbye to all this. It would be your nice fur recliner, a bottle of Scotch on ice, Players High Tar to hand and something young and blonde and cuddly on his knee.

Because you could buy anything if you had the money. And he would have the money. Oh yes. For the first time in his life he would have the money. A modest amount at first. Be reasonable. No point in frightening people unnecessarily. But there would be more where that came from. Plenty more. Enough to keep him nice and comfortable for the rest of his life.

As nothing further was mentioned about the trouble at the Misbourne weir on the nine o'clock local news, the clientele of the Red Lion decided it had all been some sort of joke and turned their attention to matters more substantial. The discovery of six pheasants in old Gordon Cherry's outhouse. And the shameful matter of Ada Lucas's grandma's tea set which had been valued, while still in her front room cabinet, by an itinerant dealer for fifty pounds when everyone knew it was hallmarked Rockingham and worth all of a hundred.

By turning-out time the business on the river had been practically forgotten. People wandered off in the moonlight or drove home, their minds full of other things. As the landlord said to his wife while she was funnelling the drips tray back into the cellar jug, 'I reckon we've had our ration of excitement for this year.'

Which just goes to show how cosmically wrong a man can be.

CHAPTER THREE

Ann Lawrence checked over her husband's breakfast tray. Weak china tea. A four-minute egg. Fresh toast. An apple. Some Flora and Cooper's Oxford marmalade. She put a sprig of lady's mantle in a little flowered jug.

'Would you mind taking this up, Hetty?'

Ann had called Mrs Leathers Hetty since she was a toddler and Mrs Leathers had always called her either Annie or Pickle or one of several other affectionate nicknames. But, on the day she married, Ann had mysteriously become Mrs Lawrence and no amount of argument, whether teasing or serious, could persuade Hetty to address her otherwise. It simply wouldn't be right.

'Course not,' replied Mrs Leathers, immediately wondering where on earth she would put herself if the vicar (as she still thought of him) opened the door in his nightshirt. Or worse.

'Just knock and leave it outside his room.'

Ann poured herself a third cup of coffee and took it into the library. It was almost ten o'clock, but she had thought it best to let Lionel sleep. He had been out very late checking various refuge centres, hostels and halfway houses and pestering his contacts in the probation service. Eventually, alarm for Carlotta's wellbeing had overcome his anxiety not to offend her and he had called at Causton police station to report the girl missing. Back at home he had described at some length and in disgust their 'complete and inhuman lack of interest'.

Ann had listened consumed by misery and guilt. She longed to turn back the clock and recall the ease of spirit and absence of anxiety with which she had once lived her life. How dull this state had sometimes seemed. Now she yearned for it to return.

The postman's van was driving away. Ann went into the hall and emptied the large wire cage on the back of the door. There was always plenty of post. Lionel believed in keeping in touch – sometimes, Ann felt, with every person he had ever met in his entire life. Fortunately a great many of them appeared to have no wish to keep in touch with him. A common complaint at breakfast was that so and so had still not replied to his second (or third) letter.

Diocesan business had long ago tailed off but there was always correspondence relating to the various charities Lionel was involved with, journals (today the *New Statesman*) and begging letters. There were two for her. One she recognised as from an aged great-aunt in Northumberland who always wrote in August to remind her that it would soon be her mother's birthday and she must not forget to pray for her. The other simply had her name on. No address. Someone must have pushed it through the door. People often did, especially in the evening when they did not like to disturb. Ann took the letter to the window seat in the dining room and opened it.

She was to remember that moment for the rest of

her life: the vividness of deep pink hollyhocks pressing against the window, the raised petit point upholstery rough against the backs of her legs, a rim of dust next to her slippered foot, and herself unfolding the thin, slightly dirty paper out into a single sheet.

For one blessed fraction of a second she stared at the strange cut-out words, stuck on haphazardly, in bewilderment. Was it yet another sample of junk mail? Some new sort of advertisement? Then she read the words consecutively to see if they made sense.

There was a rush of sound inside her head. Then a staggering of the heart as if it had received a blow from a powerful fist. She sucked in air. And read the words again. 'I Saw You Push Her In.'

Ann became aware of extreme cold. A quick upsurge of sour liquid filled her mouth. Struggling not to vomit or faint she rested her head on her knees. As she crouched, trembling, a shadow fell across the carpet.

'You all right, Mrs Lawrence?'

'What?' Ann lifted her head. Then jumped to her feet. The paper fell, butter side up, onto the carpet. 'What are you doing in here?'

A man was standing in the doorway, one hand resting casually on the frame. An extremely good-looking young man with short, curly hair so blond it was almost white and dazzling dark-blue eyes. There was a tattoo – suprisingly delicate – on his forearm. A dragonfly, azure and vivid green, the body a black exclamation point. He removed his battered denim cap, managing somehow to make this seeming courtesy an insult.

'Lionel wanted the car at eleven but it won't start. I think it's the carburettor.'

'You're supposed to phone through.' Her voice ran off the scale. He'd never done this before. Come into the house. Of all the times for him to choose.

'The blower's fucked.' He smiled as Ann's cheeks went scarlet. 'I went to the kitchen to tell Mrs L but she's not there.'

Having explained himself, the young man made no attempt to leave, just slipped both thumbs into the waistband of his jeans and stared at her with mock respect. The room suddenly became a lot smaller, crammed with tensions she willed herself not to understand.

'I'll tell my husband.'

'Yeah. Right.' Still he did not move.

There was no way Ann could leave. No way she would ease past that slender body, lounging so gracefully in the doorway. She forced herself to look at him, seeing insolence, even hatred in that brilliant glance then put it down to her present state of mind.

'Dropped your letter.'

She snatched it up, crumpled it in her hand. Had he seen what it said? Impossible at that distance. She rammed the paper into the pocket of her housecoat and spoke with great effort.

'You can go . . . um . . . Jax.'

'I know that, Mrs Lawrence. No need to point that out.'

Ann stepped back, groping behind her for the window seat, lowering herself gradually down. What should she do now? Paralysed by indecision and alarm, she was saved by the arrival of Hetty Leathers.

'Excuse *me*.' Mrs Leathers, carrying a plastic tidy full of polish and dusters, pushed firmly past the chauffeur. 'Some of us got work to do.'

A blink and he'd gone. One single flowing movement, like a polecat. Mrs Leathers couldn't help noticing Ann's distress.

'You don't want to let that load of old rubbish upset you.' It was a mystery to Mrs Leathers that the Reverend could expose his wife to such riffraff. She started to remove the worn lace tablecloth, folding it carefully. 'The sooner he slings his hook the better.'

'It wasn't just him.' Ann braced herself. 'Carlotta's run away.'

'She'll fall on her feet. That sort always do.' Mrs Leathers was not usually so forthright. She liked to think she was loyal to the Reverend as well as to his wife but today she just had to speak out. Ann was looking really ill. 'I've finished in the kitchen. Why don't you go and make yourself a nice cup of tea?'

Ann half ran from the room. She did not go into the kitchen but hurried blindly through the house with no sense of direction or understanding of where she was going. Eventually she found herself in the linen closet staring blankly at stacks of folded sheets on slatted wooden shelves fragrant with the scent of dried lemon verbena.

She took the letter from her pocket and smoothed it out. Her hand was trembling so much the cut and pasted words jumped up and down as if in some mad dance. She felt she was holding something obscene. Coated with filth. Crawling with slimy invisible life.

She ran to the bathroom and tore the letter into dozens of tiny pieces then did the same with the envelope. She dropped them into the lavatory, working the handle over and over again until every scrap had disappeared.

Then she undressed, turned on the shower, and scrubbed herself fiercely all over with the hand mitt. She cleaned inside her ears and inside her nostrils and under her nails. She washed her hair, rinsing it over and over again. When she had finished, she folded up her housecoat and everything else she had been wearing when she had first touched the letter, crammed them into a bin liner and threw the lot away.

Afterwards, looking back, Ann was surprised she had not anticipated her correspondent's next step. She had seen enough thrillers, read enough crime novels. But the telephone call still came as a complete and utter shock. Almost as strong a shock as the letter itself.

He seemed to be speaking through a mouthful of cotton wool. An accentless, half-choking mumble. He wanted money. A thousand pounds or he'd go to the police. He told her exactly when and where to leave it. Ann started to protest. Tried to say he wasn't giving her enough time but the phone was banged down.

She never for a moment considered not paying and not only because of the danger of discovery. Consumed by guilt, Ann recognised that she and she alone had been directly responsible for the whole tragic situation. She had driven Carlotta from the house, pursued the girl to the river and failed, in spite of all her efforts, to stop her jumping in.

In fact Ann had now started to ask herself just how genuine these efforts had been. She remembered Carlotta crying, 'You've never wanted me here, you'll be glad to get rid of me,' and knew it was the truth.

The girl's despair, her determination to jump had made her very strong but surely if she had tried just that little bit harder . . . And then that cry, 'Don't push . . .' She hadn't pushed Carlotta. *Had she?*

But whether she had or not, the fact remained the whole business was her fault. And it was only right that she should pay. It would be the first step towards salving her conscience. She could raise that amount by a visit to the bank. They knew her there and the balance in her current account would easily cover it. And if there were more demands, she would sell what was left of her mother's jewellery. Surely that would balance the scales a little in her direction? The sad symmetry of this conclusion made her want to weep.

That night Ann took a torch to light her way through Carter's Wood. There was a little picnic area with wooden benches and two long tables. She had been told to leave the money, sealed in an envelope and wrapped in a polythene carrier bag, in the litter bin.

She was more frightened of doing something wrong than of being alone among the dark rustling trees. Nor was she afraid for her own safety. The blackmailer would hardly wish to harm his golden goose and, not wanting to be seen, would be keeping well out of her way.

There were two litter bins. One was empty and Ann dropped the packet in. It made a gentle thump as it fell and she wondered if he was close enough to hear. A small animal screamed suddenly as she ran away.

CHAPTER FOUR

When her husband did not return at his usual time from his late-night walk with the dog, Mrs Leathers went to bed. Occasionally he would do this. Call in at the Red Lion where closing time was elastic to say the least, have a throw of darts and cadge a drink or a smoke. Sometimes she thought he'd stay the night if they'd let him. So she drifted off to sleep, pleasurably aware of the empty space by her side.

When she woke, the room was full of brightness. Mrs Leathers sat up blinking, looking round. She seized the bedside clock. It was ten past eight!

Mrs Leathers gasped and climbed quickly out of bed. Charlie never forgot to set the alarm. Six thirty on the dot, always. And he never got up until he'd drunk his tea either.

More puzzled than worried, Mrs Leathers put on a shabby candlewick dressing gown. She glanced back at the room as she was leaving, as if he might have slipped down between the furniture. The bed looked huge. She hadn't realised quite how much space it took up.

Down the narrow, twisting stairs and into the kitchen where the harsh smell of Charlie's cigarettes fouled the air, killing the fragrance of bread left to rise overnight on the Raeburn. Automatically Mrs Leathers filled the kettle and put two Typhoo tea bags in the pot.

She had never thought of herself as an imaginative woman but now her mind started running every which way. All those stupid soaps – that's what Charlie would have said. They turn your mind, woman. And it was true that she was constantly enthralled by their exciting twists and turns. If this was television, her husband would have run off with another woman. Mrs Leathers' heart, which had leapt briefly in her flat chest at the very notion, got a grip on reality and thudded back into its usual place. Let's face it, she sighed aloud, who in their right mind would want Charlie?

Perhaps he had secretly become involved in a crime and had had to run away. That was more likely although he was so stupid he'd probably never know it was time to run away until it was too late. And who would he be involved with? A handful of boozy cronies down at the pub? He didn't have a real friend in the world.

The kettle boiled over. Mrs Leathers filled the pot and called, 'Tea time, Candy.'

But the dog did not come out of her basket. Mrs Leathers bent down, wheezing slightly, to peer under the table. Candy was not there. Which meant they had both been out all night.

Much more alarmed at the absence of the little dog than she had been over her husband, Mrs Leathers took the big iron key from behind the door and ran out into the front garden.

She stood at the gate under a lovely hibiscus (a Mother's Day present from her daughter Pauline over twenty years ago) but its beauty, and indeed the beauty of the whole morning, was wasted on her. All she could think about was the whereabouts of Candy.

The red mail van appeared at the end of the lane.

There was rarely any post for the Leathers and what they did get was usually addressed to Occupier, urging bookkeeping courses or the building of a double-glazed conservatory. And today was no different. The van wasn't coming down.

Mrs Leathers ran out to stop the postman and just caught him. He couldn't help staring. She looked so wild, grey hair sticking out everywhere, the bottom of her dressing gown caught up on brambles, slippers soaking wet.

'Morning, Mrs Leathers. You all right?'

'You haven't seen my little Jack Russell, have you?' Then, when the postman hesitated, 'She's mainly tan with black markings and white paws.'

'I'll keep an eye out,' he promised through the van window. 'Cheer up. Dogs – they're always running off.'

Not my Candy. Mrs Leathers flung on some clothes, buttoned any old how, pulled on her gardening clogs and ran off leaving the gate ajar, just in case.

She hurried onto the Green, her face screwed up with anxiety, staring first into the distance and then almost at her feet as if she might fall over the dog without noticing. One or two people, including Evadne Pleat, were out with their own dogs and all were deeply sympathetic. They asked if there was any special place they could search and promised to check with their neighbours the minute they returned home. Evadne offered to do some posters in bright colours to put on trees and the village noticeboard.

Mrs Leathers could only guess at her husband's exact route the previous evening. But whether turning left or right at the top of Tall Trees Lane, he would have covered roughly the same territory, working his way round in a circle to come home.

Arriving at the churchyard she decided to go all the way through and down the Pingles. This was a narrow alley running along the backs of around a dozen houses and much favoured by lovers and youngsters sniffing, swallowing or jabbing assorted illegal substances.

And as she walked, Mrs Leathers continued to call. Occasionally a garden shed was within reach and then she would tap on the walls and cry out, 'Candy?' She knew it was usually cats that got trapped in sheds but you couldn't not try.

The Pingles led almost directly into a small coppiced wood which backed onto fields of wheat and barley now harvested and bound into vast, golden wheels to be rolled away for winter storage.

Mrs Leathers entered the wood making the soft clicking sound, tongue behind teeth, that she knew the dog would recognise. She stood very still, listening intently. There was the river gurgling and rushing over the stones. A swift scuttering by some frightened animal. Creaking branches and whispering leaves. A sudden whirring and a cloud of wood pigeons exploded into the air, fanning out and wheeling away like aircraft in formation.

Mrs Leathers wondered whether to venture more deeply, penetrating the heart of the wood. She knew it was unlikely that her husband would have been walking there in the dark but could not bear to leave even the most implausible area uninvestigated. She stepped forward a few paces, silent on the thick leaf mould, called again. And waited.

There was a thread of fragile sound. Almost in-audible. You couldn't even call it a whimper. Mrs

Leathers' first impulse was to rush about madly, looking, calling, looking. Then, realising she might tread on the dog, she forced herself to stand still and be calm.

She tiptoed, murmuring gentle reassurances, backwards and forwards, parting nettles and dry old cow parsley, delicately shifting dead twigs and the occasional drinks can. She found Candy lying behind a fallen branch from an oak tree. The branch was large and very heavy and Mrs Leathers could not reach the dog without dragging it away. The sensible thing was fetch help but she could not bear to leave Candy for a single minute. So she struggled and heaved and pushed. Splinters rammed down her nails and into the palms of her hands until she wept with pain and frustration.

Eventually she was able to move the log just enough to climb through. Until she could see Candy properly. Could bend down and lift the little dog into her arms. And then she wept indeed.

That morning being dry, bright and sunny, Valentine Fainlight had ridden his twenty miles in the open. He had just re-entered Ferne Basset and was slowing down when a woman ran out from between some houses and straight into the road. He swerved, braked hard and was about to yell at her when he recognised the Lawrences' cleaner. She was cradling something, pressing it to her breast which was spattered with bright red stains.

'Mrs Leathers? What on earth . . .' He came closer. 'Oh God.'

'It's my . . . I have to . . . the vet . . . must . . . must . . .'

'Stay there. I'll get the car. Two minutes – all right?'

But she was making her way towards the house as he backed out the Alvis, no doubt hoping to save precious seconds. He had brought a travelling rug, for she was shivering with distress and cold, and tucked it round her knees.

'My sister's ringing to say it's an emergency.'

He put his foot down and the car leapt forward and shot out of the village. Causton was twelve miles away and he covered it in under ten minutes.

Mrs Leathers didn't move during the journey. Or speak. Just murmured crooningly to the sad wreckage in her arms.

Valentine wondered if it was still alive. After all, it was not unknown for the newly bereft to carry on talking to their loved ones when they could no longer hear. Presumably it had been run over. But in that case, why was she carrying it out of a siding?

A woman with a tortoiseshell kitten, having been told what had happened, gladly gave up her own appointment. She sat in silent sympathy next to Mrs Leathers, even taking her hand at one point. Val, never having owned a pet of any sort, felt rather awkward.

After about ten minutes the vet, looking rather like an animal himself with his long nose, excessively hairy hands and dark-brown intelligent eyes, came out. Mrs Leathers sprang up and ran over to him.

'Well, Mrs Leathers,' said the vet. 'She's still with us.'

'Ohh . . . Thank you, Mr Bailey. *Thank you.*'

'Don't thank me. I haven't done anything yet.'

'I just thought . . . all that blood.'

'You found her like this?'

Mrs Leathers nodded. 'In a wood not far from where we live.'

'Water nearby?'

'A river, yes. What happened to Candy, Mr Bailey?'

A tremendous blow to the head, a savage kicking which had damaged all her ribs and broken one of her back legs, then thrown into the river to drown. That's what had happened to Candy.

'I'll examine her more closely when she's had a good rest. She's not in any pain. Don't worry – we'll look after her.'

'When will you . . .?'

'Ring in the morning. That would be best.'

As they were getting into the car, Hetty Leathers said, 'What day is it, Mr Fainlight?'

'Wednesday.'

'I should be at work. I'll have to let Mrs Lawrence know what's happened.' She hesitated then said, 'He sounded very optimistic, didn't you think? The vet?'

'Very optimistic indeed,' lied Valentine, seeing her safely settled before climbing into the driving seat. 'You must be very relieved. And I expect your husband will be too.'

Ann had not expected to sleep after delivering the blackmail money. She had run wildly away from Carter's Wood, round the house into the conservatory and straight up to her room.

Having flung off her coat and shoes she jumped into bed fully clothed, pulled the duvet over her head and buried her face in the pillow, overwhelmed by fear and the sense of a narrow escape from unknown terrors. To her later amazement she immediately fell into a deep, dreamless sleep.

It was nearly eight o'clock when she came round and sat up in bed staring down at arms encased in green knitted wool and a rumpled tweed skirt. She remembered everything immediately. Every emotion, every movement, every frightened breath.

Ann got up straightaway, washed, put on a clean linen shirt, jeans and a rather felted Fair Isle cardigan and went down to the kitchen. It was beautifully warm from the Aga. There were evening primroses in a stone jug on the table, and on the dresser what was left of the willow pattern plates, cups and saucers her parents had always used. Almost everything in the room gave the comfort of continuity right down to the old-fashioned wall clock with the Roman numerals her father had bought when the village school closed.

Usually this was a favourite time. Lionel not yet down, Hetty still to arrive. The day advanced enough to vanquish any anxieties that had beset her mind when night fell but not yet so busy she had lost all understanding of herself as an individual with interests and dreams and a will of her own. Sometimes this precious sense of self was so fractured by what everyone else seemed to want and need, Ann felt she might never reassemble it again.

But this morning was something different. No peace in the kitchen today. Or perhaps ever again. She walked over to the window and stared out at the cedar tree. Early sunlight spilled over the autumn crocus scattered around its massive trunk. And threads of silvery mist still clung to the great upper shelves of spreading branches. When she was a little girl it had seemed to her that the vast tree never ended but grew upwards for ever and ever, finally disappearing into the heavens.

Suddenly she had a tremendous longing to call back those times. The years before her mother died now seemed to Ann full of golden simplicities. Tears over the death of a pet were tenderly mopped and a convincing story told of its continuing happiness in a better world. Squabbles with friends were sorted without blame or punishment.

Where was the person who could help her now? Who could kiss wickedness better? No human being, certainly. Rather did it flourish, if memory of her father's sermons did not lie, as did the green bay tree. She had never felt so lonely.

'Good morning, my dear.'

'Oh!' Ann wheeled round. 'I didn't hear you.'

'Where's my tea?'

'I'm sorry.' She looked at the clock. It was nearly nine. 'Good gracious. I wonder what's happened to Hetty?'

As Lionel had no idea, he remained silent. Just stood in the doorway in his checked dressing gown and slippers, looking expectant.

'Tea, yes.' Ann filled the electric kettle. 'Do you want it down here?' She hoped he would say no. There was something very depressing about his unshaven cheeks, the snowy stubble catching the light and the tousle of whitish locks. Somehow he always looked older in his dressing gown.

'No. I don't have time to sit and chat,' said Lionel, holding up his right hand with beneficent sternness. He looked like a Vatican official holding back hordes of agitated supplicants. 'Bring it up and I'll drink it while

I dress. There's a great deal to do. We must start the search again immediately after breakfast.'

Ann stared at him. Search?

'I'll just have bacon and egg today with a small piece of fried bread and tomatoes.' He was already turning to go. Then, over his shoulder, 'And some of those mushrooms growing in the churchyard, if they haven't already been stolen.'

It was on the tip of Ann's tongue to point out that, as her husband no longer had any connection with the church or its surroundings, he also had no divine right to the mushrooms. But, like so much that was constantly on the tip of her tongue, it was swallowed or just withered on the air, unspoken and unsung.

She went to the fridge and got out the Tupperware container of back bacon and two eggs. Returning to the table, her eye was caught by the red mail van. An image of letters falling into the wire cage caused a rush of nausea which threatened to overwhelm her. Ridiculous, she told herself. Get a grip. The vile thing you received was hand delivered. And anyway, you've done what he wanted. Why should he be writing to you again?

She watched the postman get out of the van and, as he did so, Jax turned into the gate returning from his jog. He stopped and collected the letters, running up the drive and pushing them through the flap in the front door before jogging off to his own apartment.

Ann made herself get on with the breakfast. There would be nothing for her. There hardly ever was. Lionel would pick up the post, study it importantly as he ate his toast, getting buttery crumbs over everything, then take it to his writing desk and study it importantly some more.

So, that was all right then. Ann put the eggs in boiling water, set the kitchen timer for four minutes and slid the bacon under the grill. By the time Lionel came down it would all be sorted.

She imagined him, surprised, calling from the hall, 'Something today for you, Ann.' If he did, and if it proved to be more of the same, how would she dissemble? She would give herself away, unable to help it. How much more sensible then to anticipate such a situation by checking the post herself.

Now it seemed to Ann impossible that she should have contemplated any other course. Quickly, before her husband could come back downstairs, she ran to the hall.

Although she could see straightaway that there was nothing to disturb or frighten her – all the envelopes had some company logo or professional heading and all were franked – she turned them over once or twice in trembling hands, even studying the back lest they had been opened and resealed after something wholly foreign to their normal sane enclosures had been slipped inside.

But all was well. Not realising she had been holding her breath, Ann now let it out: a slow, steady exhalation. She relaxed, leaning back against the door. This peaceful moment was interrupted by an angry shout coming from the direction of the kitchen. There was a strange smell, too, which she recognised as burning bacon. An apology already on her lips, Ann hurried away.

'I seem to be putting you to an awful lot of trouble.'

'Not at all. I wasn't doing anything special this morning.'

To tell the truth, Valentine was quite enjoying himself. Few things, he thought, were more satisfying than vicarious involvement in other people's misfortunes. No cost of any kind to oneself, lots of interesting running about and the sort of emotionally vibrant conversation that he would, in normal crcumstances, run a mile from.

He only wished he'd had a camera at the moment his remark to Mrs Leathers about her husband had sunk in. In spite of a gift for mimicry, Val knew he would never be able to capture exactly that priceless expression of guilty remembrance. She actually said, 'I knew there was something else.' How he kept a straight face he would never know.

It was generally agreed then that as they were in Causton it would be sensible to go to the police station and report Charlie missing. They took the precaution of ringing home first to check he had not turned up while they'd been out.

Val thought they would be taken to a special room but a constable in reception simply put a yellow form down on the counter for Mrs Leathers to complete after indicating that he was available if she needed any assistance.

'There's a lot of weird questions here,' remarked Mrs Leathers, dutifully filling it in. 'Scars, stammering and suchlike. Ethnic appearance code. Charlie wouldn't like that.'

Val studied the posters, none of them very cheery. A young girl's stitched up, cut and battered face: Have None For The Road. A golden labrador panting behind a closed car window: By The Time You Get Back She Could Be Dead. And a broken syringe over a

Crackdown Hotline number. He had just begun to discover more than he actually needed to know about the Colorado beetle when he realised Mrs Leathers was asking a question.

'What do they mean, peculiarities?'

'Oh, you know. Wearing a tutu or a mink G-string at evensong. That sort of thing.'

A mistake. Mrs Leathers moved just a little distance away and never quite met his eye again. She wrote for almost another ten minutes then handed the form over.

'Section four, madam,' said the constable, easing it back. 'Informant?'

'Oh, yes. Sorry.' Mrs Leathers included her own name, address and telephone number. 'Do I let you know if he turns up?'

'If you would, please.'

'He only went out for a walk.'

The constable smiled, wishing he had a fiver for every time he'd heard that one. He'd be snorkelling in the Caribbean before you could say Piña Colada. He felt sorry for the old duck, though. She'd obviously been having a good old cry before she'd been able to bring herself to come in.

He retrieved the four two eight, passed it to a civilian clerk who was answering a non-stop telephone and was just going about his business when the bloke with the old lady spoke up.

'Excuse me.'

'Sir?'

But it was not the policeman Valentine was speaking to. He had taken Mrs Leathers' arm and was gently drawing her back towards the counter. He said, 'Tell them about the dog.'

* * *

This made all the difference, as Mrs Leathers explained to Evadne shortly after she had been brought back home. Evadne, unaware that Candy had been found, had called round to check on Mrs Leathers' telephone number to add to her poster.

As it was nearly lunchtime Mrs Leathers had offered a bowl of soup and some toast. Evadne, who wanted to hear exactly what had happened, accepted. She felt rather apprehensive when a tin was produced but thought one bowl wouldn't hurt. The soup was vivid orange-red, velvety in texture and rather sweet. It resembled no vegetable she had ever tasted in her life.

But Evadne's curiosity as to the origins of her lunch vanished as soon as Mrs Leathers began to tell the story of Candy's misfortune. She listened in empathetic horror, imagining it happening to one of her beloved Pekes and wondering how on earth she would bear it.

'She will recover, Hetty. She's a brave dog with great heart.'

'Yes,' said Mrs Leathers and burst into tears.

Evadne abandoned her exotic lunch, came round the table and took Mrs Leathers in her arms. She rocked her backwards and forwards murmuring, 'There, there,' just as she did for Piers when he became melancholy, overwhelmed by all the troubles of the world.

'You must let me know when she's coming home. I'll take you to Causton myself.'

'Thank you.'

'And are you . . .? Forgive me but these things can be . . . I mean, aftercare, medicines. I hope . . . any problem . . . um . . .'

'You're very kind, Evadne, but I am insured for her.' And what a fight there had been with Charlie over that.

'Excellent.'

Mrs Leathers took a deep breath, mopped the moisture from her cheeks and said, 'Oh dear, your soup's got cold.'

'Not to worry. What was it, by the way?'

'Tomato.'

'Good heavens,' said Evadne. 'Now, are you going to be all right? Would you like me to stay for a while? Or I can come back after I've walked the boys.'

'Actually, my daughter should be here soon. From Great Missenden.' Mrs Leathers was quite used now to Evadne's dogs being called the boys when one of them was a girl. Evadne had explained that Mazeppa was very sensitive and would hate to be singled out. 'Pauline's just sorting out someone to look after the children.'

There was a knock at the door and Mrs Leathers said, 'That'll be either her or the police.'

'My dear.' Evadne was entranced and intrigued. 'Why on earth are they coming?'

'They want me to show them exactly where I found Candy.'

'Well, I must say,' said Evadne, 'that is encouraging. To show such concern over a little dog.'

'Charlie's missing too,' explained Mrs Leathers, checking her tear-stained face in a small mirror before opening the door.

'Oh, yes?' Evadne had seen Mr Leathers dragging Candy furiously back and forth across the Green and sincerely hoped he stayed missing.

A uniformed sergeant and a young policewoman were on the step. Mrs Leathers asked them in to wait while she got her coat on. Evadne engaged them in conversation, putting them at their ease. When Mrs Leathers returned, the policewoman seemed to be having some sort of coughing fit.

'I will come with you,' said Evadne firmly. Then, when Mrs Leathers hesitated, 'Pauline would if she were here.'

Mrs Leathers had to admit this was true and that she would be glad of the company. The police car was parked at the top of the lane and a couple of women with pushchairs were already standing nearby staring curiously.

Mrs Leathers stumbled over a tussock of grass as the four of them emerged and the sergeant took her arm. Convinced everyone would think she was being arrested, she blushed scarlet. Evadne, on the other hand, stepped out with great panache, striding along and waving at any passerby. It was she who led the way to Carter's Wood.

Once inside Mrs Leathers took over. But the closer she got to the spot where she found Candy the more reluctant her steps became. During the final moments she had to hold Evadne's hand. To her surprise, once she had pointed the place out, the policewoman said she could go home.

Evadne was rather disappointed that the adventure seemed to be over almost before it had begun. A small crowd had gathered at the building site next to the pub, gazing around with the happy nosiness of the completely uninvolved. As Mrs Leathers pushed through, several people asked her questions.

Seeing her daughter's car parked beside the Green, Mrs Leathers hurried home. Evadne did the same, making a pot of Lapsang Souchong as soon as she got in to wash away the extraordinary taste of her lunch-time snack. After this she took the Pekes out for a long run. Every few yards, remembering Candy, she would stop, pick one of them up and squeeze it to her relieved bosom. Though surprised, the dogs, courteous as always, did not protest.

On the way back she noticed several more police cars and one or two plain ones. The crowd was much larger now but was being compelled to keep its distance behind a barrier of fluttering blue and white tape.

Charlie Leathers lay in a leafy hollow about fifty yards from where Candy had been found. The video team and photographer had already left. And George Bullard, the Force Medical Examiner, had also almost finished doing what he had to do. Two mortuary attendants sat on a nearby log smoking, cracking jokes and guessing at the best way to pick a lottery winner.

Detective Chief Inspector Tom Barnaby, having taken one quick look at the corpse, did not feel inclined to take a second.

'Sometimes, George, I don't know how you keep your food down.'

'It's a knack.'

'What happened to his face?' asked Sergeant Troy, bag carrier and persistent gadfly to the DCI. 'What's left of it.'

'Midnight feast in the dorm,' said Dr Bullard. 'Some sort of animal, I'd say.'

'Christ, I hope it is a bloody animal.' Barnaby sounded ready to explode. 'Cannibalism we can well do without.'

'OK, boys.' Dr Bullard peeled off his gloves and stuffed them into a disposable bag. 'You can cart him off.'

'How long's he been lying there, do you think?' asked Barnaby.

'Ohh . . . probably since last night. Certainly no longer than twenty-four hours. That's the joy of the garrotte. Immediate asphyxiation helps pin the time down.' He got up, brushing leaf mould off his trousers. 'Well, I'm off. Give my best to Joyce. How's the sprog?'

'Thriving, thank you.'

'Should have something on your desk by morning.'

Barnaby watched the doctor stride away, head back, gazing at the sky, inhaling the peaty autumn scents with every appearance of satisfaction.

'That would make a good title for the autobiography I've no doubt he's secretly scribbling.'

'What would?' Sergeant Troy stood well aside to let the graveyard shift get moving.

'The Joy of the Garrotte. Come on, let's get back to the station.'

'It's gone lunchtime, chief. What about the pub? I could just get outside some sausage, egg and chips.'

'Your guts must be made of cast iron.'

The news spread through Ferne Basset like lightning. A body had been removed from Carter's Wood. The Scene of Crime officers arrived and, after removing all sorts of interesting paraphernalia from the back of their van, put on plastic overalls, gloves and bootees and disappeared into the trees.

The sergeant and young policewoman who had called on Mrs Leathers before called again. This time the door was opened by a stout, dark-haired girl who looked about sixteen but turned out to be Mrs Leathers' 23-year-old daughter.

'Now what?' she said, arms akimbo.

'Could we have a word with your mother?' asked the policewoman. She was still at the stage where she put on a special voice as the possible bearer of bad news. Kind, gentle, slightly solemn. A dead giveaway, the sergeant thought, but you had to make allowances. She'd grow out of it.

'I reckon she's had enough upset for one day, don't you?'

'It's all right, Pauline,' called Mrs Leathers from the kitchen.

They all went into the front room where the sergeant declined the offer of a cup of tea. Just as well, thought Pauline, 'cause I certainly won't be making any.

'You reported your husband missing earlier today, Mrs Leathers. We were wondering if you have a photograph of him.'

'Not a recent one, I'm afraid.' She looked nervously at the sergeant then went over to the sideboard and took out an album. 'Why do you ask?'

'Just to help us with our inquiries, Mrs Leathers.'

'Is this something to do with all those cars over by the Green?' asked Pauline.

'That's the latest.' Mrs Leathers handed over a picture of a choleric little man glowering at the camera. He was holding a shotgun and there were several dead birds at his feet. 'Taken about eight years ago.'

'Thank you.' The sergeant stowed the photograph in his wallet.

Pauline said, 'I asked you a question.'

'Yes, it is.' No point denying it. Half the village would have seen the stretcher brought out. The sergeant chose his next words carefully. 'We have actually discovered the body of a man in the woods. Who he is or how he died we can't say at the moment.'

Mrs Leathers tried to speak but her lips had become suddenly stiff. She couldn't form the words. She stared at Pauline who reached out, took her hand and squeezed it hard.

'I'll show them out, Mum. Be right back.' On the doorstep she said, 'It's him, isn't it?'

'We don't know for—'

'Best not to get excited though, eh? Just fingers crossed.'

'Pardon?' said the policewoman.

'The life that bugger's led her. Tell you the truth, I'd have done it meself years ago if I'd thought I could get away with it.'

Valentine and Louise were having dinner on the top floor of their crystal palace. The house was extremely flexible and sleeping could be accomplished or food consumed almost anywhere.

Beds were in all the rooms: single divans covered with brilliantly coloured silk or fur throws. The kitchen was in the basement on a level with the garage. Sometimes they ate there. More often they would make use of the dumb waiter, an elegant heated cube of stainless steel suspended on black rubber cables. This glided smoothly up and down inside a transparent shaft which thrust, like a powerful obelisk, straight up through the centre of the house.

Most days they shared the cooking but tonight Valentine had spent so much of his time looking after Mrs Leathers that Louise had shopped and prepared the meal. A guinea fowl cooked in white wine with fondant potatoes and a watercress salad. Grilled peaches with Amaretto and homemade Sable biscuits. The wine was Kesselstatt Riesling.

Usually the conversation meandered easily about, touching on books or music or the theatre. Sometimes absent friends would be gently maltreated. Once upon a time, before the hearts of the couple had been chastened by the pain of their own unhappiness, such friends would have been savaged without mercy.

Sometimes Val would talk about his work but these occasions were not frequent. Barley Roscoe, the boy who had made Val's fortune, was only seven and inevitably his daily experiences, though wildly, magically adventurous in comparison with the average child of a similar age, could not sustain much in the way of adult conversation.

But tonight, like everyone else in the village (except the Lawrences), Val and Louise were mulling over the grisly discovery in Carter's Wood. Also like everyone else, they were convinced the dead person was Charlie Leathers.

'One, he's missing.' Valentine ticked the points off on his fingers. 'Two, it was his dog found nearby, badly beaten. And three, absolutely nobody likes him.'

'Not liking is no reason—'

'It's a damn nuisance. We're going to have to find someone else to do the garden.'

'He only does – did a couple of hours a week. I can manage that. It's the Old Rectory that'll feel the pinch. Which reminds me . . .' She told Valentine about her meeting with Ann Lawrence the previous afternoon when they had discussed Carlotta's disappearance.

'There is no way she would have got into that state over just a row. Trembling and shaking – she could hardly speak.'

'Perhaps she's the one who bumped off Charlie.'

'That's not very funny, Val.'

'Murder's not supposed to be very funny.'

'More likely to be—'

Louise stopped, realising immediately it was too late. The time to stop had been when the words were still in her mouth. And she had been so careful. Always thinking, anticipating. Ever since the night, months ago, when she had first spoken her mind on the subject in question and Val had spoken his mind and it was plain there could be no meeting of the two minds, ever. She had never seen her brother behave as he had then. He was like a man possessed. Which, of course, he was.

'More likely to be?'

The words lay across her heart like lashes from a whip. 'I'm sorry, Val.'

'One mistake and he pays for the rest of his life, is that it?' He got up, taking a leather jacket from the back of his chair, cramming an arm into one sleeve, shrugging it over his shoulders.

'Don't!' She ran round the table, not caring what she said now that the damage had been done. 'Don't go over there. *Please*.'

'I shall go where I like.' He was running down the

curved glass staircase. At the bottom he turned round and stared back up at her, his face quite expressionless, his eyes burning. 'If all you can find to do is criticise the one person who makes me glad to be alive then I suggest you find another place to do it in.'

Of course, someone had phoned the Old Rectory. The caller seemed to think that Lionel Lawrence, whom she insisted on addressing as 'Your Reverend', would wish to visit Mrs Leathers in his role as 'our living Lord's rod and staff and comforter'.

Much to Lionel's irritation the general view around the village seemed to be, once a cleric, always a cleric. He was still frequently addressed as Vicar and from time to time called upon to involve himself in deeply fraught situations that were none of his making. He always declined but people could be extremely, sometimes quite unpleasantly, persistent. In the present case, after a few judicious questions, Lionel felt obliged to refuse. It seemed the body had not yet been positively identified. Lionel was not easily embarrassed but even he drew the line at offering solace to a widow whose husband might pop his head round the door at any minute.

His main concern at the moment was his own wife. When he told her the news, Ann's reaction was deeply disturbing. She leapt up and seized his arm, asking him over and over again just where the dead man had been found and when exactly it had all happened. She was in a feverish state, wild-eyed, her skin so hot that he suggested calling the doctor. She calmed down then. Or pretended to. He could see her struggling to appear more tranquil but her eyes, dazed with alarm, danced and flickered round the room.

Eventually he persuaded her to go to bed. Then he went into the study, placed some applewood logs carefully on the fire and immersed himself in the Gospel according to St Paul. But his mind soon drifted back to its previous occupation and, for the millionth time, he wondered where Carlotta was now and what she could be doing. Had she made her way to London and fallen among thieves? Attempted to hitch hike and been picked up by a man who made it his business to prey on young girls? Was she even now lying lifeless on some scrubby wasteland, her clothes torn, her skirt over her head—

Lionel gasped with shock at the vivid image the thought provoked and turned his scarlet cheeks away from the fire. More safely, he dwelt on the girl's time in his house. The talks they'd had walking around the garden or in the tumultuous chaos of her room. A compassionate outpouring of paternal concern on his part which poor, affection-starved Carlotta had soaked up like a thirsty sponge. All you need is love – the naive anthem of his adolescent years – was no more than the simple truth. And he had so much to give.

All this anxiety was affecting his stomach. Lionel went to warm some milk. Settling once more in his wing chair and noting sadly that his wife was still pacing about above his head, he returned to the chaste austerities of St Paul.

Charity suffereth long and is kind . . .

Charity never faileth . . .

And now abideth faith, hope, charity, these three; but the greatest of these is charity.

It was good to know one was on the right track.

* * *

Evadne Pleat was also preparing to retire. She had taken the dogs for their final frolic, exchanged grave greetings with the occasional villager still out and about and had now settled the Pekes comfortably for the night. They slept in assorted beds and baskets in the kitchen. An early experiment with them sleeping in her bedroom had regretfully to be abandoned. There was so much jealousy. Everyone wanted to get under the blankets at once. And then the jostling for position started. After this had been more or less sulkily agreed upon, one or the other would start washing itself or get up for a drink of water. All in all it was worse than the benching area at Crufts.

Having said her prayers, making sure to include both Hetty and her pet, Evadne plumped up her pillows and nestled down under a beautiful handmade patchwork quilt. (She would have no truck with duvets, considering them merely eiderdowns under a fancy name, stuffed into a quite unnecessary bag.)

For once sleep did not come easily. The discovery of a body in the woods preyed on her mind. As did the even more dreadful discovery of Candy, more dead than alive, nearby. Evadne felt humbled by her new insight into Mr Fainlight whom she had always thought rather a sneery sort of man. Such kindness he had shown to Hetty in her hour of need.

Moonshine flooded into the room. Illuminating though the hard, cold radiance was, outlining Evadne's ornaments and pictures, she also found it a touch distracting and got up to close her curtains.

Across the way light flooded the Old Rectory's garden. Some animal on the prowl must have set off the halogen lamp. This often happened. A nuisance, Evadne remembered Ann Lawrence saying, but a price worth paying for security.

Evadne screwed up her eyes and looked more closely. With increasing frequency over the past few weeks a man would come by night to stand beneath the cedar tree. And here he was again. She could see, even from a distance, how tense the outline of his body was. Taut as a bowstring. She wondered how long he would wait this time. Suddenly a window opened, not Carlotta's which Evadne had expected but one in the flat over the garage. The young man who lived there leaned out. Evadne heard laughter, and a moment or two later the dark blue wooden door in the wall was eased open. To her surprise the figure beneath the tree almost ran across the drive and went inside. As he turned to close the door, the light fell full across his face and she recognised Valentine Fainlight.

Evadne closed the window and wandered over to a little velvet nursing chair near her bed. She sat down, feeling uneasy without any reason that she could have easily explained. She had barely spoken to the man who drove Lionel Lawrence around but she knew he was not allowed in the house and could not believe Ann Lawrence would enforce such a rule without a very good reason. Also Hetty Leathers, one of the kindest souls alive, had actually said she hated him.

Eventually Evadne took to her bed but she could not settle. It was as if her mind had been suddenly cast over by a dark shadow. She wished now she had not witnessed that sudden urgent sprint across the grass.

The main bar of the Red Lion was full to bursting but

the atmosphere was not what you'd call lively. Far from generating excited gossip and noisy speculation, the day's events appeared to have subdued the pub's clientele; people spoke in muted murmurs.

Valentine Fainlight had been quite right when he said that no one had much liked Charlie Leathers. Even so, his presumed demise seemed to have diminished them all. Everyone knew that sudden death was something that always happened to other people, fair enough. But this was a bit near home. Still not understanding quite how it had come about, the company was very ill at ease.

The landlord suggested getting up a collection for his widow, which was well received, for people both liked and sympathised with Hetty. He put a large glass collecting bottle on the counter and by the end of the evening it was half full. In fact, he reflected somewhat sourly, there seemed to be more in it than there was in his till. Soberly the bar emptied. The customers left quietly and went quickly home in small clusters. No one walked alone.

CHAPTER FIVE

For once George Bullard was as good as his word. When Barnaby reached his desk the next morning the postmortem report was already there. And so was Sergeant Troy, engrossedly reading.

'What's going on?'

'Sir?'

'You're never here first.'

'I know. You're always having a go at me about it. So I thought I'd make a special effort.'

'I like consistency in my staff, Troy. Don't start messing me about, all right?'

'Yes, chief.'

'OK. What's the verdict?'

'Garrotted, which we know already. Just "very thin wire" it says here. I expect SOCO will have more details. A heavy smoker. When discovered, four thirty yesterday afternoon, he'd been dead about sixteen hours.'

'Roughly midnight Tuesday, then.'

'Eaten a solid meal earlier that evening. Some meat dish, vegetables, rice probably in a pudding. Then later beer mixed up with pork scratchings—'

'Do you mind? I'm still trying to digest my breakfast.' Barnaby reached out for the report, flicking a page over. He read for a few more moments then put it down and opened a large envelope which had been resting against a silver-framed photograph of his wife and daughter. He drew out several large black and white prints and spread them over his desk top.

'I don't like the look of this, Troy.'

Who would? thought Sergeant Troy, staring at the bulging, terrified eyes, what remained of the goulashed cheeks, and a thrusting, blackened tongue also pretty well gnawed on. Reminded him of those weird gargoyles you saw on old churches. Either them or Maureen's mother.

'Apparently,' Barnaby tapped the PM report, 'there was no other bruising. And no skin, hair or fibres under the nails.'

'So he didn't fight back.'

'Everyone fights back, given the chance. But here, once the wire was round his neck, this man didn't have a chance.'

'Blimey. Strong-arm stuff.'

'Yes. Leathers was in his early sixties. Not young but hardly frail or elderly. To strangle the life out of someone in this specific manner takes a lot of muscular strength. Plus, I would think, a certain amount of know-how.'

'You think he's done it before, chief?'

'I wouldn't go as far as that. But it's certainly not a method one finds in your common or garden domestic.'

'Perhaps he's been practising on a melon.'

'What?'

'Like the killer in the *Day of the Jackal.*'

Barnaby closed his eyes briefly, placed the two centre fingers of his left hand on his forehead and drew a deep breath. Then he gathered up the photographs.

'Get these displayed in the incident room. They're setting up in four one nine on the ground floor. First briefing two thirty, by which time we should have something from SOCO.'

'Sir.'

'And get me a Mars Bar while you're at it.'

By the time DCI Barnaby's team had gathered for their briefing, Dr Jim Mahoney, Charlie Leathers' GP, had visited the morgue at Stoke Mandeville hospital and positively identified his patient's body. SOCO had also divvied up their preliminary conclusions.

Barnaby's team included eight CID officers, one of whom was the delectable Sergeant Brierley, after whom Troy had hopelessly lusted from the moment, seven years earlier, when he had first clapped eyes on her. And twelve uniformed coppers. Less than half the strength the DCI would have liked but that was nothing new.

'Scene of Crime report,' Barnaby waved it in the air. 'Copies available. Make yourselves familiar. He was killed by a piece of wire, possibly already looped, slipped over the head from behind and pulled tight. Dense leaf mould underfoot means we've no impression clear enough to be of use, even if the wildlife hadn't been scuffing around. A torch was found a few feet from the body with Leathers' fingerprints.'

'Have we got anything at all on him, sir?' asked Detective Inspector 'Happy' Carson, a lugubrious man, newly made up in rank and longing to shine.

'Not much at this stage. He seems to have been an unpleasant piece of work. Bullied his wife. His daughter's on record as saying she would have done the job herself given half the chance.'

'And didn't something happen to his dog?' asked Sergeant Brierley. 'I heard someone talking in the canteen.'

'That's right. Badly kicked about and thrown into the river.'

'Bastard,' said Sergeant Troy, who loved dogs. There were several murmurs of agreement. 'By the bloke who did the killing?'

'Presumably.'

'Doesn't this indicate whoever it was is still around, sir?' asked Carson. 'That it's someone the dog would recognise. And react to.'

'A good point.' DCI Barnaby liked to encourage quick thinkers. Unlike many senior officers, he did not assume that anyone holding a rank junior to his own would automatically be less intelligent.

'Why didn't it just run away?' asked a young uniformed constable. More than one incredulous face turned in his direction.

'You don't know much about dogs, do you, Phillips?' Sergeant Troy spoke coldly. Constable Phillips blushed.

'We can see from the postmortem that he probably spent some time in a pub the night he died. Fingers crossed it was his local. That should save a bit of legwork. Two of you could start your house-to-house there. It's not a large village, which is all to the good. I want every bit of gossip you can pick up. Everything everyone knows or thinks they know about Charlie Leathers. Work, life – as far back as you can go – hobbies, family. Who saw him on the night he died. Any unusual behaviour leading up to that time. Nothing, *nothing* is too trivial. I shall be talking to his widow myself. Next briefing tomorrow, nine a.m., and I don't mean five past. Right, off you go.'

The press had already picked up during their daily siftings through the Police Public Relations Office that a dead man had been found in a wood in Ferne Basset. Discovering the following day the man's name and manner of his death brought them out in force.

Newspaper reporters and cameramen vied with reporters and cameramen from the local television news. They all asked the same questions, received the same answers and generally got in each other's way.

Any television interviews took place in front of the Fainlights' amazing house. Not that it had any relevance to the crime, as far as anyone knew. It was just that it was too wonderful not to use. The second most attractive backdrop was the forecourt of the Red Lion, the deceased's favourite watering hole. The landlord and several habitués hung around by tubs of drooping pansies hoping to be asked to hold forth. The ones who did were bitterly disappointed to find themselves either missing altogether or snipped down to a few unflattering seconds on the local evening news. Unfortunately the really important interviews – those with the victim's immediate family – were unobtainable.

No sooner had this particular circus left town than the police arrived for the house-to-house and the questions started all over again. Few people really minded. The ones who did had ignored the press and felt superior, saying how sad it was that some people would do anything to get themselves noticed.

Detective Chief Inspector Barnaby and Sergeant Troy were a little ahead of their support team. Plain clothes and an unmarked car (the chief's own Vauxhall Astra) meant they could slide discreetly to a stop at the end of Tall Trees Lane unmolested. Barnaby, pausing only to admire the ravishing mauve hibiscus, walked briskly up the path to the Leathers' bungalow and rapped on the door. It was immediately flung open.

'What did I tell you buggers? She's not talking to anyone. Now piss off before I call the police.'

'You must be Mrs Leathers' daughter.' Barnaby produced his warrant card. 'Detective Chief Inspector Barnaby. And this is Sergeant Troy.'

Troy flashed his credentials and a reassuring smile.

'Sorry. I've had reporters on the doorstep all morning.' She stepped back to let them in. 'How's she supposed to rest?'

'I'm afraid we do need to disturb your mother, Miss Leathers.'

'Mrs Grantham. Pauline. She won't mind that. You've got your job to do.'

Pauline led the way into the snug kitchen. Mrs Leathers was sitting in a rocker by the Raeburn drinking a cup of tea. She had her feet up and a shawl round her shoulders.

'It's the police, Mum.'

'Ohh . . .'

'Please, don't get up, Mrs Leathers. May I . . .?' Barnaby indicated a shabby fireside chair and eased it a little closer to the warm.

'Yes, of course. Sit where you feel comfortable.'

Sergeant Troy took a wheelback to the table, turning a little away from the couple by the hearth. Unobtrusively he produced his biro and a notebook, laying them on the green and white gingham cloth.

'I'm afraid I have bad news, Mrs Leathers,' began Barnaby. 'Dr Mahoney has positively identified the man found dead yesterday in Carter's Wood as your husband.'

'We sort of expected that. Didn't we, Mum?' Pauline had drawn up a raffia stool and sat close to her mother, holding her hand.

'Yes. We're coming to terms with it a bit now.' Mrs Leathers moved quickly on. 'Would you like a cup of tea?'

'Not at the moment, thank you.'

'How exactly did he die, my dad?'

'I'm afraid he was deliberately killed, Mrs Grantham. This is a murder investigation.'

'They were saying that on the Green.' Pauline spoke to her mother. 'I couldn't believe it.'

'Do you have any idea at all who might have been responsible?'

Barnaby addressed his question to both women, looking from one to the other, drawing them into a circle of intimacy. His voice was low and calm. He looked and sounded both sympathetic and genuinely interested. It was this ability, which the DCI was able to draw on anytime and anywhere, that Sergeant Troy envied most. Troy aped Barnaby's manner sometimes but people saw straight through him and never responded in the same way. He sensed he was not trusted.

'It can't have been anyone Charlie knew,' insisted Mrs Leathers.

Troy thought this hardly worth making a note of. From what he'd heard of the miserable sod, there was every chance it was someone he knew. In fact almost anyone he knew. But this was hardly the time to point this out and naturally the chief did not do so.

'But why would he be attacked by a complete stranger?' Pauline asked her mother. 'It's not as if he was carrying lots of money. And what was he doing in the wood in the first place?'

'Walking Candy,' said Mrs Leathers.

'In the pitch dark? At that hour?'

'Did he say why he was going out so much later than usual, Mrs Leathers?'

'It wasn't that much later. Around ten instead of half nine. When he never come back I assumed he'd settled down in the Red Lion.'

'Too right,' said Pauline bitterly. 'Spending the housekeeping he'd never give you.'

'Did he say he might be meeting someone?' Then, when Mrs Leathers shook her head, 'Or behave in some way differently in the days leading up to his death? Did he do anything out of the ordinary?'

'No.' She hesitated for a moment then added, 'Just went to work as usual.'

'Where was that?'

'Mostly at the Old Rectory, where I work myself. And he put in an hour or two at the Fainlights' over the road.'

There was nothing else she could add and the policemen, having discovered where the Fainlights lived, prepared to leave. Barnaby said again how much he regretted being the bearer of such sad news. Sergeant Troy paused at the door.

'How's the dog, Mrs Leathers?'

'Hanging on.' Mrs Leathers' face was now awash with the sorrow so markedly absent when they had been discussing her husband. 'Mr Bailey says it's a bit early to predict the outcome.'

Troy knew what that meant. That's what the vet had said to him when his German Shepherd had eaten some poisoned meat put out for rats. He said, 'I'm really sorry.'

After the police had gone, Pauline asked what it was her mum wasn't telling them.

'What do you mean?' Mrs Leathers sounded quite indignant.

'You were going to say something when they asked if Dad did anything strange before he died. Then you didn't.'

'If you were any sharper you'd cut yourself.'

'Come on, Mum.'

'It weren't nothing relevant.' Mrs Leathers hesitated, recalling her husband's furious red-faced shouting when she had intruded into the front room. 'They'd've just laughed.'

'Tell me.'

'He was making a sort of . . . scrapbook.'

'A *scrapbook*? *Dad*?'

At the sight of the Old Rectory, Barnaby was instantly entranced, for it was a truly harmonious and beautiful house. Tall narrow windows (Holland blinds at half mast), an exquisite fanlight and elegant mouldings over the front door. Not in good repair, though. The mellow rose-gold brickwork, supported by a rambling Virginia creeper, was porous and fretted and in bad need of repointing. The paintwork was dirty and quite a bit of it had peeled off. The guttering was broken in several places and the attractive wrought-iron double gates were rusty.

Troy was reminded of a setting for one of the telly costume dramas his mum was so keen on. He could just see a pony and trap wheeling up the drive guided by a coachman in a tall hat, shiny boots and tight trousers. A servant would run from the house to let the little coach step down. Then a pretty girl, all flirty curls and ribbons, wearing a dress covering her ankles but showing plenty of—

'Are we going to stand here all bloody day?'

'Sorry, sir.'

Troy tugged at the griffin's head bell pull – the old-fashioned sort on a wire. As he let go, he briefly wondered what would happen if he didn't let go. Would the wire just keep on coming? Could he walk away winding it round and round his arm? Would it bring the house down? He had a quiet chuckle at the exuberance of this notion.

'And wipe that smirk off your face.'

'Sir.'

'No one in,' said the DCI who was not a patient man.

'They're in,' said Sergeant Troy. 'They're waiting for us to go round the back.'

'What?'

'Tradesmen and deliveries.' Troy's lip curled as it always did when reckoning the bourgeoisie. 'Yes, sir, no, sir. Three bags full.'

'Rubbish. It's just the local vicar as was. Lionel Lawrence.'

'You know him then?'

'I know a bit about him. He married the chief constable twenty-odd years ago.'

'Blimey,' said Sergeant Troy. 'They kept that quiet

down the Masons' lodge.' He raised his arm to give a good bang on the knocker but Barnaby stayed his hand.

'Someone's coming.'

Ann Lawrence opened the door. Barnaby took in a faded blue dress and grey hair so clumsily pinned up it was falling down. Her skin was almost translucent and the eyes so pale it was impossible to guess at their colour. The chief inspector thought he had never seen anyone so washed out. He wondered if she was ill. Perhaps seriously anaemic.

'Mrs Lawrence?'

'Yes.' There was an air about her as of someone awaiting a blow. She seemed almost to be holding her breath. Her glance moved anxiously between the two men. 'Who are you?'

'Detective Chief Inspector Barnaby. Causton CID. And this is Sergeant Troy.' As Barnaby held up his warrant card, Ann Lawrence made an involuntary little sound then covered her mouth with her hand. Such colour as there was drained from her face.

'Might we have a word with you? And your husband, if he's here.'

'What about? What do you want?' She made an obvious effort to collect herself, realising perhaps how strange her behaviour might appear. 'I'm so sorry. Come in, please.' She stood back, swinging the heavy door wide. 'Lionel's in his study. I'll take you.'

The way led through a black and white tiled hall. A great star lantern hung down over the stairwell on a heavy looped chain. A copper jug, crammed with beech leaves and achillea and dried tansies, stood on an oval table next to a little stack of outgoing mail.

The study was a quiet, peaceful room overlooking

the back of the house. Curtains of faded amber silk, so old as to be almost threadbare. Bowls of hyacinths, books and newspapers. A fire crackled with the sweet smell of applewood.

Lionel Lawrence got up eagerly when they were announced, hurrying round from behind his desk to shake Barnaby's hand.

'My dear Chief Inspector! We've met before, I think.'

'Once or twice, sir,' agreed Barnaby. 'At the magistrate's court, I believe.'

'Have you come about Carlotta?'

'Carlotta?'

'A young friend in our care. There was a disagreement – an argument with my wife – and she ran away. We're both extremely worried.'

'I'm afraid not.' Barnaby wondered if this explained Mrs Lawrence's distraught behaviour on their arrival. It seemed a bit over the top. Most young people, even from stable backgrounds, were inclined to absent themselves occasionally. Smuggled into a friend's house overnight maybe, after a row at home. A comfortable doss while their frantic parents rang every number in the book or walked the streets, calling and searching. He noticed she had now become much calmer.

'Please, do sit down.'

Ann Lawrence indicated an olive-green Knole settee then sat down herself, facing them. Caught in a shaft of sunlight, Barnaby saw that her hair was not grey, as he had first thought, but a delicate ash-blonde. She wore a poorly cut green tweed skirt and hand-knitted jumper. He noticed with a frisson of pleasurable surprise that she had absolutely lovely legs, albeit encased in tobacco-brown woollen tights. Now that the nervy tension had vanished, her skin looked smooth and relatively unlined. She could still be in her thirties.

'I expect you're already aware that Charlie Leathers has been found dead.'

'Yes.' Ann Lawrence shuddered. 'It's dreadful.'

'Have you been to see Hetty?' asked Lionel.

'Of course I have.' Ann spoke sharply. 'Her daughter is there at the moment. They'll let me know if I'm needed.'

'Whoever did this must be found,' said Lionel. This instruction was sternly directed at Barnaby. 'Such a person is in desperate need of help.'

Sergeant Troy stared, open-mouthed, at the tall, elderly man with shoulder-length, flowing pepper and salt hair who had now started pacing up and down. Bony ankles protruded from rumpled Harris tweeds and disappeared into elastic-sided boots. His long, corncrake legs bent and stretched in a scissor-like movement. His hands, locked together in anguished indecision, twisted and turned.

'What can *I* do?' he cried, eventually jerking to a halt near a pretty inlaid escritoire. 'There must be something.'

'Answering our questions is all that's needed at the moment.' Barnaby's tone was crisp. He had no intention of indulging this kind of behaviour. 'I understand that you employed Mr Leathers.'

'Yes. He helped keep the garden in order. Did odd jobs – that kind of thing.'

'Has he worked here long?'

'I believe over thirty years.'

'What sort of man was he?'

'Good heavens, I don't know. I had very little to do

with him. Ann would probably...' He turned inquiringly to his wife.

'We didn't talk much. Only about work.'

'So you knew nothing about his private life?'

'I'm afraid not.' Ann had no intention of betraying Hetty's unhappy confidences.

'You'd know if he was in trouble, though, sir?' Sergeant Troy heard aggression kick-starting the words but couldn't stop himself. He avoided the chief's eye. 'I mean, you'd sense it. And he'd want to talk. You being known for helping people, like.'

'I suppose so.' Irony, even as leaden-footed as Troy's, sailed past Lionel. He nodded, parting his thin lips in a complacent smile.

'What about money troubles?' asked Barnaby. 'Did he ever ask for a rise? Or maybe a loan?'

'He had a rise every year,' said Ann. 'As did Hetty. And no, he never mentioned money troubles.'

'Did anyone – a stranger – ever call here asking for him? Or perhaps ring up?'

'No, they didn't.' Lionel Lawrence was getting testy. 'Look, these questions are pointless and time-wasting. Leathers was plainly attacked by some poor, deranged soul who may well be compelled to cause further mischief if you don't get out there and find him.'

At this, perhaps sensing exasperation rising in both their interrogators, Mrs Lawrence rose and made an awkward sideways movement towards the door, indicating with a slight movement of her slender hand that they should follow. A moment later and Barnaby and Troy found themselves on the front steps, once more cheek by jowl with the Virginia creeper.

'Mischief!' said Troy. 'Jesus Christ. Talk about – aah.'

His forearm had been seized in a steely grip.

'Listen. Don't *ever* do that again.'

'Bloody do-gooders. They make me want to throw up.'

'Our feelings during any interview are irrelevant. Antagonise people and the information dries up – remember that.'

'We should show him some of the photographs of the victim.' Troy painfully eased himself free. 'Run him round the morgue a few times.'

He could imagine the reaction back at the station once the ex-Rev's point of view was known. Support for the death penalty was pretty solid and the subject was frequently booted around the canteen. A favourite diversion was a top five hit list compiled and updated in wistful anticipation of the happy practice being restored. Last week some joker had included Lord Longford and there was a long and quite serious argument before he was reluctantly crossed off.

As Barnaby started to walk away with Troy bringing up a sulky rear, his eye was caught by a movement near the garage. A man washing the Humber car. He had not thought to ask the Lawrences if they had any other staff. And, interestingly, they had not thought to tell him.

'A chauffeur,' said Troy, with deep scorn. 'Huh! And I thought the clergy lived plain and simple.'

'I've already told you, Lawrence is not the clergy. Gave it up years ago.'

'Cushy,' murmured Troy. 'You think Mrs L's got money?'

'Not if the state of this place is anything to go by.'

The car was almost a museum piece. A Humber

Hawk, its number plate four figures, three letters. Almost forty years old, heavy, Bible black, well-worn chestnut leather and brown cord upholstery. It was so precisely the type of car one would expect an elderly country clergyman to be trundling about in that Barnaby couldn't help smiling. There were even little silver flower vases, shaped like ice-cream cornets.

Though the man must have been aware of their approach, he didn't look up. Just kept circling the bonnet evenly and smoothly with a duster then giving it another squirt with the aerosol. He wore a tight, white singlet and even tighter jeans that looked genuinely battered rather than trendily drabbed down. He was in excellent shape and extremely good-looking. Sergeant Troy, already out of temper, glared at him.

'Good afternoon,' said Barnaby and introduced himself. The man looked directly into Barnaby's eyes, his own warm with synthetic friendliness. He gave a wide, frank smile and held out his hand.

Barnaby replaced his warrant card, not seeming to see the hand. His nostrils recognised the delicate scent of hypocrisy. He would not have bought a used bag of chips from this man, let alone a haddock fillet.

'Afternoon, gentlemen.' As the smile gradually deepened, the warmth drained from his eyes. Plainly not enough acting talent to keep both on the boil at once. 'What can I do for you?'

'Name?' said Sergeant Troy.

'Jax.'

Troy carefully wrote 'Jacks'.

'Christian name?'

'Don't have one. That's J-A-X, by the way.'

'Is it really?' asked Troy.

'We're making inquiries following the death of Charlie Leathers,' said Barnaby. 'I presume you must have known him?'

'Oh, yeah. Poor old guy. I got on brilliant with Charlie.'

'You were the only one then,' said Sergeant Troy.

'Did he confide in you at all?' asked Barnaby.

'More or less. He was dead worried, I'll tell you that.'

'What about?'

'Gambling, weren't it? A little flutter – got out of hand.'

'What sort of gambling? Horses?'

'Never said. But it was really getting to him.'

'How's that then?' asked Troy.

'One night last week he swore he copped a bloke standing over there.' Jax nodded his head in the direction of a dark clump of trees. 'I went and had a shufty. Weren't nobody.'

'So you think he was imagining things?'

'I did till today. Now I'm not so sure.'

'Did he talk to you about anything else?' said Barnaby. 'Plans he was making perhaps? His family? Other friends?'

'Charlie didn't have no friends.'

'But he got on brilliant with you?' Sergeant Troy was disbelief personified.

'I'm that sort of person.' Jax gave the bonnet a final ruthless scrutiny and started to pack his cleaning kit – chamois leather, aerosol and dusters – into a transparent zip-up holder.

'Where were you between ten and twelve o'clock the night before last, Jax?'

'You asking everybody that?' The man stared hard at Barnaby. 'Or have I been specially selected?'

'Just answer the question,' said Troy.

'In the flat.' He jerked his thumb towards the garage roof. 'It's where I live.'

'We may need to talk to you again,' said Barnaby. 'Don't move without letting us know.'

The man picked up his bag and turned away then hesitated and turned back. 'Look, you'll find this out anyway. I've been in a bit of trouble but Lionel, he's given me a second chance. I can start fresh here. There's no way I'm going to blow it.'

'That's what we like to hear,' said the chief inspector.

After this there were only the Fainlights to be interviewed. Barnaby did not have much hope in this direction. According to Hetty Leathers, Charlie had worked there only two hours a week and, given his taciturn nature, it wasn't likely he spent much of it chatting about his inner self.

'Blimey O'Riley,' said Sergeant Troy as they approached the formidable glass structure. 'I wonder how that got past the planning department.'

Barnaby wondered too. He thought the building stunningly beautiful. It was now almost dusk and nearly every room was illuminated. Not all of the pale, faintly greenish glass slabs of which the house was constructed were transparent. Some were semi-opaque and behind these the glow from the many lamps and hanging lights shifted and spread in the air like so many dissolving stars.

The front door also appeared at first glance to be made of glass but Barnaby, studying the huge, wide-ribbed rectangle, decided it was probably some very tough synthetic substance. The doorknob was a shimmering opalescent sphere. There was no letterbox. Neither did there seem to be a bell. Or a name, though he discovered later that it was called simply after the inhabitants, Fainlights.

'We'll have to knock, chief.' Troy couldn't wait to see inside.

'Hang on.' Barnaby studied the surrounding architrave and found, embedded, a narrow strip of shining steel. He pressed it and waited. There had been no responding sound from inside the house.

'That's not a door bell,' said Sergeant Troy. 'That's the Doberman release button.'

Inside the house Louise, unhappily recalling the previous evening, ignored the bell. She was staring at, but not seeing, the review pages of the *Guardian*. These rested against a cup of cold bitter coffee and a little blue glazed dish of ripe apricots.

When Val had walked out with such an air of savage finality the previous evening she had been driven to follow him. She knew where he was going and that she would learn nothing new. And that there was nothing she could do to stop him. She also knew that he would be even more angry than he was already if he saw her. Yet Louise had not been able to help herself.

When she saw him enter the Old Rectory's garden she waited with no idea of what she should do if he discovered her. After the door to the garage flat had opened, she had turned, sick at heart, and gone home.

Val had come in about an hour later. Louise had watched him through a space between the rugs on her floor. He had sat very still for some time with his head resting in his hands then gone quietly upstairs to bed.

She had hardly slept and had woken full of deep apprehension. For the first time in her life that she could remember she dreaded coming face to face with her brother. Even so, as soon as she heard him moving about, she made a pot of the Assam Orange Pekoe tea he always liked on rising and made her way to his room.

She knocked, received no reply and gently turned the handle. Valentine was in his bathroom. He had apparently just come out of the shower and was standing in front of the mirror, towel round his waist, shaving. The door was half open. She was about to call out when he bent to splash his face with water and she saw a dreadful mark, bluish crimson with almost black edges, on the back of his neck.

Louise moved clumsily backwards onto the landing. Everything on her tray shook or trembled. The lid on the teapot, the fragile cup in its saucer, the surface of the milk. Carefully she put the tray on the floor and slowly straightened. She placed her quivering hands by her sides and breathed deeply, struggling to recover her equilibrium.

She knew who was responsible for the disfigurement and told herself perhaps it wasn't as bad as it looked, even as she knew it was much worse. The phrase 'love bites' jumped into her mind. She remembered how, if you could flash one of these innocent, exuberant bruises on the school bus, the other girls were envious.

But this was something else. This was a deeply unloving bite. A hate bite. A wound. She wondered if it had bled when first inflicted, if Valentine had had to reach awkwardly over his shoulder and bathe and dry it when he got home. If it had hurt when he lay down.

Half an hour later, when her brother came into the kitchen carrying the tea tray, she could hardly bring herself to look at him. Not because of their argument, which now seemed utterly trivial, but because of what she might read in his face.

He was moving around very calmly, as if in a dream – putting his cup and saucer in the dishwasher, peeling an orange. Then he sat at the table, separating the fruit into segments, placing them carefully on a plate but making no attempt to eat.

Louise moved out of Valentine's sightline so she could look at him directly. Then she understood this was quite unnecessary for he had plainly forgotten she was there. He was staring out of the window, his gaze clear-eyed, knowledgeable, quiescent. Everything about him spoke of resignation. His hands rested sadly on his knees, his back curved beneath an invisible load.

Another memory, this time from early childhood. Sitting with her grandfather looking through a scrapbook of photographs. There were postcards too, several from the Great War. The Angel of Mons looking sorrowfully down on a soldier kneeling by a cross. The soldier looked bravely back, knowing his fate and courageously preparing to meet it. Just so did Valentine look.

More chiming finally brought her back to the present. Louise sighed, heaved herself upright and pushed the newspaper away. A distorted burly shape was outlined through the heavy ribbed door. And, just behind it, a slimmer one.

'Mrs Fainlight?'

'Mrs Forbes. Valentine Fainlight is my brother. Who are you?'

As he produced his warrant card Barnaby regarded the woman facing him with admiration. Anyone more different from Ann Lawrence would be hard to imagine. A wide, narrow-lipped mouth, perfectly painted vermilion. High cheekbones, slightly tilted hazel eyes with very long lashes and skin the colour and texture of thick cream. She reminded him of Lauren Bacall in the days when Bogie could still boogie.

'May we come in?'

'Why?' Despite the blunt response, her voice had a throaty sweetness.

'A couple of questions about Charlie Leathers. I understand he worked for you.'

'Only just.'

But she stood aside for them to come in. Barnaby entered and waited, completely at home as he was almost anywhere. Troy stared about him in wonderment. At the glorious fall of curtains, the single stunning central light, the suspended Arabian lamps and patterned silk wall hangings. At the whole elaborate fairytale structure.

She led them behind a curved linen screen which concealed a couple of vast chestnut leather sofas and a low, black, glass table supporting exotic chessmen. There was also a strange-looking lamp with a flat, thrusting head like a snake.

'So,' said Louise, crossing her legs and staring rather aggressively at the two policemen. 'What do you actually want to know?'

'How long have you employed Mr Leathers?'

Before she could reply, they heard footsteps running

quickly above their heads then down some stairs.

'Louise? Was that someone at the door?'

There was more than simple curiosity behind the question. Barnaby heard eagerness, perhaps even excitement. Valentine Fainlight came round the screen, pulling up short at the sight of the two policemen.

You would never have known, thought the chief inspector, that they were brother and sister. Valentine had thick, straight hair the colour of butter, a squarish face, pale green eyes and a large nose. He was shorter than Louise and chunky with it.

'They're asking about Charlie Leathers.'

'Really?' He sat next to his sister, pulled out a packet of Karelias and lit up. 'I can't imagine we'll be much use.'

Troy's nostrils twitched. Earlier that year he had given up smoking for the sake of his little girl Talisa Leanne, now four. For some months up to then he had been inhaling just in the bathroom then blowing the results out of the window. Maureen thought smoking only in the shower might break the habit. She was like that. Very sarcastic.

'What can you tell me about Mr Leathers?' asked the chief inspector.

'Next to nothing,' said Valentine. 'We told him what to do and he got on with it. Once a month we paid him. End of story.'

'Did he work inside the house?'

'No. Just in the garden.'

Barnaby had noticed the garden, which lay at the back of the house. A serene, extremely formal arrange-ment of golden gravel swirled into nautilus circles. Several huge earthenware amphorae were carefully positioned and there was a long, rectangular pool lined with black tiles on which floated several white lilies. The whole was enclosed by a wall holding many alcoves in which statues posed in positions that were excessively formal, even for statues.

The chief inspector, who was a keen gardener, wouldn't have liked to work there at all. A bloodless, even slightly sinister environment, he thought, and was reminded of a film he had seen when courting Joyce in the sixties. Last Year in something or other.

Seeing the boss momentarily distracted and keenly aware of the blank pages in his notebook, Troy leapt into the breach.

'No mid-morning chats over a cosy cuppa, then.'

They stared at him, then at each other and snorted with laughter. Troy flushed a dull pink. He thought of pretending he'd only been kidding (naturally they wouldn't be mingling with the hired help) but knew he wouldn't be confident enough to pull it off. The stain on his cheeks deepened. He decided he hated snotty-nosed clever dicks almost as much as he did do-gooders.

'So you have no idea who might have wanted to kill him?'

'That's right.' Louise, who was feeling rather mean, gave Troy a friendly smile. 'I don't suppose it's any help but I did see him the night he was killed.'

'It might be,' said Barnaby. 'What time was this?'

'About half ten. I think on his way to the Red Lion, dragging that poor little dog behind him.'

'Ah, yes. I believe you were involved when the animal was found, Mr Fainlight.'

Valentine shrugged. 'I ran them to the vet's, that's all.'

Sensibly, that should have been the end of the interview. It was plain that Leathers had hardly impinged upon their lives at all. And they knew nothing of his. But Barnaby was reluctant to leave. It wasn't just the extraordinariness of his surroundings. Or his pleasure, which was still going strong, in looking at Louise Fainlight. It was the feeling that there was present here what the jargon-ridden social services would have called a hidden agenda. It could be that whatever was running underneath the surface had no connection with the current investigation. In fact, that was more likely than not. But you never knew.

Barnaby assessed his next move. A link with Charlie boy if possible but anything that could open the matter out.

'Does Mrs Leathers work here as well?'

'No,' said Louise before the words were even out of his mouth. 'We use an agency in Aylesbury.'

'That's useful.' Barnaby noted the flashing speed of the denial. What was she trying to head him off from? Discussing Hetty Leathers? Surely not. Hetty Leathers' work? Maybe. 'I expect she's got more than enough to keep her busy at the Old Rectory.'

Something walked into the room then. A dark, breathing presence exposing that which had gone before for the mere chimera that it was. So, thought Barnaby, leaning back comfortably against his chestnut leather padding, whatever it is, it's over there.

'She can't half talk, that woman,' said Troy when they were once more passing beneath the sign with the wheatsheaves and cricket bats and cocky badger on their way to the car. 'Once she gets going.'

'Yes. It's a pity she didn't say anything relevant to our investigation.'

'We don't know that, sir. Best keep an open mind.' Though Troy carefully kept the satisfaction from his voice he felt the chief's sharp glance between his shoulder blades. Worth it, though. He had heard that little homily about a dozen times a day over the past ten years and for the first time in the history of the universe had managed to slip it into the conversation first. Ho, ho, ho.

Louise had talked about her years in banking. The problems of buying and selling property in London. She had discussed the building of Fainlights, describing how the conservative resistance of Causton town planning department had given way to snobbish pride when the eminence of the award-winning architect was drawn to their attention. She had described her own and her brother's childhood in Hong Kong and touched briefly on how she came to be living with him now. The creation of Barley Roscoe was mentioned, his growing fame and the new television adaptation.

Authors. Sergeant Troy sniffed, consigning yet another subspecies to his personal limbo. Fleetingly he marvelled at the chief's patience as he sat through all this irrelevant stuff then realised that he was not listening under duress but because he wanted to. When he had had enough – halfway through the saga of Louise's fight to extract a golden handshake from Goshawk Freres commensurate to her twelve-year input as a stocks and shares analyst, he made an excuse and left.

As Barnaby and his bagman reached the car, Troy said, 'Very tasty, Muzz Fainlight.'

'She certainly is.'

'What was the point of all that, d'you think?'

Barnaby climbed into the passenger seat, leaned back and closed his eyes. It was a good question but, at the moment, unanswerable. All he knew was that Valentine Fainlight had walked off the moment his sister started speaking to answer a telephone that Barnaby had not heard ring. Neither, he suspected, had Fainlight. And then Louise had simply talked. And talked. He had been – what was the word? Distracted? Diverted? No, filibustered, that was it. Obstructed even before he had made any attempt to ask any serious or relevant questions, had he known what they were.

At this stage it didn't matter. He could catch up with either or both again any time he chose. But what had been the point of such a forceful and elaborate diversion? Not, the chief inspector felt sure, to avoid further talk of Charlie Leathers. And why drag up all that stuff about her financial background? She struck him as someone who would naturally be rather discreet. Was it to deflect him from asking about her brother? A man who could tighten a garrotte if ever there was one. Probably, given those tremendously muscular arms and shoulders, with one hand tied behind his back. Whatever the reason, Barnaby was intrigued.

Troy released the handbrake, took first and lumbered out of the Red Lion car park.

'Try and avoid that camper van.'

Troy's lips tightened at the injustice. He was an excellent driver, first class. It was just being with the chief. The criticism made him nervous. It was the same with Maureen. And his mum. And his dad, come to that. In fact he only really drove well when he was by himself. But you couldn't tell people that. They'd never believe you.

A wonderful smell greeted the chief inspector when he walked into 17 Arbury Crescent. Which meant his beloved wife, Joyce, was not cooking. So who could be? Probably Mr Marks and Mr Spencer. Or, if he was really lucky . . .

'Cully!'

'Hello, Dad.' She gave him a big, unselfconscious hug and turned back to the pot. 'You've lost weight.'

'Really?' Barnaby spoke casually but was secretly delighted. He had been told by George Bullard at his last check-up that around thirty pounds had to go. No problem eating less at home but he was inclined to recover from any domestic ordeal by topping up in the canteen. 'I've been on the cabbage soup diet.'

'Ugh.' Cully gave a theatrical shudder. 'So, how's the new case going?'

'So-so. Interviewed a famous personage this afternoon.'

'Who was that, then?'

'Valentine Fainlight. He writes—'

'I know. I've met him.'

'You have?'

'First night party, three, maybe four years ago. He was with Bruno Magellan.'

'Who?'

'Wonderful theatre designer. I think they were together for quite a while.'

'He's living with his sister now.'

'Yes, Bruno died of Aids. It was very sad.'

Barnaby went into the hall to get some wine. Came

back with a bottle of Montzinger Dindarello '96, opened it and poured some.

'Any news on the commercial?'

'Nope. Still waiting. Still not cutting my hair. But Nico's up for the National on Saturday.'

'Good for Nicolas.' They clinked glasses. 'Where is he anyway?'

'Out with Mum buying "the present".' Cully's voice was a sarcastic drum roll. She hooked ironical quotation marks out of the air. Her parents' silver wedding was less than a month away.

'I thought presents were supposed to be a surprise.'

'They are. This will be yours from Mum. You buy one for her—'

'I know, I know. Thanks for your help, by the way.'

Cully had introduced her father to a friend from her student days, Dodie McIntosh, now a successful silversmith, and Barnaby had commissioned an oval, silver-backed hand mirror for his wife. The design was very lovely. Joyce's initials, flowingly interwined, were set in a heart, itself surrounded by a border of her favourite flowers, lily of the valley. The detail on every tiny bell was exquisite as the flowers continued, twisting round the handle of the mirror.

'And me and Nicolas get one for both of you.'

'Good grief.'

'I think it's brilliant,' Cully sniffed, stirred, tasted, 'especially with us going to this special place all over again. It sort of closes the circle.'

They had been talking about engagements a few nights earlier. Nicolas had thought the whole business passé. Cully had been rather scathing about wasting money on what she called 'some skinny little diamond chipping' when you could roll in the Caribbean surf with your best babe for a whole fortnight on the same money.

Joyce was still wearing her skinny chipping which was all Barnaby had been able to afford on a young constable's pay. He had given her the ring in its cheap leather box over dinner at a little French bistro in London. They had eaten boeuf bourguignon and tarte framboise washed down with the red house wine. Appreciating the significance of the occasion, the patron had let them take the menu away.

As their finances improved, Barnaby had offered to replace the tiny solitaire but Joyce would have none of it. She wore it with her band of gold and the beautiful emerald eternity ring bought to celebrate Cully's arrival, and insisted she would do so until the day she died.

It was Nicolas who had pointed out that the bistro in question, Mon Plaisir, was still thriving in Monmouth Street. Then Cully said they absolutely must go there to celebrate their silver wedding. Barnaby immediately agreed, relishing the wonderful synchronicity of the idea. Only Joyce hesitated, unsure about returning to a place of which she had such perfect memories.

'What's in this?' Barnaby took the wooden spoon from Cully's hand and gave the casserole a stir.

'Lamb, new potatoes, onions and baby turnips. Those peas go in at the last minute.'

'Couldn't you make huge amounts of everything every time you come and put it in the freezer?'

'No. How d'you think that would make Mum feel?'

'I know how it would make me feel.'

They both laughed. Barnaby heard a car in the drive, wandered into the sitting room and looked through the window. A Garden Centre van swung into the drive, closely followed by Joyce's Punto. She and Nicolas got out and conferred with the van driver. Then two men dragged a huge crated object from the back of the vehicle and carried it into the garage. Barnaby stared through the window in amazement then made his way back to the kitchen.

'Did you see that?' Joyce came in, gave her husband a kiss and found herself a glass.

'Of course I saw it.' Barnaby poured. 'It's as big as a house.'

'Well, it's nothing to do with you. In case you were wondering.' Joyce drank a little wine, pronounced it delicious, wandered over to her daughter and slipped an arm round her waist. 'That an Elizabeth David?'

'Mm. The Navarin Printanier.'

'I thought so.' She tasted the juice. 'Lovely. You're really coming on, darling.'

'Thanks, Mum.'

Barnaby went back to his window. The giant crate had been put down while Nico swung up the garage door. The chief inspector, quite sure it was his present, wracked his brains. There was only one thing he really needed, garden wise, and surely even in these stylish and sybaritic times no one made silver lawn mowers.

CHAPTER SIX

Before his 9 a.m. Friday briefing Barnaby had a quick read through the first of the house-to-house reports. They were disappointing. Apart from a statement from the landlord of the Red Lion that Charlie Leathers had been in the Smoking Bar until gone eleven, there was nothing really helpful. Confirmation that Charlie was a miserable old sod who wasn't too fussy where his fists landed came from several sources.

Apparently on the night in question he had also been boasting about coming into some money and how he was going to spend it. But as he was forever on about how he would spend his pools winnings or lottery handouts, no one paid him any mind. No mention anywhere that he gambled on anything else.

Barnaby pushed the sheets of paper irritably aside and sent up a quick prayer to the gods of cause and effect that this was not going to be 'a random'. Every investigating officer's dread, a stranger killing a stranger. No motive that any sane person could understand although, if caught, the murderer would often have passionately argued reasons why he had been driven to do it. Of course, with no single thread to instigate a search, they frequently weren't caught and huge amounts of time and money were poured away to no effect whatsoever.

Pushing this negative state of mind aside, the chief inspector got up quickly, scraped back his chair and shouted for coffee. There was no response and he remembered that Troy was running a computer search on the character who gave his name as simply Jax. It would be interesting to discover just what 'little bit of trouble' the man had been involved in.

Barnaby wandered into the main office, poured himself a cup of strong Colombian and looked around for his assistant. He spotted Troy at the far end of the room with one eye on his VDU and the other on a pretty telephonist. The chief inspector soft-footed over and slapped Troy hard on the back.

'Bloody hell!'

'How's it going?'

'I wish you wouldn't do that, sir.' Troy pushed and pulled on the lightly padded shoulders of his Cero Cerruti jacket. 'Not so good, actually.'

'What have you tried?'

'Jax, just in case. Jacks with a CK. Jacklin. Now working through Jackman, which seems to include about half the prison population.'

Barnaby watched over his sergeant's shoulder as faces flashed rapidly on and off the screen. Faces of unparalleled viciousness and kindly, snug little fellows you could put in your pocket and take home to mother. Black and white and all shades of brown. Tattooed and be-ringed or baby pink, round-eyed and smooth. Ugly shaven heads, all bumps and stubble and neat grey thatches.

'Blimey, get a load of this one.' Sergeant Troy held the button and they both studied the mug shot. A more depraved personality it would be hard to imagine.

Cannon ball head growing directly out of bullish shoulders. A spreading, deeply porous nose, thin lips drawn back from gappy, snarling teeth, ragged hair, the whole charming arrangement topped off with a leering squint of pure avarice.

'What's he done?'

'Bent solicitor.'

Shortly after this they came to the end of the Jackmans.

'Maybe,' suggested Sergeant Troy, 'our man's gone right away from his real name. You know – Saunders, Greenfield?'

'Doubt it. They don't have much imagination when it comes to an alias, fortunately for us. Try Jackson.'

There were a lot of Jacksons too but at last they found their quarry, dark-haired at the time of recording his matchless profile and with quite a heavy moustache but the same man nonetheless.

'Gotcha!' said Barnaby. 'So, what does his "bit of trouble" amount to?'

Troy tapped some more. Both men studied the screen then turned to each other with expressions of disturbed bewilderment.

'I don't believe this,' said Sergeant Troy.

'I do.' Barnaby remembered how his skin had tightened at the first sight of the chauffeur. His repulsion at the thought of gripping the outstretched hand deepened as he read the list of offences. 'What I can't believe is that old fool Lawrence letting the wicked bastard anywhere near his family.'

'Perhaps he doesn't know.'

'Of course he knows. He's on the resettlement board.'

＊　＊　＊

It was a pleasant drive to Ferne Basset. A warm wash of autumn sunshine drenched the hedgerows and patchily reflected light from the road, still damp after a recent shower. The fields were already being ploughed. Shining seams of rich brown earth curled up and over behind the harrow's teeth, to be picked over by a flock of screaming gulls.

The village was looking almost its old self. The police presence had departed, as had the fourth estate. A group of youngsters were acting the fool on the fringe of Carter's Wood where the crime had occurred. Running in and out of the trees making creepy 'whaah, whaah' noises, pretending to strangle themselves and each other, walking around stiff-armed and legged like Frankenstein's monster.

It was nearly one o'clock when they drove up to the Old Rectory. Troy, remembering Lionel Lawrence's long ago link with the chief constable, half expected a courtesy call at the house first with an explanation of what they were doing there. But Barnaby indicated that he should park right over the far side of the drive, as near to the chauffeur's flat as possible. As they got out, Troy spotted the Humber Hawk squatting heavily in the garage and said, 'Looks as if he's in, sir.'

Barnaby rapped loudly on the dark blue door. Around it clung a rich-smelling late honeysuckle and on the step were tubs of creamy petunias and salvias. Over their heads a window swung open.

'What do *you* want?'

'A word, Mr Jackson,' called up Troy.

Their knowledge of his name was a blow, Troy could

see. But surely the bloke had known they would be checking up on him?

'Didn't take you long to ferret that out.'

'Here or at the station, it's up to you,' said Barnaby. 'And get a move on. I don't like standing on doorsteps.'

The window closed but the door was not opened for several more minutes. Troy saw this as an 'in your face, make them wait, up yours' gesture. Barnaby was more concerned that something which had been on view was being tidied away. He wished now he had come with a search warrant but the circumstances hardly seemed to justify it. They had discovered nothing to connect Jackson with the death of Charlie Leathers. Merely that he was the sort of man whose past activities indicated a murderous lack of self-control.

They followed him up warmly carpeted stairs into a long, L-shaped bed-sitting room. This was comfortably furnished with, Barnaby could not help noticing, much newer pieces than the Rectory. There was an oatmeal carpet, attractive flower prints on the wall and cream curtains patterned with scarlet poppies. Several sets of weights were stacked against the skirting board. Two doors led off, presumably to the kitchen and bathroom.

Sergeant Troy stared at all this, his face flushing angrily. He thought of beggars lying in doorways open to all weather and any abuse that passing thugs might feel like dishing out. Of youngsters, dossing down at night in damp cardboard boxes. Of his own grandparents living on their state pension, counting every penny, proud of never being in debt. While this jammy bastard—

'Sergeant?'

'Sir.' Troy collected himself. He got out a notebook then sat in a comfortable fireside chair with orange cushions. Barnaby took its opposite number. Jackson stood leaning against the door.

'Make yourselves at home, why don't you?'

'You seem to have fallen on your feet, Terry.'

'Mr Jackson to you.'

'Now, the night Charlie Leathers died.'

'We've been through all that.'

'Well, we're going through it again.' Sergeant Troy ground out the words through clenched teeth.

'I was here from around seven. Watched the soaps.' He nodded towards a Sony portable television. 'Had a couple of beers, mixed up some Pot Noodles. Listened to John Peel on the radio. Went to bed.'

Barnaby nodded. He wouldn't be able to move Jackson from that. And the man was sharp enough to know they had nothing to place him at the scene of the crime or he'd have been down Causton nick long since. The chief inspector moved to more flexible matters.

'This gambling Charlie told you about, how did he place his bets?'

'Phone.'

'Who was the bookie?' asked Sergeant Troy.

'Dunno.'

'But they were pursuing him and he was frightened?'

'That's right.'

'Funny nobody else seems to know about this,' said Troy. 'Not even his wife.'

'That sour old bitch?' Jackson laughed. 'All he dreamt about, poor old Charlie, was buttered crumpet. Know what I mean?'

'Or his cronies in the Red Lion.'

Jackson shrugged.

'I think you made it all up.'

'Thinking's free.'

'Was he familiar with your background, Terry?' asked the chief inspector.

'I'm starting from scratch here. I told you.'

'That must be nice. Wipe out the past, just like that.'

'Yeah.' Jackson looked wary, not sure he liked the way the conversation was going. He painted on an ingratiating smile. His incisors, so sharply pointed they could have been filed, twinkled and gleamed.

'Not what you'd call a tasty past, is it?' continued Barnaby.

'I've done my time.'

'You've done little else. Juvenile courts from day one. Thieving, lying, runner for the big boys. Look-out for dealers and pushers. Actual and grievous bodily harm, beating up a pensioner and leaving him more dead than alive. A stabbing—'

'I were egged on. There were a whole crowd of us.'

'You held the knife.'

'So? Everybody deserves a second chance.'

It wasn't a whine, just a simple statement of fact. Barnaby wondered if the pensioner might have liked a second chance. Or the guy left lying in the gutter with a punctured lung. He said, 'If you got what you deserved, Jackson, the world might be a sweeter smelling place.'

Downstairs the flat door opened and closed. Barnaby, watching Terry Jackson, marvelled at what happened next. A strong and heartless man was transformed, before his very eyes, into a persecuted, hunted creature driven by cruel fate to the very end of its despairing tether. All the steel dissolved from his muscular frame which had now become so soft and boneless it could no longer support him. His legs buckled. He crouched on the floor hugging his knees to his chest, hiding his face.

'What on earth is happening here, Jax?'

The boy (yes, boy, for so he had become) slowly lifted his head and gazed with great agitation at the Reverend Lawrence. Both policemen stared in disbelief at the pale and fearful countenance, the troubled eyes now swimming with moisture, the shaking, tremulous mouth.

'They just pushed in and started on me, Lionel. I ain't done nothing.'

'I know that, Jax. It's all right.'

'I promised you I'd never let you down.'

Lionel Lawrence turned and faced Barnaby. He looked severe and disappointed, giving the impression that if anyone had let him down it was Her Majesty's Police Inspectorate.

'Why are you persecuting this young man?'

'There's no question of persecution, sir. We are simply pursuing our inquiries into the death of Mr Leathers.'

'I'd've thought,' suggested Sergeant Troy, 'you'd want that thoroughly gone into. Him being your employee, so to speak.'

'This is my property. If you need to speak to Jax again, you call at the Rectory first. I shall come over here with you. There'll be no more bullying. He has that right.'

'Actually, he doesn't.' Barnaby nodded angrily to his sergeant who put away his notebook and got up to leave. The chief inspector followed, glancing back just once.

Lionel Lawrence was bending over, helping Jackson to his feet. Jackson was clinging to the older man's arm for support. His tear-stained face glowed with pious gratitude as if he had received a blessing.

Barnaby, nauseated, slammed the door and hurried down the stairs.

'Gay as a bent banana, that old geezer.' Sergeant Troy strode towards the car, giving vent to his feelings by kicking furiously at the gravel.

'I don't think so.'

'What, then? What's he doing it *for*?'

What was Lionel Lawrence doing it for? Barnaby let the question occupy his mind as Troy churned up the drive and zoomed into the main road.

Unlike many of his colleagues, the chief inspector did not automatically lump all 'do-gooders' together and despise the lot. He had met very many, both professional and amateur, during his long career as a policeman and grown to recognise the different types and the many different angles from which they approached the business. There were always quite a few who denied they had any angle at all. And many more who were extremely muddled as to what their angle actually was.

Many were in it for the power it gave them, the opportunity to forge relationships where they would always be in charge. These were the sort of people whose personality and talents made it highly unlikely that, in the normal run of things, they would ever have authority over anything more charismatic than the office cat. With them, compassion was merely a mask for condescension.

This same rationale applied to the socially inept. Usually without stable, happy relationships in their own lives, these emotional inadequates would start off with the huge advantage of being able to call the psychological shots. Frequently for the first time in their lives someone needed them.

Then there were those romantically drawn to what they saw as the glamour of violence. Never, in reality, having been on the receiving end, these people sometimes excitedly took up prison visiting. With a warder always close by they could spend quality time with what they believed would be some of the wildest and most dangerous specimens of humanity. Barnaby had once had dealings with a Quaker visitor, a pacifist, who preferred to befriend only murderers. When this paradox was drawn to his attention, he saw nothing odd in it at all.

One could add to this the early retired with woolly, undirected feelings of altruism and the small number of comfortably off who still had a social conscience. Then one was left with the few, the very few remarkable human beings who, without a single string attached, simply loved their fellow man. Barnaby had met many who saw themselves in this role. In actual fact, in over thirty years, he had come across two.

So, where did that leave Lionel Lawrence? The chief inspector decided to find out more about the man. For instance, did the Lawrences have children? If the answer was no, this might be the reason he so consistently offered sanctuary to the young. (Didn't someone mention a girl who had run away?) Had he always been in the Church? Was this his first marriage? If so, how did he live before it took place? And did this warm bath of unreasoned sentiment he was presently wallowing in ever splash over to console the plain, the middle-aged or elderly of either sex? And if not, why not?

The DCI's attention was rudely catapulted back to the present when Sergeant Troy honked furiously and jerked his head towards a man with a red setter. Both were patiently waiting to cross the road and did so with understandable speed while Troy, still seething at the repulsive tableau he had just witnessed, violently revved the engine.

As the policemen left the village, they passed Evadne Pleat's Morris Minor coupé just turning into Tall Trees Lane. She trundled inch by inch down the narrow space, crushing thistles and nettles and getting various sticky bits and assorted fungi attached to the wheels. She tried not to think about reversing back up.

Many would think it the height of foolishness to have driven down in the first place but Evadne had a precious cargo that could not safely be otherwise transported. Hetty Leathers and Candy were in the back. Hetty held the dog in her arms. She could not bear the thought of shutting her away in a box or basket after what she had suffered. And carrying her down the lane, however carefully, would still involve the risk of stumbling, maybe even falling, and dropping her precious burden.

Evadne parked directly outside the cottage and

Hetty passed over the key. When the front door was unlocked she climbed out very, very carefully.

Both women stood inside the kitchen smiling at each other. Hetty was reluctant to let go of the dog and eventually sat down by the Raeburn with Candy on her lap while Evadne made them all some tea.

'Do you think she'll be able to get in and out of her basket?'

'Not really,' replied Evadne. 'I think it will be easier to just put a cushion on the floor.'

They both studied the dog who lay awkwardly on her back gazing up at Hetty. Her back leg was in plaster and stuck straight up in the air. The wound on her head and the tattered ear had been extensively stitched and she wore a deep, stiff white collar to stop her scratching. Her ribs were tightly bound with an elastic bandage. Hetty thought she looked quite comical, in a quaint, dog Toby sort of way. Hetty could afford that sort of frivolous observation now that she knew Candy would survive.

'Is . . . um . . .' Evadne lowered her nose into a canister celebrating the Queen and Prince Philip's Silver Wedding. It held some very black, powerfully pungent dusty stuff. She sniffed daintily, recoiling in disbelief. 'Is this . . .?'

'That's it,' said Hetty cheerfully. 'One each and one for the pot.'

'Right ho.' Evadne added boiling water, unhooked two jolly Tower of London mugs from a pine stand and looked around for a strainer.

'You have to wait for it to brew, Evadne. At least five minutes.'

'This will be fine for me.'

114

Evadne poured half a mug for herself, waited until Hetty gave the nod then poured her friend's drink. Inky black with a lot of milk and two large sugars.

'Are you sure this is what you want?'

'Beautiful.' Hetty took a long swig. 'Tea you could trot a mouse on, as my dad used to say.'

Evadne had a happy moment picturing the mouse skating back and forth across the surface of Hetty's drink, its arms folded neatly behind its back, then sat down and attempted to stroke Candy. But so little of the dog was exposed she had to settle for gently patting her nose.

'Will you be all right now?' Evadne meant both of them, which Hetty immediately understood.

'We will. You've been so kind.'

'Nonsense.' Evadne gruffly dismissed the idea of being kind as genuinely kind people always do. 'Well, I'd better get back to my family.'

Hetty decided to walk Evadne to the gate. But she was no sooner out of Candy's sight than the dog started to softly howl. Awful, whimpering cries that smote both women to the heart. Hetty turned back.

'She's frightened,' said Evadne. 'You won't be able to leave her alone for a while. Will you be able to manage?'

'Yes. Pauline can help with the shopping.'

'I'll call round tomorrow.'

But the door was already closing. Evadne regarded her Morris coupé uncertainly. It seemed as fastly stuck between hedge and hedge as a cork in a bottle. She could not imagine how on earth she ever drove down there and plainly it was out of the question for her to reverse back up. Help was needed.

She fought her way, pushing and struggling, past the car, then strode off towards the village street picking goosegrass off her pale green linen Oxford bags. She thought of calling in at the Red Lion. They were a jolly crew there. Very friendly, always letting fly some merry banter as she strode by with the Pekes.

On the other hand there might be a fair bit of chat about who was or wasn't safe to drive. Who could spare the time. And who would be perfect if only he wasn't over Aylesbury way visiting his mother. In other words, delay.

Evadne was anxious to get the matter sorted so she could return home and prepare the Pekes' lunch. Mazeppa liked her warm jelly starter out of the marrow bone and onto a nice bit of fresh toast by midday or her digestion, always delicate, became positively flimsy.

And then Evadne thought of Valentine Fainlight. Of how kind he had been when he had come across Hetty stumbling around with her injured burden. He would help. In fact he would probably be glad to have the opportunity to call at the bungalow and see how Candy was getting along.

Valentine was only pretending to work. He had been messing about – cleaning brushes, half sketching illustrations for scenes as yet unwritten that would in all likelihood remain so – all morning. And when the mysterious echo of door chimes shivered around the glass walls, his brain was so crammed with erotic images that he heard nothing. Electrically charged sights and sounds and sensations and smells from the previous night ran constantly over and through his mind.

Mingled with these thrilling reflections were memories of the first time Jax had let him into the flat. This had been nearly four months ago. Until that evening they had barely spoken and then only to exchange the banal courtesies of strangers. But they had also exchanged looks which had left Valentine, entranced by the man's beauty, in an agony of calculation as to when and where and how it might happen.

When it did, when the blue door was finally left open, he had set one foot carefully on the staircase bearing with him the anticipation of weeks, believing yet not quite believing, half expecting still that the interior door would be locked.

It wasn't. He had entered the room and stood, hesitant and trembling with emotion, on the threshold. He called quietly 'Hello' and sensed a movement behind him. A strong smooth arm slid across his chest, gripping him tight, pulling him backwards. Warm lips burned the back of his neck, a tongue outlined his ear then slid, flickering like a snake's, deeply inside. Very slowly his shirt was pulled free and unbuttoned.

Valentine, suddenly and blindingly happy, tried to turn round. To embrace the other's firm sweating flesh, to speak, but the naked arm tightened and he could not move. No longer wished to move.

Jax started to whisper, pouring a stream of filth into his captive's ear, then moved savagely and suddenly inside him. Valentine, gasping and sobbing for breath, descended into a nightmare of excitement and pain.

Why had he thought there might be kindness? Watching Jax wander over to the bathroom, listening to the shower running, slowly putting on his own clothes, Valentine asked the question then despised himself for a weakling. What had he expected? It had been a thrilling experience, joy and alarm in equal proportions – anyone up for casual sex should be so lucky.

Jax came out wearing a robe and a conqueror's smile. He was tired and had to rest now so Val must excuse him. Valentine, concealing his disappointment that post-coital ciggies were not on the menu, hesitated. He had brought money even while hoping it would prove to be unnecessary. Not because he was mean but because he was looking for something money could not buy. But he had to be sure he would be welcome again.

'I wonder . . .' He opened his jacket. The outline of the well-filled wallet in the inside breast pocket was plain to see. 'That is . . .'

'Very good of you, Val.'

'I wouldn't wish.'

'I'll be honest. Money's too tight to mention at the moment.'

'Perhaps I can.'

'The Giro goes nowhere.'

Val simply removed all the notes from the wallet and placed them carefully on the coffee table. Jax, calm and relaxed, did not even glance their way. And though he said goodnight, he did not say thank you.

After barely twenty-four hours, Val had been desperate to get into the garage flat again. And so it had continued.

Valentine had never thought of himself as masochistic. Had never sought or enjoyed pain. But he soon recognised, with a little thrill of horror, that this man could do anything to him, anything at all, and he would not resist. Would even welcome whatever situation developed between them.

Finally the sound of the bell penetrated this dense fog of recollection. Louise would not ring. She had a key. It must be him! Valentine jumped up from his desk, flew down the barley sugar stick spiral staircase and flung open the front door.

The woman with all the dogs at Mulberry Cottage stood outside. She was wearing an extraordinary outfit and her wildly snagged hair was full of pollen and leaves and seeds and even a couple of blackberries.

It took Valentine a moment to collect his wits and a moment more to grasp what she was saying. It was some garbled tale about a motor car that would not reverse, yet another injured dog and someone called Piers who needed to be let out on the stroke of twelve if he was to maintain his natural position as team leader.

Valentine went to get his jacket. Whatever the drama actually involved, sorting it out would help pass the time until evening – when dusk would fall and he could once more present himself at the blue painted door.

Being invited to the Old Rectory for coffee, though not a rare occurrence, did not happen all that often. When Ann had rung up yesterday evening and suggested it, Louise had said yes straightaway although she had planned that morning to drive to the library at Causton. She could do so later in the day and was unhappy to find herself seeing this as 'filling the afternoon up'. Needing to kill time was an unpleasant novelty. When working she had frequently prayed for a forty-eight-hour day.

She spent the time before leaving attempting to assess her relationship with Ann Lawrence honestly. Almost testing it for strength. As terms of friendship went, she hadn't really known Ann very long. Their mutual confidences were not what some women might call intimate. But Louise had experienced a genuine degree of warmth in these exchanges and also felt that Ann would prove to be both discreet and loyal.

The fact of the matter was that she was longing to share with someone sympathetic her worries about Valentine. There were other friends she could have talked to, but none nearby and no one who had actually stood face to face with the individual at the heart of the matter. She knew Ann loathed Jax, although this had never been put into words, and also suspected she was afraid of him.

For a while, sleepless in the middle of the night, Louise toyed with the idea of ringing the Samaritans. The service was confidential and perhaps it would be easier to talk to a kindly, anonymous listener, especially by telephone.

But Louise had no sooner started to dial than she had second thoughts. What could she say? My brother is homosexual and is seeing a man I believe to be dangerously violent. What would they say? Are you quite sure about that? No. How well do you know this man? Not at all. What age is your brother? Forty-three. Have you tried to talk to him about this? Once. It caused such a rift in our relationship I swore I'd never try again. Do you think he might be persuaded to talk to us himself? Under no circumstances.

End of story.

Now she checked the clock. Almost eleven. Louise got ready to leave in a half-hearted way, not bothering with make-up, just pinning her hair loosely on top of her head. She put on a loose-fitting, long-sleeved apricot linen dress and some dark glasses. The day was not really sunny enough to merit them but lack of sleep had left bruised-looking smudges beneath her eyes.

When no one appeared at the front of the Old Rectory, Louise made her way round the side of the house, relieved to see the garage door wide open and the car missing.

The back entrance was reached through a conservatory. Very large and very old, it held garden paraphernalia. Wellingtons, old jackets, a couple of straw hats and dozens of flowering plants. A well-established Hamburg vine as thick and tough as a man's arm and planted directly in the earth twined, pale and splintery, across the roof. The whole place had a rich earthy fragrance that was very pleasant. Louise lingered a moment, taking pleasure in the dense almost oppressive silence broken only by the hiss and trickle of a garden hose.

She pushed open the back door and called 'Hello?' There was no reply. Louise wondered if Ann had simply forgotten her invitation and gone out, leaving the door unlocked. She often did this, to Louise's city-bred incredulity.

But although Ann proved to be in the kitchen, it was plain she had indeed forgotten the invitation. When Louise put her head round the door, Ann stared blankly across the room as if at a complete stranger – only for a fraction of a second but long enough for Louise to recognise that this was not going to be the person to whom she could unburden her heart. Driven by need, she must have been fantasising earlier, investing what she saw now was merely a pleasantly amiable acquaintance with qualities it did not have. Louise, even while recognising how unfair this was to Ann, was surprised by how disappointed she felt.

'Louise! Oh, I'm sorry. I quite – Oh dear . . .'

'It doesn't matter.'

'Of course it does. Please, sit down.'

Ann, surely more distressed, it seemed to Louise, than the occasion warranted, started to hurry about, collecting the cafetière, washing out the grounds, finding some deep yellow breakfast cups. And all with a flurried unhappy air of determination that seemed further to demonstrate just how unwelcome the interruption actually was.

'Look,' said Louise, who had not sat down, 'we can do this another time.'

'No, no. You must stay.'

'Could we just have tea then?' She pulled out a ladderback chair. 'A bag in a mug would be fine.'

Ann immediately abandoned the coffee-making preparations and switched on the electric kettle which straightaway switched itself off. She stared at Louise. 'I don't know. This morning everything seems . . .' The rest of the sentence was lost to her.

'Let me.' Louise got up and filled the kettle. The sink was full of dirty dishes. She looked around for tea bags and made the drinks while at the same time keeping an eye on Ann, now sitting at the table, pale-faced and trembling slightly from head to foot.

Louise took the tea over, sat down and took Ann's hand. It was dry and cold. They sat silently for quite a long time. Comfortable at first, Louise eventually began to feel awkward in the continuing silence.

'What is it, Ann? Are you ill?'

'No.'

'You're shaking.'

'Oh, yes.' Ann began to contradict herself. 'I think it's the flu. A cold. Something like that.'

Whatever it was, it was nothing like that. Louise wondered if there had been some sad family news. A death, maybe. But then remembered that Ann had no close living relatives. Or friends, except in the village. Could it be a delayed reaction to Charlie Leathers' murder? It seemed unlikely. Like everyone else, she had not liked the man.

'Do you want to talk about it?' She released the hand.

Ann lifted her head and looked at Louise. Then stared vacantly at the mugs of tea, the stale toast crumbs, the branches of purple berberis in a jug. Did she want to talk about it? God, yes. Sometimes she wanted to talk about it so desperately she feared she would not be able to control herself. That she would be driven, like the poor wandering rejects from mental hospitals, to seize a total stranger in the street and force on him her dreadful secret.

But could she trust Louise? How well did she really know her? Ann thought she would probably be safer with the passerby. They would simply assume she was mad and that would be an end to it.

What had happened was this. Earlier that morning, just before ten thirty to be precise, Ann found a second letter lying in the little cage behind the front door. Strangely, considering she was still reeling from the shock of receiving the first, she did not immediately recognise it for what it was.

The post proper had been delivered half an hour earlier and had proved as boringly innocuous as ever. Most of it was junk and Ann threw it into the bin. Lionel, running around gathering his wits and his papers in readiness for a working lunch with the Caritas Trust Committee, pushed what was left into his briefcase.

After breakfast Ann helped Lionel on with his coat, found him a light Paisley muffler to protect his chest and left him still dithering over his papers to see how Mrs Leathers and Candy were keeping. On the way back she called at Brian's Emporium for some fresh bread and oranges and bought stamps at the post office. Altogether she was away from the house for probably half an hour.

During that time anyone in the village could have seen her and quite a few probably had. The thought of one of them watching and waiting until the house was empty and she had safely turned into Hetty's lane or joined the post office queue then slipping their poisonous message through her letter box was chilling, to put it mildly.

Her name was printed in full on the envelope. The words inside, once more cut and pasted, looked different. This time they were all from newspaper headlines. Ann stared at the large black threatening capitals: **'FIVE GRAND THIS TIME MURDERER SAME PLACE SAME TIME TOMORROW'**.

She had walked unseeingly to the kitchen, dropped

the letter and envelope into the Aga then sat bolt upright at the table. Where could she possibly find five thousand pounds in the next twenty-four hours? Even if she sold all her mother's jewellery, so very dear to her, it would not raise so much.

Of course, she owned the house. Compared to what the Old Rectory was worth, even in its present shabby state, a few thousand was a drop in the ocean. She had no doubt the bank would lend against such sterling security. But then what? Interest would be charged straightaway. She would have to repay this and the loan which she could only do by cashing in some of her securities, thus reducing the only income she had. It was already barely sufficient for two people to live on. And what if another demand turned up?

She had just reached this wretched stage in her reasonings when Louise appeared. She was concerned, kind. Made some tea. And was now asking if she, Ann, wanted to talk about it.

The temptation was terrible. Ann could feel her mouth filling up with words. Explanations, excuses. How the whole terrible business with Carlotta had flared into life and run wild – totally out of her control. The first sentence 'it wasn't my fault' was on her lips, just about to spill over and run when the telephone rang.

It was only a message for Lionel but afterwards Ann saw the interruption as miraculously timely. What a fool she had been even to contemplate confiding in Louise. How well did she really know the woman? The Fainlights' house almost overlooked the Rectory. Louise would be in a perfect position to see just when she went out, leaving the coast clear. How easy to run over, deliver the letter, watch for the victim's return then come round to gloat. Look how sneakily she had entered the house, not even ringing the front door bell.

Ann stared suspiciously across the table, quite forgetting that she herself had invited Louise. Now Louise was withdrawing, preparing to leave. Just as well. From this moment Ann would keep a very sharp curb on her tongue. And trust absolutely no one.

The 9 p.m. briefing was just that, brief. And as disheartening as Barnaby feared it would be. There were no leads at all. The house-to-house, now concluded, had come up with virtually nothing they didn't know already. There seemed to be no dark secrets in Charlie Leathers' past. He was born and raised in the village and everyone knew everything about him. His life was an open, if not very pleasant, book.

The DCI left the incident room and its wall of hideous blow-ups for the much more pleasant surroundings of the press office where he was due to record a television appeal for information, to be shown at ten thirty at the end of the local evening news summary.

He sat stoically being powdered against shine – a procedure he loathed – while wondering how Nicolas could stand putting the muck all over his face two afternoons and six nights a week. Having done his stuff and washed his face he was on the point of leaving the building when Sergeant Troy put his head round the door to say there was someone waiting to see him in reception.

'I'm really sorry to come so late.' It was Hetty

Leathers' daughter. 'Tell the truth, I thought you might be gone.'

'Not at all, Mrs Grantham.' Barnaby led the way to a couple of worn leather seats at the far end of the reception area.

'It won't take a minute.'

Actually Pauline was now in rather a different frame of mind from when she had first heard about Charlie's 'scrapbook' from her mother. Coming so close to the discovery of the murder, it had appeared extremely significant. Then, gradually, its possible significance had faded and now she sat with her carrier bag full of chopped about newspaper feeling a bit of a fool. In fact she had almost chucked the stuff back in the bin and forgotten the whole idea.

Hurriedly she explained all this to Barnaby, adding several flurried apologies for wasting his time. But he seemed grateful that she had come in. Far from taking the bag with a quick thank you, he questioned her closely as to what had led up to the discovery.

'Well, it was when you asked if Dad had done anything out of the ordinary in the last couple of days.'

'I remember.'

'Apparently the night before he . . . it happened he went into the front room with the paper and some scissors. He was in there ages. When Mum went to see if he wanted a cup of tea he flew at her.'

'What made your mother think he was compiling a scrapbook?'

'He was cutting things out. And there was a pot of glue on the table. And another funny thing, Pauline continued hastily as Barnaby seemed about to speak, 'he cleared up after himself. And that's not just a first, it's a bloody miracle.'

'And these sheets are what was left?'

'Yes – trimmings, everything. He put them in the dustbin. Lucky it was Tuesday not Monday or the bin men would have had it.'

Back in his office Barnaby pulled some chopped-about sheets of *The People* from the KwikSave plastic bag. The front page – 'Massacre of the Innocents' – was dated Sunday, 16 August. Troy, still hanging about and welcoming the overtime, handled the sheets in some bewilderment.

'Don't see how making a scrapbook can get a man knocked off.'

'He wasn't making a scrapbook.'

'What then?'

'Use your brains.'

Troy flirted with that one for a moment, tucking his eyebrows into a serious pleat and looking intense. He was about to give up when something occurred to him.

'Whatever Leathers cut out, he did it for a reason. So we won't find the missing pieces in here.'

'They'll be in the original. Take this to the incident room before you go and get somebody from the night shift on to it. Then we can compare.'

'Ah. Nice one, chief.'

It seemed so obvious when pointed out. So why couldn't he, Troy, just once come up with something startling and original and perceptive. See a link that everyone else had overlooked. Place a piece of evidence in just the right position to shed a light over the whole case and bring it to a successful conclusion. Once was all he asked. A chance to pip the DCI to the post before he retired. Dream on, sunshine. Dream on.

CHAPTER SEVEN

Barnaby took the lift down to the incident room the following morning metaphorically crossing his fingers for a lucky break. Few things were more frustrating than an absolutely static case with not a single apparent weakness that could be leaned on and worried into revelation. Perhaps Charlie's 'scrapbook' would prove to be that weakness. If so, it would transform Barnaby's temper, well to the bad after a sharp exchange with Joyce during breakfast.

'You're not going to the station, Tom.' He had got up from the table, picked up his jacket and was craftily easing his way towards the door.

'Tom!'

'Uh huh?'

'It's your rest day.'

'Something really important turned up as I was leaving yesterday.'

'So?'

'I thought you'd rather I handled it today than spend half last night chasing things up.'

'Can't someone else "handle it" and phone through?'

'I'd rather do it my—'

'When you've got your teeth into something you're like a dog with a bone. Frightened to death someone else is going to get a bite.'

'Rubbish.' Barnaby fumbled for his car keys and wondered if it was true. 'Anyway, I'm home all day tomorrow.'

'You know the Gavestons are coming for dinner?'

He had quite forgotten. 'Yes.'

'Half past six, latest.'

'Yes!' shouted Barnaby then was sorry and attempted a conciliatory kiss.

Joyce turned her cheek away and slammed the kitchen door. Barnaby slammed the front door. He got into his Astra and slammed that door then drove aggressively to the station, which was quite unlike him. At the station he strode first to the lift and then to his office where, just to make the numbers even, he slammed that door as well.

He hoped this latest set-to didn't mean his wife and daughter would be ganging up on him, as they were wont to do from time to time, urging early retirement. Not that he hadn't occasionally longed for an easier life himself. In spite of the team spirit and boozy, post-shift camaraderie, the sometimes umbilically close connections and protecting of each other's backs, the fact remained that, at least in its upper echelons, the force was a pool of sharks. Great powerful beasts swimming around, jaws snapping, tails athwack. Egoistic, fiercely competitive individuals determined to strive ahead. To divide and rule.

And old sharks had better beware. No wonder so many of these sad, exhausted creatures ended up, long before it was strictly necessary, sheltered from the fighting behind a desk at headquarters. But not this one. Too many years at the sharp end had spoiled DCI Barnaby for such cushy, toothless repose.

Emerging from the lift, the chief inspector ran into his sergeant coming out of the Gents and reeking of high tar nicotine.

'Still testing your resistance, Troy?'

'It's all very well for you, sir. An addiction can be really . . .'

'Addictive?'

'Yeah. Nobody ever praises you, do they?'

'What?'

'People who've never smoked. Maureen, for example. They don't know what it's like.'

Barnaby was in no mood for such whingeing. He strode ahead to the incident room, slapped a near-empty folder of notes onto his desk and stared at his dejected-looking team. It was not only dejected but somewhat depleted. He stared fiercely round the room.

'Where's WPC Mitchell?'

'On her way,' said Inspector Carter. 'She's been working—'

'She shouldn't be on her bloody way! She should be here. You.' He jabbed a finger at a constable perched on a table. 'Go and—'

But at that moment Katie Mitchell rushed in. All smiles, all excitement.

'Sir! I've—'

'You're late.'

'The courier didn't bring the original till half five this morning. And there were so many shreds and bits, assembling it took for ever.'

'Ah,' said Barnaby. 'I see.'

'And after all that there were only six words.'

Barnaby held out his hand. WPC Mitchell came forward and placed a sheet of A4 paper in it.

'I've stuck them on in the only order that makes sense, sir.'

'So you have,' said Barnaby, taking the 'only order' in. And his heart sang.

'*I saw you push her in.*'

Barnaby read out the words aloud again into the silence. He could see and feel the whole room becoming charged with interest and vitality. Lethargy and disappointment were wiped out in this one single moment of revelation.

The anonymous telephone call, it now seemed, was not a hoax. The strong likelihood was that someone actually had fallen or been pushed into the Misbourne at some period shortly before 10.32 p.m. on Sunday, 16 August.

'Does anyone have any ideas,' asked Barnaby, 'as to how this breakthrough might put us on fast forward?'

Sergeant Troy did not hesitate. Although his thoughts and opinions were rarely canvassed, nevertheless he kept his mind in good trim. He could not bear to be found wanting.

'Leathers saw someone being shoved into the river and tried a spot of financial arm-twisting. Instead of paying up, whoever it was gave him a nice wire collar. Also, as one of Lionel Lawrence's bleeding hearts disappeared at roughly the same time, I'd say the two incidents were definitely connected.' Troy paused, suddenly feeling very exposed, and stared hard at the nearest computer screen. The analysis seemed pretty sound to him but he knew the gaffer. Barnaby had a way of slicing through a presentation, finding the weak link and snapping it back hard under your nose, like a rubber band with a pebble in it.

'Good.'

'Sir.' Troy received this with a certain amount of caution. He'd been here before. Something nice then a sting from the scorpion's tail – e.g., good – for someone with three per cent of a dead amoeba's single brain cell.

'Although . . .'

Here we go.

'The idea that this,' Barnaby waved the paper, 'is the first step to blackmail, though extremely likely, must be only supposition at this stage.'

He smiled happily around at his officers, lifted right out of his previous mood of despondency. 'Anyone else? Yes, Inspector Carter.'

'This nine, nine, nine call, sir. Maybe it was made by whoever did the pushing. They might have panicked. Had second thoughts.'

'A rescue would hardly be in their interest,' said Sergeant Brierley. 'They could end up being accused of assault, or worse.'

'Whoever it was could have fallen in accidentally,' suggested Troy. 'During a fight, say.'

'That's no lever for blackmail.'

'Oh, yeah. Got it.' I'm not saying another word during this briefing. Not a bloody word.

'Right,' said Barnaby. 'Now, I want the tape of this anonymous call from force headquarters, so somebody get on to Kidlington. Also a copy of the report submitted by the investigation team who were called out to the river. Then we'll start yet another house-to-house at Ferne Basset – leave out the Old Rectory, I'll be calling there myself – plus the other two villages in the triangle, Swan Myrren and Martyr Bunting. Check on any sounds of disturbance heard between the hours of nine o'clock, say, and midnight. Bear in mind that could be anywhere – not necessarily on or near the river. Arguments travel.

'As do floaters. So we'll have to fax not just all our stations but borderline counties as well – Oxford, Wiltshire. And notify the river authorities. They might even run a search if we're in luck. And I want an examination of the river bank as far as the weir but starting in the village. This is where Leathers walked his dog so I should imagine this is where he saw her pushed in. Plus a check on all the hospitals and morgues in that area. They may have had a drowning during the past six days. Don't forget the outpatients' register. She could well have climbed out or been fished out, needed medical treatment then been sent home. Wherever that proves to be.'

'Do we specifically ask about a young woman, sir?' asked Constable Phillips.

'No. I don't want it narrowed down at this stage. We're still only guessing.' Barnaby waved his A4 sheet with the six-word message briefly in the air before laying it on his desk. 'I want copies of this on the board. Will someone please get Mrs Pauline Grantham's prints, for elimination, and Leathers' for confirmation. Also I want the phone box at Ferne Basset printed though I suspect after six days it'll be a waste of time.'

As they all moved off, Barnaby sat back in his chair, eyes closed for a few moments of recapitulation. He decided to apply for a search warrant. It might be a good idea to look over the girl's room and he could imagine Lawrence's reaction should he turn up without the correct authority. Meanwhile . . .

'Troy.'

'Sir.' Sergeant Troy scrambled quickly to his feet.

'Mars Bar.'

Hetty Leathers was anxious to get back to work. She was surprised, after Pauline had returned home to her husband and children, how much she missed the company. Though Hetty would be the last person to suggest that an unhappy marriage was better than no marriage at all, there was no doubt you got used to having another human being around the place. Pauline rang every evening and the whole family would be over at the weekend but it wasn't quite the same.

The second reason was money. Hetty was in the deeply embarrassing position of being unable to pay for her husband's funeral. She had been horrified to discover exactly how much it would cost. Her only savings, just over two hundred pounds, had been penny-pinched from the housekeeping over the years. Occasionally there was a pound or two left at the end of the week; mainly there was nothing.

Candy was still showing great distress if Hetty as much as left the room so Ann Lawrence suggested she brought the dog to work with her. Ann drove down to the end of the lane, Hetty carried the dog to the car wrapped in her blanket and Candy spent the day in an old armchair by the Aga.

This was where she was lying, fast asleep, when Barnaby and Troy arrived. Barnaby noticed the garage was empty and was not entirely displeased. Presumably Jackson was driving the Reverend Lawrence about his business, which meant that Mrs Lawrence would be by herself.

He recalled their first meeting. Her shocked recoil when she understood who they were. Her extreme wariness during their questioning and hasty willingness to show them out. This time he would have a button to press. And he would press it. Hard.

But it was Hetty Leathers who opened the door and explained that both the Lawrences were out. She was very apologetic.

'We'd also like a word with you, Mrs Leathers.' Barnaby smiled, suddenly in the hall. 'If that's all right?'

'Well.' She stared anxiously at Sergeant Troy who was closing the heavy front door behind him. 'I am working.'

'Kitchen, is it?'

Now they were just as suddenly in the kitchen. Troy exclaimed with genuine pleasure at the sight of the little dog.

'She's getting better?'

'Yes. The vet said . . .'

Barnaby let them run on for a moment. It would relax Mrs Leathers, which might help when it came to answering questions. For himself, he was not really interested in animals unless well-stuffed, preferably with sage and onion and a nice strip of crackling on the side.

'Would you like a cup of tea?'

Both policemen said yes and sat round the long, worn deal table to drink it. There was a plate of biscuits too. Hetty, looking puzzled but interested, passed the sugar bowl. Troy took several spoonfuls, stirred then discreetly removed his notebook from his jacket pocket and placed it on his knee.

'What did you want, Inspector? Is it about Charlie again?'

'Not directly, Mrs Leathers. I'd like you to tell us, if you would, about the young girl who was recently staying here.'

'Carlotta?'

'I understand she ran away.'

'Good riddance,' said Hetty. 'She should never have been here in the first place, a girl like that.'

'Was she here long?' asked Sergeant Troy.

'Too long,' said Hetty. Then, when Barnaby smiled encouragingly, 'A couple of months.'

'What sort of person was she?'

'Two-faced. Talked to people like dirt unless the Rev was around, then butter wouldn't melt.'

The performance sounded familiar. Barnaby picked up the connection and followed it through. 'What about Jax, though? Two young people – I presume they got on?'

'No.' Hetty, deeply grudging, added, 'It's the one good thing you could say about the girl. She couldn't stand him.'

'Not one of your favourites either, then?' asked Sergeant Troy.

'Gives me the creeps. Mrs Lawrence won't have him in the house and I don't blame her.'

'Has that always been the case?'

'Pardon?'

'I mean, did something specific happen to cause it?'

'No. She put her foot down right from the beginning. Mind you, he got in the other day – Wednesday morning, I think it was. I went into the dining room to clear and there he was, leaning up against the door as if he owned the place. And poor Mrs Lawrence trembling and shaking like a leaf. I soon saw him off, I can tell you.'

Troy wrote Wednesday's date down, catching the chief's eye. It was gleaming with interested curiosity.

'Did she say what he wanted?'

'Something about the connecting phone not working. Load of rubbish.'

Barnaby waited a moment but nothing more seemed to be forthcoming on the subject so he turned the conversation back to Carlotta.

'Do you know anything about this girl's background? Where she originally came from, perhaps?'

'She come from where they all come from. That charity trust what the vicar's involved with.' Hetty drank some of her own tea and pushed the hazelnut biscuits in Sergeant Troy's direction. 'Ask me, it's money chucked down the drain. Why can't it go towards decent kids trying to make their way in the world?'

'You're right there, Mrs Leathers.' Sergeant Troy wolfed three biscuits.

'I understand that Carlotta disappeared after an argument,' said Barnaby. 'Do you happen to know what it was about?'

'No I don't and if I did I wouldn't tell you. I'm not discussing Mrs Lawrence behind her back.'

'I wouldn't expect—'

'That woman's a saint, what she's had to put up with.'

Ruffled feathers. There was a small silence. Barnaby nodded at the last statement, looking extremely sympathetic. Troy smiled and winked at the dog who had woken up. Candy yawned back at him. The chief inspector tentatively put another question.

'Did visitors call here to see Carlotta? Friends or relatives?'

'Not that I know of. She had the odd letter – airmail, from abroad. I won't tell you what she did with them.'

Plainly this was a threat without foundation. Both policemen waited patiently.

Hetty said, 'Straight in the fire.'

'Good heavens,' said Barnaby.

'Never even opened. I said to her one day, that might be important. What if someone's died?'

'How did she take that?' asked Troy, stirring it.

'Told me to mind my own blankety-blank business.' Hetty got up quickly then and started collecting the teacups. 'I've got to get on.'

She put the rest of the biscuits back in the tin under Troy's wistful gaze then took the teapot to the sink. Barnaby guessed that, although she had actually said very little, she was worried about having said too much. Perhaps of being disloyal. He decided to leave it for now. Should there be a next time he would talk to her at home where there might be less constraint. Troy replaced his notebook and started re-buttoning his jacket.

'Do you have any idea when Mrs Lawrence might be back?'

'She shouldn't be too long,' said Hetty. She had turned the taps full on now and Barnaby did not catch the words: 'She's had to go to the bank.'

He waited until she had turned them off then asked if he might look over Carlotta's room.

There was a deeply embarrassed silence. Finally Hetty, not looking him in the eye, said, 'I don't want to seem rude, Inspector, but aren't you supposed to have a . . . er . . . something . . .'

'I shall have a warrant later today, Mrs Leathers, but it would really save time if we could—'

'I just don't think the Reverend would like it.'

He'll have to lump it then, thought Sergeant Troy. He spent a pleasant few moments picturing Lionel lumping it and rather hoped Mrs L would stand firm. But he was to be disappointed.

'He won't have a choice,' warned Barnaby, 'when we come back after lunch.'

'Well . . . I should have to be present,' said Hetty, adding quickly, 'No offence.'

'We would expect you to be,' Sergeant Troy assured her.

And Barnaby said, 'Could you show us the way, please?'

It was a long climb to the attic. The first two sweeping staircases had wide and shallow steps, carpeted with deep blue and red Axminster patterned in the Turkish style and so faded in places its backing showed through. The banisters were solid dark oak ending in huge octagonal lantern shapes with large carved acorns on top.

'Mrs Lawrence used to slide down these,' said Hetty.

'Mrs Lawrence?' Troy stared at the wide gleaming bars in amazement.

'When she was little.'

'Ah.' He felt foolish and covered up quickly. 'I didn't realise you'd been here so long.'

'She used to put a cushion at the end. One day her father took it away and she really hurt herself.'

'What, on purpose?'

Hetty chose not to reply.

Having paused on the first landing for a breather, Barnaby said, 'You must have started straight from school.'

'That's right,' said Hetty. 'Fifteen I was. All my friends thought I was daft, coming to work here. They were off getting jobs in Boots or Woollies or some office or other.'

'So why didn't you?'

'I don't like those big places, full of people crowding you – foreigners as like as not – all gossip and back-biting. I wanted a quiet, orderly job with a nice family.'

Barnaby had started climbing again. Hetty followed, with Troy bringing up the rear, gazing about him. He was amazed at how much old stuff there was about. Dark, dreary oil paintings like you get in museums. Little carved brass tables. A big gong on a stand and a padded drumstick, the head wrapped in linen. Plus a fully-grown crocodile in a glass case. It was covered all over by cracked squares of shiny caramel-coloured skin. The beast was smiling, flashing hundreds of winky, twinkly teeth.

'Keep up, Sergeant.'

'Sorry.' Troy hurried across the second landing. The chief and Hetty Leathers were about to ascend a much more steep and narrow set of stairs covered in fawn haircord. There were only about a dozen steps leading to a white painted door. This was of the cheapest type, available from any B & Q. Plywood, hollow inside, with a silver-coloured oxide handle. It was closed.

143

As Hetty reached out, Barnaby touched her arm.

'Have you been in here since Carlotta disappeared?'

'No. She wouldn't let me – Mrs Lawrence. Said she'd see to it.'

'Is that unusual?'

'It certainly is.' Hetty clucked gently. 'I was quite put out, I don't mind admitting.'

'And has she? Seen to it?'

'Not to my understanding. But then, I don't live in so I wouldn't know everything she does.' She turned the handle and opened the door. All three stood staring into the room's interior.

Eventually Hetty said, 'Well! I've seen some messes in my time but I've never seen anything like this.' She sucked in another highly indignant breath. 'Filthy young madam.'

Troy, never one to create a newly minted epigram when a well-worn one was to hand, muttered, 'Looks like a bomb's gone off.'

Barnaby said nothing. He was recalling what the Lawrences had said at their first interview. He remembered Lionel putting the blame for Carlotta's departure on his wife. There had been a disturbance. She and the girl had had 'an argument'. Some argument.

Once again he put his hand on Hetty's arm, this time as she was about to step inside the room.

'I think the fewer people walking around the better, Mrs Leathers.'

'If that's what you want, Inspector.' Hetty positioned herself firmly in the centre of the doorway. She kept her eye on both policemen while they were together and on Troy when they had separated to different parts of the room. He didn't know whether to be flattered or insulted.

If Barnaby had not known the circumstances he would have assumed he was looking at the aftermath of a burglary. There was the same sense of wild, angry searching, clothes ripped from hangers and flung all over the floor, magazines – *Minx*, *Sugar*, *19* – torn to shreds, posters ripped off the walls and torn across. He picked up a couple. The names – All Saints, Kavana, Puff Daddy – meant nothing to him. Since Cully had left home eight years ago, he was totally out of touch.

All the drawers from a small chest had been pulled out and flung across the room, the contents lying where they fell. Cosmetics, underwear, a loose tangle of tights, a pink plastic hair dryer. Brushes, rollers, combs. The place smelt pungently of cheap hair spray overlying a more pleasant, peachy fragrance.

Troy, agitating the corner of the prettily flowered duvet, released a cloud of tawny dust. Then he saw several little piles of it on the bed and the floor. If this was junk it was a new one on him. He bent down and sniffed.

'She's been chucking face powder about, chief.'

'There doesn't seem to be much that she hasn't chucked about.'

'That girl always did have a paddy on her,' said Hetty. 'There's the box – look.'

Barnaby picked up the box, Rimmel's Honeybun, and put it carefully on the bedside table. Troy, noticing this, went to the far side of the room, retrieved a cushion that belonged to the single armchair and just as carefully replaced it.

'Don't touch anything, Sergeant.'

The times I have to bite my tongue, thought Troy, it could double as a sieve. He watched the chief, who was standing by the little porthole window, apparently lost in thought.

But Troy knew what the DCI was really doing. And there was a time, some years since admitted, when he would have attempted to do the same. To observe the scene, noticing every minute detail, to attempt to bring the drama which had brought such destruction about to life. To put flesh on the antagonist's bones.

Yes, Troy had had a go at all that. But he had so rarely been right and so often monumentally wrong (once he had arrested a shady antiques dealer on suspicion of stealing the local church's ornaments, only to find it was the vicar) that he soon gave up. As he put it to Maureen, 'With an ace fishmonger on the doorstep why struggle to catch your own?'

Barnaby was wondering if he had made a mistake asking Mrs Leathers to show him Carlotta's room. He thought about the coming interview with Ann Lawrence and was beginning to feel it might have been better to arrive with a search warrant and enter the place with her at his side. He would have had a reaction then. Been able to watch the play of expression on her face as he moved around. Getting warmish, warm, warmer! Getting cool, no – cold, icy, brrr!

Irritated, he put the image aside. This was pure fantasy. If she had anything at all to hide there'd been ample time to clean up the place. But perhaps it had never occurred to her that the police might wish to see where Carlotta had lived. Possibly the experience of their extremely violent parting had left her unwilling, perhaps even unable, to enter the room again. Yes, that was more like it.

A heavy sigh and an ostentatious clearing of the throat from the doorway returned him to the present.

'Mrs Leathers,' said the chief inspector, 'thank you for being so patient.' He nodded at Troy and both men moved towards the door.

'No trouble, Inspector. Only I must get on.'

As they walked away from the house, Troy, father of one, female, four years, three months, nine days, said, 'You've got a daughter, sir. Was her room ever like that?'

'Pretty near,' said Barnaby. 'The cat had kittens in it once and we didn't find them for three weeks.'

'Blimey.' Troy looked sideways at the boss. He seemed to be smiling but you could never be sure. 'You're exaggerating. Aren't you?'

'Only slightly.'

Ann's branch of Lloyd's in Causton not only still had a manager actually in residence but was also open for three hours on alternate Saturday mornings. Richard Ainsley had an office with his designation on the door and a polished wooden Toblerone on his desk with his name printed in gold. Ainsley had known Ann a long time, as he had her father. He had met her husband too, whom he didn't much like. As Ann had anticipated, he was prepared to lend her what she needed against the security of the house. But she was very surprised at the high rate of interest.

'It won't take long to draw up the agreement. If you'll call in perhaps next Thursday, Mrs Lawrence—'

'I have to have it now!' Ann realised she was almost

147

shouting, leaning over the manager's desk. 'I'm so sorry, Mr Ainsley.' She sat back, her face scarlet. 'I don't know what . . . I'm sorry.'

Mr Ainsley was not unused to emotional outbursts. Money was the fulcrum on which most people's lives turned. When it seemed to be slipping away, they panicked. Understandably. But he had handled Ann Lawrence's financial affairs since the death of her father and was both surprised and mildly distressed to find her in such a predicament. Naturally he wondered what the money could be for. Hardly a conservatory or a new kitchen, two of the most common seductions currently turning up on loan applications. Or a holiday in the Bahamas, though heaven knows she looked as if she could do with one. None of these would give rise to such desperation.

'This is quite a lot of money, Ann.' He decided not to mention the withdrawal, only days ago, of a thousand from her current account. 'Over what sort of period do you see it being repaid?'

'Oh – very quickly.' Ann stared across the desk at this round little man with his neat hair and neat, gold-rimmed glasses and neat moustache. All puffed out with his own importance. Pompous, stuffy, fatuous, long-winded roly-poly pudding. And to think in a previous life she had rather liked him. Even been grateful for his kindness. 'Actually, someone has died. There are funeral expenses to look after. But I am mentioned in the . . . er . . . will. Remembered, that is. So there won't be any . . . problem . . .'

Concerned though he was, Richard Ainsley decided to call a halt to this wretched business. He could not bear to hear her lying. He suggested a repayment period of six months and, when she agreed, produced a form, quickly filled it in and asked her to sign it. Then he rang the chief cashier to clear payment.

'I need it in cash, Mr Ainsley.'

'Cash?'

Ann was hurrying blindly away from the bank, the envelope safely in the bottom of her handbag, when she collided with Louise Fainlight who was just turning away from the cash point.

After the automatic apologies and awkward hellos, neither woman knew what to say. Both were recalling their last meeting. Louise remembered that Ann had asked her to the house and then not wanted her there. Ann remembered thinking it could well be Louise who was doing the blackmailing.

She thought it again now. Thought it with the money held close to her side, burning through the soft beige leather of her handbag. Was this meeting really a coincidence? Or a determined attempt to check that she was actually doing what she had been instructed to do. A sudden wild impulse seized Ann. A mad urge to confront Louise. Brandish the notes in her face. Shout, 'Here it is! Is this what you want? Is it?'

Appalled, she turned away, mumbling something vague. Pretending she needed the cash machine herself; standing in front of it while Louise walked away. Then, becoming aware that a small queue had formed and that people were staring at her strangely, she stepped aside. Blushing, and on the verge of tears, she affected to look in her handbag for some lost item.

She felt she was losing her mind. The events of the previous few days suddenly overwhelmed her with a kaleidoscope of fear-filled, violent images and sly murmurings. She stared suspiciously at people passing her on the pavement. Coolly they turned aside, pretending indifference and that the whispering was none of their doing, but she knew that secretly they were all laughing at her.

Shortly after their strange encounter outside the bank, Louise was driving out of Causton when she saw Ann crossing the road in a wandering sort of way. Her immediate impulse was to offer a lift. She even took her foot off the accelerator and started to brake. But there was something so strange about Ann's appearance. One hand gripped the edges of her coat, pulling them fiercely together although the day was quite mild. The other was hovering in front of her mouth like a fluttering bird. Even so, Louise could see her lips moving. She was frowning, too, and shaking her head.

Louise drove on. She had her own problems which were rapidly becoming quite severe. This was no time to try and cope with a person not only plainly distraught but who also, Louise was now convinced, didn't even like her.

She had not expected to have to come into Causton, especially on market day, and had no ready cash. From the first, Louise had insisted on sharing all the bills at her brother's house and paying the housekeeping alternate weeks. This was her week. She had run out of various items and, a certain cautious friendliness having been re-established between herself and Val, last night she had asked him for some money to tide her over. He said he didn't have any. Unthinking and genuinely puzzled, Louise said, 'But you went to the bank only the other day.' She remembered picking up the withdrawal slip from the the kitchen floor and throwing it in the bin. It had been for four hundred pounds.

Within seconds the atmosphere changed, becoming thick with anger and resentment.

'I am getting absolutely sick of this!' Valentine almost spat out the words.

'Of what?'

'Of *you*. And your constant bloody criticism.'

'I didn't mean to—'

'It is your week to pay for the food. Right?'

'Forget it. I'll drive into town.'

'If you don't want to pay your way—'

'That's a rotten thing to say.' Now she was raising her voice. 'I've paid my way ever since I arrived, as well you know.'

'Really?'

'Where else d'you think my savings have been going?' As she spoke, Louise had a sudden sickening knowledge of what had happened to Valentine's four hundred pounds. And knew that the awareness showed on her face.

There was a formidable quietness between them then Valentine said, 'I can't cope with all these rows. I have work to do.' Deliberately he turned his back on her, walking away towards the stairs. 'I mean it, Lou. I've just about had enough.'

Louise, shaking with resentment and distress, couldn't bear to remain in the house. She made her way to the garden and sat down by the pool. What was she to do now?

Anger at the injustice of her brother's remarks had already evaporated. In its place flooded childhood memories. Always their parents' favourite, Valentine had rarely taken advantage of his position. Appreciating the unfairness of the situation even when very young, he had constantly attempted to rejig the balance, praising paintings she brought home from school that her mother barely glanced at, helping with her homework, talking his father into letting her tag along when they went fishing. For her fifth birthday he had made a little wooden box painted with starfish and baby seals which she still treasured. And, nicest of all, he had always been able to make her laugh.

At this final recollection, Louise started to cry. She wept bitterly, her eyes open and without wiping her tears away, as children do. At her feet, glittering in the dark reflected water, the golden carp swam heavily up and down.

Watching them was quite hypnotic. Gradually, the austere formality of the garden laid a calming hold on her emotions. The weeping became spasmodic then dried to a sad sniffle. Her heartbeats were more measured. She sat on for perhaps another half-hour, gradually becoming more peaceful.

But what to do now? Plainly Valentine was very unhappy, which meant Louise was unhappy too. But if he did not want her around, how could she properly stay? Surely this strangely violent transformation must be temporary – the alternative did not bear thinking of – and when it was over, he would be quite alone. Perhaps she could move just a short way away, to one of the neighbouring villages. She could afford to rent a small house or flat.

Anger seized her at the thought of the man responsible for all this disruption and her brother's wretched state. Before Jax came, they had been contented, their lives orderly and pleasurable. Then the anger drained away and she began to feel frightened, as if her whole life had been suddenly menaced.

DCI Barnaby and Sergeant Troy were having a very pleasant lunch at the Red Lion: steak and kidney pudding with fluffy mashed potatoes and garden peas. And a dessert made from tinned fruit salad, sponge cake and raspberry jam, grandly calling itself Raspberry and Apricot Pavlova.

'Know anything about Pavlova, Sergeant?' asked the chief inspector, moving a dirty ashtray from a table by the window.

'I know you don't get much for three quid.'

'One of the greatest dancers that ever lived.'

'That right?' Troy seized his irons and set to.

'Famous for her interpretation of a dying swan.'

'Sounds good,' said Troy politely.

'It's said that people who saw it were never quite the same again.' Barnaby drank a little of his Russian stout which was delicious. 'And she was at it till the day she died.'

'Why is it,' asked Sergeant Troy, sawing gently away, 'that kidneys always squeak when you cut into them?'

Although Barnaby had not introduced himself at the bar and was wearing an ordinary, dark blue business suit and plain tie and polished black Oxfords, he knew that they knew he was a copper. And not just because he had already been seen around the village questioning people.

Sometimes Barnaby thought he wore an insignia, like the mark of Cain. Invisible to himself but screaming to the rest of the world This Man Is A Policeman. He did not exaggerate. Once he had been having dinner with Joyce in a restaurant they had never been to before. Halfway through his Lobster Armoricaine the manager had come over to say they were having a bit of trouble with a drunk who would not pay his bill and what did Barnaby advise?

Here in the Red Lion they were being not noticed in the studied way people sometimes decide not to notice if a famous person happens to be within their sight range. Not impressed, not even interested. Better things to do with their time.

'They're quick on the house-to-house.' Sergeant Troy, who had just started on his raspberry sponge, nodded, grinning towards the door. 'Our wooden tops.'

Two uniformed constables from Barnaby's team had come in and were talking to the landlord and a couple of locals at the bar. Troy noticed, to his chagrin, that the landlord was offering the plods a drink. Which they refused. Quite right too.

'You were one yourself once.'

Troy, scraping his bowl, did not respond. He preferred to forget this inglorious period in his glittering career. Instructed now to 'drink up', he drained his boring alcohol-free lager and shrugged into his elegant, lightweight jacket.

As he made his way towards the door, he noticed two very attractive women at the bar. The force was with them, having a laugh and a joke. One of the policemen caught Troy's eye. The sergeant moved his head slightly to indicate who was bringing up the rear. One look of dismayed disbelief and the uniform scrambled to its feet, thanked the landlord loudly for his help and legged it.

'What are you chortling at?'

Chortling. Where did he find them? Troy decided to look it up in Talisa Leanne's dictionary when he got home. Chortling. The more you said it, the wonkier it sounded.

'You going to follow up on Mrs Lawrence now, sir?'

Barnaby mumbled something inaudible. He was seething with bad temper and all directed against himself. Throughout lunch he had become more and more convinced that the apprehension he had entertained while in Carlotta's room – that perhaps he should have waited until Mrs Lawrence returned to see it with him – had been correct.

He knew now he should have waited if it took all day. And interviewed her before she had had a chance to find out from Hetty Leathers why the police were in the house. Now he had thrown away one of the most important weapons in the interrogator's armoury – surprise.

As it happens, he was wrong. Hetty and Candy had been collected by Evadne Pleat just before twelve for a lift to the vet's. Ann did not return for another hour and so knew nothing about his earlier visit. Even so, luck was still against the chief inspector, though for quite a different reason.

The Humber Hawk was in the drive and a light on in the garage flat. But Barnaby decided to tackle the Lawrences first, feeling it more likely that information would be revealed that would be of use in Jackson's interview than the other way round.

Once more Troy swung on the old-fashioned bell. If anything, the paintwork on the front door looked even more flaky. On the bottom section there was a strip of it actually curling away from the wood.

Lionel Lawrence himself opened the door. He gazed at them with a puzzled expression, as if he was sure he had seen them somewhere before but not quite where. His white hair was slightly more tidy than the last time but he had compensated for this by wearing an extremely colourful, very long hand-knitted scarf, fraying not only at the edges but all down one side.

'DCI Barnaby.'

'Sergeant Troy.'

'Hmm,' said Lionel, turning and striding back into the house. His floor-length lovat overcoat, divided at the back from the waist down, flapped vigorously behind flashing a Black Watch tartan lining.

As the door had been left standing open, the policemen followed and found their way to Lionel Lawrence's study. Ann Lawrence was sitting in a pale blue wing chair by the window. Very still and calm. Unnaturally so, thought Barnaby. He saw her frown and struggle to remember who they were. For a moment he thought she was drunk.

'Have you found out something?' asked Lionel Lawrence. 'Is there news of Carlotta?'

This bloke wants to get his priorities right. Sergeant Troy dug out his notebook and stared severely at the dishevelled parson. We've got a murder on our plate here. Then he remembered they might have two murders on their plate if the girl had really drowned and felt minimally less impatient.

Barnaby said, 'It's possible.'

'Oh! Did you hear that, my dear?' Lionel beamed at

his wife who turned her head slowly and with great care towards all of them. 'There is news about Carlotta.'

'Carlotta. How lovely.' The words were slow and thick and unnaturally isolated, one from the other. There was a long pause. 'Lovely.'

Ann had to struggle to hold the three figures in the room in some sort of focus. Although solid enough in themselves, they seemed to move in an improbable way. Looming forward and retreating, like people in a dream. Their voices echoed slightly.

She had overheard the doctor warning Lionel that she might feel slightly disoriented at first. He had given her an injection and there were some tablets to take three times a day. They were tranquillisers and they certainly worked. She had never felt so tranquil in her life. In fact she felt so tranquil she would have been happy to slip into unconsciousness and never come round again.

It was Jax who had spotted his employer's wife as he was driving Lionel home. Ann was pacing round and round the taxi rank outside Causton library, her head wagging like a broken doll's. Lionel leapt out of the car and ran to her. Ann flung herself at him, locked her arms round his neck and started shrieking. Jax had helped get her into the car then driven directly to the doctor's.

'Is your wife not well, Mr Lawrence?' Barnaby asked.

'Ann?' inquired Lionel, as if she was only one of many. 'Just a little run down. Tell me—'

'I was hoping to talk to her about the day Carlotta disappeared.'

Carlotta . . . Something swam to the surface of Ann's mind. A slender white shape. A human arm. It curved upwards, a half-moon gleaming against the dark, then sank without a trace.

'Mrs Lawrence, do you remember what happened before she left? I believe there was an argument.'

Hopeless. Whatever she'd been given was powerful stuff. Barnaby thought it seemed to have been ideally timed to stop her talking to him then told himself not to be melodramatic. No one at the Old Rectory could have known about the police's reconstruction of the blackmail letter. Or the new direction the case had taken. He turned his attention to Lionel Lawrence.

'Could *you* give me any details, sir?'

'I'm afraid not. The night it happened I was at a meeting till quite late. When I got home, Ann was asleep. How she could have just gone to bed with that poor child . . .' Lionel shook his head at this sad abrogation of his wife's duty. 'The foxes have holes and the birds of the air—'

'But surely you discussed it the next day.'

Lionel's face became set in a moonish stubbornness. The chief inspector simply raised an interrogatory eyebrow and waited. Troy, seated with his notebook at a satinwood card table, inhaled with pleasure the mellow natural scent of beeswax. And watched.

He was good at waiting, the gaffer. Once he'd kept it up for nearly ten minutes. Troy, who had no more patience than a two-year-old, asked him how he did it. Barnaby explained that he simply absented himself. Naturally one had to keep eye contact and maintain an intent, sometimes even slightly threatening posture but within these limits the mind could do its own thing. One of the most useful, he found, was listing gardening jobs for the weekend.

Poor old Lawrence just wasn't up to it. He didn't last ten seconds, let alone ten minutes.

'Apparently Ann thought Carlotta had borrowed some earrings. She questioned the girl, obviously very clumsily. Naturally Carlotta got frightened—'

'I don't see why,' said Sergeant Troy. 'If she hadn't—'

'You don't *understand*,' cried the Reverend Lawrence. 'For someone of her background to be wrongfully accused is a deeply traumatic—'

'And you believe it was wrongfully, Mr Lawrence?' asked Barnaby.

'I know it was.' Sounding unchristianly smug and self-righteous. 'Ann is notoriously careless. People are who've never known want.'

'Still, such things do happen,' said Troy, feeling sorry for the devastated, long gone Mrs Lawrence. In return he got an incredulous stare awarding him ten out of ten for sensitivity plus bonus points for tender loving care.

'Could you tell us something about her background, Mr Lawrence?' asked the chief inspector.

'It's all on record at the Caritas Agency.'

'Yes, and we shall be talking to them. But right now I'm talking to you.'

The Reverend looked rather taken aback at the sudden hardening of his interrogator's voice.

'I don't see how prying into the girl's past will help find her.' He blinked weakly. 'Everyone has a clean slate here.'

'I believe she often received airmail letters.'

'Oh, I doubt that, you know.' Lawrence smiled indulgently.

'Apparently she threw them away unopened,' added Sergeant Troy.

'Who on earth told you such a story?' It didn't take him long to run through the possible suspects. 'I'm surprised you attend to servants' gossip, Inspector.'

This brought a response from the blue armchair. Ann Lawrence gave a muffled cry and struggled to sit up. She tried to speak but her tongue, a huge lump of inert flesh in her mouth, would hardly move.

'Herry . . . no . . . not . . . serv . . .'

'Now look what you've done!' He crossed over to his wife, propelled, it seemed to Barnaby, more by annoyance at her behaviour than care for her wellbeing. 'We must get you upstairs, Ann.' He glared at the two policemen who stared stolidly back. 'If you want to talk to myself or my wife again you can make an appointment in the proper manner.'

'That's not how it works, I'm afraid, sir,' said the chief inspector. 'And I have to inform you that if you remain uncooperative, any future interviews could well be taking place at the station.'

'We'll have to watch our step there, chief,' said Troy with a chuckle in his voice as they were crossing the gravel. 'Him and his fancy handshake connections.'

Barnaby commented briefly on the Reverend Lawrence's Masonic connections, employing the vividly concise gift for imagery and pithy dialogue that made his subordinates so apprehensive of getting a summons to his office.

Troy had a good laugh and went over the retort a few times to make sure he remembered it to pass on in the canteen. By the time he'd got this well and truly sorted, they were standing by the door of the garage flat.

This time he had seen them coming. Seen the car, seen them go into the main house. He would be well prepared. Barnaby, recalling the interruption from Lawrence on the last occasion they talked to Jackson, trusted the Reverend would be spending the next twenty minutes or so remonstrating with his wife.

Sergeant Troy's thoughts were running along precisely the same lines. One more up-chucking display of snivelling hypocrisy from the chauffeur and he could see the Red Lion's Apricot and Raspberry Pavlova suddenly forming a tasteful mosaic on the smart cream carpet. And he would not be cleaning it up.

The door was opened. Jackson stood there wearing a silvery tweed jacket and black cotton polo neck sweater. His face wore an expression of unguarded candour. 'And to think when you said you'd be back, Inspector, I thought you was just stringing me along.'

'Mr Jackson.'

'Terry to you.' He stood politely aside and they all went upstairs.

The flat looked pretty much the same as the last time they were here except for a new ironing board leaning up against a wall by the kitchen. Both the kitchen and bathroom doors were wide open as if to deny they had anything to conceal. There was a copy of yesterday's *Daily Star* sunny side up on the coffee table.

Jackson sat on the settee. His manner was bland and compliant. But his eyes were keenly focused and Barnaby noticed he sat well forward, hands resting lightly on his knees, the fingers curled like a sprinter.

'Do you always drive Mr Lawrence, Terry?'

Jackson looked surprised then wary. Whatever he had expected, it had not been this.

'Yes. Me or Mrs L. He never got round to learning.'

'Tell me what happened today.'

'How do you mean?'

'Everything leading up to this doctor's visit.'

Jackson hesitated. 'I don't know that Mr Lawrence would like that.'

'I'll either get it here or down the nick,' said Chief Inspector Barnaby. 'It's up to you.'

So Terry Jackson told them how he had been bringing Lionel back from a meeting at Causton council offices to discuss improvements to the training of magistrates. Driving along the High Street they had spotted his wife wandering about in a high old state. Lionel had tried to get her into the car but she had started shouting and waving her arms about.

'Shouting about what?'

'Nothing that made any sense.'

'Come on. Something must have made sense.'

'No, honestly. It was all jumbled up. Then I got out to help but that just seemed to make her worse.'

'Surprise, surprise,' muttered Sergeant Troy.

'At first Lionel asked me to drive home but then he changed his mind. Their doctor's at Swan Myrren, Patterson, and we went directly there. He saw her straightaway. Must have given her a whacking shot of something. She was like a zombie when she came out.'

'Then what?'

'Stopped off at the chemist's for a prescription and drove back here.'

'Do you know why she went into Causton?'

'No.'

A hair's breadth of hesitation. He knew and he didn't want to tell them. Good. A minuscule scrap of progress. Barnaby paused, considering whether to make anything of this now or save it for later. He decided to wait, noting, with some satisfaction, that Jackson's forehead was now lightly beaded with sweat.

Changing tack entirely, he said, 'There was a young girl staying here until a few days ago.'

'That's right.'

'What was she like?'

'Carlotta? A stuck-up bitch.'

'You didn't hit it off then?' said Sergeant Troy.

'Thought she was above me. And she was nobody, right? Come through the system same as I did.'

'Turned you down, did she?' suggested Barnaby.

'She didn't get a fucking chance!'

'That make you angry?'

Having responded to the jibe apparently without thinking, they now watched Jackson step back. He said, carefully, 'I never came on to her. I told you. She weren't my type.'

'D'you know why she ran away?'

'No.'

'Lawrence never discussed it with you?'

'None of my business, was it?'

'What about Mrs Lawrence?'

'Do me a favour.'

'Oh, of course.' Troy's fingers gave a little snap of pretend recollection. 'She won't have you in the house. That right?'

'Bollocks.' Jackson sullenly turned away from them and started chewing the inside of his right cheek.

'There is a possibility that she may not have run away at all,' said Barnaby.

'You what?'

Sergeant Troy took up the story. 'We received a report, at roughly the same time she was supposed to have gone, that someone had fallen into the river.'

'That wouldn't have been Carlotta.' Jackson laughed for the first time. 'She's far too sharp. Always looking out for number one.'

Look who's talking, thought Troy. He repeated himself: 'Fallen. Or been pushed.'

'Well, it weren't me. I were in Causton the night you're on about. Waiting to collect Lionel from a meeting.'

'Is that a fact?'

'Pure as the driven, I am.'

Barnaby remembered his mother saying that when he was little. Pure as the driven slush. He wasn't unduly depressed by Jackson's story. Presumably the man had had time to squander while hanging around and Ferne Basset was only a twenty-minute drive at the most. Less if you put your foot down. And he had no alibi for the crime that truly did exist. The murder of Charlie Leathers.

Barnaby got up then and Troy, rather disappointed, did the same. Almost at the door the DCI turned with one of his 'gosh I almost forgot' starts. These were invariably followed by a laboured rendering of 'by the way'. Troy always got a kick out of this little number. An absolute hoot which would not have deceived a baby.

'Oh, by the way . . .'

'You're not going?' said Jackson. 'I was about to put

the kettle on.' He gave a shout of spiteful laughter.

'A bit of news about Mr Leathers,' Barnaby pressed on.

'Charlie?' Jackson spoke absently. He seemed miles away. 'You got anybody in the frame yet for that, Inspector?'

You had to hand it to the bastard, thought Sergeant Troy. He'd got more front than Wembley Stadium.

'I've started fancying you in that position actually, Terence.'

'*Me?*'

'He was blackmailing you, wasn't he?'

At that single word, the atmosphere changed. They watched Jackson making a great effort to pull himself together and sharpen his concentration. A struggle which showed in the jumping jack nerve in his temple and the rigid line of his jaw.

'That's a lie.'

'We have grounds for thinking it's true.'

'Oh, sure. The grounds that I'm the only one round here with a record. The only one whose face fits. The only one you can take down the slammer and work on just because I'm vulnerable.' Jackson was recovering fast. He looked about as vulnerable as a puff adder. He sauntered away into the kitchen, calling over his shoulder, 'Come back when you know what the fuck you're on about.'

Barnaby put a quick hand on Troy's arm and half eased, half dragged him out of the flat. As they were crossing the drive, he saw the Reverend Lawrence's startled face through the dining room window and lengthened his stride.

'Can I say something, sir?'

'Of course you can "say something", Troy. What d'you think this is, the Stasi?'

'It's not a criticism—'

'OK. It's a criticism. I expect I'll survive.'

'I just wonder if it was a good idea to tell Jackson we know about the blackmail. I mean, he's on his guard now but we still can't book him for anything.'

'I wanted to spring it before he picked it up somewhere else. To see his reaction.'

'Which was very satisfactory.'

'Indeed. I don't know what exactly is going on here but I'd say whatever it is he's in it up to his greasy neck.'

It was almost dusk as they made their way back to the Red Lion car park. Halfway across the Green, an extraordinary thing occurred. Barnaby stopped walking and peered into the pearly mist of early evening.

'What on earth is that?'

'I can't see . . .' Troy squinted, frowning hard. 'Blimey!'

A strangely fluid outline was looming, retreating, shifting and hovering some distance away. It emitted shrill little calls and cries and seemed to be somehow perched on waves of surging foam. Gradually the whole mysterious presence came closer.

'If we were in the desert,' said DCI Barnaby, 'this would be Omar Sharif.'

A woman approached them. Stout, middle-aged and wearing floppy green trousers, a crimson velvet poncho and a trilby hat with peacock feathers in the brim. The foam resolved itself into several cream-coloured Pekinese dogs who continued to surge as the woman introduced herself.

'Evadne Pleat, good afternoon. Aren't you Hetty's chief inspector?'

'Good afternoon,' replied Barnaby, and gave his name.

'And I'm Sergeant Troy,' said Sergeant Troy, already enamoured of the dogs, daft-looking things though they were.

'I heard you were going round. I just wanted to say that if there is anything, anything at all, that I can do to help, you must call.' Her round rosy face shone with earnestness. She had a sweet smile. Nothing like the common or garden smirk of daily exchange that barely reaches the lips, let alone the eyes. She smiled as a child will, enthusiastically, quite without calculation and confident of a friendly response. 'It's Mulberry Cottage. Over there by the Rectory.'

'I see.' Barnaby glanced over at the small, pretty house. 'Hasn't someone already visited you?'

'Oh yes. A very efficient young man if somewhat fussy about his clothing.' She had watched Constable Phillips standing at her gate for ages, frowning crossly and picking balls of pale fluffy stuff off his uniform trousers. 'I've told him my ideas though I'm not sure he quite appreciated the wide range of my knowledge and experience.'

'Would that be in some special subject then?' asked Sergeant Troy politely.

'Personal relationships,' replied Evadne, beaming at them both. 'The ebb and flow of emotion in the human heart. And really, isn't that what all your investigations come down to in the end?'

During this conversation the Pekes had been lunging about and Evadne had lunged with them, hanging on to her trilby as best she could.

'I'll certainly keep what you say in mind, Miss Pleat,' muttered Barnaby. 'Now, if there's nothing else . . .?'

'Not at the moment. But if there is anything specific you need help with, you only have to ask. Say goodbye to the nice policemen,' instructed Evadne.

Although they had not stopped barking since the conversation started, the dogs now redoubled their efforts, yapping and leaping and tumbling about and getting their leads mixed up.

'What are they called?' Sergeant Troy lingered and heard an irritated snarl somewhere in the region of his left ear.

'Piers, Dido, Blossom, Mazeppa – don't *do* that, darling. Then there's Nero and the one right at the back is Kenneth.' She indicated a tiny white chrysanthemum, squeaking and jumping straight up and down into the air.

Troy had to run halfway across the Green to catch up the chief.

'You're a fast mover, sir.'

'I am when I want to get away from something.' Barnaby approached the car with feelings of relief. 'How does she ever hear herself think?'

'They were only being friendly.'

Barnaby gave him a look to turn the milk. They got in the car. Troy switched on the ignition and tried to think of a conciliatory remark to jolly up their homeward journey.

'Unusual name, Evadne Pleat.'

'You think so?' Barnaby could afford to sound superior. He was recalling the occasion, some years back, when he and Joyce had visited her brother in

America. Colin, exchange teaching in California, was living in an apartment owned by a woman called Zorrest Milchmain. You had to get up early to beat that one.

Joyce was laying the table. A pretty blue and yellow Provençal cloth, honeysuckle in a tall crystal vase, narrow elegant wine glasses.

Everything except the soup (carrot and coriander) was cold tonight. Joyce had popped into Fortnum's on her way to Marylebone station and had set out wild smoked salmon, steak and chestnut pie, artichoke hearts and Greek salad.

She had been to London for lunch at the National Theatre. Nico's audition was at eleven thirty. Joyce and Cully met him in the Lyttelton foyer. They sat for a while listening to a flute, viola and piano trio playing a Fauré romance then went up to the Olivier restaurant where Joyce had booked a table.

Everyone had a glass of champagne because, although Nicolas wouldn't know the results of the audition for at least another week, it had still been a wonderfully exciting day. He had auditioned for Trevor Nunn on the *Jean Brodie* set and was high as a kite simply on the strength of having stood on the same spot and walked the same boards as the greatest theatrical names of the century: Scofield and McKellan; Gielgud, Judi Dench and Maggie Smith. This was the place where Ian Holm had played King Lear. Had Joyce seen Lear? It was the most breathtaking display of bravura ... ohhh ... heartrending ... you just couldn't believe ...

Joyce smiled, content to let him run on. That was

one of the comfortable things about actors. They were so easy. You were never short of a subject for conversation.

She watched Cully kiss her husband's cheek, raise her glass, happy and excited. But having a daughter in the business had made Joyce sharply aware of the vagaries of the artist's life. Up one minute, down the next. And she knew Nicolas, too, quite well enough to understand that by the evening doubts would gradually be breaking the surface of all this sparkling ebullience. Even now having just said that Trevor Nunn seemed really encouraging, he added, 'Of course, *seemed* . . .'

Joyce looked out of the window at the sun glittering on the river and at London's great iron bridges and sighed with pleasure. She had the gift of always knowing she was having a wonderful time while she was actually having it, not just in retrospect like so many people. It would be such fun telling Tom. When he came into the kitchen she was still lost in reverie.

'I say!' He was staring at the table. 'This looks a bit of all right. What's that?' He pointed to a spectacular pudding.

'Pear Charlotte. You can just have the pears.'

'Where d'you get all this?'

'Fortnum's.' Then, when her husband looked puzzled, 'I've been to London.'

'What for?'

'Tom, honestly.'

'Don't remind me.'

'I'm not going to.'

'There's some Chardonnay in the hall that would go a treat with this. D'you mind, love?'

When Joyce returned from the wine rack, a bottle

of Glen Carlou in her hand, Barnaby said, 'Nico's audition.'

'You looked at the calendar.'

'Has he got in?'

'I'll tell you all about it over supper.' She opened the wine. 'The Gavestons cancelled, by the way.'

'Jolly good. So . . .' he waved his hand at the crystal and glasses and flowers. 'What's all this for?'

'It's for us.' Joyce gave him a glass of wine and a brisk kiss on the cheek.

'Mm.' Barnaby drank deep. 'Very nice. A cheeky little number with a warm undertow and a steely backbone. Reminds me of someone not a million miles away.' He started to sing 'The Air That I Breathe' quietly, under his breath. It had been their song, years ago, played at their wedding. ' "If I could make a wish I think I'd pass . . ." '

Joyce passed him a napkin.

'Remember that, darling?'

'What?' She had started eating.

'The Hollies?'

'Mm. Vaguely.'

CHAPTER EIGHT

It was nearly ten the following morning when Ann Lawrence regained consciousness. No way could you call it simply 'waking up'. The Hoover on the landing outside her room buzzed faintly at first, no louder than a bee. Gradually the level of the sound increased. There was knocking as the machine banged against the skirting board.

Ann felt as if she was swimming up from the depths of the ocean. On and on she swam, struggling through dark layers of muddy mind swamp until finally somehow heaving back her swollen eyelids. She found herself in semi-darkness. For a moment, lying on the pillow, she stared at the uncertain outlines of heavy furniture. It all looked completely unfamiliar. Then she made the mistake of trying to lift her head.

'Ahhh . . .' A searing pain flared behind her eyes. Gasping from the shock of it, she closed her eyes and waited for the agony to pass. Then, keeping her head very steady and pressing down weakly on the mattress, Ann levered herself up the bed until she was leaning against the headboard and rested there, absolutely still.

The vacuum cleaner had been switched off. There was a very gentle tap at the door. Hetty Leathers put her head round then came cautiously into the room.

'Thank goodness. I thought you was never waking

up.' She crossed over to the window and drew the curtains. A grey dullness crept into the room.

'Don't put the light on!'

'I wasn't going to.' She sat on the side of the bed and took Ann's hand. 'My goodness, Mrs Lawrence, what on earth happened to you?'

'I . . . don't know.'

'I said you should never have had two of them tablets. I told him.'

'What?'

'Last night. When you went to bed.'

'But . . . you're not here . . .' Ann sighed deeply, made another effort to complete the sentence but failed.

'In the evening? That's right. But he rang nine o'clock yesterday wanting to know what to do about his supper.' Hetty's voice still quivered with an echo of the irritation she had felt. As if the man couldn't have opened a tin of soup and made himself a sandwich. 'So I thought I'd better come back this morning or you wouldn't have a bite all day.'

'Who rang?'

'Who?' Hetty stared in amazement. 'Why, Mr Lawrence, of course.'

'Ah.'

'Had to ask my neighbour to sit with Candy. I wouldn't of come only he said you were ill.'

'Yes.' Ann's cheeks became hot as certain vivid scenes, disjointed and seemingly quite disconnected, started jerkily running through her mind. A distraught woman being seized and bundled, struggling, into a car. The same woman, weeping, pushing a man away as he tried to calm her, fighting a woman in a nurse's uniform who was trying to hold her arm. Then the whole set-up becoming stable but distant, as if being viewed through the wrong end of a telescope. Finally the woman seated in surroundings which seemed vaguely familiar but also intangible like a room in a dream. The place was crammed with bulky but strangely insubstantial furniture. She was slopping tea against her lips and tipping it everywhere.

'I can't stay here!' A sudden movement and nausea possessed her. Ann clapped a hand to her mouth.

'What do you mean, Mrs Lawrence? Where would you go?'

'I . . . don't know.'

'You try and rest. There's nothing downstairs to worry about.' Hetty got up from the bed. 'Everything's running smoothly. Now, what if I make you a nice hot drink?'

'Feel sick.'

'Listen.' Hetty hesitated. 'It may be none of my business but them trankerlisers don't suit everybody. If I were you I'd chuck the lot out the window.'

Ann eased her way back down the bed and rested on the pillow. She lay flat on her back staring at a single spot on the ceiling and gradually the sickness passed. She began to feel better. A little bit stronger. But only in her body.

Her mind was still a rag bag of jumbled sounds, pictures and impressions that seemed quite meaningless. Then a single spear of light pierced the tangled mess and Ann understood that she was the woman in the strange, dream-like sequence.

If this recognition was alarming – she really had made a public exhibition of herself, been forced into her husband's car and made to submit to treatment in a doctor's surgery – it was also consoling. Memory had played her true and there was nothing seriously wrong with her mind.

But how had she got into this state in the first place? Ann tried to concentrate. Before being found and made to get into the car, she had met someone – Louise Fainlight! And there had been some unpleasantness – no, *she* had been unpleasant. Louise had been simply friendly in a perfectly normal way. Yet Ann had seen her as some sort of threat. Why?

Ann gently agitated a head packed with scrunched-up barbed wire. Struck her forehead with the heel of her hand and grunted with frustration. Causton. The market. Louise at a cash point. Herself leaving a building. The bank. What had she been doing in—

Oh God. It all returned, like a noxious stream of water flooding her consciousness. She sat up quickly, the swimming in her head hardly noticed. She breathed quickly, almost panting with emotion and fear, swung her legs out of bed, reached for her handbag. The envelope was still there. She scrabbled at the flap of the brown envelope, pulled out the rubber-banded wads of notes and stared at them. *Five grand this time murderer same place same time tomorrow.*

At midnight the 'same time' she had been lying unconscious in a drugged sleep. But he wouldn't know that. He would think she was defying him. What would he do? Send another note? Ring up and threaten? Should she perhaps take the money to Carter's Wood tonight and leave it in the litter bin anyway?

But what if he did not return? Anyone might find it. Or the bin might be emptied and the money lost. Ann recalled her humiliating interview with the bank manager. She couldn't bear to go through that again.

On the other side of the room on an old walnut chest of drawers was a large photograph of her father in a silver frame. She wished with all her heart that he was still alive. He would have had no truck with blackmailers. She could just see him sailing out to confront whoever it was, flailing around with his heavy ash stick and cursing fluently in the full glory of his rage.

That this would have been foolish, Ann had to admit. Here was no passing tramp or layabout to be subdued by bullish authority. What they were dealing with contained a dark authority of its own that would not be easily overcome. And she could do nothing.

It was as this knowledge of her own helplessness slowly took hold that Ann felt in herself the first beginnings of resentment quickly followed by a warming flicker of anger.

Was this her lot then? To just sit, meek and trembling, awaiting instructions like some pathetic Victorian skivvy. Running to obey these the minute they were issued. Selling more and more of her precious possessions to satisfy the outrageous greed of an unknown persecutor. She could not bear it. She *wouldn't* bear it.

Yet what was the alternative? For the first time she sat and considered, not unthinkingly in a panic-stricken rush but with calm seriousness, what would happen if she did not pay.

He would tell the police. An anonymous tip-off at no risk to himself. They would come and ask questions. She could not lie or brazen it out. It was against her nature and everything she had been taught to believe in. So she would tell them the truth.

How terrible would the consequences be? Would she be arrested? Perhaps. Questioned? Certainly. Lionel would be devastated and the village would have something really exciting to gossip about. But this would pass and Ann was surprised to realise that she was not all that concerned about Lionel's possible devastation. After all, he had spent years running around after people in trouble, so he should be able to cope with a spot of his own.

As if she was already being interviewed, Ann started to go through the dreadful course of events once more. The missing earrings, Carlotta's wild response and flight, the struggle on the bridge. The terrible moment when the girl fell in. Her own frantic running and searching along the river bank. The 999 call.

Surely the police would see that she was not the sort of person to deliberately harm someone. And Carlotta's ... Ann flinched from the word. Carlotta had not been found. She may have scrambled ashore even while Ann was urgently calling her name. Though the moon had been bright, there were dark patches that would have given cover.

It was an accident. That was the truth of it and they would have to believe her. She would return the money to the bank and her unknown persecutor could do his worst.

Louise, heavy-hearted and dull from lack of sleep, was getting dressed. She had not seen her brother since their row on Friday evening. He had left before she got up the next day, leaving a note saying simply that he had gone to London. Lying wide awake at nearly 3 a.m., she had heard him come in. Usually she would have waited up, wanting to know how his day had gone, but last night she had hesitated, afraid it would make him angry.

Louise, tying the belt of the first dress she laid hands on, stood suddenly still, jolted by the sheer novelty of such an observation. She had never been afraid of Valentine in her life. Bewilderment was slowly transformed into a quiet rage. She got up and strode over to the wall facing the village street. Pressing her hands flat against the glass, she stared across at the Old Rectory garden, at the giant cedar and the flat over the garage and felt her rage harden into hatred.

Why couldn't it have been Jax instead of Charlie Leathers? A miserable, not very pleasant old man would have lived and a foul young one, at the very beginning of his havoc-dealing life, would have been destroyed. I could have done it myself, thought Louise, truly believing at that moment that she was capable of murder. Not hand-to-hand, of course, she could not have borne to touch him. But say there had been a remote control – a button to be simply pressed. Well, that might have been a different matter.

She lifted her hands, studied the blurred imprint of her palms and finger span then wiped her forearm quickly across the glass, obliterating all trace. If she could do it like that, with no more concern than squashing a greenfly on the roses . . .

'What are you thinking?'

'Ah!' Louise jumped away from the window then moved quickly back. She stood in front of the smeared handprint as if it was readable, making her malevolence plain. 'You made me . . . I didn't hear you come in.'

'I'm just going for a shower.' Val was wearing his cycling gear. Black Lycra knee shorts and yellow top, both dripping wet, plastered to his powerful shoulders and muscular thighs. He looked at her without expression. 'Put some coffee on, Lou.'

In the kitchen, waiting for him to come down, Louise breathed evenly and deeply. She was determined not to be drawn into an argument; she would remain uncritical and calm. It was his life. Only, prayed Louise silently, let me not be driven from it.

There was coffee on the table and brioche with pale butter and Swiss black cherry jam. When Valentine came in he sat straight down and poured the coffee without looking at her and Louise knew what was coming.

'I'm sorry about yesterday.'

'That's all right. Everyone has—'

'I was very unfair. You've always more than paid your way here.'

'That's all right, Val. We were both upset.'

'But,' Valentine put his cup down, 'we do need to talk.'

'Yes,' said Louise, as the floor fell away beneath her chair. 'I do see that.'

'I spoke in anger, suggesting you move out. But I've thought about it and, you know, I still think it might be a good idea.'

'Yes,' said Louise again through stiff lips. 'I . . . er . . . I've been thinking pretty much the same thing, actually. After all, I only came here temporarily, to lick my wounds, so to speak. And I'm feeling so much better now. Time I dived back into real life – or is it dove – before I ossify. I thought I'd rent somewhere between here and London while I look round for a place more permanent. It might take me a few days to get my things sorted. Is that OK?'

'Oh, Lou.' And Valentine put down his cup, reached out and took his sister's hand. 'Don't cry.'

'I remember when you first started calling me Lou.' She had been twelve and head over heels entranced by a beautiful youth who was staying in their parents' house. In her innocence Louise had believed him to be simply her brother's friend. 'It was when Carey Foster—'

'Please. Not the "do you remember" game.'

'Sorry. Below the belt?'

'A bit.'

'I can come and see you?' Louise's voice sounded strained and childish, even to herself. 'And ring?'

'Of course you can ring, idiot. And we'll meet in town, like we always used to. Have lunch, go to the theatre.'

'In town.' She was being banished then. Louise sipped nearly cold coffee, sour on her tongue, and already the pain of separation began to make itself felt. Every cell in her body ached. 'Yes. That would be lovely.'

After a quiet Sunday spent in the garden lifting and storing tulip and lily bulbs, splitting and replanting hardy perennials and cutting back summer-flowering shrubs, Barnaby prepared for his 8.30 a.m. briefing the next morning feeling physically relaxed and in a positive frame of mind. He made a note that a ten o'clock appointment with the Caritas Trust was listed in his desk diary.

Troy, who was waiting by the door trying to appear cool and alert, was chewing on a Twix. He had taken them up as a substitute for cigarettes and it was working pretty well except he was still smoking.

As Barnaby tapped his papers neatly end to end and slipped them into an envelope file, he frowned at the sight of his sergeant's chomping jaws.

'Don't you ever stop eating?' It was a sore point. No matter what Troy ate or how much of it, he never put on an ounce.

'Certainly I do.' Troy was aggrieved. If it wasn't one thing it was another. First thing in the morning too. What was the old bugger going to be like by six o'clock?

'I can't imagine when.'

'When I'm asleep. And also when I'm—'

'Spare me the grisly details of your sex life, Sergeant.'

Troy maintained a dignified silence. He had been going to say, 'When I'm reading to Talisa Leanne.' He rolled the chocolate wrapper into a pellet and flicked it into the waste basket.

Thinking of his daughter reminded him of 'chortling'. He had indeed looked the word up in her dictionary and found it to be a cross between chuckling and snorting. Pretty stupid, Troy decided. Why not the other way round? Hey, let's hear it for the snucklers.

Everyone in Room 419 was sitting up and looking alert, notebooks open, print-outs everywhere. Only Inspector Carter appeared crumpled as if he hadn't been to bed and rather depressed. Perversely, Barnaby decided to start with him.

'Piss all, actually, sir,' responded Carter, having been asked what he'd got. 'We did a very thorough house-to-house in all three villages, going back in the evening to catch anyone at work during the day.'

'And those who were in the pub?'

'Oh, yes. No one seems to have heard any disturbance last Sunday night. All inside, curtains drawn, watching the telly. One person, a Mr . . . um . . . Gerry Lovatt was out walking his greyhound, Constanza, just yards from the weir at quarter to eleven and he heard nothing either.'

'That is surprising,' said Barnaby.

'There was that lady—'

'Yes, I'm coming to you, Phillips. Thanks very much.'

'Sorry, Inspector.'

'Carry on then.'

Constable Phillips's Adam's apple bobbed nervously. He blushed and Sergeant Brierley gave him a kindly, encouraging smile. Troy, entranced simply by being in the same room with the girl he fancied rotten, sent his own smile winging across the desk tops. He had named his daughter's kitten Audrey merely for the pleasure of constantly repeating her name. That ignored him as well. Maybe he should rechristen it Constanza.

'A Miss Pleat,' began Constable Phillips.

'I've met Miss Pleat,' said Barnaby. 'You're not telling me I'm going to meet her again, are you?'

'Not necessarily, sir.'

'Thank God for that.'

There was a certain amount of nervous laughter in which Constable Phillips laggardly joined.

'Only I think she might have something. Not facts, I'm afraid, just ideas.'

'Don't tell me, the ebb and flow of the human heart?'

'Something like that, sir. Well, she seems to think that Valentine Fainlight, the man in that amazing—'

'I know who Fainlight is.'

'Sorry. That he's in love with the girl who ran away, Carlotta.'

'Valentine Fainlight is a homosexual, Constable Phillips.'

'Oh. I didn't realise. Sor—'

'On what does Miss Pleat base this remarkable assumption?'

'He goes over to the Old Rectory night after night and stands looking up at her window.'

The room exchanged amused but slightly wary glances, holding back any vocal expression of mirth. Watching the chief, waiting to see which way the wind blew.

After a few moments during which he appeared lost in thought, Barnaby said, 'Is that all?'

'Yes, sir,' said Constable Phillips, praying that it was.

'Right. What's next?'

Print-outs were consulted. Barnaby was informed that according to hospital and police information no person matching Carlotta Ryan's description had been found dead, in or out of water, accidentally or on purpose, during the past seven days.

The search of the river bank was hardly fruitful. On the whole it was pristine but a rough patch of scrub and thorn bushes owned up to a few crisp packets and Cola cans, an old motor tyre once used as a swing and the frame of a baby's pushchair. A retired brigadier, chairman of the Ferne Basset Conservation Society, presented himself at the search and began explaining that the 'cess pit' under observation was used as a dumping ground by council house tenants. It was cleared every week by a member of the Society and was promptly fouled again. Courteous requests to refrain from this habit had been ignored. He insisted that a note to this effect be added to the police report. Village pride was at stake.

Responses to the station's television appeal were still being followed up. The usual attention seekers were being weeded out and what was left was not encouraging.

Sergeant Jimmy Agnew and WPC Muldoon, checking up on the background of Lionel Lawrence, had come up with what was surely the dullest CV on record. Born in 1941 in Uttoxeter, grammar school education with O levels in five subjects, including Religious Education. Dip Theology at the Open University. Not even a suspicious passion for scouting.

DS Harris, detailed to lay his hands on the recording of the anonymous telephone call the night Carlotta disappeared, explained that Kidlington had a backlog, always being short-staffed on Sunday, but it would be over for sure later in the day.

As the DCI had feared, SOCO's print check in the phone box at Ferne Basset proved that the whole procedure had been a pointless waste of their valuable time.

Barnaby was looking forward to meeting Ms Vivienne Calthrop of the Caritas Trust for the Resettlement of Young Offenders. He was about to talk not only to someone who had known Carlotta but who, with a bit of luck, might describe the girl from a reasonably disinterested viewpoint.

Lionel Lawrence, squinting and blinking behind his rose-tinted glasses, was worse than useless. Jax was full of spite because Carlotta had rejected him. Mrs Leathers resented the girl's presence on behalf of her employer and Ann Lawrence had, so far, been unavailable.

They arrived ten minutes early and Troy took advantage of this by getting out of the car and striking up. He did so in a mood of bitter resentfulness both against himself and the bloody fags. So far Maureen still didn't know he'd started again. Somehow or other he had managed not to do it in the house. A brisk walk before bedtime accounted for three saturating smokes and he just about held on till leaving the house the next morning. Gargling with mouthwash, ferociously brushing his teeth and chewing on a bag of parsley from Sainsbury's seemed to have disguised this underhand activity so far. The fact that his clothes still reeked of nicotine was easily explained by their daily exposure to the tasteful ambience in the station toilets.

'Come on!'

Troy stubbed out his cigarette and hurried after the chief. 'Is it kosher, this place?'

They were mounting some heavily stained concrete steps then pushing through metal swing doors painted khaki. The paint was badly chipped and the right door caved in at the bottom as if someone had given it a good kicking.

'Oh, yes. We checked it out. On their headed paper there's a circuit judge noted for his interest in rehabilitation plus two members of the Howard League, as well as our Lionel. The funding's from several impeccable philanthropic sources and a small amount comes from the government.'

At the end of a dreary corridor a large white notice

announced Reception. The letters were very carefully written with a curly flourish here and there and bordered with brightly coloured flowers. The pinned-up card was enclosed in a transparent freezer bag.

A tiny, thin little girl was inside. She hardly looked old enough to go out to play, never mind run a switchboard. She had hair like canary feathers, silver rings through her eyebrows and a chirrupy little Cockney voice.

''Ello.'

'Hello,' said Barnaby, wondering what it signified when receptionists seemed to be getting younger all the time. 'We're—'

'Miss Calthrop's ten o'clock, right?'

'That's it,' said Sergeant Troy. He was wondering if she had made the card on the door. 'And you are?'

'Cheryl. I'll take you over.'

She ignored the phone which had just started to ring and led them out of the building and across the tarmac parking lot towards a rackety old Portacabin lifted from the ground on breeze blocks.

'You don't look much like a copper,' said Cheryl, tripping along in absurd little boots with leopardskin cuffs and four-inch heels. She gave Sergeant Troy a friendly nudge.

'What're we supposed to look like then?'

'Him.' She jerked her soft, lemon-coloured curls towards the chief inspector lumbering along behind.

'Catch me in twenty years,' said Troy.

'Nah,' said Cheryl. 'You ain't never going to weigh that much. You ain't the sort.'

They climbed three wobbly wooden steps. Cheryl rapped on an ill-fitting door. Immediately a wonderful humming sound, like the rich vibration of a viol, rippled under the door and ebbed and shimmered around their heads.

'What was that?' asked Barnaby.

'She's just saying come in.' Cheryl skipped away, adding over her shoulder, 'Deep breath and 'old your nose.'

The two policemen went inside.

Oh boy, thought Troy, inhaling deeply a one hundred per cent genuine gold-carat bred-in-the-bone fug. The wonderfully stale and putrid atmosphere, the concentrated essence of fag that tells an addict he has come home. Except home could never smell this good. Behind him Troy noted a muted moan of protest.

Barnaby, wishing he had indeed taken a deep breath, looked about him. There had been no attempt to disguise or decorate the walls. Metal frames and screws held together panels of hammered grey flat stuff which looked suspiciously like asbestos. There were old-fashioned metal filing cabinets though a dusty computer was just visible behind stacks of files on an extremely cluttered desk. An electric extractor fan let into one of the panels stuttered and coughed. Behind the desk, in a neat reversal of the usual no-smoking sign, a handmade effort had a glowing cigarette with a large, black tick drawn through it.

Someone had attempted to make the foul ambience less offensive by liberal squirtings with a sickly sweet freshener. This further clashed with the fragrance of monosodium glutamate from some takeaway empties in the waste basket and the bold, sultry perfume the woman behind the desk was wearing.

Vivienne Calthrop made no attempt to rise as the

police presented their credentials, just glanced at the warrant cards and waved them away. Rising in any case would not have been easy for she was hugely overweight. She was, in fact, one of the largest women Barnaby had ever seen.

'If you'd like coffee the gubbins is over there.' She jerked a thumb first towards a white, rather dirty Formica table then at a couple of battered armchairs.

'No . . . um . . . really. . .' If Barnaby was thrown it was not because of the woman's appearance but her truly remarkable voice. Very husky, extremely melodious, luxuriant and warm, it crackled with vitality. My God, thought the chief inspector, sinking into one of the armchairs, what my daughter wouldn't give to sound like that.

'Feel free to indulge,' said Miss Calthrop, shaking a Gitane out of a cellophane-wrapped packet and lighting up.

'Thank you,' said Sergeant Troy, reaching inside his jacket before catching the chief's eye and thinking better of it.

'So, what's all this about Carlotta?'

'I don't know what you've been told, Miss Calthrop—'

'Next to nothing. Just that the police wanted some information on her background. What's she done now?'

'Run away,' said Sergeant Troy.

'Oh, come on. The CID fronting the show and she's "run away"?'

'Obviously there's slightly more to it than that.'

'Bet your Aunt Fanny,' said Miss Calthrop.

'There was an argument where she was staying—'

'Old Rectory, Ferne Basset.' She tapped a file on

her desk with a huge white sausagey finger in which were embedded several beautiful rings. 'One of dear Lionel's many benisons.'

'She was accused of taking a pair of diamond earrings,' Barnaby took up the story. 'In some distress apparently, she ran away. Very soon after this we received anonymous information saying someone had fallen into the river.'

'Or jumped,' said Troy.

'She would never have jumped,' said Miss Calthrop. 'She was far too fond of herself.'

This was so like what Jackson had said that Barnaby was both surprised and impressed. Surprised because he had assumed the man had been offering a Carlotta of his own making to fit in with whatever story he had in mind.

'Tell me about her,' said the chief inspector, relaxing in his chair and looking forward to the next few minutes provided he could only surface breathe. He always enjoyed the process of trawling for new information.

Troy dug out his notebook while also trying to relax in his chair. As he had a spring sticking in his bottom this was not so easy. Still sulking over the lack of a ciggie, he produced his biro and started clicking it on and off, much to Barnaby's annoyance.

'Some of the young people that have sat where you're sitting now, Inspector . . .' began Miss Calthrop, 'the wonder is not that they have grown up delinquent but that they have managed to grow up at all. To read their files, to understand the poverty, cruelty and total lack of love which has been their lot since the day they were born is to despair of human nature.'

Barnaby did not doubt Miss Calthrop for a minute.

He, too, had listened to some appalling stories as the background of the accused had been read out in court. But, although not unsympathetic, he was compelled to keep an emotional distance. It was not part of his job to try and help or heal a fragmented personality. That was for the social services, probation officers and prison psychiatrists. And he did not envy them.

'But Carlotta Ryan,' continued Vivienne Calthrop, 'had no such excuse. Her background was comfortably middle class and I understand her childhood to have been reasonably happy until her parents broke up when she was thirteen. Her mother remarried and Carlotta lived with them for a while but she was very unhappy and ran away more than once. Naturally one wonders if the husband was abusing her . . .'

Naturally? thought Barnaby. God, what a world we live in.

Troy was easier now he had something to do and scribbled happily. He had also noticed an Amaretti biscuit tin on the filing cabinet and wondered if he could persuade a few to walk his way.

'But Carlotta assured me this was not the case. Her father was working in Beirut – not the safest of places to take a child – but she decided she wanted to be with him. Her mother agreed and off she went. She was very rebellious and, as I expect you know, the Lebanon is not a country where women, even foreigners, can behave as they do here.' She tugged at some frizzy fronds of hair like ruby-coloured seaweed on her forehead. 'Her father was very concerned she might end up in serious trouble and both parents decided the solution might be to send her to boarding school.'

'How old would she be then?' asked Barnaby.

'About fourteen. Carlotta asked to go to somewhere that concentrated on drama training but her parents were afraid the educational standards might not be too high so they put her in a place near Ambleside.' Miss Calthrop paused for an inhalation so cavernously deep and powerful that her eyes almost crossed themselves with surprise and pleasure at the shock of it. The fat cheeks didn't even dimple.

'Why a stage school?' asked Troy, breathing deeply alongside. 'Did she want to be an actress or something?'

'Yes, she was very keen. I got the impression that if they'd let her go, she wouldn't have veered quite so wildly off the rails.'

Always an excuse. Sergeant Troy swiftly transcribed all these details. As he did so he tried to think as he knew the boss would be thinking. Bring the girl alive in his mind, picture her flouncing, arguing, determined to get her own way. What his gran would have called 'a right young madam'.

Actually, he was wrong. Despite his good intentions, Barnaby was having quite a struggle keeping his mind on the meaning of what Vivienne Calthrop was saying. Seduced by the remarkable beauty of her voice and the extraordinary and exotic grandeur of her appearance, his curiosity was given over to speculating by what circuitous route she could possibly have arrived in this sordid den.

He watched her stub her cigarette into an ashtray already brimming with crimsoned dog ends and re-arrange the marquee of rose and turquoise silk draped around her person. All this jelly wobbling made her earrings dance. They were very long, reaching almost to her shoulders, delicate chandeliers of sequinned discs, enamelled flowers and tiny moonstones all trembling on a fan of golden wire.

Barnaby became aware that he was being severely looked at. 'I'm sorry?'

'I'm not going through all this for nothing, I hope, Chief Inspector?'

'Of course not, Miss Calthrop. I was just engrossed in that last point you made. It raises interesting . . .'

Vivienne Calthrop sniffed. 'You're with us now, I trust?'

'Of course.'

'Then she ran away for the third time and on this occasion they didn't get her back.'

Troy's arm ached. He was dying for a cuppa and some of that interestingly named confectionery. All right for some, with nothing to do but loll back in an armchair with no broken springs and stare out of the window. Nice to see him ticked off for once though.

'Our file,' she picked a folder from the tottering pile on her desk, 'covers the time from when she first came to the attention of the social services until her stay with the Lawrences. There are solid facts here and there are statements from Carlotta which could be truth or fantasy or a mixture of both.'

'What do you think, Miss Calthrop?' asked Barnaby.

'It's difficult to say. She enjoyed . . . how can I put this . . . presenting herself. She would never just come into a room, sit down and simply talk. Every time there had to be a different Carlotta. Wronged, unhappy daughter. Talented girl denied her chance of fame. Once she appeared with a tale about being stopped in Bond Street by a scout for a model agency. Gave her a card, asked to see a portfolio of photographs. All nonsense. She was nowhere near tall enough, for a start.'

'And what about her record?'

'Persistent shoplifting. I don't know how long she'd been at it when she was caught. She swore that was the first time. Don't they all? She was cautioned then caught again a few weeks later with a shopping bag full of Armani tights and T-shirts. Shortly after this she was spotted on camera taking a Ghost evening dress from Liberty's. A woman had been in the day before, trying it on, taking ages over the business, attempting to get them to reduce the price, and it was thought Carlotta might be stealing to order. A much more serious business than the odd impulse snatch. When the police took her home they found a roomful of stuff, all very classy. Molton Brown, Donna Karan, Butler and Wilson jewellery.'

Troy gave his pen a rest. He saw no point in writing down all these names which, in any case, were Greek to him. No wonder Mrs Lawrence had suspected the girl when her earrings had disappeared. She was lucky to have a rag left on her back.

'Would that be the last address you have for her?'

'Yes. Close to Stepney Green.' She was already writing. 'I hope you find her. Alive, I mean.'

'So do I,' said Barnaby. As Miss Calthrop handed the slip of paper over, a concentrated whoosh of a perfume that dare not speak its name zoomed up the inspector's nostrils. Bordello Nights, thought Barnaby, or some copywriter's missed his vocation. On recovering, he asked if they might take Carlotta's file away and extract any information that could be of help to them.

'Certainly not,' replied Miss Calthrop. 'I have told

you everything relevant to your inquiries. Our clients may be on the lowest rung of society, Chief Inspector, but they're still entitled to some privacy.'

Barnaby did not pursue the matter. He could always make a special application should he feel it necessary. He smiled across at Miss Calthrop as warmly as if she had been fully cooperative and changed tack.

'Have you sent many . . . clients to the Old Rectory, Miss Calthrop?'

'Over the past ten years or so, yes. Regrettably, not all have benefited. Several have even betrayed the Lawrences' trust.'

'No,' said Sergeant Troy on a drawn-in breath. He thought he might run with this line in mock amazement for a bit then remembered the chief's nagging about alienating interviewees.

'Hard to understand, I know,' said Vivienne Calthrop. 'You would expect them to be so grateful that they would seize any opportunity to transform their lives. But I'm afraid it rarely seems to work like that.'

'That's very sad,' said Barnaby. And meant it.

'They're like animals, you see, who have never known anything but cruelty and neglect. Sudden kindness is often viewed either with suspicion or disbelief. Even contempt. Of course,' she smiled, 'we do have our successes.'

'Young Cheryl, perhaps?' asked Barnaby. Then in the pause that followed. 'Sorry. Confidential?'

'Just so, Chief Inspector.'

'What about Terry Jackson?'

'Not one of ours.'

Barnaby looked surprised.

'Lionel sits on at least two rehab. boards. The young man may have become known to him that way.'

'They're all young, are they?' asked Sergeant Troy. 'These people Mr L takes on.'

Miss Calthrop turned and stared at him. 'What is the implication behind that remark?'

'Just a question.' Troy remembered the chief putting the same one, to himself as it were, a couple of days ago. 'No offence.'

'Lionel Lawrence is a saint among men.' Miss Calthrop's bulk started to agitate itself, heaving and trembling like a mountain on the move. Her magnificent voice developed a volcanic rumble. 'His wife's inability to have children is a tragedy. Do you wonder he is paternalistically inclined?'

'Yes. Well, I think that's—' Barnaby, rising, was cut off.

'And now they are old—'

'Old?' said Sergeant Troy. 'Mrs Lawrence isn't old. Thirty-five if she's a day.'

'*Thirty*—'

'Nice looking, too.' On their way to the door Troy stopped at the tacky white table and peered into the Amaretti tin. It was full of rubber bands. 'Slim, blonde. Lovely—'

'Open the door, Sergeant.'

Miss Calthrop was still vibrating at full throttle as the DCI thanked her and the two men left.

As they got into the car Troy said, 'Talk about well built. I bet one of her legs weighs more than our garden shed.' Then, when there was no reply, 'We're really meeting them today.'

'We meet them all the time, Sergeant. The trouble

with you is, you've no relish for eccentrics.'

'If you say so, sir.'

Relish, huh. What's to relish? As far as Sergeant Troy was concerned, eccentrics was just a poncy word for weirdos. He liked people who ran along predictable lines. The others just tossed a spanner in the works and screwed up life for everybody else. He put the keys in the ignition, revved hard with showy and quite unnecessary vigour and asked if they would be going straight to the address they had just been given for Carlotta Ryan.

'May as well.'

'Good. I like driving in London. It's a real challenge.'

Barnaby winced. Then, as they drove away, his thoughts turned again to Vivienne Calthrop. Her pretty face: blue eyes, perfect small nose and soft, rosy lips lost in a surrounding sea of wobbly fat and double chins. The wonderful hennaed hair tumbling over her shoulders, and eyebrows dyed exactly to match. It was the eyebrows, Barnaby decided, that got to him. There was something touching about the trouble taken.

'I'd love to hear her sing.'

'Yeah, great.' Troy spoke absently. He was watching the mirror, signalling, pulling out. 'Who?'

'Who? Didn't you hear that woman's voice? It was practically operatic.'

'Me and opera, chief.' Troy sighed then shook his head, feigning regret at this mutual lack of enchantment.

'You don't know what the word Philistine means, do you, Troy?'

'Certainly I do,' Sergeant Troy responded quickly,

on solid ground for once. 'My Auntie Doll takes it for her blood pressure.'

Lomax Road was a turning to the left halfway down Whitechapel just past the London Hospital. A tall narrow house which looked to be as grotty inside as it was out. A blanket was pinned up at the ground-floor window, grimy nets at the one upstairs.

'Be a laugh if she's in there, won't it? Feet up, watching the box, having a bevvy.'

'Nothing would please me more.' Barnaby studied the various bells. The wooden backing was half hanging off the wall, the wires rusty. Benson. Ducane (Chas). Walker. Ryan. He pressed them all. A few minutes later a small sash window was pushed up and a young girl looked out.

'Whaddya want?'

'Police,' said Sergeant Troy.

'No police in here. Sorry.'

'We're looking for Carlotta Ryan.'

'She's gone.'

'Could you perhaps spare a minute?' asked DCI Barnaby.

''Ang about.' The window slammed shut.

Troy muttered, 'What a dump. Just look at that.' The concrete front garden was full of splitting bin bags, festering rubbish and dog mess. 'I bet the rats queue up to have it away on that lot.'

They could hear her clattering downstairs, clopetty clop, clopetty clop, like a little pony. Which meant stone steps or old lino, about what you'd expect in a dump like this.

A tall, slim girl stood facing them. She wore sprayed-on leather hipsters and a once-white jumper, well short of her waist. Her hair was apricot with bronze tips, in a rough poodle cut. Glitter dust bloomed and sparkled on her cheeks and eyelids. Her navel was pierced with a ring from which depended a very large, shiny stone. Her hands were grubby with bitten nails. Barnaby thought she looked like a shop-soiled angel.

He introduced himself and Troy then asked if they might come in for a minute. She looked up and down the road, for all the world like a suburban housewife embarrassed at having the police on the doorstep. A comparison dispelled by her first words.

'You gotta be sharp round 'ere.' She closed the door behind them. 'They see you co-operating with the old Bill . . .'

The stairs were stone and the walls covered with dirty anaglypta. They had been painted so often that the original pattern of swirling feathers had been almost obliterated, at the moment by an unpleasant brownish yellow gloss.

It was not a large house – there were two doors on the ground floor and two on the top – but it was tall and the stairs were very steep. As they climbed after the girl, Barnaby, holding the banister, huffed and puffed. Troy enjoyed his rear view of the leather trousers. Halfway up they passed what looked like a very grotty bathroom and toilet. The window which the girl had looked through was still open.

'Which . . . which flat is Miss Ryan's?' wheezed the chief inspector.

'You all right?'

'Huhh . . . huhh . . .'

'I should come and sit down before you fall down.'

'I'm fine. Thank you.' Barnaby hated to reveal any physical weakness and he made a point of wandering round the girl's room for several moments before he actually did find a seat on a zebra-striped Dralon settee, splitting its sides with fair wear and tear.

'Carlotta lived next door.'

'Could you give me your name, please?' Sergeant Troy lowered himself carefully onto a pink furry stool with purple leatherette trim and a little sequin fringe. He felt like a poser in a clip joint showered by sardonic abuse along the lines of 'get your kit off, sailor' or 'ooh, look – a chipolata'.

'Tanya.'

'Very exotic.' He smiled across at her. 'Russian.'

'Yeah. If me mum could've said no to the Smirnoff, I wouldn't be here today.'

Barnaby laughed and Troy turned his head, surprised and resentful. He had lost count of the little witticisms he had polished up and delivered to the chief to ease the boredom of the daily grind. If he got a half smile he reckoned he'd won the jackpot. Now he couldn't even console himself with the thought that the DCI had no sense of humour.

'Surname?'

'Walker.' She stared at them both. 'What's she done now then, Carlotta?'

'How well did you know her?' asked Barnaby, leaning forward in his usual friendly fashion.

'We got on OK, considering.'

'Considering what?'

'Different backgrounds and that. I were at Bethnal Green Comprehensive, she went to some posh school in the Lake District. Way she described it, you'd've been better off slagging round the Pentonville Road.'

'Did you ever think she might be making it all up?'

'Oh, yeah. She were a dreadful liar, except she called it imagination. "You can imagine yourself anybody, Tarn," she used to say. And I'd say, like, "Get real, Lottie." 'Cause when you've finished imagining, it's the real world you're stuck with, right?'

'Right,' said Sergeant Troy and smiled again. He couldn't help it. In spite of the screwy gunge decorating her face and the stridently sexy clothes, there was something almost innocent about her. Her gelled hair stuck up in little points all over her head, like the soft spines of a baby porcupine.

'We've been given some background from the Caritas office.'

'You what?'

'An organisation that helps young offenders.' Barnaby read over the main points of his notes. 'Could you add anything to that?'

'Not really. I know she'd been thieving for ages before she were caught. And then she goes straight back to it. Seemed to think she were invisible. Like I said, living in a dream.'

'Did Carlotta talk much about the theatre?' Barnaby waved his hands in a vaguely all-inclusive gesture. 'Acting, that sort of thing.'

'She were dead keen. Had this paper with jobs in—'

'*The Stage*?'

'Mind reader, ain'tcha?'

'My daughter's in the business.'

'She'd follow the ads up but never get anywhere. Reckoned you had to have this special card.'

'Equity.' Barnaby remembered the excitement and delight on the day Cully got hers.

'Spent all her money on classes. Dancing, working on her voice. I mean, who needs it these days? That lot in *EastEnders* sound like they was dragged up in Limehouse.'

'Do you have any idea where she went for lessons?'

'Somewhere up West. Look, you still ain't told me what this is about. Is she OK, Lottie?'

'We don't know,' said Troy. 'She's disappeared.'

'I ain't surprised. She were bored rigid down in Fern whatsit. Bugger all to do. The old man always jawin' and his wife treating her like dirt.'

Barnaby thought that didn't sound like Ann Lawrence. 'You talked to her, then?'

'She'd ring up sometimes.'

Barnaby glanced around the cluttered little room.

'There's a pay phone in the 'all.'

'And she didn't come back here?'

Tanya shook her head. 'I'd've heard her moving about.'

'Maybe you were at work.'

'I only work nights. Lap dancing in a club off Wardour Street.' Tanya noticed Troy's expression change and added, with affecting dignity, 'It's nothin' like that. They're not even allowed to touch you.'

'How about visitors? Did Carlotta have any?'

'Men, I suppose you mean.'

'Not necessarily. We're looking to contact anyone who knew her.'

'Well, the answer's no. She went out a lot but nobody came to the flat.'

'Who has the place now?'

'Nobody. You have to pay three months in advance so it ain't run out yet.'

'Do you have a spare key?'

Another head shake. 'I can give you the landlord's number if you want.'

As Troy wrote it down, Barnaby wandered over to the window. The back view was only slightly less depressing than the front. Tiny concrete yards or squares of hard-packed earth almost invisible under abandoned domestic detritus. There was a rusty fire escape that he wouldn't have liked to trust his life to. He turned back into the room and asked Tanya about the people in the downstairs flat.

'Benson's a Rasta, spends most of his time over at Peckham with his girl friend and the baby. Charlie's a porter at Seven Dials. But they both moved in after Carlotta left so they won't know nothing.'

'I believe she received several airmail letters at the Rectory.'

'They'd be from her dad. In Bahrain.'

'We heard,' said Sergeant Troy, 'she threw them away unopened.'

'Blimey.' Tanya's face became pinched and wistful. 'Catch me chucking letters from my dad away. Always assuming I could find out who he was.'

'If you can think of anything else, Tanya, give me a call.' Barnaby gave her his card. 'And, of course, if Carlotta turns up. Day or night – there's an answering machine.'

On their way out Troy took down the number of the pay phone. Barnaby opened the front door and the two policemen were once more exposed to the weak autumn sunshine.

Sergeant Troy thought of his family: parents, grand-parents, aunts, uncles. Although at any given moment at least half of these assorted relatives would be driving him up the wall he couldn't imagine life without them.

'Poor kid. Not much of a start, is it? Not even knowing who your dad is.'

'You're not going soft on me, are you, Sergeant?'

Tanya stood at the window watching them walk away. She let the curtain fall and heard a soft click as the wardrobe door was opened in the bedroom. Then someone moving about.

'It's all right,' she called over her shoulder. 'You can come out now. They've gone.'

As Barnaby and Troy were driving along the City Road on their way to Camden Town, Ann Lawrence was in the kitchen of the Old Rectory brushing a leg of lamb with branches of rosemary soaked in olive oil. Hetty Leathers sat next to her at the table shelling peas. Candy had twisted and rolled off her cushion and was now hobbling and hopping towards them.

'She can smell the meat.' Ann smiled down at the little dog.

'We're a bit dot and carry one today, I'm afraid,' said Hetty and produced a biscuit from the pocket of her flowered overall. While Candy snapped it up, she looked at Ann with some concern. 'Are you sure you're up to things, Mrs Lawrence? You look ever so flushed.'

'I'm all right,' said Ann. 'I feel much better, honestly.'

She meant this and for more than one reason. First, her vow to tell the truth and shame the devil had not faltered throughout yesterday and when she woke up this morning the resolve was as strong as ever.

Secondly, although she could never have admitted this to Hetty the flush was actually one of emotional intoxication following an argument with her husband.

'It was ever so good of the Reverend to agree to take Charlie's funeral,' said Hetty, uncannily picking up her train of thought. 'Him being retired and everything.'

'He was only too pleased.'

This was not quite true. Lionel had been really put out when Ann had made the suggestion. Had argued that to appear publicly in his vestments when for the last ten years he had been regarded by the village as a lay person would confuse everyone. She told him not to be ridiculous and a free and frank exchange of views occurred, to Lionel's alarm and Ann's surprise and increasing exhilaration.

'This man worked at the Old Rectory for years.'

'I'm aware of that, my dear.'

'It would mean a great deal to Hetty. The day will be painful enough without a complete stranger holding forth from the altar steps. And it's not as if you've pulled much weight on the pastoral front so far.'

'What *do* you mean, Ann?'

'I mean the counselling, Lionel. The tender loving care, the patient listening and ongoing support – I thought that was your speciality.'

'I fear little will be gained by continuing this conversation.'

'No doubt if she was eighteen and pretty and accused of selling drugs Hetty'd have had all that plus pocket money, a nice little flat and a new ironing board.'

'You're shouting.'

'If you think I'm shouting now just keep walking towards the door.'

'I can't think what has got into you.'

Ann stood very still and a feeling of tremendous caution possessed her. She realised it was not so much something getting into her but something that was already in her about to get out. Was that what she really wanted? But after a moment her mind, so recently tumultuous and chaotic, clarified. Resentments and desires that she had not even known she possessed came into focus.

How grey and sterile her gentle, orderly life suddenly seemed. How spineless her behaviour. For years she had struggled to accommodate her husband's way of life. Had seen him, if not as a good person, at least as a better human being than herself. Now this self-imposed martyrdom was coming to an end.

Lionel had stopped walking. Perched on the edge of the nearest chair, he had started patting the arm in a soothing manner as if the very furniture might be the next thing to turn against him.

Ann watched with a lack of emotion which quite disturbed her. Lionel had gone his own way without let or hindrance for so long that she had forgotten how he reacted when crossed. The mouth had become petulant, the lower lip, soft and rather wet, pouted in a sulk that might have been appealing in a tiny child. In a 58-year-old man it was simply pathetic.

'We can't go on like this, Lionel.'

'Like what?' Genuinely puzzled, he gaped at her. 'What's wrong with you, Ann?'

'I'm not blaming you—'

'I should hope not.' Lionel was righteously indignant. 'I haven't done anything.'

'If anyone's to blame it's myself. I've let things drift

partly out of laziness but also because I wanted us to be happy—'

'We *are* happy.'

'I haven't been happy for years,' said Ann.

Lionel gulped and said, 'Then I think it's high time you started counting your blessings, my dear.' He levered himself upright, his eyes sliding anxiously towards the door. 'Perhaps you should take one of your tranquillisers.'

'I've thrown them down the lavatory.'

'Was that altogether wise?' When his wife did not reply, Lionel took a cautious step sideways. 'And now I really must go. I'm due at the juvenile court by ten thirty.'

'Why are other people's troubles always more important to you than our own?'

'This is a special case.'

'I'm a special case.'

'I shouldn't be late back.'

'Ring them up. Tell them you've got a crisis in the family.'

'I can't do that.'

'I will, then.'

'No.'

Lionel had spoken so quickly and so quickly sat down again that Ann knew the court appointment was a lie. She felt the first flicker of pity yet never considered for a moment letting things go. There was too much at stake. She took a deep breath to calm herself. Though her heart was full, she found herself wondering if the words to clearly express her feelings could be found. The main thing to remember was there was to be no going back. Or forward either, if that meant treading the old, well-worn, soul-crushing path.

'Lionel, I came to a decision a little while ago. There are various things I need to say and I hope you'll hear me out.'

Lionel had decided to take a leaf out of the book of Job. Long-suffering, patient, eyes glazed with inattention, fingers drumming an awkward rhythm on bony knees.

'First, I can no longer agree to have strangers staying here.'

'Well, that's no surprise.' The tone was condescending and would-be jovial. Plainly he planned to humour her. 'The way you treat—'

'In any case, maintaining a nine-roomed house and a very large garden is beyond my means.'

'Help costs nothing in the country—'

'The place is falling to bits. I can't afford to keep it on.' She was determined not to use the royal pronoun. Lionel had contributed nothing financially to their marriage since he had surrendered his stipend and she would not pretend that he had. 'And there's no reason why I should.'

'We have a position in the village—'

'What do you know of the village?' Ann looked through the window at the cedar tree, part of her existence since the day she was born, and her courage faltered. But there were other trees and freedom never came without a price. 'The Rectory will have to be sold.'

'You can't do that!'

'Why not? It belongs to me.' Thank God. And thank God I never let him near my trust fund, such as it is. How awful, thought Ann. Here's the only life I've ever known breaking up in huge chunks around me and all I can think about is whether I'll have any money. But then – she experienced a sad instant of comprehension – it's not as if there's any love involved.

'And where are we going to live? Or haven't you given that trivial little matter any thought?'

'I hope to get a job. Perhaps train for something.'

'At your age?'

'I'm only thirty-eight.'

'People are retired at forty these days.' He gave a bitter, sarcastic laugh. 'Easy to see you've never had to cope with the real world.'

Ann sensed genuine spite behind the words. Understandable. It was not only her world that was being shaken up today. But it was still a shock to realise that the person to whom she had given almost half her life didn't even like her.

'Anyway,' Lionel continued sulkily, 'you haven't answered my question. And I can tell you right now we won't be moving far from this area. My work must and will continue even though I may no longer be able to offer a refuge to those in need.'

'I don't see why not,' replied Ann, driven to bluntness by this blithe assumption that they would still be rolling merrily along in double harness. 'You'll just have to find somewhere with enough space.'

'Find . . . enough . . .'

'With a spare room.'

'What?' Lionel's face showed utter bewilderment which gradually dissolved into an alarmed understanding. 'You can't mean.'

'You don't listen, do you, Lionel? It's been all of two minutes since I told you I haven't been happy for years.'

A long pause.

'Well, we'll just have to do something about that, won't we?' said Lionel, adding an awkward and tentative, 'dear'.

Faced with this grating sycophancy, Ann winced. 'It's too late.'

'I see.' At this Lionel gradually became so puffed up with outrage it seemed he might rise naturally into the air and float to the ceiling. 'So this is the reward I get for a lifetime of devoted service?'

Unfortunately at this moment Ann's eye alighted on the ebony ormolu clock on the mantelpiece. She saw herself crossing the room, picking it up and handing it to Lionel with every good wish for a happy retirement. Her mouth twitched and she had to bite hard on her bottom lip. Covering her face with her hand she turned away.

'I'm glad to see you still have some decent feelings, Ann.' Lionel, now safely grounded, moved with hunted dignity towards the door.

'One more thing,' said Ann as she heard the handle turn. 'I want that man out of the garage flat.'

'I can't get anywhere without Jax,' said Lionel firmly. Then, with a little stab of triumph, '*You'll* have to drive the car.'

'There won't be any car, Lionel.'

Kemel Mahoud, contacted on Barnaby's mobile, gave his office address as 14a Kelly Street, just off Kentish Town Road.

He was a wiry little man with a smooth, fawn skin, almost bald but flashing a huge brigand moustache, two silky blue-black swags of hair waxed up at the ends into curly commas. He was obsequiously anxious to be helpful – suspiciously so, in Troy's opinion.

'A first-class tenant, Miss Ryan. First rate. No troubles. Rent paid. Spot on.'

'She was a thief, Mr Mahoud,' said Troy. 'When the police followed her home, they found the place full of stolen goods.'

'Ah!' He gasped in what appeared to be real amazement. 'I can't believe. Such a nice girl.'

'You knew her?'

'No, my God. Just saw her one time. She gives deposit, three months' rent, I give key. Two minutes – done.'

'Well, now I'd like you to give me the key,' said Barnaby. 'We need to gain entrance to the flat.'

'Won't she let you in?'

'Miss Ryan has disappeared,' said Sergeant Troy.

'But rent is due, two weeks.'

'That's not our concern. You'll get the key back, don't worry.'

'No problem.' He crossed to the far wall, three-quarters covered by a huge peg board on which hung masses of neatly labelled keys. 'Always I wish to help.'

'Slimy toerag,' said Sergeant Troy, climbing into the Astra and ramming the key into the ignition. 'Foreigners. They're practically running the place.'

'Watch that florist's van.'

Crawling back down Whitechapel past the Bangladeshi stalls of wild-looking vegetables and ripe mangoes and glittering saris and cooking pots, Barnaby started to keep his eye out for a place to lunch.

'Oh, look, chief! What about there?'

'Keep your eye on the road.'

'It's the Blind Beggar. Where it all happened.'

'Nearly thirty years ago.'

'Couldn't we, though? Please?'

Troy's enthusiasm was great and his disappointment commensurate. A comfy, bright, clean pub with a nice thick carpet and all the expected furnishings. There was even a paved garden with white furniture and a dark green awning tacked onto one side. It being a pleasant day, this was where they took their hefty beef sandwiches and halves of Ruddles.

'Your face.' Barnaby was laughing.

'What?'

'Like a kid on Christmas morning with an empty sock. What did you expect, blood on the floor?'

'Sawdust, maybe.'

'Look, one Kray's snuffed it, the other's in for life and Frankie Fraser's making a bomb on the celebrity circuit. It's a different world.'

Troy smeared horseradish onto his sandwich and looked out at the crowded pavements and roaring traffic. This was life and no mistake. He started to relax and enjoy himself.

'Actually, chief, I've been thinking about putting in for a transfer to the Met.'

'You've been *what*?'

'Why not?'

'Because they'll chew you up in two minutes flat then spit out the fur and gristle, that's why not.'

'It can't be that bad.'

'Can't it?' Barnaby laughed. 'What put such a daft idea into your head in the first place?'

'They get to drive a Porsche 968 Club Sport on patrol.'

'Rubbish.'

'It's true. Inspector Carter told me in the canteen.'

'Take out a second mortgage and buy your own.'

'Maureen'd kill me.'

'It's still a safer option.'

When they returned at three o'clock to 17 Lomax Road, it seemed deserted. Before letting themselves in, Barnaby had tried the bell for Benson and Ducane (Chas) with no success. Troy rapped on Tanya Walker's door and got the same result.

The chief inspector hesitated a few seconds before entering Carlotta's room. Over the years he had come to savour moments like this for their sheer unpredictability. You turn the key, you open the box and you find . . . what? Good news that could unexpectedly turn a deadlocked, impenetrable case inside out; bad news that could make all the work that had gone before a waste of time. Or nothing at all.

'Blimey,' said Sergeant Troy who entered first. 'The locusts have landed.'

'They certainly have,' agreed Barnaby.

The rooms were empty except for the furniture. A wooden table with extending leaves and two hard-backed chairs, a shabby armchair and a scarred chest of drawers with two knobs missing. In the corner of the room was a sink, a Baby Belling and a tiny fridge. On the metal draining board were a few chipped cups and saucers and a battered frying pan. Behind a greasy-looking bead curtain was a second very small room with a single bed, the sort of dressing table that had become obsolete sometime in the swinging sixties and a narrow wardrobe.

'I wonder how much that oily tosser screwed her for this dump.'

Barnaby shrugged. 'A hundred. One twenty.'

'Daylight robbery.' Troy moved over to the chest of drawers and made to open one.

'Use your handkerchief!'

'Right, chief.' Troy wrapped it round his fingers and pulled. 'You think we've got a suspicious here, then?'

'I don't know what I think.' Barnaby walked around, staring at the walls. Lumps of Blu-Tack were plentiful, posters were not.

Troy called out from the smaller room, 'Drawers in here empty. And the wardrobe.'

'Why would someone strip a place when they haven't permanently moved out and there's still some rent left?'

'Search me.'

'Even the bedding's disappeared.'

'Maybe Tanya's borrowed it.'

'No key, remember?'

Troy sat in the armchair. It made the one with the broken spring in Vivienne Calthrop's office feel like cloud nine.

'Maybe she thought she was permanently moving out,' suggested Troy.

'Yes,' said Barnaby. 'Maybe she did. And there's something else.' Barnaby sniffed then breathed more deeply as he came to a halt by the window. 'How long did Lawrence say Carlotta had been at the Rectory?'

'Couple of months.'

'There's no way this place has been shut up for two months. The air's fresh. This window's been opened within the last day or so.'

'Crikey,' said Sergeant Troy.

214

'We'll drive over to Bethnal Green nick. See if they'll do us a favour and get any prints lifted. And seal that door.'

'Pity the horse has bolted,' said Troy.

By the time his team had assembled for their early evening briefing, Barnaby had discovered that the Met's forensics could not be of assistance in the matter of Carlotta's flat.

'I asked if they'd dust the place but they've already got a backlog processing prints so we'll have to get our lot out there a.s.a.p. Then we'll be able to match what they get against the landlord and anyone else with access to the keys. Plus, of course, the three other residents in the house.'

'Do we have the girl's own prints, sir?' asked Sergeant Brierley.

'We should have by this time tomorrow.'

Barnaby was looking forward to telling Lionel Lawrence that a couple of forensic officers would be entering the Rectory, with or without his permission, within the next twenty-four hours and smothering all resistable surfaces in his attic bedsit with aluminium powder.

As soon as the briefing was concluded, he retired to his office and did just that. When the agitated burble about police states and the harassment of innocent citizens was in full flow, Barnaby interrupted somewhat forcefully.

'I'm surprised to hear you taking this attitude, Mr Lawrence. I thought you would be a hundred per cent behind anything that helped establish the possible whereabouts and wellbeing of Miss Ryan.'

There was a longish pause during which Barnaby smiled quietly to himself. Wrong-footing the pompous was a small pleasure but some days a man needed all the small pleasures he could gather.

Lionel made a strange noise which sounded as if he was gargling with an extremely unpleasant substance.

'Well, naturally . . .'

'That's all right then.' Barnaby drew a cheerful line under the subject.

'Will they clean everything up before they go?'

'No.'

'Ah.'

'I also need to speak to your wife. I hope she's now fully recovered.'

'She certainly is.'

Barnaby absorbed this quick, unconsidered response, shot through with bad-tempered resentment, and wondered what had brought it about. Perhaps he'd find out tomorrow. With a bit of luck it might be conflict over Jackson. A lever to prise the lid off that particular can of worms.

'So perhaps we might fix a time tomorrow when Mrs Lawrence is sure to be in.'

'Well, the Mothers' Union meet at five thirty. She'll be here five at the latest to sort out the crockery and stuff. Never misses. Otherwise she's in Causton most of the day on business.'

A lot of 'she's' there, thought the chief inspector. You'd think the poor woman didn't have a name to call her own. 'If you'd kindly tell her—'

'Tell her yourself. She's just coming.'

A moment later Ann Lawrence picked up the phone, agreed in a calm voice that 5 p.m. would be a good time and that she was looking forward to talking to him.

Barnaby hung up, shrugged into his overcoat, peered through the dusty cream slats on his Venetian blind and discovered a slight drizzle misting the evening air. It did nothing to damp his spirits. In half an hour he would be home and sitting in his favourite chair in front of the fire with a glass of wine and the daily paper while the wife of his bosom cooked up a storm in the kitchen. Yes, well, maybe in that case, two glasses of wine.

It had been a good day on the whole. He had found out quite a lot about Carlotta. He had met two people who knew her, he had seen where she lived. And tomorrow he would be talking to the one person who knew exactly what had happened on the night she disappeared.

CHAPTER NINE

Forty-eight hours after she had made her momentous decision, Ann was getting ready to go into Causton. Lionel was sulking in his study. She had knocked and said lunch was ready and he had not replied. Where she would once have taken a tray in for him, she now ate her own meal and left his to get cold on the table.

She had four hours before the police came. Although her resolve to tell them everything had not faltered she did not want to spend the intervening time dwelling on how the interview might go. Or on what might happen to her when it was over.

There was plenty to do. First she would go to the bank and pay back the five thousand pounds. (She had already rung Mr Ainsley to say she would be doing this and asking him to cancel their loan agreement.) Then she would do the rounds of estate agents. There were several in Causton and she hoped to cover them all. Or at least as many as it took to take her up to half past four.

In her bedroom, having changed into a flowered dress and jacket, Ann was drawn by the beauty of the day to her window. She noticed that the gravel drive, barely a week since Charlie Leathers raked it over, was already sprouting weeds. And the wonderful thing was she would not have to go and tug them all out. No one would. As Ann relished this satisfactory observation, the sun vanished behind a cloud. A nice sense of timing, for it was then that Ann saw Jax. That is, she saw the lower section of him. The rest was hidden beneath the bonnet of the Humber which was half in and half out of the garage. She needed the car to drive into Causton.

At the thought of walking up to the man, looking into those cold, radiant eyes, being exposed to that suggestive leering voice, her courage, so steadfast until then, faltered. And what if Lionel had already told him of her demands that he should leave. What might he say then?

What a pity Mrs Leathers wasn't still here. She would have stridden across, told him the car was wanted right away and he'd better look sharp about it. Perhaps, Ann thought, I could just open the window and call.

Then, upset and agitated, she remembered the telephone. There was an extension from the main house to his flat. If she rehearsed what she had to say, there would be no need to get involved in any sort of conversation. Keep it short, she instructed herself, picking up the telephone and pressing the connecting button. She watched him stop what he was doing, wipe his hands on a cloth and disappear through the painted blue door. And the instruction worked. After all that queasy anxiety, the exchange was simplicity itself.

Ann said, 'This is Mrs Lawrence. I shall need the car in five minutes. Will it be ready then?'

And he said, 'No problem, Mrs Lawrence.'

A ridiculously overwhelming rush of relief (after all, what could he actually *do*?) receded and Ann began to feel calmer. She washed her face and hands, brushed her hair and tied it away from her face with a black silk ribbon then collected her handbag, checking that the money was still inside. She hesitated whether to take a coat – the sun had come out again – and decided against it.

She left the house and walked in what she hoped was an unflustered way towards the garage. There was no sign of Jax. The interior of the car was heavy with the smell of polish, the chestnut leather gleamed. Telling herself she had been watching too many movies, Ann still couldn't help checking out the back of the car. She even turned over a travelling rug on the carpeted floor to make sure the interior was empty.

As she drove out of the gates and turned left towards the road to Causton, everything about her suddenly seemed transformed. The whole world seemed light and airy and free from care. That was the world – carefree.

'I am carefree,' said Ann aloud. And she started to sing.

'Penny Lane', the song her mother had loved, the song she half remembered from her childhood.

'Penny Lane is in my ears and in my eyes . . . there beneath the blue suburban skies . . .'

And, as the distance between herself and the Old Rectory increased, so did the dizzy feeling of exhilaration. She was cutting herself loose. Floating away from the self-centred, querulous man around whom she had organized her life for so many years and from the huge, crumbling millstone of a house. A source of financial worry for as long as she could remember. To paraphrase a title from Lionel's huge collection on his counselling bookshelf, this was the first day of the rest of her life.

She covered the last few miles to the outskirts of Causton anticipating her meeting with the estate agents. And wondered how soon they would be able to come and give a valuation. That they would jump at the chance she was sure. A house the same size as hers, though admittedly in much better repair, had been sold at Martyr Bunting the previous week for three hundred thousand pounds.

A roundabout was coming up. Ann started to concentrate on the road ahead. She negotiated her way round the war memorial in the main market square and down Causton High Street past Boots and Woolworths and Minnie's Pantry. She decided to go there for tea around four o'clock, then there would be no need to have anything at home. She could stay out until almost the minute the police were due to arrive. She hoped it would be the big, burly detective who came after Charlie was killed. She had liked him and not only because he had shown impatience with Lionel's affectations. Ann had guessed at a man unclouded by sentiment but not without kindness. Solid, self-contained and passionately interested in whatever was going on around him.

She turned left at the town hall, behind which stood the new three-storey car park. This had been built only after two years of the most ferocious opposition. Causton, population twenty-seven thousand and eighty-three souls at the last electoral listing, reckoned it did not want or need a public car park. When it was mooted, Middle England took to the streets with banners and besieged the *Causton Echo* with abusive or heavily ironical why oh why? correspondence. Sit-ins took place at the municipal offices and when the town planning department bravely organised a public meeting, it ended in a riot. Several people lay down when the diggers came in. It was built anyway, of course, and the moment it was open the council painted double yellow lines all over the town centre and outlying streets so people had no choice but to use it.

At three o'clock on a weekday afternoon, the car park was almost full. Ann drove slowly round the first and second tier but there was not a single empty space. At the third she found one between a Land Rover and a Robin Reliant, miles away from the exit.

Ann didn't really like using the place except at ground level which had plenty of natural light and people passing just a few feet away. Artificial lights were installed in the rest of the building but often didn't work. Sometimes this was due to slack maintenance but more often to vandalism

Like any public space with ease of access, lack of supervision and an opportunity for concealment, the car park had attracted those with something to conceal. Only the week before, several men had been caught after holding their very own car boot sale, swapping small bags of dream dust for large bags of used currency. They did not realise a pair of lovers were practically on the floor of a car just a few feet away. The ardent couple, passion spent, memorised the dealer's number plate before wisely putting, and keeping, their heads down.

Ann had read about this in the paper. As she got out

and locked all four doors, recalling the drug handlers' capture made her feel slightly more confident in the way air passengers will when travelling immediately after a major disaster, aware not only that the odds against a second disaster happening so soon were astronomical but also feeling everyone on the flight deck would be concentrating one thousand and one per cent.

The long space between her and the lift was crammed with cars but apparently empty of human beings. Ann started to walk, looking around as she did so. How ugly concrete was. The bleak grey walls were already stained with running dark seams, like black tear tracks.

She found herself counting the vehicles. Two, three, four . . . On seven – lucky seven – there was a sound behind her. A creak as if someone was opening a door. Ann wheeled round. Nothing. Had someone got out of one of the seemingly empty cars? Were they even now creeping along behind her, keeping pace with her movements? Or drawing level and catching up?

She shook her head with irritation at her own timidity. Where was all the courage that had filled her heart and mind when she had sung those words a mere half-hour ago? She took a deep breath, lifted her chin and lengthened her stride. Eleven, twelve, thirteen – nearly halfway there.

He must have been wearing soft shoes, or no shoes. She didn't hear a thing but glimpsed a sudden great pouncing out of the corner of her eye. Then he was on her. She felt the weight of him, the grunting curse of his breath. His arm was clamped so fiercely round her throat that, even in her terror, she could not cry out.

She was dragged over to the nearest car. Then, before she understood what was happening, he seized her hair, gathering it tightly in his fist, and yanked her head right back then swung it forward with tremendous force hard down against the edge of the bonnet.

Valentine Fainlight was working. That is, he was going through the motions. The proofs for *Barley Roscoe and the Hopscotch Kid* had finally arrived and Val was vaguely turning over the pages, thinking they looked all right to him. Once upon a time, in another life it sometimes seemed, he would have noticed that the margins on more than one page were not quite even and that Barley's magic cap was too dark a shade in the scene where he transformed hopscotch squares into blocks of honey fudge. (The cap, a pale, delicate blue when Barley was simply going about his day-to-day affairs, deepened according to the degree of catastrophe his transformations wrought.)

Valentine saw none of these things. He saw only Jax's face: cruel, beautiful, enigmatic. He had found himself wondering briefly yesterday evening how a person not all that intelligent could actually manage to look enigmatic then felt ashamed. Val had had thoughts like this once before and had immediately berated himself for being snobbish and unfair. And in any case, they were irrelevant. For who was ever cured of a fever by dispassionate analysis?

He felt bad about Louise. He loved his sister and knew that his apparent rejection was hurting her. The only thing to be said in his defence was that if she continued to live with him, she would be hurt much, much more.

Sometimes, at moments like this when Val acknowledged that the word relationship was meaningless and what he had really been infected by was a fatal disease, he remembered Bruno. Val had had the good fortune to live for seven years with a complex, gifted, difficult, funny, kind and completely loyal man. The sex had been great, the fights never vicious. When Bruno died, Valentine felt he had fallen into a bottomless chasm of despair.

His partner's parents, one or two very close friends, his work but, most of all, Louise had pulled him back to life. Now, when she was struggling to recover from her own smash-up, he was turning her out. A month ago he would not have thought himself capable. This morning, when she had cried in the kitchen, he felt so terrible he almost changed his mind. But then a wonderful idea occurred to him. A week ago, when Louise had gone to London for the day, he had asked Jax over to see the house. It had been warm and they had had wine and sandwiches in the garden. Jax had loved Fainlights and could hardly tear himself away. With Louise gone, Jax could not just visit, he could actually come and stay.

The telephone rang. Val snatched it up and cried, 'Yes, yes?'

'Hello, Val.'

'Jax! What do you—' He stopped, gulped in some air. 'I mean, how are things? How are *you*?'

'I'm just going to have a shower, actually.'

Oh God, if this is a tease I'll go over there and kill him.

'You one of them green people?'

'What?'

'You know, save water, shower with a friend.'

'Do you mean you'd like . . .'

'Only if you want.'

Louise saw him go. She had heard the phone ring, once. Now she watched her brother, her lovable, intelligent brother, capering in his excitement, fumbling with the front gates and racing into the road. Dancing at the end of this odious man's leash like some sad performing bear.

As Valentine hurried through the blue door and up the stairs, he realised he had not brought any money. But he could put that right. He could explain.

The door of the flat was slightly open. He could hear the shower running. Was Jax already in there? Or maybe he was moving silently behind him on the cream carpet, creeping up to jump. To grab Val hard round the throat as he had once before. Already excited, Val deliberately didn't turn his head.

But then Jax walked out of his bedroom wearing a loosely tied towelling robe. Came straight up to Val and put the end of the belt in his hand. Then, using both his own hands, ripped open Val's shirt, sending the buttons flying.

Hetty Leathers, having now confirmed the time and date of her husband's funeral, invited Evadne both to the church and afterwards for a light lunch at the bungalow.

And so Evadne was laying out her black. It was not a colour she enjoyed wearing, consequently there was very little to choose from. However, having been brought up to observe the traditional formalities, she felt unable to attend such a function in any other colour.

A lot depended on the weather. A late August day could be extremely warm or unexpectedly nippy. Evadne removed a fine wool coat and skirt from her wardrobe and gave the outfit a good shake. The coat smelt of moth balls and the lingering fragrance of Coco, her favourite scent. Then she picked out a long-sleeved anthracite velvet tunic and matching trousers and studied them thoughtfully. They were certainly dark enough to be acceptable and extremely elegant but her mother would have fainted with horror at the idea of a woman wearing trousers in church. Aware that her parent's benign but strict attention could beam down unannounced at any time, Evadne put the ensemble back.

The hat was not a problem. Well, it was and it wasn't. That is, she had a hat and it was the proper colour but it was not what you would call funereal. She had bought the organza confection for a favourite niece's wedding a year ago. It had a high crown, a wide, down-curving brim and was trimmed with dark floppy peonies made of shiny silk. However, as one could no more enter church without a hat than one could wearing masculine attire, it would have to do.

Evadne carried the clothes downstairs and hung them in the kitchen near an open window to freshen up. Then she set about making a cup of lemon verbena tea which she always enjoyed with her morning paper.

Soon there was a scratching at the front door. Evadne opened it to admit Mazeppa carrying a basket holding *The Times*. She was standing in for Piers who was having a lie-in.

Mazeppa was a good girl, even famous – one of her puppies had won Best in Show at Crufts – but she had never got the hang of carrying a newspaper in her mouth. She felt this inability keenly and was deeply ashamed of being sent out with a basket. Evadne had never thought to explain that Piers only carried the local paper in his mouth. Even he needed a little help with the heavies.

Now Mazeppa, determined to impress, tipped the basket onto its side, pulled out a section of the journal, mangled it between her teeth, dragged it into the kitchen and laid it carefully down.

'What have I told you?' Evadne picked up the paper, poking her finger through an extremely soggy patch and wagging it at the dog. 'How am I supposed to read this?'

Mazeppa beat her feathery, fleur-de-lys of a tail hard against the table leg panting and sighing with pleasure at all this attention.

'Now I suppose you think you're getting a biscuit.'

The thumping rhythm slowed, becoming less certain. Mazeppa's face, already squashed by nature into a crumpled landscape of ridges, tucks and frowns, became even more scrunched up by anxiety. Evadne patted the dog, tossed it a chocolate Bourbon and took her tea into the sitting room. She opened the remains of the newspaper at the arts section.

There was an exhibition of early English mezzotints and watercolours at the V & A. Evadne loved watercolours. She wondered if the museum would accommodate the dogs. Mrs Craven had taken her poodle, a fractious little show-off, to a horticultural display at St Vincent's Square. The Pekes, by comparison, were as good as gold. Perhaps they could be left briefly with the cloakroom attendant? She decided to ring the very next day.

Already consumed by a happy glow of anticipation, Evadne skipped the theatre reviews – why on earth would anyone need theatre with the drama of daily life all about them? – and found the book pages.

She always kept a little notebook and propelling pencil by her chair to write down new titles that appealed. Not that she could afford many of them but Causton library, even in its present state of constant penury, usually managed to raise or borrow a copy from somewhere.

Today there was a full page on children's literature. It was divided into boxes relating to the child's age and showed illustrations from the books, some funny, some charming, some so frightening Evadne wondered at the parent who would let them into the house. She wished she had a young friend or relation to climb on her knee and listen to *The Tale of Peter Rabbit* or *Babar the Elephant*. Perhaps the newly married niece would eventually oblige.

In the seven to nine years section she found a new title from the Barley Roscoe series. Evadne knew all about Barley. Valentine Fainlight had donated a signed copy of his young hero's adventures in aid of the church fete and Evadne had won it on the tombola. Barley was an appealing child, frequently in trouble yet always starting out with the best of intentions. He reminded her of William Brown but without William's stunning insouciance when standing amidst the wreckage of his confident attempts to be helpful.

Evadne put the paper aside, rather sorry now she had opened it. She had been trying to put the name Fainlight from her mind. Trying not to dwell on the sad fact of Carlotta's disappearance. Her heart went out to Valentine. When the nice young constable had asked her if she had known the girl or could give any information about her disappearance, Evadne had mentioned her lovelorn suitor. Then, fearing that she had implied some involvement on Valentine's part, hurriedly explained that this was purely a matter of observation rather than actual knowledge.

And his poor sister. Oh dear. Evadne sighed aloud. She had heard Louise weeping in the garden of their house on Friday. Evadne had called on behalf of Christian Aid and had hovered uncertainly for several minutes, torn between a natural longing to offer comfort and an anxiety that an intrusion might embarrass or annoy. Louise had always struck her as a very private person. In the end she had walked quietly away. So much unhappiness. Evadne picked up *The Times* hoping to recapture her pleasant feelings of a few moments ago. She turned to the music page. This was largely taken up by an appreciation of a young and gifted jazz musician who had recently committed suicide.

Evadne sighed again, rather more loudly this time. Mazeppa jumped into her lap, gazed intently into her eyes and gave a long moan of sympathy.

At five fifteen precisely, when Louise Fainlight was quietly breaking her heart and her brother was kneeling on a tiled shower floor in a state of worshipful ecstasy; when Hetty Leathers and her daughter were cracking a bottle of Guinness to celebrate having scraped together the necessary to pay for fifty per cent of Charlie's funeral (thanks to the Red Lion collection bottle) and the members of the Mothers' Union were preparing their hearts and minds for their genteel and philanthropic endeavours, Detective Chief Inspector Tom Barnaby and Sergeant Gavin Troy presented themselves on the crumbling steps of the Old Rectory.

Lionel Lawrence hardly heard the bell and in any case was in such a state of inner turmoil that he had quite forgotten his telephone conversation earlier that day with the police. Lionel felt like a man who has owned a kitten for years, devotedly caring for it in a kindly if absent-minded manner, only to have it turn into a panther behind his back and bite a great chunk out of his hand.

Obviously Ann would calm down. He would have to be patient, talk to her, maybe even listen a bit. She plainly felt she had some sort of legitimate grievance although Lionel could not imagine what this could possibly be. But he would make whatever promises she wanted and even do his best to keep them. Anything else was unthinkable. To be cut adrift at his time of life, homeless, penniless. What would he do? Where would he go? After years of dedicated compassion towards society's cast-offs, Lionel realised that now that he was in need of a spot of it himself, there seemed to be no one to turn to. Furious at his wife for putting him in such a position while knowing he could never afford to let it show, Lionel decided to forgive her, as a Christian should, and work hard towards their reconciliation.

The bell rang again and this time it registered. Lionel, still consumed with apprehensive visions as to his future, drifted across the black and white tiled hall and opened the door.

To his annoyance it was the policemen who had been so insolent only a few days ago. He couldn't quite find the courage to tick off the senior officer and the younger was nosily peering over his shoulder into the house so Lionel settled for staring severely into the gap between them.

'Sorry to interrupt,' said Barnaby, looking about as unsorry as a man could be, 'but I believe you're expecting us.'

'I most certainly am not,' said Lionel. 'What I am expecting in,' he removed a pocket watch from his waistcoat pocket and locked onto it as if spellbound, 'roughly twenty minutes is the Ferne Basset Mothers' Union monthly committee meeting.'

'We spoke on the telephone yesterday.' Barnaby stepped forward as he said this and Lionel, taken by surprise at the sudden brisk movement, moved hurriedly to his right, investing this brief sidle with an air of intolerable persecution.

'Arranged to talk to Mrs Lawrence,' explained Sergeant Troy, by now also in the hall. 'Fivish.'

'Ah.' Lionel did not close the door. 'Well, she isn't here.'

'But will be shortly?' suggested the chief inspector. 'You did say she always attended the meetings.'

'Indeed. It is one of the high spots of her monthly calendar.'

Good grief, thought Sergeant Troy. What a life. He tried to imagine Talisa Leanne's mother joining a union.

Poor buggers wouldn't know what had hit them. Maureen'd argue the hind leg off a donkey, persuade you black was white. You'd believe a man could fly and if he'd got any sense the minute he saw her coming that's exactly what he'd do.

Lionel marched off, leaving them standing in the hall. Although they had not been asked either to wait or to make themselves at home, Barnaby and Troy sat on two small wrought-iron seats on either side of the large copper vase. The chairs were extremely uncomfortable.

Troy, straightaway bored, peered through the arrangement of beech leaves and tansies only to realise the chief was already in one of his 'do not disturb' moods.

But Barnaby's thoughts were by no means as tranquil as his calm exterior would suggest. He was thinking of the coming meeting with Ann Lawrence. Third time lucky, he had confidently told himself during the journey over. At their first brief meeting he had not even known that the missing girl would be relevant to the Leathers murder case. On Saturday, Mrs Lawrence had been so full of dope, no interview had been possible. Now she had had all of Sunday and Monday to recover. When he'd spoken to her yesterday she had sounded calm and not at all apprehensive. He recalled her actual words: 'Yes, Inspector. And I want to speak to you. In fact, I'm looking forward to it.'

He murmured the last sentence aloud and Troy quickly said, 'Sir?'

'She said, "I'm looking forward to it" – our meeting. What do you make of that?'

'Got something on her mind. Wants to talk it over.' Troy glanced at his watch. 'She'll miss all the fun if she don't get her skates on. The place'll be swarming with mothers any minute.'

'I don't like it.'

'*I* shan't like it,' said Troy. 'It's an aspect of life I could well do without.'

'Be quiet.' Barnaby was experiencing a slight feeling of sickness. The cold clutch of tension in the pit of his stomach. A moment of inexplicable and fearful recognition, like finding the lavatory chain swinging when you believed you were alone in the house. 'Can you see anyone coming?'

Troy got up, stretched his legs and went over to the long window by the side of the front door. In the drive, striding with brisk determination towards the Rectory, were several women. They were not the stodgy matriarchs Troy had been expecting, tweed-wrapped and bluff-complexioned. Some wore bright trousers and jackets. One wore what looked like a green Homburg, a long purple mohair jumper and Fair Isle shooting stockings. See them coming? Ray Charles could see them coming.

Troy opened the door, stood to one side and let them swarm in. They didn't hang about. Just legged it for the interior where they could be heard talking loudly to Lionel. Amidst this distant uproar was the clatter of china and teaspoons.

'Get hold of Lawrence, Sergeant.'

Troy tried. Lionel was in the kitchen pretending to help and having his half-hearted, clumsy efforts laughed at with kindly indulgence. When it was understood that Ann was not present, the lady in the hat offered to

235

make him some bacon and eggs. People were swarming all over the place. Someone said, 'Ah, there you are' to Sergeant Troy and asked if he would take a tray loaded with cups into the sitting room.

'Mr Lawrence? Would you—' Troy dodged back to let a sliced cherry cake past. 'The chief inspector would like a word.'

'What?' shouted Lionel, taking the cling film off a plate of cucumber sandwiches and cramming two in his mouth.

'In the hall, sir, if you would.' Troy eased his way round the deal table and cupped his hand, gently but firmly, round Lionel's nearest elbow. Wrong.

'Have you ever come across the phrase "civil liberties", Sergeant?'

'Yes, Mr Lawrence.'

'Well, if you don't want a summons for assault, I suggest you take your hand away.'

Troy removed his hand. 'And perhaps you are aware, sir, that refusing to assist the police in a murder inquiry is a punishable offence.'

'There's no question of that.' Lionel, though still munching, moved briskly towards the exit. 'Simply that every man is entitled to defend himself.'

They got into the hall just in time to bump into the chief striding out to find them.

'Where the hell have you been?'

'Sorry, sir. It's a bit hectic—'

'In here.' Barnaby turned into the first doorway to present itself. A small octagonal room with a few hardback chairs, some piles of sheet music and hi-fi equipment and an old Bechstein grand. Troy drifted over to the piano, produced his notebook, just in case, and rested it on the rich, mottled walnut lid.

Nearby was a silver-framed photograph of a fierce old man in a dog collar. Though almost bald, grey hair sprouted profusely from his ears and nose and he sported a fine pair of Dundrearys. He glared at the camera. His dog, a piggy-eyed bull terrier, rolled back its leathery lip presumably to free the teeth for a good nip. They looked made for each other.

'So, Mr Lawrence. When did you last see your wife?'

'What on earth—'

'Answer the question, man!'

'Mid-morning.' Lionel gulped the words in some alarm. 'Around eleven.'

'Did she say what her plans were for later?'

'Drive into Causton. I suppose she was going shopping. She didn't say.'

'Did you have an argument?'

'How did— You have my assurance that our . . . discussion yesterday has nothing to do with your present inquiry.'

'Point is, sir,' said Sergeant Troy, who had started scribbling, 'it might help us to know what her frame of mind was.'

'Why?' Lionel appeared mystified. 'How, help?'

'I understood from you that Mrs Lawrence has never missed a Mothers' Union meeting.'

'There's a first time for everything.'

'Aren't you worried?'

Lionel now appeared not only mystified but slightly alarmed. And Barnaby, realising that he had raised his voice, checked himself. Another decibel or two and he would have been shouting.

Lionel's honest bewilderment pulled him back. He

saw how his behaviour must appear. For the truth was he had no logical reason for feeling some harm had come to Ann Lawrence. She could have run into a friend, be choosing books at the library, trying on clothes . . . No logical reason. Just the icicle slowly stirring his guts.

He tried to speak more calmly. 'Could you tell us what time she left?'

'I'm afraid not. I was in my study. We didn't lunch together today.'

Blimey, must have been quite a corker, that discussion, thought Sergeant Troy. He put a question of his own, knowing the answer but hoping to stir things to good effect.

'Would Mrs Lawrence have driven to town, sir? Or might your Mr Jackson have taken her?'

'No.' Sadly, Lawrence didn't rise. 'She liked to drive herself. Although . . .' Suddenly he could not be helpful enough. It was painfully clear that he wanted to get rid of them. 'Jax might be able to tell you what time she left. I believe he was working on the Humber just before lunch.'

'They talk to you?' asked Jax. 'The police?'

'Yes. That is, they came round.' Valentine was sitting on the edge of the divan. Now that the wrestling and fighting and subduing was over and blood had returned to his crushed limbs and strained muscles, all was pain and confusion. But the happiness, the dark shining, was in there somewhere.

'About Charlie?'

'That's right.'

'What sort of thing they want to know?'

'It was Louise who saw them. I sloped off.'

'They'll catch up with you.'

'We hardly knew the man.'

'Makes no difference.' Jax sauntered across the room and flung himself into the orange fireside chair. He spread his legs and leaned back, grinning. 'Suppose I'd better put some clothes on.'

'No,' cried Val quickly. 'Don't, please.'

'Ready for some more, then?'

'It's not that. I just like looking at you.' He eased himself off the divan, reached down, wincing, to pick up his boxer shorts.

'I know that shop.'

'Sorry?'

'Sulka. In the West End, right?'

'Yes. Bond Street.'

'I met this bloke got his dressing gowns there.'

'Really?' Valentine felt a quite different sort of pain at the thought of the unknown man. 'If you want I'll take you. On your next day off.'

'No, thanks. They're crap. I like something with a bit of style. Like that jacket you got me.'

'Jax . . .' He hesitated, searching for the right words, desperate not to offend. 'What are the conditions under which you have to stay here? I mean, is it for a specific time like, um . . .'

'Community service?' The phrase was invested with scornful disgust.

'I just hate the thought of turning up one day to find you've gone.'

'I wouldn't leave you, Val boy.'

'Don't say that if you don't mean it.' Val waited but the longed-for assurance was not forthcoming. And what would it have been worth if it had? 'The thing is, my sister—'

'She don't like me.'

'Louise is moving out. She'll be starting work again soon and wants to be nearer town. So, if you need somewhere to stay . . .'

'Might be useful.'

'I'd love to have you.' Climbing into his khaki chinos, Valentine tried to sound casual even as his mind flooded with images of compelling happiness. He would cook marvellous food for himself and Jax. Play Mozart for him. And Palestrina. Read to him – Austen or Balzac. At night they would lie in each other's arms, yellow stars shining through the glass roof, dazzling their eyes.

Jax said, 'In an emergency.'

'Of course.' Valentine buttoned his shirt with stiff, clumsy fingers. 'That's what I meant.' He tried to keep his eyes off Jax who was running the tip of his index finger along soft, tan-gold skin on the inside of his thighs, crinkling it gently, first one way then the other. Up and down, up and down.

'It was lovely to hear from you.' Val was pleased and surprised that his voice came out so smooth. He was expecting a croak. 'Out of the blue like that.'

'I crave it sometimes, Val. Special times. And at those times I just gotta have it – know what I mean?'

'Christ, yes.'

'Today was, like, one of those days.'

'And is it something special that sets you off?'

'It is. Always the same thing.'

'You wouldn't like to . . . If I knew what it was, maybe—'

'One day, Val boy.' Jax got up then, crossed to the window and stared out. Then suddenly started to laugh.

'Look.' Sergeant Troy jerked his head across the drive as Barnaby closed the Old Rectory door.

'A garage, yes. I have seen one before.'

'No, upstairs.'

Barnaby lifted his head. Terry Jackson was standing at the window of his flat. Either he was completely nude or wearing the lowest pair of hipsters since Randolph Scott hung up his spurs.

'Pity,' said Troy. 'Another couple of inches and we could have got him for indecent exposure.'

'Sniggering bastard,' said Barnaby and it was true the chauffeur was laughing at them. The chief inspector slowed his footsteps to a dawdle to give the man time to get his clobber on. 'I wouldn't put it past him to open the door bollock naked.'

'I hope not,' said Sergeant Troy. 'We're having toad in the hole tonight.'

Jax opened the window above their heads and called down, 'It's not locked.'

For the third time Barnaby made his way up the smartly carpeted stairs. He recalled his first visit which had ended in a sickening display of cringing and weeping by Jackson once his protector arrived. And the second, three days ago, when the chauffeur had been questioned about Carlotta Ryan and had nearly jumped out of his skin the moment Barnaby released the word 'blackmail' into the conversation.

So, what were they in for this time? Barnaby, passionate proselytiser on the necessity to keep an open mind all his professional life, had never found it as hard as he did now. In fact, if he was honest, in the case of Terry Jackson he had given up trying. He believed on next to no evidence that this man had killed Charlie Leathers and was involved, up to the hilt, in the disappearance of Carlotta Ryan.

He opened the door to the main flat without knocking and walked in. Jackson was once more leaning against the window, this time facing into the room. He seemed quietly pleased with himself. Glossy and replete like some smartly groomed, newly gorged animal. He wore a French matelot jersey and skin-tight white 501s. His feet were bare and damp hair was plastered to his head in minute, springy curls. Dyed and permed, thought Barnaby, remembering the dark, greasy hanks on Jackson's earlier mug shot. It gave him a moment of brief, petty satisfaction. Then Jackson smiled at him, a smile like a Tyson upper cut, and the satisfaction faltered and died.

'You're after me, Inspector,' said Jackson. 'I know you are. Admit it.'

'No problem admitting that, Terry.' Because there was a third party in the room, Barnaby made the statement semi-jocular. 'Good afternoon, Mr Fainlight.'

Valentine Fainlight mumbled something in Barnaby's direction. He looked embarrassed, defiant and also mildly exasperated. No need to ask what they had interrupted. The whole place reeked of sex.

'Well, Jax, I'll be—'

'Don't go, sir,' said Barnaby. 'We still haven't managed to talk to you about Carlotta Ryan's disappearance. One of our officers called again on Saturday, I believe.'

'I was in London all day.'

'Well, now you're here,' said Sergeant Troy. He sat in the orange armchair and got out his notebook. There was no way he could produce a civil greeting, let alone a smile. If there was one species of human being he despised it was arse bandits.

'Two birds, y'see, Val,' said Terry Jackson.

'I really don't understand why you're asking me. I barely exchanged half a dozen words with the girl.'

'We're asking everyone, sir,' said Troy. 'It's called a house-to-house.'

'The night she disappeared,' continued Barnaby, 'was two nights before Charlie Leathers was killed. She ran away from the Old Rectory and we now believe that she fell or, more likely, was pushed into the river.'

'Good heavens.' Valentine stared across the room in amazement. 'Did you know about this, Jax?'

'Oh yeah.' Jackson winked at Barnaby. 'They keep me well informed.'

'So we wondered,' said Sergeant Troy, 'if you saw or heard anything latish that evening that might help us.'

'And that was?'

'Sunday, August the sixteenth.'

'We were both at home but I honestly – oh, hang on. That was the night we saw Charlie and his dog. I remember because *Betty Blue* was on the box. But I don't see how that could possibly help you with Carlotta.'

'That's not the point,' said Jackson. 'You gotta be crossed off their little list, see? So things are nice and tidy.'

'We've also got some questions to ask you,' said Sergeant Troy, turning to Jackson.

'Notice I don't get any "sir".'

'Like, do you happen to know what time Mrs Lawrence left for Causton this afternoon?'

'Is something up?'

'Do you or don't you?' snapped Barnaby.

'She rang through here just after lunch – twoish. Said she wanted the car. Drove off, oohh, ten, fifteen minutes later.'

'Did you notice what she was wearing?'

Jackson shrugged, puzzled. 'Some sort of flowered thing.'

'Did she say why she was going into town?'

'We're not on those terms.'

Barnaby had known that and that the question was probably a waste of time. But sometimes timid people like Ann Lawrence, ill at ease with more powerful personalities, would offer unasked-for information in a futile attempt to disarm.

'That it, then?' said Jackson. 'Hardly worth wearing out your tyres for.'

'Where were you this afternoon?'

'Here, gardening. Round the back mainly. Now Charlie's gone, it's getting a bit jungly.'

'And what time did you come over, sir?'

'Oh, I don't . . .' Valentine's cheeks were suddenly crimson. 'Maybe around half three.'

'Nearer three o'clock,' said Jackson. He smiled directly, brilliantly, across the room at Fainlight, shamelessly exerting his power. Then he turned back to Barnaby. 'Anyway, what's it to do with you?'

Barnaby hoped it would prove to be nothing to do with him. He hoped that more than he had hoped for anything for a very long time. As Troy slipped in the ignition key, Barnaby was punching figures into his mobile.

'Where to, chief?'

'Hang on a minute.' As Barnaby waited, something of his unease communicated itself to Sergeant Troy.

'D'you think something's happened to her?'

'Hello? Control room? DCI Barnaby. Have you had any casualties reported today p.m.?' Pause. 'Yes, a woman. Mid to late thirties. Perhaps wearing a flowered dress.'

A much longer pause. Sergeant Troy watched Barnaby's profile. Saw the bones suddenly become more prominent, noticed the frown lines deepen and the beetling brows draw so tightly together they were almost one thick, grey-black line.

'I'm afraid it does, Andy. Could you fill me in on the background?' He listened for a few moments then switched off. 'Drive to Stoke Mandeville hospital.'

'What's happened?'

'Fast.'

Troy put his foot well down. There was no siren but police business was police business. He asked again what had happened.

'A woman was found in Causton multi-storey car park. Just before three o'clock and unconscious from a tremendous blow on the head. As she'd been robbed they had no way of identifying her.'

'If it's Ann Lawrence—'

'It's Ann Lawrence all right. The attack happened barely seconds before she was found otherwise I've no doubt the bastard would have finished her off.'

'Bloody hell.'

'Apparently someone was driving up to the top layer almost as it was taking place. The attacker heard the car coming and ran.'

'What, down the stairs?'

'No, he rang for the lift and hung around filing his nails and whistling Dixie. Of course down the bloody stairs!'

'Sorry.'

'The motorist saw her lying there and rang for an ambulance. She's in intensive care.'

'That's a miserable coincidence, chief.'

'You reckon?'

'We seem fated— Pardon?'

'Bag-snatchers snatch and bugger off. They don't hang around to beat their victims to death.'

'You think all this is connected to the Charlie Leathers business?'

'Bet your Aunt Fanny,' said Barnaby, stealing without shame from the redoubtable Miss Calthrop.

It was hard to believe, thought the chief inspector, looking down at the motionless, deathly pale form of Ann Lawrence, that she was still alive.

As Barnaby gazed at the figure on the bed, his sergeant was observing him. Some emotion, which Troy could not easily decipher, swept over Barnaby's face then disappeared, leaving it expressionless. Abruptly he turned aside and spoke to the nurse who had admitted them.

'Who do I talk to about this?'

'Dr Miller. I'll see if I can find him.'

While they were waiting, Barnaby remained silent, staring out of the window. Troy also averted his eyes from the white metal bed. He hated hospitals almost as much as he hated graveyards. Not that he had anything against the dead or dying personally. Just that they and he didn't seem to have much in common. Having said that, this year he was thirty and a couple of months ago his grandma had died. The two incidents coming so close together had given him pause for thought. Of course he had all the time in the world to go yet – his parents were only fifty – even so, immortality, practically a dead cert a mere five years ago, now seemed a much more dodgy option. He was just thinking about waiting outside in the corridor when the nurse returned with a stressed-out-looking man wearing steel-rimmed glasses. He had a great frizz of very fair hair and wore a crumpled white coat.

As Barnaby started to speak, Dr Miller eased the two policemen out of the room, saying that, at least as far as he was concerned, the theory that unconscious patients heard and understood nothing was far from proven.

'So what are her chances?' said Barnaby.

'Too early to say.' He stood there on the balls of his feet, a busy man, ready to run. 'She's got a deep cut across the head and massive bruising which could mean brain trauma. We'll know more when we've done a scan. We've got her stabilised, which is the first step.'

'I see.'

'The big danger is a subdural haemorrhage.' He tugged on his stethoscope. 'This means draining off blood beneath the outer membrane – always risky.'

'Yes.' Barnaby, his stomach playing pitch and toss, swallowed hard. 'Thank you, Dr Miller. We do know who she is, by the way.'

'Excellent.' He was already striding off. 'Tell admin. on your way out.'

There were quite a lot of bad-tempered motorists hanging around the multi-storey car park waiting for their vehicles as uniformed officers made a note of each and every registration.

There was also a police presence on the top level under the direction of Colin Willoughby. Barnaby did not like Inspector Willoughby. He was a rigid man. A toady and a snob without imagination, sensitivity or a shred of human understanding. The last sort of person, to the chief inspector's thinking, to make a good police officer.

'Good heavens,' said Willoughby as they approached. He sounded so amazed they could have been visitors from another planet. 'What are you doing here? Sir.'

'The woman who's been attacked is involved in a case I'm currently investigating. Charlie Leathers' murder.'

'An identification already?' He was plainly more resentful than relieved.

'Ann Lawrence,' said Sergeant Troy. 'The Old Rectory, Ferne Basset.'

'Hm.'

'I've just come from Stoke Mandeville,' said Barnaby.

'Popped her clogs, has she?'

The DCI's lips tightened with distaste. 'Do you have an accurate time on the assault?'

'Five to three the bloke found her.'

'I see.' Barnaby looked about him. 'So, what stage are you at here?'

'Oh, we're doing everything by the book. No need to worry. Sir.'

'I'm not worried. I'm just asking a straightforward question.'

'All the numbers are being noted. And we're—'

'Who let those people up here?' Barnaby jerked his head angrily towards a man and women stepping out of the lift. 'Don't you know enough to protect a scene where a savage assault has taken place?'

'Go back down,' shouted Inspector Willoughby at the top of his voice. He waved his arms furiously at the couple. 'Go away! Now!'

They leapt back into the lift.

'This approach, this whole level should have been taped off. And the stairs, which is how he escaped. What the hell are you playing at, man?'

'It's all happening. Sir.'

'It's not happening fast enough, is it?'

'Her car's a Humber Hawk, by the way,' said Sergeant Troy. 'Very old.'

Willoughby glared. He did not like being interrupted, even by someone of his own rank. As for this plain-clothes upstart . . .

'It's just down there,' nodded Troy, compounding his insolence.

'I've got eyes, Sergeant. Thank you.'

'I'd like it roped off,' said Barnaby. 'And gone over by SOCO. Every inch.'

'What?'

He may have eyes, thought Sergeant Troy, but his ears don't seem to be up to much.

'I'm not in the habit of repeating myself, Willoughby. Just see to it.'

'Sir.'

'Where was she found?'

'Over here.' Willoughby led the way towards a scarlet Megane. 'Lying in front of the car. I'd say a couple of feet from the radiator grille.'

Barnaby looked more closely at the car. There was a slight but definite indentation on the rim of the bonnet. Vividly he saw Ann Lawrence's head being swung down against it with tremendous force and felt sick again. Then told himself not to run with such vivid fantasies. She could have been coshed by anything. But then why bother to drag her over to the car? Also the wound was high. Partly on the forehead but also on the front section of the skull. In any case, how often do attackers walk up to their mark, look them in the face and strike? They creep and sidle and slink. They pad up silently behind and let them have it. Barnaby looked about him.

'She got as far as here,' he stood in the aisle between the cars some distance away, 'presumably making for the lift. He followed and jumped her, dragging her over to the Renault. You can see the heel marks through this oily tyre track. And nearer the car as well.'

'I had made a note of that, actually, sir.'

'Good for you, Willoughby,' said the chief inspector, disbelief sticking to the words like toffee. 'So we'll have to hang on to the Megane, get it properly examined.'

'Absolutely.'

There was an exquisite pause which Barnaby delighted in extending. It was plain that Willoughby did not know exactly why the red car had to be tested. Fear of being thought stupid meant he could not bring himself to ask. But if he didn't ask, when SOCO asked him if they were looking for anything specific, he wouldn't know. It was moments like this, sighed the chief inspector contentedly to himself, that made what was often a mundane job really worthwhile.

Sergeant Troy said, 'Look here.'

'What?' Inspector Willoughby moved quickly to the car, pushing Troy aside.

'How d'you get a dent in a place like that?' Troy, having nodded at the bonnet, spoke over his shoulder to the DCI. 'Not from a collision, that's for sure.'

'That's right.' Barnaby smiled. 'Well spotted, Sergeant.'

Willoughby, ferociously envious and annoyed, stared at the car with burning eyes. He'll melt the paint, thought Barnaby, if he keeps that up.

'Make sure everything she was wearing goes to SOCO.'

'Naturally, Chief Inspector.'

'And I'll want a tape of the interview with the man who found her. Right,' he turned away, 'that seems to be it. For now.'

'I'll check the pay ticket on the Humber, sir. It'll give us Mrs Lawrence's exact time of arrival.'

'You're on form today, Sergeant, and no mistake.'

And Troy made his way towards the Humber with a swing and a swagger, the tips of his ears glowing with pleasure.

As both men were leaving the building, Barnaby's mobile rang. It was Sergeant Brierley ringing from the incident room to inform him that the tape of the anonymous 999 call on the night of Carlotta Ryan's disappearance had finally arrived.

After she had finished speaking, Barnaby asked if

she would get a further matter sorted. Troy listened in some bewilderment. He did not ask for an explanation, he had his pride. In any case it would probably be, 'Work it out, Sergeant,' then, when he couldn't, he'd feel twice as bad as if he'd never asked in the first place. But *bicycles*?

Within half an hour of Barnaby and Troy leaving the hospital, the news of a murderous attack on Ann Lawrence was all round the village. Not much later the dreadful details also became available via Connie Dale, the postmistress, whose daughter was a nurse in the geriatric ward.

Ferne Basset's reaction this time was very different to its response when Charlie Leathers was killed. Morbid relish was replaced by genuine distress, for most of the villagers had known Ann since she was a little girl. Known and liked her for her gentle, inoffensive ways and unobtrusive kindness. Many remarks were made along the lines of "Thank God her father isn't here today", and "Her poor mother must be turning in her grave". People wondered aloud how on earth the Reverend would manage.

It would be hard to pinpoint just when the precise situation at the Old Rectory became common knowledge. Either someone called at the house and was rebuffed. Or concerned inquiries, made by telephone, were handled in a strange and deeply unsatisfactory manner. One or two people were simply cut off. Another was answered by a stranger's voice. Having promised to fetch Mr Lawrence, the phone was laid down and no one returned to pick it up although the caller could overhear masculine voices and loud laughter. Later it was discovered that the Reverend had not even visited the hospital where his wife lay at death's door.

Hearing this, Hetty Leathers was deeply upset. She wanted very much to be there if only so that Mrs Lawrence knew there was at least one person who cared. Pauline's husband Alan was standing by to drive her to Stoke Mandeville but the ward sister, once she had discovered Hetty was not a close relative, said there was really little point as things were at the moment. So Hetty picked a large bunch of flowers and branches of autumn leaves that Mrs Lawrence loved and Alan drove in and left it at reception with a card from all of them.

That evening Evadne fed the Pekes, gave them a drink, read a story (*Laka – the Timberwolf*) till they were settled then made her concerned way to Hetty's bungalow.

The night was cool and the Raeburn was glowing, transforming the kitchen into a snug little cave. Candy, without her plastic collar and elastic bandage but still in plaster, rocked and staggered happily towards Evadne, licking her hand and barking.

'How's our small miracle?' said Evadne, sitting in the rocker and accepting a glass of Lucozade.

'So much better,' said Hetty, taking the shabby fireside chair opposite her friend. 'It's wonderful to see her gradually becoming less timid. Although we haven't been out for a proper walk yet.'

'That will be the test, I've no doubt.'

They sat for a few moments in companionable silence. The silence lengthened and the longer it lasted, the more impossible it seemed that either would wish to speak. For there was only one possible subject of conversation and who would want to talk about that? But it could not be contained for ever.

Suddenly Hetty burst out, 'It was Charlie! Ever since he was . . . that's when it started. What's going on, Evadne? What's behind it all?'

'My dear, I wish I knew.'

'First him, now poor Mrs Lawrence. I've never heard that women say an unkind word about a living soul. And now she's . . .'

'There, Hetty.' Evadne reached out and took her friend's hand. 'We must pray for another miracle.'

'But it's so frightening. What will happen next? I feel we're gradually being pushed towards the edge of a great black hole.'

Evadne could not have expressed it better or – given the fearful accuracy of the image – worse, herself. She knew exactly what Hetty meant.

Like most people in Ferne Basset, she had been convinced that the murder of Hetty's husband had been a random act of violence. Probably committed by some deranged soul mistakenly released from a mental institution before his time. The man had been asleep in Carter's Wood. Charlie had stumbled over him and, enraged and terrified, the lunatic had sprung up, killed him and run away. Understandable, inasmuch as madness ever is. That had been the going theory and everyone had accepted it with alacrity and not a little relief.

And now this. But wasn't the attack on Ann Lawrence also random? Someone had suggested it was a bag-snatcher. And miles away from Ferne Basset. So didn't that, once more, put the village in the clear?

Evadne realised she was regarding the place where she had been so happy for so long almost as a character in a story. A clear and sunlit haven, beautiful in all its seasons, sustaining and secure when the tale begins then gradually, as the narrative becomes more opaque, tangled and disquieting, so the village, too, becomes transformed into a wilderness full of unknown dangers. They truly had awoken to find themselves in a dark wood, where the right road was wholly lost and gone.

'What's that, Evadne?'

'Oh . . .' She had not realised she was murmuring aloud. 'A line from a poem which seems to sum up our predicament.'

Hetty gave the impression of taking a deep breath. Then she said, 'There is something I haven't told you.'

'What's that, Hetty?'

'Pauline knows but the police don't seem to have made it public so . . .'

'You know I never repeat anything.'

'Apparently Charlie was trying to blackmail someone.'

'Oh!' Evadne went very pale. 'And they think that was the motive?'

'Yes.'

'So it *was* someone he knew?'

'Not just someone he knew, Evadne . . .' Hetty was trembling, shaking from the crown of her head to her shabby, slippered feet while Candy quivered in sympathy. 'Don't you see, it must be someone we all know.'

When the news about Ann Lawrence reached the

Fainlights, they were pussyfooting around each other with great caution, determinedly avoiding a quarrel.

About an hour earlier Valentine had returned from Jackson's flat and disappeared into his room to work. While she sat nervously waiting for him to re-emerge, Louise had vowed to behave with nothing but supportive, loving, uncritical kindness. She would keep this up until the moment she left the house. And for ever after. She and Val would not be divided. *He* would not divide them.

And, after all, everything passes. Louise took this stark consolation to her heart as she spent the next half-hour alternately tormenting and comforting herself by wondering how this wretched union would eventually be severed.

Perhaps Jax would simply get bored. No, she was quite sure that feelings of either interest or boredom were simply not relevant as far as this affair was concerned. He could be bored to tears but as long as there was something to be gained from the relationship, it would continue. Valentine might hope that he was a special person to Jax but Louise was sure that the great cold landscape of the boy's heart was impregnable. The only special person in Jax's life was himself.

Neither could she imagine Valentine getting bored with Jax. One did not tire of an obsession. It burned itself out or it burned you out. For the same reason it was impossible to picture Val falling in love with another person.

Fleetingly Louise remembered how happy her brother had been during his years with Bruno Magellan. So distraught was Val for months after his partner's death, endlessly reliving all their earlier joys and pleasures while sliding further and further into a pit of depression, she had despaired of ever seeing him find the will, energy or courage to start another relationship. And then, after months of slowly struggling back into the light, to be seized by a passion so sterile and reckless it appeared to be hurling him once more into the depths of despair was heartbreaking.

Was that Val coming down? Louise, sitting by the window, turned her head sharply towards the stairs. It struck her that for weeks now that was all she had been doing. Either constantly watching her brother, or listening for him.

She listened for Val's return when he was out and for signs that he was about to leave when he was in. She listened to him on the telephone and tried to guess who the caller was. She listened to his voice when they spoke, attempting to anticipate the twists and turns of his emotions before they were made manifest to twist and turn against herself. To her shame she had even looked through her brother's correspondence which was how she discovered a credit slip from Simpson's in Piccadilly for a leather blouson (American Tan) costing eight hundred and fifty pounds.

Now Louise thought for the first time of how her behaviour might appear to Val. She had assumed, blinded as he was by his frenzied attachment, that he had never noticed this close surveillance. But what if he had? How then would it make him feel? Crowded, that's how. Spied on. Unable to escape, like a prisoner in a cell with a little peephole. Helpless to avoid observation any time the jailer chose. No wonder, thought Louise, with a quick, blinding intuition, he wants me gone.

And she couldn't stop observing because she couldn't stop caring. Because that meant she had stopped loving. And I shall do that, she vowed silently, when I'm in my grave.

A movement in the road caught her eye. A blue car was turning into the Old Rectory drive, drawing up at the front door. She recognised the two men who got out. They were the same policemen who had come to interview herself and Val. Louise wondered what they wanted. She noticed they didn't ring the bell for the main house but crossed over to the garage flat.

Louise arranged the expression on her face, tried various opening gambits on for size and mentally tuned her voice to a note of amiable casualness. She had heard Val's footsteps dragging down the stairs. Not all that long ago he would have bounded down two steps at a time.

When his bowed head came into view, Louise said, 'Hi.'

'Waiting up?'

Louise ignored the gibe. 'I was just going to make tea. Would you like some?'

'I'd rather have a drink.'

'OK.'

'OK.' Val caught the wary passivity with spear-like accuracy. 'Do I hear a whiff of "sun not quite over the yardarm"?'

'No. You can pour Jack Daniel's on your cornflakes and throw up all over Richard and Judy for all I care.'

'That's more like it. I was wondering where the

real Louise had gone for a minute.'

'So.' She crossed to the drinks table. 'What'll you have?'

'Don't care. Just make it strong.'

'Jameson's?'

'The very man.' He watched her rattling around in the ice bucket. Observed her cast-down face, noticed the slight thickening under her chin, hollowed cheeks and tired lines, which he had never noticed before, printing the fine skin beneath her eyes. Poor Lou. She hadn't asked for any of this.

'So, as we seem to be playing house, what did you do today, Mrs Forbes?'

'Well,' Louise drew a deep breath like a child about to recite in front of the grown-ups, 'I worked in the garden. Made several phone calls – putting out feelers for work. This afternoon I went to Causton and had my ends trimmed.'

'I don't like the sound of that.'

'They give you some coffee afterwards.'

'I'd need an anaesthetic first.'

'What about you?'

'I didn't garden. I made no phone calls. And my ends are absolute hell.'

'Come on, Val. You must have done something.'

'Looked over the proofs of the *Hopscotch Kid*. Messed about generally. Then Jax rang around three and I went over.'

'Uh huh.' Louise took a deep breath. 'How is he then, Jax?'

'Fighting fit.'

'So you had a good time?'

'Brilliant.'

'Good. Actually when I was in Causton I—'

'Until the bloody police turned up.'

'Oh? What did they want?'

'What do they ever want? Bullying him with endless questions. Once you've slipped up in this country, Lou, you're done for. It's a waste of time even trying to go straight. I didn't used to believe that. I thought it was just criminals, you know, whining. But it's true.'

'What a shame it's happening now.' Louise gagged on the words but somehow managed to squeeze them out. 'Being down here, well away from the sort of people who got him into trouble, could have given him a completely new start.'

'Exactly!' Valentine drained half the Irish in one swallow. 'I don't have much time for Lionel, as you know, but his idea of sanctuary for youngsters in trouble is really great.'

Youngsters? That man was never a youngster. Cunning like his is as old as the hills.

'I think I'll join you.' Casually Louise turned away to pour herself a drink. She knew it would be a mistake to show how pleased she was at the way the conversation was progressing. And an even bigger one to try and build on it. She said, 'I got a partridge for tonight.'

'Lovely.' Val drained his glass and walked over. 'You could freshen my drink.'

'You haven't got a drink.' Louise laughed, letting go a little with relief at the first hurdle cleared.

'My ice cubes then.'

After she had refilled the glass, Valentine carried it across the room, flung himself onto the huge pale sofa and put his feet up. He already looked slightly less tired. His face was smoothing out. As he stretched his legs and flexed his toes, Louise sensed a quickening of vitality. Could it really be possible that a few transparent lies on her part could accomplish such a transformation? Lies which his sharp intelligence would normally see straight through?

It seemed so. Oh, why hadn't she realised months ago how hard her fear and dislike of Jax had been for her brother to handle? Even obsessives have moments of clarity and it must have seemed to Val that she had withdrawn her love and support just when he needed it the most. If only she had made allowances for his irrational state of mind. Listened more sympathetically. Bided her time. But, because there had never been pretence between them, this had simply not occurred to her. Not until now, when it was too late.

'Sorry, Val.' The sound of his voice had registered but not the words.

'I cut you off when we were talking before. Something or other happened in Causton?'

'Oh, yes. You'll never guess who—'

But then the telephone rang. And after the call it was impossible to continue that or any other conversation. The terrible news about Ann Lawrence not only stopped Louise's mouth but was so devastating in the light of what she had been about to relate that it almost stopped her heart as well.

'Are you all right, Lionel?'

'What?'

'How do you feel? I mean, *really*?'

'I'm not sure.'

It was a good question. Very perceptive. How did he feel, really? He knew how he ought to feel. And perhaps, if Ann hadn't been so cruel to him, he would appropriately be feeling it. Frantically worried, praying to God for her recovery, dreading the heartbreak that follows the loss of a beloved spouse.

And he had loved her. All these years he had been a good and faithful husband. The trouble was, as the ugly scene the previous day had so clearly illustrated, she didn't love him. So he could hardly be blamed if his response to the dreadful news he had just received was somewhat muted.

'I should go, shouldn't I?'

'Fact is, Lionel, she won't know whether you're there or not.'

'That's true.'

'If she comes round, well . . .'

'Then, of course.'

'Obviously. And if it's not out of line, I'd like to say you have my deepest sympathy.'

'I know that, Jax. It means a lot having you here.'

'For some reason unknown, Mrs Lawrence never took to me.'

'She had – has a nervous disposition.'

'But I'm not the sort to take offence. And I can only pray that God is on our side at this moment in time.'

'Thank you.'

An hour or so earlier, after the person at the other end of the line had explained what had happened and Lionel had listened in thunderstruck silence, he had stood for a long while with the phone glued to his ear staring at the faded wallpaper.

Then, when the first shock had passed, he felt curiously empty. He sat down and waited to see what would happen next. What happened next was that

Lionel found he very much needed to pass the information on. Any suggestion that this was nothing more than the normal human response when receiving disastrous or exciting news would have outraged him. Lionel knew himself to be purely in need of consolation and support. But where to find it?

The only person he could think of was dear Vivienne at the Caritas Trust. She had always been most *simpatico* on the increasingly frequent occasions when he had felt the need to unburden his heart.

Lionel dialled the number with what he was pleased to see was a very steady hand. But he had hardly begun to speak before Vivienne cut him short. She was interviewing and also had someone waiting. When Lionel suggested he should ring later, she said she would call him but not to hold his breath.

Bewildered, he hung up. So who else was there? It was a moment or two before he thought of Jax largely because, in his understanding of their relationship, he himself was always firmly cast in the role of comforter. But he had nothing to lose by asking. Jax might even welcome the opportunity to repay some of the kindness he had been shown.

And so it proved to be. He had rushed over within minutes, bringing a bottle. Lionel had been so grateful he had not demurred when Jax opened the red wine straightaway and insisted that he drink some. And Jax, 'as this is rather an unusual occasion', agreed to join him. Now the bottle was nearly empty.

'This is really delicious.' Lionel drained his third glass, not noticing that Jax's remained almost untouched. 'It certainly seems to take the edge off the pain.'

'Mr Fainlight gave it me,' said Jax. 'I did a little job for him.'

Lionel looked at his watch. 'D'you think . . .'

'It's not vintage or nothing.'

'Perhaps I should ring.'

'They said they'd contact you if there was any change.'

Lionel didn't remember that. He stared around the room, frowning. Jax crossed over, bringing his glass, to sit next to his benefactor on the sofa.

'I can see I'm going to have to look after you, Lionel.'

'Oh, Jax.'

'Just till Mrs Lawrence gets better.' Jackson hesitated. 'Perhaps I should stay over here tonight.'

'Oh, would you? I get so lonely sometimes.'

'I've noticed that, Lionel. And many's the time I've wanted to make an overture of friendship, believe you me. Just been afraid to overstep the mark.'

'I don't know how to express my gratitude.'

Jackson prided himself on his sense of timing. There would be a moment to suggest how Lionel could best express his gratitude but this was not it; it was too soon after the sad event and the Rev was more than a little swacked. It was not drunken promises that Jackson was after. Such promises frequently did not survive the harsh scrutiny of the morning after. Thankfulness recollected in sober tranquillity was the ultimate aim.

Lionel's glass once more being empty, Jackson offered to exchange it for his own, even going as far as to place it in Lionel's hand. He curled the limp fingers round the stem and his eyes shone with encouragement and approval.

The doorbell rang. Lionel gave a great jump and his wine went everywhere. Jackson stepped back, his expression one of controlled rage, and left the room.

Even in his present state Lionel recognised the two men Jackson showed in. He struggled to get up, making indignant incomprehensible gurgles. Reeled, steadied himself with one hand.

'Mr Lawrence?' Barnaby stared in amazement.

'He does live here,' said Jackson.

Barnaby, who had only rung the main house bell after getting no joy at the garage, said, 'Why aren't you at the hospital, sir?'

'What . . . what?'

'Haven't you heard from Stoke Mandeville?'

'Yes . . . that is . . .' He turned to Jackson.

'They said Mrs L was unconscious.' Jackson spoke directly to Barnaby. 'And that they'd ring if there was any change. If there is, naturally he'll be straight down there.'

The patronising scorn with which he spoke was deeply disturbing. As was Lionel's attitude. A dishevelled, shambolic figure covered in stains that looked appallingly like blood, he sat beaming at Jackson, nodding eagerly at everything he said.

'Anyway,' Barnaby made no effort to conceal his contempt, 'it's you I'm here to see, Jackson.'

'Anything, Inspector. You've only got to ask.'

'How are you on a bike?'

'Never tried it. I went straight from skateboarding to TDA. Anything else?'

'Yes,' said Sergeant Troy. 'We're asking for your clothes. Top layer, underwear, socks, shoes. Contents of pockets. The lot.'

'That's fetishism, that is.'

'Just get on with it.' Barnaby seemed to have endless patience.

'You mean . . .' Jackson touched the edge of a beautiful leather jacket. 'These clothes?'

'If those are what you were wearing at three o'clock this afternoon,' said Barnaby, 'yes.'

'I've told you earlier, I were gardening this afternoon. You don't think I'd do a dirty job in clobber like this.'

'So we'll have the clobber you did do the job in,' said Sergeant Troy. He was taking a leaf out of the chief's book and speaking calmly and quietly. What he really wanted to do was run across the room, get his hands round the fucker's throat and squeeze till moisture showered from his baby blues like rain.

'It's in the flat, Inspector.'

'So get it,' said Barnaby. 'And stop calling me Inspector.'

'No problem,' said Jackson, strolling towards the door. 'The cycle should be through by now.'

'The what?'

'The wash cycle. After I'd finished work I put everything in the machine. Like I say, it was a dirty job.'

Barnaby was twenty minutes late for his seven o'clock briefing and arrived flushed with annoyance after a wrangle with the money men on the top floor. The incident room was bristling with people lively and animated on two counts. First, the situation, which had appeared to be in grave danger of becoming totally moribund, had now taken a totally unexpected and dramatic turn. Secondly, the tape had arrived. Everyone had heard it except the chief and his bagman. Inspector Carter waited till they were seated, wound back and pressed Play.

The moment she spoke Barnaby knew who it was.

'... help ... you must help ... me ... someone has fallen— no, no, into the water ... the river ... she disappeared so fast ... just swept ... I ran up and down ... all the way to the weir ... What? Oh, Ferne Basset ... I don't know, half an hour, maybe less ... For God's sake! Does it matter when? Just come, you must come now...'

When asked for her name, the woman caught her breath. There was a moment of absolute silence then the receiver fell. They could all hear it, clattering and banging against the side of the box. Then she started to cry. Just over a minute later the phone was placed very gently back on the rest.

Barnaby sat very still, his eyes closed. There was no point in bemoaning the tragic twists and turns in the case that had kept Ann Lawrence from his grasp until it was too late. 'If only' were words outside his vocabulary. Even so, it was bloody hard.

The room was still. Someone switched the machine off. Sergeant Troy, struggling with a deep sense of unease, looked sideways at the brooding figure under the Anglepoise. He saw a profile that seemed to sag rather than relax, blue veins prominent in the wrists (why had he never noticed them before?) and a heavy droop of skin above each eyelid.

Of course the chief often looked knackered, that was nothing new. Sergeant Troy had seen him look tired and disappointed many times. Cheated. Betrayed even. But not beaten like this. And never old.

Barnaby lifted his head, heavily at first as if it was a

ball of stone, then more freely. His burly shoulders, freed from tension, set themselves firmly back.

'Well,' he said and smiled, warming to life again before their very eyes. 'Here's a turn-up for the book.'

The whole room was reactivated as well then, like a film when the freeze frame is released. People started to move, gesture, talk. Someone even laughed. It was Sergeant Troy actually. Part nerves, part just bloody relief.

'Ties her well in, doesn't it, sir?' said Audrey Brierley. 'Mrs Lawrence.'

There were murmurs of agreement. Plain as the nose on your face, it seemed now. The missing girl had lived in the woman's house, as did the prime suspect. Or as good as. The murdered man had worked for her. Everything was becoming satisfyingly intertwined.

'Certainly,' said Barnaby, 'we now know she saw what happened when the girl went into the river. But that's all we know at this stage, OK?'

There were a few murmurs of reluctant agreement.

'Let's not get over-excited,' continued the chief inspector. 'She may simply have been an observer.'

'Presumably a secret observer,' suggested DI Carter, 'or someone would have shut her up long before this.'

'But if that was not the case,' Barnaby carried on smoothly, 'and Mrs Lawrence was the only person involved, then Leathers must have been blackmailing *her*.'

This suggestion, which overturned all the beliefs and theories held so far in the murder inquiry, was presented with surprising equanimity. The room, taking their cue from the top, nodded.

'First thing tomorrow we chase up her bank. And if she's been drawing out large sums of money...' Barnaby shrugged, letting the rest of the sentence tail eloquently away.

Troy liked this idea of open-ended dialogue, if only so that someone else could make a fool of themselves for a change by finishing it. He said, 'So our assumption that the blackmail victim murdered Leathers...' He shrugged, letting the rest of the sentence tail eloquently away.

'Yes?' said Barnaby.

'Um.' A pause.

'Hurry up. We haven't got all day.'

'I think Gavin means,' said Sergeant Brierley, 'that it's very hard to picture Mrs Lawrence garrotting someone.'

'Very hard indeed,' said the chief inspector. 'Though not impossible.'

'But she's been attacked herself, sir,' said Constable Phillips. 'There aren't two murderers involved in this case surely?'

Barnaby did not reply. Just sat looking round the room. Roughly ten minutes into the meeting and so far sympathy for Ann Lawrence was not particularly in evidence. The chief inspector was not surprised. As far as he knew, no one present, apart from Troy, had met her. They had certainly not witnessed her lying unconscious and hanging on to life, breath by fragile breath, in a lonely hospital bed.

'So where does Jackson fit into this, chief?' asked Troy. 'D'you think he was involved in the assault on Mrs Lawrence?'

'I don't think, I know.'

'But why?'

'Presumably because we were going to meet her later this afternoon.'

'But would he know that?' asked Inspector Carter. 'Given the total lack of communication between them.'

'He could have listened in – there's a connecting line from his flat to the house. Or got it from Lionel. He's putty in Jackson's hands.'

Troy snorted in disgust. Putty wasn't the word he'd use. Something soft, yes. Flexible, yes. Something you could step in that would leave an impression on the sole of your shoe. But not putty. He snorted again just to emphasise his complete and utter disdain.

'Whatever,' said Barnaby. 'But I'm convinced these two crimes are back to back and skin-tight. Solve one, you solve both.'

'All due respect, sir—'

'No genuflexions, please, Phillips. Anyone on my team is encouraged to speak their mind.'

And God help them, said his team silently to itself, if he's running a moody.

'It's just that,' continued Phillips with a quail in his voice, 'as the girl's body has never been found, how do we know we have a serious crime at all?'

'Because whatever Leathers saw gave him a genuine lever for blackmail. And trying it on got him killed.'

'Oh yes, sir.' Constable Phillips, not a tall person at the best of times, folded himself down into his chair until he almost vanished. 'Thank you.'

'Any time,' said Barnaby.

'Could she have just swum to the other side, climbed out and run away?' asked DS Griggs.

'Hardly,' said Inspector Carter. 'You've read Jackson's record. Can you see him being that incompetent?'

'Not if the attack on Mrs Lawrence is anything to go by,' agreed Sergeant Agnew. He turned to Barnaby. 'How do you think he managed to work that, sir?'

'Yes,' said Audrey. 'Like, how could he know in advance where she was going to park?'

'He drove in with her,' said Barnaby. 'Though of course without her knowledge.'

'That's right,' agreed Troy. 'She'd never have got into a crowded double-decker bus with him, let alone a car.'

'He wouldn't risk hiding in the back, surely.'

'No, no, he used the boot,' explained Barnaby. 'Climb in at the very last minute, pull the lid down, hold on to the latch. And bingo, he's on the spot when she gets out.'

'Unlucky for Mrs L there was no one around,' pointed out Inspector Carter.

'That would merely have delayed the attempt,' said the chief inspector. 'He'd have got her later – waiting at the traffic lights, walking too near the kerb. One hard push when a bus was coming would do it.'

'Plus he might be carrying,' added Troy. 'He's been done for using a blade.'

'Lovely,' murmured Audrey Brierley.

'And all because she knew exactly what happened the night Carlotta disappeared?'

'I'm sure of it,' said Barnaby.

'He must be desperate.'

'Yes,' said Barnaby. 'Which makes him doubly dangerous.'

271

'We should get a result this time, though, sir. Broad daylight? Someone must have seen him.'

'Maybe,' said Barnaby. 'But I think it'll be forensics who are going to nail this one.'

'They're working on the Humber,' added Sergeant Troy. 'And they've got his clothes. Though he'd already put them through the wash.'

'That's a giveaway if you like,' said Constable Peggy Marlin, a stout, comfortable women in her late thirties with several sons. 'I've never known a bloke that age wash his clothes at all, never mind the minute he takes them off. They're all over the floor for the next three weeks.'

'We might have more luck with the shoes,' said Barnaby. 'We've got all those that were in his flat plus the sneakers he was wearing.'

'He'll have cold feet.' Policewoman Marlin laughed.

'He'll have more than cold feet before I've done with him.'

'There's an oily smear through which Mrs Lawrence was dragged,' explained Sergeant Troy. 'Just a pinpoint on one of his shoes and we've got him.'

'Did you see any trace, sir?' asked Sergeant Brierley.

Barnaby hesitated. 'Not with the naked eye. But of course that doesn't mean the lab won't.'

There was a longish pause. Looking around, the chief inspector sensed their excitement seeping away. Saw them thinking that if the bloke had stepped in it the evidence would have been plain enough. Knew his words had provoked diminishing enthusiasm, disappointment even. Well, that was not his fault. He couldn't offer what he didn't have.

'No doubt the slimy sod's sorted himself an alibi,' said DS Griggs.

'According to him he spent the entire time weeding the Rectory back garden.'

'Anyone see him?' asked Inspector Carter.

'Fortunately, no.' A small cheer. Barnaby went on to explain how, having hung around for half an hour pouring black coffee into Lionel, they had finally got the information they wanted.

'It seems Lionel was working in his study on a funeral address for Charlie Leathers. Being out of practice, he reckons it took him a good hour and a half. The study faces the front of the house.'

There were a few soft whistles, raised eyebrows and incredulous glances. Inspector Carter put the general feeling into words.

'Jackson's wire-walking this one. What if the old guy had come looking for him?'

'Oh, there'd be some tale about him falling asleep or shopping in the village. Lawrence believes every word he says.'

'Loosely wrapped, is he?'

'To put it kindly.'

'So when can we prove Jackson was there?'

'For sure, just gone three thirty. He asked Valentine Fainlight to come over.'

There were jeering 'ooohs' at this, some crude and deeply unfunny gestures and one simple request to God that the 'slimy pair of penile warts' should disappear up each other's bottoms.

Constable Phillips said, 'I didn't realise Jackson was gay.'

'He's not gay,' said Sergeant Troy, in a voice so thick

with contempt he sounded about to choke. 'Just rents it out to the highest bidder.'

'This puts Evadne Pleat's romantic musings in a quite different light,' said Barnaby. 'D'you recall she saw Fainlight hanging round at night in the Lawrences' garden?'

'And thought he was after Carlotta,' reminded Audrey Brierley. 'He must be absolutely besotted.'

'Yes,' agreed Barnaby. 'Let's just hope he's not so besotted he's prepared to lie.'

'You mean cover for Jackson?'

'There's already a discrepancy over time. Fainlight thought he got to the garage flat about half three. Jackson said it was nearer three o'clock.'

'Well, he would, wouldn't he?' Constable Phillips, gradually unfolding from his chair, peeped out of his shell.

'Does he know the score, Fainlight?' said DS Griggs. Barnaby shook his head.

'That'll make a difference,' said WPC Marlin. 'Wait till he discovers what he's giving an alibi for.'

'Which brings us to the most important question,' said Barnaby. 'On which everything, *everything* will depend.'

'How he got back?' said Sergeant Troy. And suddenly twigged the message on the mobile from the car park.

'Exactly.'

The room broke out into general conversation. Everyone talking, offering ideas and suggestions. Chairs were scraped as people turned round to agree or disagree.

'He wouldn't take a cab, that's for sure.'

'Nobody could be that stupid.'

'Would he risk thumbing a car?'

Cries of 'oh, please' and 'I thought you said he wasn't stupid' followed by 'the driver'd remember him'.

'Steal one then?'

'He'd have to leave it on the outskirts of the village.'

'Well, he used something. You don't walk twelve miles in half an hour.'

'He used a bike, of course,' said Sergeant Troy, cutting into the general hubbub with a self-satisfied smirk. 'I believe we've already run a check on thefts, isn't that right, sir?'

Barnaby fished out a sheet of A4 from the clutter on his desk. He waved it with a hint of smugness rather in the manner of television cooks producing out of the oven a dish they'd prepared earlier.

'There were three stolen in Causton today. A kid's mountain bike, a bone-rattler some poor old pensioner took to his allotment and a Peugeot Leader Sprint left outside the Soft Shoe Cafe. They're really lightweight. They can be ridden hard and fast and I reckon that must be the one we're looking for.'

One or two officers looked rather disgruntled at this conjuring trick. If the chief had worked it out and checked it out, why couldn't he have just spoken out? Barnaby smiled, indifferent to their discomfiture. If time permitted, he always liked the team to suss things for themselves.

'A bit of a risk, sir,' said Sergeant Brierley. 'What if he hadn't found one?'

'Bound to. There's always several on display outside Halfords, for a start. He was probably making for there when he came across this one.'

'It's brilliant, that,' said DS Griggs. 'Covers the

distance, easy to dump and you can jump off and hide if you have to.'

'Exactly,' agreed Barnaby. 'The machine can't be far away. I shall organise a search first light in the morning.'

'Won't he have nipped out by then and disposed of it properly?'

'I hope he tries. I've a man on the house. From now on wherever Jackson goes, we go.' No point in spelling out the problems he'd had obtaining this temporary surveillance. His positive conviction sounded like mere suspicion unsupported by a single shred of evidence to the powers that held the purse strings. The lookout having been grudgingly given, Barnaby was told the situation would be reviewed every twenty-four hours. This time tomorrow, Jackson could once more be as free as the lark ascending. If that happens, thought Barnaby, I shall put one of my own team in his place and keep quiet about it.

'So are we going to give him a tug, sir?' asked Charlie Agnew.

'No. He'd walk. There's nothing to hold him.' Barnaby stared grimly through his team and directly at the back wall with its hideous montage showing the mangled remains of Charlie Leathers. 'When I bring that bugger in, he stays in.'

Louise was getting ready for bed. So far she had taken over an hour about it and could well take another, the procedure being so utterly pointless. For she would never sleep. She might as well stay where she was now, wrapped in a cream velvet robe and curled into the deep hollow centre of a leather armchair. The chair was a perfect oval without arms or legs, suspended by transparent silk ropes from a glass beam in the roof of the house.

Swinging gently backwards and forwards often helped her to relax, sometimes even induced a dream-like drowsiness. But not tonight. Tonight it would take a pharmacist of genius or an opiate not yet discovered to bring an intermission to her tormented consciousness.

The news about Ann had been bad enough. Hearing it, imagining the pain and the terror, understanding how near she now lay to death – that was bad enough. But the other thing . . .

When he had first heard the news, Val was deeply shocked and genuinely sorry to hear what had happened. But later that evening, following a phone call from the Rectory, all this emotion was transformed in a crucible of furious indignation to something approaching rage.

'God Almighty! When are they going to leave that poor devil alone?'

'What are you talking about?'

'Those sodding policemen. They'll hound him and hound him until he can't take any more.'

'Who?' She knew, of course.

'Then he'll strike out in sheer desperation. Re-offend probably. And they'll rub their disgusting hands together and throw him back inside.' Valentine stared hard at his sister, sheer desperation not entirely absent from his own countenance.

'Poor Jax,' said Louise quickly. She had almost forgotten the role she had so recently started to play. 'What is it this time?'

'The usual. Trying to tie something on him he

couldn't possibly have done.'

'Not . . .' Louise had to reach blindly behind her then for support, waving her arm through the air before half sitting, half falling into a seat.

'That's right, the attack on Ann Lawrence. They've even taken the clothes he was wearing when it happened.'

'Oh no.' Dizziness overwhelmed her. 'Val, it can't be true.'

'Of course it isn't true. He was at the Rectory all day. Try telling them that.' Finally his sister's ghastly pallor registered. 'Sorry, Lou. I'm a selfish sod. She was your friend, wasn't she?'

'Yes.' Louise was perfectly clear on that one. Ann had been her friend. How could she ever have thought otherwise?

'I'm going to get you some brandy.'

Louise remembered now that she had drunk the brandy. Swallowed it like water and with much the same effect. When the shock had receded enough for her to be able to stand, she had excused herself and come upstairs. She had bathed, wrapped her still shaking limbs in the cream robe then rocked endlessly back and forth to a lonely rhythm of desolation.

She told herself she might have been mistaken. He had gone by so fast. A cyclist, all in black. Leggings, long-sleeved jumper, gloves, knitted hat pulled right down covering his hair and forehead. She'd parked, just for a minute, on a double yellow outside the bank. Was on the point of getting out, even had the door slightly open, the road behind showing clear. And there he was in her wing mirror. Far away, then present, then gone. Barely a second from start to finish. But, because of the mirror, she had seen his face. And recognised it.

At least she thought she had. But now Val said he was at the Rectory all day. Said he himself was actually with Jax when the savagery took place. So she must have been wrong. In despair Louise, who had stopped believing in the Almighty even before she had stopped believing in Father Christmas, prayed. Awkwardly, with burning, passionate clumsiness, not knowing quite what to say.

'Please God,' she mumbled, 'let it not be him.' Then, feeling this was too vague, she forced herself to elaborate. She even said his name and felt it, squatting like a toad, on her tongue. 'What I mean is, let the man I saw today on a bicycle in Causton not be Jax.'

There was a cold emptiness inside her mouth. And she knew the words were sterile. What was the point? Louise climbed out of her chair and stood, staring through the roof at the almost black sky scattered with sparkling points of cold light. How could anything or anyone even exist up there, let alone be taking the slightest interest in her anguished pleading?

Even so, even while understanding that the whole procedure was a pointless, hopeless waste of time, she could not stop one final request.

'And please, God, *please* look after Val.'

As Barnaby turned into Arbury Crescent, he felt like Sisyphus finally giving up on the boulder. Standing aside, watching it roll away, bouncing and tumbling back down the mountainside while he strode on towards the summit, light of heart.

That moment in the incident room when the tape of Ann Lawrence's emergency call had started to play, when it became plain that he had possibly been barking up an entirely mistaken tree for the entire investigation, had struck the DCI hard. He knew he had given the impression of recovering quickly. He was good at that and it was important that he should be. Disheartenment was an infection that spread like lightning. But it was a false impression. In truth he was feeling very disheartened indeed.

Also he was in grave danger of becoming personally involved. Never recommended, it still sometimes happened. When the cruel mistreatment or murder of a child occurred, for instance, few policemen were able to remain completely detached. But this was not the death of a child. This was the death of an extremely unpleasant old man who had been attempting blackmail.

So why the hatred? Barnaby realised with a shock that this was the correct word. He had begun to hate Terry Jackson. Hate his merry smile and shameless posturing, his conversation which danced back and forth as lightly as a featherweight, a spiteful jab here, a feint – the sham attack which made a fool of the recipient. And, just as it did, the real attack. A serious blow, fast and heavy, to the solar plexus.

Hatred sparkled too when he thought of the man's appearance. Dwelled on that spare, tawny flesh and hard muscle, and the shining navy blue eyes with strange golden pupils. The only physical flaw in this Apollonian perfection, as far as Barnaby could see, were the teeth which had never been properly cared for. But no doubt once this need for cosmetic dentistry was brought to Fainlight's attention the omission would be quickly rectified.

Barnaby yanked his attention away from this idea. Because it would never happen. There were no up-market dentists whitening and capping and straightening in the Scrubs. Or in Albany or Strange-ways. And that's where Jackson would be ending up.

And you'd better believe that, you heap of festering slime. Realising he had spoken aloud and was now gripping the steering wheel as though his very life depended on it, Barnaby slowed down almost to a halt. Because it was not good, this feeling. Hatred could blind you, narrow your options to nothing, obscure evidence that might be right under your nose. Not to mention sending your blood pressure into a spin.

He remembered what Joyce had said to him the other morning, that, once on a case, he was like a dog with a bone, gripping it between his teeth, anxious that no other dog should get a taste. He had been angry at the time. He wondered again if it was true and decided it was. Well, partially. Barnaby had a strong sense of self-worth, he would not have risen to his present rank otherwise, but he believed he was also prepared to listen. In this, although not unique, he was very much in the minority. Still in second, he turned into the driveway of number seventeen.

And then things started to get better as they always did. Whatever foul muck he'd been up to his oxters in during working hours, this was where it started to fall away. It was a strange process, not forgetfulness so much as a psychological cleansing, and he never quite understood it.

It could have been the verdant sweetness of the

garden (even in winter there was always something irresistibly beautiful to look at) or the familiar warmth of the solid, red-brick building where he had lived contentedly for over twenty years. But overwhelmingly, of course, it was Joyce. Wherever she was, he was happy to be.

Barnaby never took this good fortune for granted. You didn't, with a job like his. Anyway, complacency was an absolute magnet for disaster. He had heard the words, I never thought this would happen to me, almost more often than any others. He would never say them. Or believe that never doing anyone any harm was a talisman against disaster. Barnaby reached out and touched the walnut dashboard before getting out of the car.

Cully's Dyane, yellow and mermaid green with a huge sunflower painted on the boot, stood under the laburnum tree. Barnaby's step, already eager, quickened. He had hardly put his key in the lock when she opened the door.

'Dad! Something wonderful's happened!' She seized his hand. 'Come on.'

'Let me take my—'

'No. You've got to come *now*.'

The kitchen door was wide open. He could see Joyce smiling, Nicolas looking tremendously proud, golden-foiled bottles and champagne glasses. Public rejoicing. He looked down at his daughter's shining face and knew what she was going to tell him. He put his arm round her and caught the sweet fragrance of her hair. His little girl.

'Cully. Oh, darling, what can I say?' Barnaby realised the backs of his eyes were prickling. So what? It wasn't every day one became a grandfather. 'Congratulations.'

'It's not me you have to congratulate, silly. It's Nico.'

'Nico?' Barnaby rearranged his expression quickly but the disappointment sliced across his heart. They went into the kitchen together.

'I've got into the National, Tom.' Nicolas laughed, raising his glass, plainly not for the first time. 'Isn't it wonderful?'

'Wonderful.' Barnaby formed the word through stiff lips. He said 'Congratulations' again.

Cully poured him a glass of Veuve Clicquot and smiled at her mother. 'Dad thought I'd got the shampoo commercial.'

'Did he?' said Joyce and caught her husband's eye. Not that she had needed to.

'I speet on shampoo commercials!' cried Nico and started laughing again, draining his wine, throwing the glass into the air.

'Do you know what you're going to play?' asked Barnaby, having long since learned the correct responses to any news of a theatrical nature.

'As cast. But that could mean anything, *anything*. They're doing Pinter, *Antony and Cleopatra*, *Peter Pan*!' cried Nico.

'And a new Terry Johnson comedy all about Sid James,' said Cully.

'Carry on Camping up the Cottesloe.'

'It's not called that surely,' said Joyce.

'You could play Barbara Windsor, darling.' Cully blew her beloved a kiss.

'Yes! I'd look brilliant in drag.'

'One way to get the notices,' said Joyce, dry as a bone. She knew the immodesty was merely a front;

even so, Nico could be somewhat trying at times. 'Have some more wine, darling.' She reached out for her husband's glass and he took her hand instead.

'I'd rather have a sandwich.'

'A sandwich?' Nicolas treated them to his Lady Bracknell, sounding more like Tim Brooke-Taylor than Edith Evans while remaining better looking than both. But then, who wasn't?

'I speet on your sandwich! We're going out to celebrate.'

'Where?'

'The River Cafe.'

'What!'

'Cool it, Dad.'

'If you think—' Barnaby stopped right there. If Cully had been pregnant they could have moved into the River Cafe bag and baggage and had breakfast, lunch and dinner there for a month. 'Anyway, I've heard about that place. You can't just turn up—'

'Nico got a cancellation.'

'It's our treat,' said Nicolas, sounding slightly truculent. 'I sold my old banger yesterday.'

'We decided it was stupid having two cars. Especially in London.'

'So, what better way to blow three hundred pounds?'

'Now, Tom,' said Joyce, observing her husband's reaction, 'calm down.'

'Out of the question. Anyway, I'm on the cabbage soup diet.'

'He hasn't heard,' said Nicolas, winking at his wife.

'Heard what?' said Barnaby.

'They're famous for it,' said Cully, passing to her mother.

'It's true, Tom,' said Joyce. 'I read only the other day. The River Cafe make the best cabbage soup in the world.'

CHAPTER TEN

It was the following morning and Barnaby was at his desk attempting to sort out his day and compose what few notes there were for the eight thirty briefing. He was finding it extremely hard to concentrate. This time yesterday, if someone had told him he would spend the best part of two hours that very evening giving his current case load barely a single consideration he would have thought they were mad. Yet such had been the case.

They had been given a table by the window over-looking a smooth stretch of grass edged by paving slabs bordered by a low wall rising directly above the Thames. The surface of the water was burnished by the setting sun and lamps gleamed along the paved walkway.

Even on an autumn evening the River Cafe was incredibly light and airy and packed with happy customers. Talking, laughing, eating, drinking. At one point a woman broke into song (*'Vissi d'Arte'*) and no one seemed to take it amiss.

The service was perfection. Friendly without being unctuous, visible the minute you needed it, absent when you did not. Suggestions tactfully made and no offence taken if they were ignored. No one endlessly re-filled your glass as if you were a toddler in a high chair. Nothing was off and what was on was utter heaven.

The cooking went on behind a long steel counter where a great many thin people in long white aprons produced the sort of food that leads a great many fat people to the brink of despair.

Barnaby ate tagliatelle fragrant with asparagus and herbs and Parmesan. This was followed by turbot, the flakes of which melted off his fork. Green salad with a bit of rocket. Some beautiful potatoes. And not a cabbage in sight. Everyone tasted everyone else's food and, when this was noticed, extra forks appeared from nowhere. For pudding Barnaby had Chocolate Nemesis which very nearly proved to be his own. They drank Torre del Falco from Sicily. Nico bought Cully the recipe book, grandly inscribed, and also one for Joyce. Barnaby was apprehensive.

'Don't worry,' said Cully to her dad as they walked, some little way behind the others, towards the taxi. 'Mum'll be fine. Nobody can burn pasta.'

Barnaby had remained silent. To his mind a woman who can burn salad can burn anything.

'You're looking a bit more cheery this morning, chief.' Sergeant Troy entered, interrupting this voluptuous reverie. He was looking less cheery himself. Rather pale and wan, in fact.

'Went out celebrating last night,' said Barnaby. 'My son-in-law took us all up the Smoke to dinner. To the River Cafe.'

'I've heard about it. By the river.'

'That's the place.'

'Maureen saw it on the telly.'

'Actually, he's just got into the National, Nico.'

'Brilliant,' enthused Troy. National? National what?

Barnaby put his papers in a bulldog clip then really clocked his sergeant for the first time.

'You all right, Troy?'

'Sir?'

'You look a bit peaky.'

The fact was that Sergeant Troy had had a strange and most disturbing dream. In the dream he had awoken, tried to rise and found himself unable to do anything other than roll his head heavily from side to side. His limbs felt extraordinary, flat and empty like an unstuffed rag doll's. Then he saw, on the floor by the bed, a neat stack of bones and knew them to be his own. Gruesome or what? Troy blamed this nightmare on the visit to the hospital. And the churchyard next to the Rectory hadn't helped matters.

'I'm all right, chief.' Cockeyed fancies, even involuntary ones, were best kept to oneself. The force didn't go a bundle on neurotics. Sergeant Troy carried his trenchcoat over to the old-fashioned hat stand and rejoiced in the sensation of warm flesh on living bone. He said, 'Have you contacted the hospital?'

'Yes. They've done the brain scan and found a clot. They're operating this morning.'

'What about feedback from our man on the spot?'

'Nothing doing,' replied Barnaby. 'Nobody in, nobody out. Not even the postman. Presumably Jackson's still in the main house, "looking after Lionel".'

'What a sick scene. Talk about decadent.' Troy was pleased to be able to make use of decadent. He'd got the word from the sleeve notes of *Cabaret* ages ago. It was surprising how difficult it was to drop it into general conversation when you considered how much of it there was about.

'If we phrase it very carefully we can try a public appeal,' said Barnaby. 'Simply describe the stolen cycle, the time it was swiped and suggest the direction it may have been taking. Someone must have seen him.'

'We could say what he was wearing.'

'For God's sake! First, we don't know what he was wearing. Second, we keep any reference to Jackson, however oblique, absolutely out of it. Once he's nailed, I want no accusations of pre-trial prejudice getting him off. Or the civil liberties mob breathing down our necks.'

'The press'll be on to it though. Nobody's going to believe a public appeal over a missing push bike.'

'So we'll stonewall. Won't be the first time.' Barnaby slipped his notes into an envelope file, took his jacket from the back of his chair and put it on. Troy held the door open and the DCI strode away from his office. The working day proper had begun.

That same morning Hetty Leathers arrived at the Old Rectory at her usual time of 9 a.m. but without Candy. The dog was coping much better now at being left alone and, as Mrs Lawrence was absent, Hetty felt she should perhaps ask the Reverend's permission to bring Candy to work.

She went in through the front door, carrying straight through to the kitchen. There she found Jackson wearing a pair of stained jeans and a sleeveless vest, scraping Marmite onto burned toast. His bare feet were up on the table. There was no sign of Lionel.

Hetty turned round and walked straight out again. Out of the kitchen and out of the house. As she made to go down the drive, a movement through the library window caught her eye. She crossed over, rested her hands on the sill and peered in. She insisted afterwards to Pauline that she had no thought of spying and this was probably true. What was also true was that she very much wished she'd walked on by.

The Reverend was crouching over Mrs Lawrence's writing desk. Letters were strewn everywhere. As Hetty watched, he tore another envelope, already opened, practically apart in his eagerness to rip out its contents. A second to stare angrily at the piece of paper and it joined the others on the floor. He paused, panting for a moment, then started to tug furiously at a little drawer at the back of the desk that would not open.

Hetty watched in shocked amazement. The Reverend's face, distorted by a fear-filled hungriness that could hardly be contained and scarlet with effort, was barely recognisable. He put his foot against the leg of the desk and this time using both hands heaved on the drawer with all his might. Hetty ran away.

As she did so, Jackson wandered into the library. Leaned against the door jamb, dark blue eyes gleaming with excitement, a happy smile barely disturbing his lips.

'I hate to see you like this, Lionel.'

Lionel, by now wailing with rage, looked fit to explode.

'Wait.' Jackson strolled across the room and rested a calming hand on Lionel's arm. 'If you must break into other people's property—'

'You don't understand!' shouted Lionel.

Jackson turned his face from the gust of sour wine and reeking, unwashed skin. He was very fastidious about that sort of thing.

'And stop shouting. You'll have half the village out.'

'It's all right for you . . .' Lionel attempted to soften his voice, with little success. 'What's going to happen to me? Where shall I go?'

'You don't even know Mrs L's made a will.' Jackson's grip tightened slightly. 'In which case, as her legal better half, you'll be laughing.'

Lionel gave a single piercing cry. 'I thought I was safe here.'

'Let go,' said Jackson. He sounded patient, not unkind just weary, like a parent who'd had enough of a favourite child's tantrums. 'I'll do it.'

Lionel released the drawer and stood, arms swinging loose by his sides, staring. Jackson produced a knife from the pocket of his jeans. A click and the short, narrow blade sprang out, shining. He inserted it behind the lock, gave a sharp twist and the drawer sprang open. It was full of papers.

Lionel seized them and started to read. Jackson could see the heading Friends Provident, the words separated by a blue rose. After a few minutes Lionel had shuffled through all the pages and flung them also to the floor.

'All to do with her trust fund.' He was very near to tears and struggling for breath. 'She's always been very tight with that, Jax. I wanted her to buy a little flat, give a temporary home to youngsters struggling to make a new life. People like yourself. But she was adamant. There's so much selfishness in the world, meanness, don't you find?'

'I don't like to hear you being disloyal, Lionel. I've always thought Mrs L basically a very sincere person.'

It was probably with her solicitor. Or the bank. 'I think you need some breakfast. Cheer you up a bit.'

'I'm not hungry.'

'Plus a wash and brush-up. OK, I got "no change" from the hospital this morning but things could have altered by dinner time. What if you was allowed to visit this afternoon? You can't go in looking like that. Come on.' He took Lionel's damp and unresisting hand. 'Jax will make you a nice piece of toast.'

'You're so good to me.'

'Richly deserved, to my mind, Lionel.'

'You won't go away?'

'Try and make me.'

Barnaby's appointment with Richard Ainsley was for ten o'clock. They were shown straight into his office and offered tea which Barnaby declined. The bank manager's face was grave as befitted the matter under discussion.

'A most dreadful business. I can still hardly believe it.' His distress was plainly genuine. A fact explained by his next words. 'I have known the family thirty years. Ann, Mrs Lawrence, was seven when I first started handling her father's affairs.'

Barnaby had not been aware of that but rejoiced in the knowledge. One never knew what would be grist to the investigative mill.

'Then I'm sure you will be doubly anxious to help us, sir.'

'Of course I am. But how is it possible? A random, violent attack—'

'We're not sure that it was random.'

'Oh.' Ainsley's expression changed then. Became

immensely cautious and somewhat apprehensive. He sniffed and stared intensely at his visitors as if etheric traces of the crime might still be drifting about their persons.

This reaction from the public was not uncommon. Barnaby smiled encouragingly and said, 'I can assure you that anything divulged during this interview will be in complete confidence.'

'Ah.' Richard Ainsley looked warily at Troy sitting near the door, notebook balanced discreetly on his knee. 'Well . . .'

Barnaby jumped in at the deep end. 'We have reason to believe that Mrs Lawrence was being blackmailed.'

'So that's—'

'That's what?'

But Ainsley withdrew immediately, like a limpet into its shell. 'You must understand, Chief Inspector, my customer's financial affairs—'

'Mrs Lawrence is undergoing an emergency operation, Mr Ainsley, even as we're sitting here. A positive outcome is far from certain. Now, I can go to a magistrate, get the relevant piece of paper and come back for the information you are withholding. But time is of the essence here. I urge you to co-operate.'

'Yes. I do see. Oh – this is all so dreadful.' He wrung his hands for a moment, then opened his desk diary, checked a date and started to speak.

'Ann came in to see me on Saturday morning. August the twenty-second. She needed to borrow five thousand pounds against the security of the house. That was acceptable, of course. The Old Rectory is worth a great deal of money. But her income is a modest one and I was concerned about her ability to make regular repayments. When I mentioned this she became almost hysterical, which naturally made me more concerned then ever. She had already drawn a thousand pounds from her current account.'

'When was this, sir?'

Richard Ainsley had almost forgotten Sergeant Troy, quietly taking notes. He studied his diary again and replied, 'Wednesday the nineteenth.' Then, turning back to Barnaby, 'I'd made a note of the date should it arise during my meeting with her.'

'So it was six altogether?'

'That's right. And she insisted on cash both times. Extremely worrying. I was so relieved to hear yesterday that she was bringing it all back.'

'What?'

'She rang in the morning, about ten thirty.' Ainsley smiled, quietly pleased that he could bring about this consternation, even under such unhappy circumstances. He was only human. 'I was to cancel the loan and she would be returning the cash that very afternoon. Oh.'

Oh indeed, thought Barnaby, watching the shock hit home.

'Did the person who attacked her . . .?'

'I'm afraid so,' said the chief inspector. 'When she said "all", did you understand this to mean all she had borrowed or just the five thousand?'

'Deary me. What a situation. We'll never get it back. What will head office say?'

'Mr Ainsley?'

'Mm?'

'Five or six?'

'I don't know. Oh, this is terrible. Terrible.'

* * *

Being economical with the truth had been an integral part of Louise's life for so long it had been years since the fact had even registered. A huge proportion of her working day was spent lying. Not that she thought of it like that. After all, who in the financial world wasn't doing it? Brokers, analysts, financial advisers – all prepared to conceal or misrepresent what they believed to be the true state of affairs while struggling to penetrate the false representations of others. So this latest small untruth, spoken earlier over the telephone to the reception desk at Stoke Mandeville, had caused her no trouble at all. Now she approached the reception area and gave her name.

'Mrs Forbes?'

'That's right. I rang earlier.'

'Ah, yes. Your sister's on the third floor. Take the lift and I'll let them know you're coming.' The receptionist, a pretty Asian woman, added, 'I'm so sorry. Such a terrible thing to happen.'

'Thank you.'

A staff nurse met Louise, said pretty much the same thing and led her along a long, silent corridor, her shoes squeaking on the rubbery surface. She opened a door at the very end and they went in.

Louise stopped in her tracks. Her heart gave a jerk then suddenly started to beat with furious speed. For no reason, she felt suddenly frightened. Ann lay quite motionless in a narrow iron bed. Precisely in the centre of the bed, Louise noticed. The same amount of space each side of her thin shoulders. You could do that, of course, when a person was deeply unconscious. Satisfy the human passion for order and balance.

The room was full of blue light. Machinery hummed, quite noisily. There were several computer screens, one of which had the shimmering green line, constantly peaking and subsiding, so familiar to viewers of hospital dramas.

There was a single bedside chair, rather office-like with a tweed seat and tubular chrome arms, but Louise did not sit down. She stood at the foot of the bed, staring. There were no what she would call signs of life. Louise had never seen a dead person but surely this was what they looked like. There was not the slightest trace of colour in Ann's skin, what one could see of it. And no rise and fall of her breast. The taut, hospital-cornered sheet did not move. A needle in her arm led to a bottle suspended on a frame. A tube disappeared into her mouth and another depended from her nostrils.

In alarm, Louise turned to the nurse. 'She's not breathing.'

'The ventilator does that for her. Have you spoken to Dr Miller?'

'No.' Louise felt her heart turn over. 'Should I have?'

'The brain scan showed a clot, I'm afraid. We'll be operating later today.'

'What chance is there—'

'The very best chance. Mrs Lawrence is in good hands.'

Louise looked anxiously around the room. 'Shouldn't someone be here all the time?'

'Someone is – almost all. And don't worry, she's monitored. The slightest change in breathing, heart-beat, pulse or blood pressure and the alarm goes off.'

Louise had brought some flowers from the Rectory

garden. She had not asked permission, simply gone in with her secateurs and cut an armful of the things that Ann loved best. Hollyhocks, apricot and cream foxgloves, the last of some floppy pink roses with a powerful, musky scent. She did not as much as glance towards the house and no one came out to stop her.

When she had rung up to see how Ann was, Louise was told that only close relatives were allowed to visit. That meant Lionel, a man who lived in a self-centred world of his own and had probably never thought to take a flower at all, let alone his wife's favourites.

Now, looking down at her friend, Louise saw how absurd and foolish her impulse had been. She had not fully understood how dangerously ill Ann was. Had imagined her coming round, maybe during her own visit, and, seeing the flowers, suddenly turning the corner. Or, unconscious, still being able to sense and recognise the heady fragrance of the roses she so lovingly cared for.

Stupid, *stupid*! Louise chided herself as she sat by the bed. She reached out, took Ann's hand and almost dropped it. So cold and lifeless. And yet Ann was still there. Whatever it was that vanishes when a person dies, the essence of themselves, their 'Ann-ness' if you will, was still there.

Louise felt she should speak. For who was to say that Ann would not hear? She tried out various sentences in her mind but they all sounded pathetic. Death a whisper away and all she could think of were banal simplicities you could hear any day of the week on a television soap. 'I'm here, Ann, it's Louise. Can you hear me? We're all thinking about you. Everyone is so sorry. They send their love. You'll be all right.' (This last surely the acme of wildly unrealistic optimism.)

In the end Louise said nothing. Just kissed Ann's cheek, gently squeezed her hand and tried not to picture what lay under the tightly wound bandages.

Jax had done this. Fact. She had seen him running away. Well, racing away. But Val had said it wasn't possible. That he had actually been with Jax when the crime occurred. It couldn't be true. Yet surely he would not lie to cover for the man – not over something as terrible as this?

Was it possible she had been mistaken? Louise closed her eyes, re-imagined the moment when she had been about to open her car door, saw again the dark figure zooming up and flashing by. It had been very quick, a lightning flash. Yet she had been so sure.

Perhaps she had been thinking of Jax at the time. That was likely. These days she seemed to think of little else. Could she have superimposed his face on the speeding cyclist. The mind plays tricks, deluding and deceiving. We all believe what we want to believe.

A soft swish as the air-locked door was pushed open. A staff nurse smiled apologetically, explaining they needed to attend to Mrs Lawrence.

Louise moved away, indicating her flowers. 'Please, could someone . . .'

'They'll be put into water, don't worry.' Then, rather awkwardly, 'We have notified Mr Lawrence of his wife's condition. I wondered perhaps if there was some domestic . . . well . . . upset?'

'I'm sorry?' Louise's expression was one of blank bewilderment.

'Some reason why he hasn't called to see her. Or even telephoned.'

* * *

Driving once more through Causton on her way to Ferne Basset, Louise realised she could not go home. She just couldn't face Val so soon after seeing Ann. Couldn't put on her false face and express concern over the future of that creature who was ruining both their lives. And she doubted if she could successfully conceal her anger at Ann's neglect by her husband.

As it was now one o'clock, she decided to stay in town for lunch. Instinctively avoiding the multi-storey, Louise left her bright yellow Seicento tucked away in a tiny back street, risking a parking fine.

There were only two cafes in Causton. One, Minnie's Pantry, was unbearably mimsy. The Soft Shoe was a greasy spoon. Louise decided on the Spread Eagle which was in the Good Pub Guide and had quite decent food. The lounge, it not being market day, was only half occupied.

There were newspapers on sticks and she tried to read the arts pages of the *Guardian* while drinking Guinness and waiting for an individual steak and kidney pudding, braised cabbage and potato croquettes. It was hard to keep her mind on the music and theatre reviews. That world, which had so recently been very much a part of her life, now seemed as remote as Mars.

A Sony portable was suspended over the far side of the bar, the volume low. When the local news came on, Louise put down her paper and took her drink across to listen. A woman in civilian clothes, referred to as a police spokesman, was voicing an appeal for information following an incident in Causton the previous day. A Peugeot bicycle had been stolen at around 3 p.m.

from Denton Street. The cyclist was thought to have made off in the direction of Great Missenden. It was possible the theft could be linked with a more serious incident. A telephone number was given. Louise wrote it down.

The response to the television news appeal was surprisingly swift and several calls had been received by two thirty when Barnaby and Sergeant Troy returned to the incident room from the canteen. Still swamped in blissful recall of his highly calorific outing the previous night, the DCI had eaten very lightly and, consequently, remained clear-headed and full of energy.

Barnaby sat at his desk in excellent spirits, in part conjured by the confirmation (at least as he saw it) that Ann Lawrence had definitely been the person blackmailed and that she had been prepared to pay up at least once and possibly twice, for had she not drawn out more money, presumably to cover a second demand?

Barnaby recalled his brief telephone conversation with her on Monday. She had seemed very calm, even cheerful. Said she was looking forward to talking to him. This, linked with the intention to return the money, implied that she had come to the decision not to pay. Also that she planned to tell the police exactly what had been going on.

Barnaby murmured again to himself at the vagaries of fate while watching Sergeant Troy, with a mass of paper in his fist, making his way down the incident room. His expression was somewhat cautious.

'What d'you want, sir? The good news or the bad news?'

'What I don't want,' snapped Barnaby, 'are stupid games. Or tired old maxims I've heard a thousand times before and never reckoned the first time.'

'Right. The good—' He was interrupted by an intemperate growling. 'Sorry. We've had nine calls. All genuine, I'd say, as the descriptions of the cyclist hardly vary. We've even got him on film—'

'Got him on film?' In his excitement Barnaby banged his fist down on the desk top. 'Then got him is right!'

'Top Gear, men's fashion next to the Soft Shoe Cafe, has a couple of mobile security cameras. One covers the shop interior, the other the door and a small area of the pavement. Our man's caught on it actually pushing the bike into the road and riding off.' Troy turned his final page and put the papers down on the desk. 'Someone's bringing the film over.'

'With news as good as this, what could be bad?' asked Barnaby.

'The man carried a small rucksack and was in black from head to foot. Gloves, knitted hat, leggings, everything.' Troy watched the chief take this in. Sit back in his chair, winded. Who wouldn't be?

'So the stuff Jackson took out of his washing machine—'

'That forensics,' Barnaby reached for the telephone and savagely punched at the dial, 'have already spent the best part of twenty-four hours working on.'

'Was completely irrelevant.' Troy watched his chief with some sympathy. 'Why did he choose the Hotpoint, d'you think? Why not just take something out of the wardrobe?'

'His idea of fun. Hoping we'd think, hey, these've

been washed pretty quickly. They must be guilty jeans. And a guilty T-shirt.'

Which we did, recalled Sergeant Troy. Silently. 'He's a clever bastard.'

'Jackson is not clever.' It was almost a shout. Heads turned, keyboards ceased to clatter, telephone calls were put on hold. There was a gathering of attention which Barnaby irritably dispersed with a vigorous swishing at the air with his hand. 'He is devious,' said the chief inspector more quietly. 'He is vicious and twisted and cruel. But he is *not* clever.'

'Right, sir.'

'No man who has spent twelve of his twenty-six years in and out of juvenile courts, remand homes, Borstal and prison is clever. Hold on to that.'

'Right,' said Troy again, this time with more conviction.

'Hello, Jim?' said Barnaby as the receiver squawked at him. 'Look, I'm sorry about this but that material on the Leathers case we sent down yesterday...'

By mid-afternoon on the day after Ann Lawrence was attacked, Ferne Basset was in a ferment of agitation. There was a good reason for this. A stranger in a dark blue Escort had arrived at dusk the previous evening, parked on the edge of the Green and sat in his car reading a paper. Highly suspicious, to say the least. He was still there when night fell.

In the morning, relief and, it must be said, a certain amount of disappointment were experienced when the car appeared to have vanished. Then it was spotted some distance away, nearer to the church. This time the occupant was drinking from a Thermos flask and smoking. Later he got out and had a walk around, neither greeting anyone nor responding to friendly civilities on the village's part with anything other than a curt nod.

The words Neighbourhood Watch could have been invented to describe Ferne Basset and it did not take long before it was generally agreed, round the counter at Brian's Emporium, that the newcomer was casing the joint. Local burglaries, in spite of endlessly inventive and costly precautions, were common and commonly successful. Straightaway the decision was taken to ring the local bobby.

PC Colin Perrot's beat covered four villages. He got more hassle from this one than all the others put together and always from what Colin had designated the 'upper strata'. This lot weren't prepared to accept the slightest deviation from what they regarded as the socially acceptable norm. He had been called out once late at night following a complaint about someone holding a rock concert. Had driven nine miles in the pouring rain to find music coming from one of the council houses that was half the level he could hear any night of the week through his own lounge walls.

'They don't know they're born,' muttered Colin to himself, putt-putting to a halt then heaving his BMW onto its stand. He went into the shop, listened, came out and made his way towards the stationary car. All the customers and staff came out and watched from the forecourt as PC Perrot rapped on the window which was promptly wound down.

'What seems to be the situation?' asked Brigadier Dampier-Jeans, a leading local worthy and chairman of the parish council, when the policeman returned.

'Ordinance survey,' replied Perrot. 'Something to do with land measurement.'

'A likely story,' said the brigadier. 'Saw his papers, did you?'

'Of course,' replied Perrot, somewhat huffily. He did not like to be told his job. 'He has government authority.'

'Why doesn't the fellow get out and survey then, 'stead of sitting in his motor like a stuffed bison.'

'There has to be two of them,' explained PC Perrot. 'The other chap's been delayed.'

While talking, he had been setting the bike straight and climbing on. Now he kicked the pedal and roared away before they could all start jawing at him again. Speeding along, Perrot wondered if the copper in the Escort would get lucky and the bloke in the big house would make a run for it. At the same time he thanked his lucky rabbit's foot it wasn't him stuck out there on the greensward till the cows came home.

Later that afternoon, Hetty visited Mulberry Cottage, only briefly for she had left Candy fast asleep in her basket. Now, sipping a cup of strange tea which was the colour of pale straw, though not unpleasant, she accepted a second piece of iced gingerbread.

'I heard,' said Hetty, 'that he was something to do with agriculture.'

'I don't think so, dear. My information was map measurement. Ground contours, that sort of thing.'

And that was saturation point as far as the man in the car was concerned. Now they reverted to the subject they had started with. Much more interesting than the stranger's occupation and certainly more worrying. What was going on at the Old Rectory?

'I couldn't believe my eyes,' said Hetty. She had said it before but so extraordinary was the scene her eyes could not believe that Evadne did not doubt her for a minute. 'Feet up on the kitchen table. And poor Mrs Lawrence, who'd never even have him in the house, lying at death's door.'

'Incredible,' said Evadne, who was really distressed. 'What can Lionel be thinking of?'

'Something's gone wrong between them,' said Hetty. 'She didn't take his lunch in for him before she went to Causton. That's never happened before. He was shut in his study. She drove off and left him to it.'

'They must have had a quarrel.'

'I hope so.'

'Hetty!'

'About time Mrs Lawrence stood up for herself. He's been ruling the roost for years. What's more – and I wouldn't want this to go any further – it's all her money. He's nothing more than a leech.'

Evadne nodded. The whole of Ferne Basset knew it was Ann's money.

'And when I left he was going at the papers in her desk like a madman. Ripping them up, flinging them about. His face was as red as a turkey cock's. Mark my words, that man's heading for a stroke.'

Which reminded Evadne to ask if she had rung the hospital that day.

'This morning. They said "no change" but if you're not a close relative they won't always tell you. I said to them, "I'm as close to her as anyone else in the world." But it didn't do any good.' Hetty's mouth slipped and trembled. 'She used to come into the kitchen when she was little: I taught her to make pastry. She'd never use the cutters. Always wanted to design her own shapes. Flowers, cats, even little houses. I used to think she'd be an artist when she grew up.'

Evadne crossed over to her friend and put an arm round her shaking shoulders.

Hetty cried out, 'How could anyone be so cruel?'

Evadne rocked Hetty backwards and forwards for a moment. 'Hetty, would you like to say a prayer for her?'

'What?'

'It may help.'

Hetty seemed uncertain. And no wonder, thought Evadne. Her life had hardly been one to engender gratitude.

'Well . . . if you really think so.' Hetty made an awkward movement, about to get out of her chair, but Evadne eased her gently down again.

'No, no. It's not necessary to kneel down. God doesn't care about that – a sincere heart is all that matters.'

'I won't know what to say.'

'No need to say anything. Just picture Ann surrounded by divine light. And hold fast.'

Quietly Evadne began to pray. Hetty tried to imagine Ann surrounded by divine light. She came up with a sort of halo, like the Bible illustrations in her Sunday school class years ago. As for brightness, the most dazzling source she could think of was the halogen light in the garden of the Old Rectory which seemed somehow appropriate.

Around the room six pale heaps of fur sat or lay in complete silence. There was not even a scratch or a yawn. Evadne's Pekes were used to moments like this and knew exactly what was required of them.

* * *

By six thirty in the evening Barnaby had been shut up in his office for nearly two hours. The incident room managed to appear both noisy and hectic even when nothing much was happening and he needed to be reasonably quiet. To be alone and think. Sergeant Troy came in from time to time with information and the occasional slug of strong Colombian.

Half an hour ago he had brought in an extremely satisfactory forensic report on the Lawrences' Humber. A tiny filament of shiny black acetate had been caught on the worn piece of carpet lining the boot. And some fragments of grit had also been present. These were coated with white material which, on closer examination, proved to be garden lime. Nothing remarkable in that, no doubt Ann Lawrence had frequently carted such stuff back from the garden centre, but if it matched precisely grit found in the cyclist's shoes, then they were really on to something.

Problem was, they didn't have the cyclist's shoes. Or his gear. Or his bike. The search for this had, so far, been fruitless. Yet the time factor meant it must have been abandoned very near the village.

As soon as reports of the black-clad figure started to come in, two officers had been sent to Jackson's flat to search for the clothes and Ann Lawrence's handbag. They had found neither. Which meant he had either taken other stuff to wear – hence the rucksack – or stashed a change of clothing where he planned to leave the bike. The handbag couldn't have just vanished. Shortly after the men left, Lionel Lawrence rang the station, rather incoherently complaining of police harassment.

Having reached this one step forward two steps back point in his reflections, the chief inspector was rather pleased by the distraction of a door opening and his sidekick's appearing this time with a steaming mug of strong Typhoo and a packet of biscuits. Fortunately they were Rich Tea, a dull morsel at the best of times. Hardly rich at all in any appreciable sense of the word.

'You know I'm watching the calories, Sergeant.'

'Yes, chief. It's just, only a salad at lunch. I thought . . .'

Barnaby grandly waved the brightly coloured packet away and asked if anything new had turned up.

'Our man's report's in from Ferne Basset. Apparently Jackson's still not put his nose outside the house. DS Bennet's taken over the shift. How long are they going to let you run this for, chief?'

'Results in thirty-six hours or else. That's the latest.'

'D'you think Jackson's spotted him?'

'What, through the Rectory walls?'

'I wouldn't put anything past that scumbag. Oh, and the film's arrived from the Top Gear shop.'

'Why didn't you say so?'

'I am saying so.'

Sergeant Troy flattened himself against the door as Barnaby, grasping his mug, hurried from the room. There was no need for him to get wound up, though Troy hadn't the heart to point this out. They had already run the film through once downstairs so there'd be no hiccup when the boss came to view, and it was pretty useless. Blink and you'd miss the bugger.

'Go on then.' Barnaby, having seated himself, leaned forward eagerly, hands on knees, gazing at the VDU. The film began. Grey-blue figures laden with bags or shopping trolleys shuffled apathetically along the pavement, two girls walked past arm in arm, giggling. A toddler was carried by on his father's shoulders. No one seemed to be aware of the camera. There was a dark flash across the screen.

'What was that?' asked Barnaby.

'Our man,' said Troy.

'Ah, shit.' The chief inspector's shoulders slumped. 'All right, run back and freeze.'

They studied the slim figure, gripping the handle-bars of the stolen machine. The bike was half on the pavement, half on the road as the cyclist prepared to jump into the saddle. Even on hold and seen only from the back the gathering of muscular energy appeared formidable.

'Same height as Jackson, same build,' said Inspector Carter.

'Of course it's the same height and build!' Angrily Barnaby pushed back his chair. 'It's the same bloody man.'

'Shall we blow the picture up, chief?' asked Sergeant Brierley.

'Might as well, though I can't see anything coming of it.'

'If only he'd been facing the other way,' said DS Griggs. Adding, 'That bastard's got the luck of the devil.'

'It'll run out sooner or later,' said Barnaby. 'Everybody's does. Even the devil's.'

Louise had not mentioned the hospital visit to her brother. She had not intended deliberately to conceal this but remembered that, during their earlier conversation, the subject of Ann's attack had immediately led to an eruption of anger quickly followed by a diatribe against the police for their continual persecution of Jax. Now the time when she could have naturally mentioned it (she had arrived home eight hours ago) had long passed.

She had answered the lunchtime news appeal, though. Rung the number given from a box outside the post office in the Market Square and described the cyclist without saying that she recognised who he was. She couldn't bring herself to do that, even anonymously. And as she was not prepared to follow up and identify him personally – partially out of fear for her own safety but mainly because of the pain it would cause Val – any such admission would be pointless. She was rather ashamed of this, her memory of the time spent in the intensive care unit was raw and painful, and Louise knew that if Ann died she would speak out whatever the cost. But of course what she really longed for was for Ann to recover and be able to tell the police herself who had attacked her.

This understanding led to an anxious few moments when Louise wondered if Jax might make his way to the hospital to make sure Ann did not recover. There seemed to be nothing to stop him. No guard outside her door, no member of staff inside. All very well to say, as the staff nurse had, that someone was nearly always there. It only needed a moment, when the someone was not there, for vital plugs to be snatched from their sockets and Ann's life to drain helplessly away. And, as the police presumably thought her the victim of a random attack, they would see no need for protection. Louise told herself she was being melodramatic. Too many movies – a scene from *The Godfather* came to mind – but the image would not fade.

She rang the hospital. She had intended to do so anyway to hear how the operation had gone but there was little for her comfort. The operation had been straightforward. Mrs Lawrence had not come round yet from the anaesthetic. There had been no visitors.

A sudden coolness in the air rather than any sound told her the front door had opened and been closed. Her brother came slowly into the room. He nodded silently then threw himself down in a scarlet velvet armchair shaped like a vast shell.

Louise was used to seeing him return from the garage flat wearing a mingled expression of joy and pain and walking as though half his bones had been mangled. It was a relief to see him looking pretty much as normal. Or as normal as he ever looked these days.

'How are things over there?'

'Jax has moved into the Rectory pro tem.' The disappointment had been keen. He had not been able even to touch the boy. 'He's taking care of Lionel.'

Louise felt a sudden deep pang of apprehension. She knew she ought to stop there. Say 'how kind' and not attempt to delve deeper. But a terrible curiosity drew her on. She longed to know why Lionel had not visited his wife. Or even contacted the hospital.

'He must be pretty upset. Lionel, I mean.'

'Distraught, poor chap. Doesn't know whether he's coming or going.'

'Has he been to see her?'

'Oh, yes. They went this morning.'

'*They?*'

'What's the matter?'

'Sorry. I just thought . . . Ann being so . . . usually more than one visitor . . .'

As her tongue floundered over the words, Louise's heart beat a little faster. By asking a question to which she already knew the answer, she had taken the single step from honesty to trickery. She stared at her brother with dismay. They had never played these sorts of games. He stared back, his glance at first speculative then thickening into suspicion.

'Someone has to drive Lionel. That's all I meant by "they".'

'Oh, yes. Sorry. I didn't think.'

'What's behind all this?'

'Nothing. Just making conversation.'

'No you're not.' He was on the verge of becoming angry. Louise tried to work out how best to extricate herself. Perhaps if she said she was tired and going to bed, he'd simply shrug and let go. With the old Val, there would have been no problem. But this new, damaged Val was so volatile, so ready to strike out blindly at real or imagined slights. And in this case he was right. She was not being straight with him and the suspicion was deserved. Wouldn't it be better simply to tell him the truth?

'I went to see Ann today.'

'What?'

'Around lunchtime.'

'Why didn't you tell me?'

'I couldn't. It was so awful, Val. Tubes and drips and machinery . . . and poor Ann hardly there at all.'

'Oh God, Lou.'

'She's dying, I know she is.' Louise burst into a

flood of tears. Val climbed out of the armchair, came over and put his arms round her as he had when she was a little girl. For a moment Louise allowed herself the comforting conceit that things were once more as they used to be. But then the longing for veracity, to have everything absolutely straight between them, drove her on.

'They said . . .' She was crying so much she could hardly speak. 'He hadn't been to see her at all . . .'

'Who?'

'Lionel.'

'That's ridiculous.'

'Or even rung up.'

'You talked to the wrong person. Reception changes all the time at these big places.'

'This was the nurse at intensive care.'

Val withdrew then. First physically, the warm muscly flesh of his arms hardening until Louise felt she was being embraced by two curved planks of wood. Then disengaging his emotions.

'I thought you'd stopped all this.' Val's voice was cold. He got up and moved away.

'Val – don't go!'

'I thought you'd changed. That you'd begun to understand.'

'I do,' cried Louise.

'Now you're calling him a liar.' He looked down at her with a detachment that was not entirely without sympathy. 'I've asked Jax to come and live here, Louise. Whether you move out or not. You'll just have to accept it.'

'How can I accept something that makes you so unhappy?'

'It's not about being happy. It's about being glad to be alive.'

After his sister had gone to bed and cried herself to sleep, Val sat near the window of his own room, gazing out at the great cedar tree in the driveway of the house opposite. Louise had wept so violently and for so long, he had thought she might make herself ill. Yet he did not go to her for he was unable to say what she longed to hear and knew his presence could only torment her further.

It was true what he had said about being glad to be alive. Equally true that, for a great deal of the time, he now experienced pain and fright. But the moment was long gone when he could have walked away. No question now of weighing distress against satisfaction and trying to decide if the game was worth the candle.

Dante had got it right. And von Aschenbach. Look, lust after, love and worship youth and beauty. Just don't touch. But what about the 'strife below the hipbones', as he had somewhere read the sexual urge memorably described. It seemed to Val the more frequently his longing for Jax was satisfied, the more powerful it became. Tonight, sitting awkwardly in the untidy sitting room of the Old Rectory asking after Lawrence's wife, Val had felt he was on fire.

Jax and Lionel sat facing him on a sofa that was splashed with red stains. Jax was drinking Coke, his tongue darting in and out of the glass like a fish. Each time he reached out for his glass, the dragonfly tattoo passed through a fall of light from a standard lamp and sprang to iridescent life. Lionel sat as in a waking dream: calm, smiling and looking at nothing and no one in particular.

Val did not stay long. He couldn't bear having Jax within arm's reach and not be able to touch him. The boy's blazing blue eyes shone with sexual invitation. The flickering tongue, nothing but a sensual wind-up, was already driving Val mad. He prayed that Jax would offer to see him to the door, perhaps even come outside for a moment and stand close to him in the darkness. But Jax did not move. Just waved an ironical goodbye, lifting his glass.

Val had no illusions about what his life would be like when the boy moved in. Though his love for Jax was immensely powerful it was also powerless. He would give and give until it hurt. Until not only his bank balance but his heart was bled white. Jax would take, physically, emotionally and fiscally, as much as he liked for as long as it suited him. Then he would be off. He would not grow to love Mozart or Palestrina. Nor would he ever be persuaded to read a grown-up newspaper, let alone Austen or Balzac. Such Pygmalion longings Val now recognised as hopelessly foolish. Yet they were not ignoble and he could not laugh at them as he could easily have done had they been held by someone else.

This bleak clairvoyance, showing no ray of light or comfort at all, did not unduly depress Val. He liked the thought that he was prepared for anything and believed he would be able to cope when the end came even though the thought filled him with despair.

There was no one to talk to about all this. Val had several good friends, straight as well as gay, but there was not one who could possibly understand. Bruno, yes, perhaps, but he was now a cloud of dust blowing across the Quantocks where they had loved to walk. And Val, who, scattering the ashes, had thought he would die any minute, torn apart by utter loneliness, now spent every waking moment of his life longing for someone else.

He got up stiffly – Louise was quiet at last – and rubbed the muscles of his calves. He had woken that morning with a blinding headache and had not cycled either on the road or on the runners in the garage, the first time he had missed for months and his legs knew about it.

The halogen light came on in the Rectory garden. The tortoiseshell cat from the Red Lion sauntered across the grass then stopped and crouched, quite motionless. Val was on the point of turning away when he noticed the blue door was only half visible. A tall wedge of dark shadow stood in for the missing section. The door was standing open.

His heart exploding with sudden joy, Val ran out of the house across the moonlit road and up the narrow carpeted stairs. Into the darkest moments of his life.

CHAPTER ELEVEN

Detective Chief Inspector Barnaby stirred his chopped banana and muesli. Gave a moody sigh. Put his spoon down.

'Is there any more coffee?'

'Doesn't look like it,' said Joyce, directing her attention to the empty cafetière. 'And I'm not making any more. You drink far too much of that stuff as it is. Have you cut down at work?'

'Yes.'

'You promised.'

'*Yes*.' Barnaby pushed his bowl aside. 'For heaven's sake.'

'What was the matter last night?'

'I couldn't sleep.'

He had had fragmentary dreams, vivid little cuttings and snippets all relating to what was overwhelmingly on his mind but juxtaposed in ridiculous combinations that made not the slightest sense. Valentine Fainlight cycling furiously on Ferne Basset village green but never moving from the spot, with Vivienne Calthrop hovering just above the ground behind him like a sequinned barrage balloon. Louise Fainlight in a wetsuit made of crocodile skin, fishing with a billhook in the weeds of a fast-flowing river and catching it on the frame of an old pushchair. Ann Lawrence, young and beautiful, wearing a flowered dress, climbing into an open red car. Straightaway a transparent canopy festooned with tubes and jars fell over her and the car turned into a hospital bed. Lionel Lawrence, in a room like yet unlike Carlotta's, threw ornaments and books around and tore up posters while Tanya, this time an angel in truth with huge feathered wings, perched on top of a bookshelf and shoved two fingers at him, grinning.

Finally there was Jackson floating up from Barnaby's subconscious in the shape of a monstrous rocking sailor doll. It was laughing, a clockwork cackle, and the more it was pushed, the more it laughed and bounced back. Beaten and thumped and pushed and beaten, the mechanical laughter became louder and louder, finally distorting into one long scream. This was when Barnaby awoke and knew it was himself that screamed.

Joyce reached out across the table and took his hand. 'You'll have to let go of this, Tom.'

'I can't.'

'You always say—'

'I know what I always say. This one's different.'

'You're like that man with the whale.'

'That's right.' Barnaby managed a bitter smile. 'Call me Ahab.'

'It'll break sooner or later.'

'Yes.'

'Try and—'

'Joycey, I'm sorry. I'm going to be late.'

If anything, he was twenty minutes early. Joyce followed her husband into the hall, helped him on with his overcoat. Took down a scarf.

'I don't want that.'

320

'Just take it with you. It's really chilly. There's mist in the garden.'

She watched him get into the car from the hall window. Heard the aggressive revving and the engine picking up speed, too early and too fast, as he drove off. Then the telephone called her away.

Something terrible had happened to Val. Louise was so used to her brother getting up first that, on waking to a silent house, she simply assumed he was away doing his daily twenty-mile run.

She flung on some warm trousers and a jersey, made some tea and took it outside. Barnaby had found the garden at Fainlights too rigidly austere for his taste. But it was precisely this constrained formality that appealed to Louise. Edges were straight, low barriers of yew were precisely angled, shrubs were shaped into unmoving elegance by skilful clipping, the dark water in the pool remained unruffled. Even overlaid as it was now by the rattle and roar of the approaching Causton and District Council's Refuse Collection lorry, the scene was very peaceful.

Louise wandered idly around, drinking her tea, stopping to admire a delightful sculpture of a hare and stroking its ears, rubbing a scented leaf between her fingers. Coming to the back wall, she noticed the key was missing from the garden door. It was a large iron key, always turned in the lock against intruders but never removed, Val's theory being that anyone who could gain access to the thing would be in the garden already and if Louise started keeping it in a safe place it would soon get lost.

Louise turned the handle and stepped out onto a

narrow grass verge bordered by a ditch. On the other side of the ditch a long field of stubble bordered by hedges stretched away to the main road. The key was not on this side either. She would look for it after breakfast and buy a bolt and padlock in Causton if it could not be found.

Moving away from the garden, she wandered round to the garage. Though the stack of bikes was there, the Alvis was missing. Then, to her surprise, Louise saw it in the road, parked neatly, close to the kerb. The refuse lorry pulled up. A man took the Fainlights' wheelie-bin and hooked it onto the lifting apparatus. There was a loud thump as the contents were emptied and the bin was banged back onto the pavement. Louise pushed it into the garage.

Returning to the house, she called her brother's name and, receiving no response, went to his room. Val was sitting on a low chair very close to a window overlooking the village street and the Old Rectory drive. On his knees were a pair of field glasses from an earlier birdwatching phase. His fingers gripped the leather strap so tightly the white knuckles seemed to be almost cracking the skin. His car keys were on the floor by his feet.

'Val?' His utter stillness frightened her. 'What is it? What's the matter?'

It was as if he hadn't heard. He didn't even turn his head. Just swayed slightly as if slipping into sleep then jerked himself upright. He still wore his clothes from yesterday.

'Have you been here all night?'

'Nothing.'

Louise stared, bewildered, then realised he

was answering her first question.

'Are you ill? Val?' She reached out and touched him then snatched her hand back. His arm was cold and heavy as a stone. 'You're frozen. I'll get you a hot drink.'

'I'm all right.'

'How long have you been sitting here?'

'Go away, Lou. No, wait! I need a pee.' He handed her the glasses. Then, walking quickly away, 'Don't take your eyes off the house.'

Louise waited for him to come back, not watching any house, with or without the glasses. When he did so he turned from her, once again staring out with feverish concentration, squinting and peering through the lenses.

Louise waited a few moments, sensing she had been forgotten. She was unsure what to do next. Making a cup of tea, the universal English panacea for everything from a headache to fire, flood and pestilence, seemed rather a futile gesture. But he was so cold. And it was better than doing nothing. But then, as she began to move away, Val started to speak.

'I can cope . . . that is, as long as I . . . I *can* cope . . . I'll be able . . . to handle . . . only I've got to . . . then . . . tell me . . . ask him . . . *ask* him . . . torment . . . I can't bear . . . not . . . not . . .'

All this anguished mumbling was punctuated by sucked-in, painful wheezes. He sounded like someone having an asthma attack. Louise waited, devastated, for this wildness to run its course. There was small comfort in knowing that none of it was meant for her. Just before she left the room he brought the glasses up quickly with a little cry then, just as quickly, dropped them. His shoulders sagged with disappointment.

Louise retreated to the kitchen. Making tea and wondering who on earth she could turn to in her dilemma brought her sharply up against the realisation that, now that Ann was not here, there was no one. She and Val had always been self-sufficient, each to the other, while living in Ferne Basset. Keeping yourself to yourself was all very fine until one of you became helpless. She considered ringing their GP then almost immediately abandoned the idea. What was the point? The man would hardly come out to see someone simply because they were utterly wretched and gabbling senselessly to themselves. And if he did, how might Val react? In this present, thoroughly unbalanced state he seemed quite capable of throwing the doctor down the stairs and himself straight after.

What could have happened since they parted company the night before to have reduced him to this pitiful condition? That it was Jax's doing she had no doubt. She wondered if she dared ask Val then quickly decided against it. Not because she feared his reaction but because she was afraid he might decide to tell her the truth.

It wasn't until she returned to his room with the tea and Val turned to her, his eyes vague and terrible, that she remembered that today was Charlie Leathers' funeral.

Straws had been drawn in the Red Lion to decide who should represent the hostelry where Charlie had spent so many miserable hours putting the jovial punters off their beer.

The obvious choice, mine host, was not prepared to

leave the pub and no one blamed him. That left five regulars who, for various reasons, were still around one minute after the suggestion had been mooted. Of these, one was in the Gents, two were playing bar billiards and so missed hearing the proposition. Another, a retired actor, was chatting up Colleen the barmaid, and the last, Harry (Ginger) Nuttings, had had a tin leg since the war and just couldn't make it to the door on time. It was Harry who drew the short straw.

He promised faithfully to turn up at St Thomas in Torment on the stroke of 11 a.m. cometh the day but never did. Explaining at lunchtime – after draining a double Whisky Mac in lieu of attendance money – he told the company that he had unbuckled his leg, as was his habit when taking a nap after breakfast, but on waking found it had rolled under the bed. By the time he had managed to fish it out, the hearse was drawing up level with the church gate and he didn't want to shame them all by turning up late.

'Must have been a small house then,' said the retired actor.

Louise thought so too as she stood, a discreet distance from the family and well away from that cold border of death, the edge of the grave. She was not wearing black, though her wardrobe was full of it, feeling such a gesture would be deeply inappropriate given her casual relationship to the deceased.

Louise wished she had not come. She felt now that Hetty Leathers had only asked her out of politeness and was as surprised to see her as she herself was to be there. Also she worried about leaving Valentine. She had looked back, going through the lych gate, and had seen him staring fixedly through the glass, lonely and abandoned in his retreat like a prisoner in a high tower.

The Leathers family was bearing up bravely. Pauline, holding her mother's hand, was on her left. Pauline's husband, a burly man with cropped red hair, linked arms on the other side. Hetty did not give much evidence of needing their support and all three were concealing their grief well.

Evadne Pleat stood next to them, her face tiny beneath a vast, gauzy meringue of a hat. While appearing to cast her eyes down gravely and respectfully at the coffin, she had actually noted Louise Fainlight's appearance with some concern. She could only see Louise's profile but noted the mouth, turned down as in a tragic mask. Also she was wearing what, for her, was an awful lot of make-up. She was screwing up her eyes and blinking. As if conscious of being watched, she tugged at the dark, satin fall of her hair, pulling it forwards, half concealing her face.

Once Lionel Lawrence had registered that his wife, being no longer in any state to order him about, was unable to force him to do his ecclesiastical duty vis-à-vis their late employee, he had promptly abandoned the whole idea. The Reverend Theo Lightdown, as shocked as anyone by the dreadful news about Mrs Lawrence, understood straightaway that her husband could not leave her side and stepped promptly into the breach.

Unfortunately he knew nothing of Charlie and had to build on the few comments Lionel gave him (rather garbled, actually, but who could blame the poor man?). So the address was not only brief but also somewhat inaccurate. The Reverend Lightdown seemed to sense as much as the five mourners stared at him, dry-eyed and somewhat bewildered. He touched on Adam the gardener, that heavenly forerunner in whose earthy footsteps Charlie had so honourably trod. His love of all growing things and the magic of his "green fingers". His convivial friendships. A dearly loved father and grandad now at peace and waiting patiently for the day when his dear wife and helpmeet of many years would be joining him. At this a look of such horror and distress shadowed the widow Leathers' countenance that the Reverend Lightdown decided to bring the eulogy to a close.

Now, at the graveside, he closed the book of Common Prayer and pressed it gravely to his bosom. Hetty watched as the coffin was slowly and evenly lowered. If tears were gathering, it was at the sight of the beautiful wreath, so thoughtfully chosen by Ann with her sweet, rather childlike, writing on the black-edged card. There was a much more modest, rather ordinary one from Hetty and the family and a bouquet of yellow chrysanthemums from the Fainlights.

The ropes strained and creaked against the varnished wood but the coffin did not tilt or tip one iota. As if all this carefulness mattered, thought Hetty. As if Charlie would care, one way or the other. Or about the floral tributes, come to that. Pauline released her mother's hand and whispered in her ear.

Hetty bent to pick up a handful of earth. She was surprised how dark and rich and crumbly it was. Just like Christmas cake. She threw it down into the grave. It fell on the inscribed brass plate, almost covering her husband's name. He was reduced to C . ar . i . Lea . . . . . now.

Hetty had seen this action done often in television dramas and now began to feel rather like an actress herself. Certainly, she felt no genuine sorrow. She just wanted to get back to the bungalow and see if the grandchildren and Candy were all right. And start serving the sliced ham and salad lunch with tinned salmon and cucumber sandwiches and Battenburg cake that Pauline and little Jenny had set out earlier.

The tiny funeral party began to move away. There was an awkward moment when Louise held out her hand to Hetty and said how very sorry she was and Hetty wasn't sure what the right thing to do was. But Pauline stepped in, simply asking Louise back to the house for a cup of tea if she'd like to come. But Louise said she had an appointment and hurried away.

Evadne was coming back to the bungalow and was looking forward to it. She liked to see her friend in the bosom of her family and the grandchildren were delightful. Once they had negotiated the lych gate, she tucked Hetty's arm in hers and they strolled in the bright autumn sunshine towards Tall Trees Lane, Pauline and Alan close behind.

Hetty mentioned her strange continuous lack of feeling to Evadne who suggested Hetty had a word with her GP. Later in the week she did and Dr Mahoney diagnosed delayed shock. He warned Hetty that grief could not be permanently denied and that she must be sure to come to the surgery if she needed any sort of help. Finally he cautioned that, 'Sorrow can come flooding in at the most unexpected moment.'

But it never did.

★　★　★

There were many things that Barnaby disliked about his work although, fortunately for him, they were outnumbered by things he liked. One of the things he disliked intensely, which almost drove him mad sometimes, was waiting. Waiting for feedback and for reports to be processed. Waiting for scene of crime and postmortem results. Waiting to see people who might or might not have some information regarding a case you were locked into and their first free space was Friday week. Waiting for faxes responding to your faxes, which never turned up, and waiting for photographs to be developed. Waiting for the next lot of perforated paper to come foaming out of the printer. Waiting for whatever lowlife chancer was facing you across the Formica-topped table in the interview room to open his mouth and say something, anything, if only 'fuck off'.

Right now Barnaby was waiting for a fingerprint match on the prints found in Carlotta's place in Stepney with those in the attic at the Old Rectory. Presumably they'd be the same but one had to be certain. There had been two other sets of prints in the attic room, presumably Ann and Lionel Lawrence's for Hetty Leathers had sworn she'd never set foot in there since Carlotta arrived. Lawrence had grudgingly agreed to come into the station at some point to have his taken for purposes of elimination. (More waiting.) Jackson's, already on file, had been compared, with negative results.

The blow-ups from the security camera film lay on Barnaby's desk, mocking him. A man in black mounting a Peugeot cycle which had since vanished. So where could it have been hidden? If you wanted to hide a book, choose a library. But a bike? There were no Halfords in Ferne Basset to slip one machine in among dozens of others. And the clothes – even more important. If they could only find the Lycra shorts, prove the thread in the Humber boot belonged, and link them to Jackson. But if they couldn't – and as time went by this was looking more and more likely – another way had to be found.

As he struggled to perceive what this other way might be, Barnaby was overcome by the haunting fear that somewhere there was one question which, if put to the right person and answered truthfully, would hand him a loose end in the vast web of information he was caught up in. He would then be able to pull on the thread and gradually unravel the mystery. Perhaps he had already asked the question but of the wrong person. More likely, he did not yet understand what the question was.

And how much clearer the way would be if he knew what to jettison. Experience told him that only a fraction of the information that had come flooding in would be of use. Yet only a small percentage could safely be discounted. Eventually (please God) he would know the truth and understand that all he had ever really needed was this simple fact from forensics, that slip of the tongue in an interview, a deliberately misleading conversation that only now could be fully understood.

But for the moment all he could do was wait. Actively wait, that was, for inaction was unbearable to him. He decided to start reading through all the case information from the very beginning. There had not been time until now and reading piecemeal as things came in could never give a cohesive view. He would read slowly, carefully but with a sharp eye. He looked at the calendar. Thursday, 27 August. Over ten days since Carlotta ran away. Eight days since Charlie Leathers died. Maybe today would be his lucky day.

Detective Sergeant Alec Bennet was getting bored. Or rather, more bored. He was bored when he started his surveillance, for nothing is more boring than knowing you are going to be sitting in a car hour after hour staring at a house in the vain hope that your quarry will rush out and drive off to somewhere incredibly glamorous and there start doing lots of very exciting things that were against the law.

In fact what happened ninety-nine times out of a hundred was that either they never came out or, if they did come out, it was to nip round to the corner shop for some fags, a six-pack and a handful of Instants then go straight back in again.

It struck Bennet that the Old Rectory could have been better placed. He could see the forecourt of the Red Lion in his left-hand wing mirror and would give a lot to be doing his lookout from a window seat in the lounge while getting to grips with a Ploughman's and a half of lager. But it was not to be.

His stomach told him it was one o'clock. He unwrapped his corned beef and Branston pickle sandwiches, put his jam turnover in its separate waxed paper to one side and spread a pretty flowered paper napkin on his knees. Julie was daintily thorough in all her wifely duties – well, nearly all.

Still observing as he unscrewed his Thermos, the policeman became uncomfortably aware that he was himself observed. There was a prickly feeling on the skin of his face and neck and his hands became unpleasantly moist. He did not look up or round. Just drank his tea and ate his sandwich.

Then he noticed, on the wall surrounding the Rectory, two discs of lemon sunlight dancing about. Field glasses. He got out of the car, made something of a show stretching his arms and legs then strolled off as if to take a turn round the Green.

The watcher was at an upstairs window at that extraordinary building that looked as if it should be housing not human beings but a small rainforest. He was motionless, his gaze riveted on the Rectory. So, thought Bennet, sauntering back and climbing into the car, that makes two of us. He wondered if this little detail was worth ringing in but as the guy was well distanced, and so still he could well be in the throes of a near-death experience, Bennet decided not to bother.

What he would do was drive to the far side of the Green. That way he would still be able to see the Rectory gates and the splendid silver car outside the glass house but Four Eyes could not see him. However, hardly had he replaced the plastic cup on his tartan Thermos when a car, very old, large and black, drove quite quickly out of the gates, turned left and set off on the road to Causton.

DS Bennet swept his napkin, jam turnover and flask to the floor with one hand and switched on the ignition with the other. He had been briefed that, should the car emerge, it would definitely be his man as no one else in the house could drive. Eyes fixed firmly on the road ahead, he did not at first notice that, within a second of his own departure, the shining Alvis was on his tail.

Barnaby, having been engrossed for over an hour reading and re-reading all interviews pertaining to the case, was staring at the wall when Sergeant Troy put his head round the door.

'God, is it lunchtime already?'

'Jackson's making a run for it.'

'Brilliant.' Barnaby said a silent thank you as he reached for his coat. Four more hours and he'd have lost the lookout. 'Let's hope he's not just popping into Causton for a bottle of something to touch up his roots.'

'Bennet says he's on the Beaconsfield road.'

'Sounds promising.' They made their way briskly to the lift. 'Has Bennet been spotted?'

'He thinks not. He's running three, four cars behind Jackson at the minute. And Fainlight's Alvis is also in the queue.'

'Really?'

'Oh, yeah. Very quick off the mark. Watching from the house, apparently. His car's even further back. Bennet gets the feeling he's anxious not to be spotted.'

'If we're going any distance we'll need petrol. Better stop at the Fall End service station.'

Within half an hour it seemed almost certain that the Humber was making for London. Jackson had bypassed Causton altogether, driving straight to Beaconsfield then linking up with the M40. Keeping him in sight would be 'a piece of piss' according to DS Bennet.

'He couldn't overtake a five-year-old on rollerskates

in that bloody hearse, sir. We're talking sixty all the way. And that's going flat out.'

'Where's Fainlight?'

'Pardon?'

'The Alvis.'

'Still behind me. Keeping a low profile. Or as low as you can driving something out of a Bond movie.'

Bennet then broke into 'Live and Let Die' and Barnaby quickly switched his mobile off. The irritation barely lasted a second. Instead he began to dwell happily on how kindly Fate was treating him for a change. For, if you had to follow someone in a car, there could be few more discreet and surefire ways of keeping them in sight than trundling along on the inside lane of a motorway.

'We never did get a London address for Jackson, did we, chief?'

'No. He went to the Lawrences almost straight from prison. Stayed a week or two in a hostel to sort his stuff out. Before then he just drifted. No fixed abode, as they say.'

'Wouldn't fancy that much.'

'Like I said, he's not clever.'

'So he could be going almost anywhere?'

'He could be. But I don't think he is.'

Somewhere between Paddington and Regent's Park the silver Alvis overtook Bennet's Escort. He didn't actually see this happen. To tell the truth, the Alvis had been several cars behind, invisible to all intents and purposes, for the last half-hour and Bennet had half forgotten it. He hadn't even noticed it jump lanes.

He wasn't worried. As long as he kept the corpse

and cart, as he had christened the Humber, in sight it was immaterial who else joined the party. He didn't even have to hang back because, as the chief had pointed out during their last exchange, to Fainlight the dark blue Escort hardly stood out. Even if noticed it would be just another car on the road.

As all three vehicles passed over Blackfriars Bridge, Troy was circling Hyde Park.

'You sure you've got the geography right, Sergeant? And don't tell me we're taking the scenic route. I've got eyes.'

'Yes, sir.' Troy remembered looking forward only the other day to driving in London. Saw it as a challenge, which it certainly was. He could handle it, no question, it was just that if he didn't get into the left-hand lane soon he'd be going round and round the Marble Arch till he was dizzy and God help him then when they finally came to a halt. He signalled, swerved out and got a trumpet blast from a foghorn up his exhaust that turned his bowels to water.

'Short cut, chief. Avoiding Blackfriars. Gets dead dodgy this time of day.'

The silence was worse than a reprimand.

'Whereas this way, nip across Waterloo Bridge and, bingo, we're in Shoreditch.'

'Looks like Oxford Street to me.'

And so it was. They crept gradually down, overtaking, at half a snail's pace, huge red doubledeckers, several of which had a notice on their backsides thanking you for letting them pull out. Troy had a fleeting but vivid picture of what might happen if they pulled out and you didn't let them and decided that, on balance, it might be best not to argue.

He couldn't help noticing the extremely hostile attitude shown by the drivers of black cabs, of which there were many. They hooted, they stopped him overtaking, they tried to cut him up. One man screwed his finger into his forehead and yelled, 'Wanker!'

'I've heard about London taxis,' said Troy. 'I didn't know they were as bad as this.'

'You're not supposed to be here.'

'What?'

'Buses and cabs only.'

'Why don't they tell you?'

'We've just passed a sign.'

They crawled round Piccadilly Circus where the steps circling Eros were invisible under a crowd of young people eating, drinking and lolling about. Two appeared to be wholeheartedly trying out the god's first principle for size.

They edged down the Haymarket and round Trafalgar Square, jam packed with tourists, most of whom were generously feeding the pigeons. The pigeons also gave without counting the cost and Barnaby regarded his car's spattered bonnet sourly as they finally made their way over into Shoreditch. DS Bennet came through on Barnaby's mobile and described his position. Just outside Whitechapel Tube.

'He'll probably be turning left any minute, Bennet. Heading for Lomax Road, number seventeen. If he enters the house, fine. Just stay close. If he tries to leave, detain him. We're only five minutes or so behind you.'

'Right, sir.'

As DS Bennet switched off, the Humber moved

away from the traffic lights, followed by about a dozen cars, including the Alvis. The Escort was held up by a red light but catching up wasn't a problem. The flow of the traffic was pretty smooth and Bennet could see well ahead. He watched the Humber turn left and, a few moments later, the Alvis did the same.

Turning himself, Bennet discovered that they were indeed at the top end of Lomax Road. But then something went wrong. Traffic moved more and more slowly and finally stopped. Car horns started to blare. Motorists were putting their heads out of the windows of their vehicles and abusing no one and nothing in particular. DS Bennet got out of his car, walked a little way looking ahead, trying to find the source of the hold up. Located it. And started to run.

The Alvis was in the middle of the road. The driver had simply come to a halt, got out and walked away. A little further down, Bennet saw the Humber awkwardly jammed into a too small parking space, the rear end sticking out.

He hurried along the pavement. The DCI had suggested number seventeen. He could hear shouting inside the house from several doors away. On his home patch an excited clutch of neighbours would already be gathering. Here passersby just passed indifferently by.

The front door was ajar. Bennet hesitated. He had been told simply to watch the house but a disturbance was a disturbance. And with the Alvis holding the traffic up, who knew how long it would take the DCI to get here? The volume of sound from the voices, both male, escalated. One was cracking with violence, the other let forth anguished screams of pain which became transmuted into grunts and snarls and panting.

Once the verbals became physical, Bennet decided to act. He wondered whether to call the DCI before going in then decided against it. This half-second hesitation was to prove fatal. As he opened the front door he looked upwards and saw two figures struggling on the landing. One fell backwards against a wooden stair rail. It splintered under his weight then gave way entirely. Bennet watched in horror as a man tumbled through the air, landing with tremendous force on the stone floor directly in front of him.

It was some considerable time before Barnaby was able to interview the survivor of this terrible confrontation. The local police were on the spot a good half-hour before the chief inspector who left his sergeant stuck opposite the White Hart and half walked, half ran to the house in Lomax Road. They had already called out their medical officer, driven the Alvis away, and were now trying to clear the still honking traffic jam.

Arrangements had been made to remove the man on the hall floor, whose skull had been crushed as a result of his fall, to the morgue of the London Hospital as soon as some transport could get through. Meanwhile he was invisible underneath a bedcover removed from the flat upstairs where the argument had started.

DS Bennet sat on the stairs, devastated with shame. When the DCI arrived he sprang up.

'Sir, Christ, I'm sorry. I don't know what to say. I heard them – how violent it was getting. I should have gone in before. I just didn't know whether – what . . . I'm so sorry.'

Barnaby crouched down, lifted a corner of the bedcover and carefully replaced it. He touched Bennet lightly on the shoulder as he went by.

'No need to be sorry, Sergeant.'

Several hours later, extensive liaising having taken place between the Thames Valley and the Metropolitan police forces, Valentine Fainlight, having been formally charged, was released into the custody of two officers from Causton CID.

At the station he washed and changed his clothes for a clean shirt and jeans his sister had brought along. She had refused to go home and had been waiting in reception now for almost two hours.

Barnaby and Troy had been sitting in a room on the ground floor at the back of the CID building for roughly half that time, attempting to get some sense out of Fainlight, with no success whatsoever. In London he had been seen by a doctor, examined, his cuts and bruises attended to and declared fit to be interviewed. He had not spoken there either.

Physically fit, that meant. As for the rest of him, Barnaby was not so sure. Grievous bodily harm was a term well understood in police circles. But where was the definition to cover grievous mental harm? For that was surely what the end of Fainlight's searingly destructive relationship had brought about.

He sat with his head in his hands, his shoulders bowed. He had been offered food, tea, water and had refused all, shaking his head without speaking. Barnaby had given up switching the tape on and off. Now he tried again.

'Mr Fainlight—?' Barnaby could see the man was

not being obdurate. He suspected that Sergeant Troy's presence and his own had hardly registered in spite of the time that had passed. Fainlight was simply consumed by quiet, impenetrable grief.

Barnaby got up, gestured to Troy to stay put and left the room. Their prisoner was not the sort of man who would refuse to talk to the police out of principle. When he had recovered from the shock, he would tell them what had happened. But when might that be?

As far as the chief inspector had been able to ascertain, until the moment Jackson fell there were no witnesses to the fight which meant only Fainlight could tell them what had actually occurred. And it was in his own interests as well as Barnaby's that the sooner he talked, the better. Presumably he would not wish to remain in a cell until his trial which could well be months away.

All of this Barnaby explained to Louise Fainlight in the reception area. She had sprung up on recognising him. She was much changed. He had never seen her without make-up and her naked face, stamped with the most wretched anxiety, was grey and lined. Asked her age now, he would have guessed around fifty.

'When can I see my brother?'

'I was hoping—'

'Has he got someone with him? What about a solicitor? That's his right, isn't it?'

'Yes. Do you have a family solicitor?'

'She's in London. When can I see Val?'

'Come and sit down, Miss Fainlight.'

Barnaby took her arm and they made for an unwelcoming wooden slatted bench. Louise sat reluctantly and on the very edge, plucking at the fringe of her jersey.

'I'm sure you want to help your brother—'

'Of course I do!'

'And we're hoping you can persuade him to talk to us.'

'What, *now*?'

'The sooner he answers—'

'You've been at him at that other place for hours. He should be resting.'

'He can't be released—'

'Is it true, about Jax?'

'Yes.'

'Oh, poor Val!' And she began soundlessly to cry.

There was no question of leaving Louise and her brother alone together. But Barnaby arranged the most discreet and unthreatening police presence possible. Sergeant Brierley sat, not at the table but on a chair by the far wall. Barnaby was sure that within minutes Fainlight and his sister would forget she was there and so it proved to be. An assurance had been demanded by Louise that no recordings would be made of any conversation with her brother. Though longing to be with him, she was determined to make no contribution that might reinforce, even inadvertently, the prosecution's case.

Barnaby was sitting in the next room along the corridor. There was a small, wire-meshed window set into the wall and through this he could see and hear Louise and her brother. They sat on hard metal chairs side by side. Louise held Valentine clumsily and at an awkward angle in her arms, rocking him back and forth like a baby. This went on for almost twenty minutes and Barnaby was just about to give up when Fainlight threw back his head and let out a terrible howl followed by a series of harsh, ratching sobs.

'We're off,' said Sergeant Troy who had only just come in. 'I've asked them to bring some tea. Do you want a Mars while they're at it?'

'So when I saw the door standing open I thought it was our signal. You can imagine, Lou, how I felt.' Tears of pain flowed down Valentine's face. He wiped them with the back of his sleeve. The table top and floor were littered with screwed-up tissues. Louise took her brother's hand and pressed it to her lips.

'I ran over – I nearly fell on the stairs I climbed so fast – but there was no one there. And I realised it must have been left open by accident.'

He gripped her fingers so tightly she almost cried out.

'God, Lou, if only I'd left then. Why didn't I just walk away? If I'd done that he'd still be alive.'

Louise closed her face against joy. Shuttered the light in her eyes. 'I know, love, I know.'

'Then there was that click on the phone you get when someone picks up an extension, and I thought it might be him. And that he might be ringing me. I swear that was it, Lou. I wasn't spying or anything. And when I heard his voice, I couldn't believe it! So tender, so loving and gentle . . . saying things I'd never dared to even dream of hearing. That she was the only one who had ever mattered, first in his heart now and always, not to worry about anything, he would be with her as soon as he could get away, everything would be all right . . .'

Louise's heart turned over with pity. She produced more tissues and once more patiently dried his face. She would need to be very patient in the weeks and months to come. Patient and disingenuous. Tender, loving and gentle.

'And then, of course, I had to know. I had to see her. Not to do harm, though I was blind with jealousy, but just to see what sort of person could bring this miracle about. So I sat and watched. And when Jax left the house I followed him.

'He drove to this place in the East End. I just stopped the car, left it where it was and ran after him. They were in a room at the top of the stairs. The door was open and I could see them hugging, laughing. You'd think they hadn't seen each other for years. And then he saw me – on the landing. And everything changed.

'I've never seen such anger in a human being. He screamed and shouted, and the more I tried to say I was sorry, the more violent he became. How dare I bring my . . . my dirt, my filth into her home. I was a sick fuck. A pile of vomit. I wasn't fit to live. I think he was half mad. And all the time she was talking quietly, trying to calm him down. And then he hit me.

'I fell down and as I was getting up I heard her cry, Terry, Terry, don't. And I saw his face and I've never been so frightened in my life. I thought, he's going to kill me. So I started to fight back, I couldn't help it, and we were on the landing when he . . .'

Louise gently rested her hand on his arm. A fragile comfort but he cringed as if battered. 'Val, it was an accident—'

'It was my fault!'

'They've got to understand that. You can't spend the rest of your life in prison.'

'I don't care where I spend the rest of my life. I just hope to God it's bloody short.' He fell silent for a moment then said, 'The joke is, Lou, the bloody tragic joke is *I* would have died for *him*.'

In the adjoining room, Troy drained his cup of lukewarm tea and Barnaby peered inside his third sandwich (rather fatty ham, pale pink tomato and salad cream) and put it back on the plate. Troy was just stacking both cups and saucers on the tray when Fainlight started to speak again. Barnaby grabbed his sergeant's arm and hissed for quiet.

'The odd thing was I'd seen her before, this girl.'

'Really?' Louise sounded incredulous. 'How could you have?'

'At the Old Rectory. It was Carlotta.'

'But . . . that's wonderful, Val! Everyone thought she'd drowned. I must tell Ann—' And then she stopped, remembering.

'Her hair was different, a funny orange colour, and cut all short and spiky. But it was Carlotta all right.'

CHAPTER TWELVE

In the end they caught her quite quickly. Barnaby had feared she would go to earth, change her appearance again and simply vanish into the city's underworld. If not London then Birmingham or Manchester or Edinburgh. And with no photograph to circulate, the chances of picking her up were practically nil.

But, to cover every exit, both of the names she had been using were flashed to all air and sea ports and rail terminals to the Continent. She was spotted by the Eurostar departure point at Waterloo, travelling under a name that Barnaby immediately recognised. The name by which she had first introduced herself, Tanya Walker.

A sorrier sight, thought Barnaby as she was brought into the interview room, he had rarely seen. When he was a constable on the beat he had sometimes had to answer calls from department stores who had found a toddler that had become separated from its mother. The same bewildered panic in her eyes, the same wailing loss. What was it about that vicious bastard Jackson that could bring this girl and Fainlight likewise to their knees in sorrow?

The tape was running. And, unlike the interview two days earlier, this time there was no difficulty extracting information. She answered all his questions unhesitatingly, without ever a pause to reflect, in a flat, colourless voice. She did not care. She had nothing left to lose. And thank God she did, thought the chief inspector, for with Jackson dead, how else would he have unravelled the tangled mess that had been jamming up his thought processes for the past two weeks.

Though Barnaby had had several hours to prepare for this interview, there was more than one aspect to the case and he had not quite decided which to broach first. He turned them over in his mind in reverse order of importance. First came the least interesting – the girl's relationship with Jackson. She was plainly in love with him, he had had power over her, she would do anything to please him – the old, old story. Then her version of what had happened in Lomax Road. Third, the background to her connection to Carlotta Ryan, the girl who had lived in the room next door. Finally her exact role in the elaborate intrigue at the Old Rectory which had culminated in the murder of Charlie Leathers. Though this last was by far the most interesting and important, Barnaby perversely chose to begin with the third.

'Tell me about Carlotta, Tanya.'

'I told you about her. When you come to the flat.'

'What happened to her?'

She looked vacantly at him.

'Is she still alive?'

'Course she's still alive. What you on about?'

'Then where is she?' asked Sergeant Troy.

'Having the time of her bloody life, I should think. Halfway round the world on a cruise ship.'

'And how did that come about?'

'An ad in that stage paper. She auditioned about ten

days before she was due to go down the Rectory. They offered her the job, topless dancing. A year's contract. She jumped at it.' Tanya looked across at Sergeant Troy and for the first time showed a spark of animation. She said, 'Wouldn't you?'

Troy did not respond. It would not have been appropriate but also he didn't want to. He remembered his first meeting with this girl and how touched he had been by her appearance and larky chatter and the sad fact that she did not know who her dad was. Probably just another lie. He tightened his lips against the chance of a smile, unaware of how sanctimonious it made him look.

'So whose idea was it that you go to the Lawrences instead?' asked Barnaby, pleased that at least he knew now why the flat had been cleaned out. 'Yours or hers?'

'Terry's. He liked the thought of being able to keep an eye on me. Mind you, he'd get up the Smoke when he could. He was here when you turned up. Hiding in the bedroom.'

Barnaby cursed silently for a moment. But his voice was even as he said, 'So you knew him before?'

'For ever. On and off.'

'Must have been mostly off,' said Sergeant Troy. 'All the time he's been banged up.'

'Yeah, mostly.' Tanya looked across at Troy then with grave contempt. Troy flushed with resentment and thought she'd got a bloody cheek. Even so, he was the first to look away.

'But you pretended otherwise?' said Barnaby.

'S'right. He didn't want the connection to show.'

'Because of the grand plan?'

'Partly. But also it's his nature to conceal things. It

was the only way he ever felt safe.'

'So how was it supposed to work?'

'It was brilliant. We had two plans, one for day, one for after dark, depending on when Mrs L took off. I lifted some jewellery, old-fashioned stuff she were keen on.'

'It belonged to her mother.'

'Yeah, whatever.'

Barnaby held out his hand. 'You wouldn't happen . . .?'

Tanya hesitated.

'Come on, Tanya. You've admitted taking them. Giving them back will look good on your sheet.'

Tanya opened her bag and put the earrings in Barnaby's hand. They looked very small. Small but beautiful.

'Now you're going to flog 'em, ain'tcha?'

'That's right,' said Sergeant Troy.

Barnaby asked what happened next.

'When she come to my room about it I went mad, tearing up stuff and screaming me life was over. Then I ran away. We knew she'd come after me 'cause she was like that.'

'Concerned,' suggested Barnaby.

'It worked perfect. If it hadn't, Terry'd got plenty other ideas up his sleeve.'

'She thought she'd pushed you in,' said Barnaby. 'She was frantic.'

'That was the *point*,' Tanya explained patiently. 'She ain't going to pay up if I'd jumped, is she?'

'Why should she pay up at all?' snapped Sergeant Troy.

'Because she can afford it. Because she's got a

bloody great house and somebody to clean it for her and somebody else to do the fucking garden. And because she's never done a stroke of work in her life!'

'I take it you didn't like her,' said Barnaby.

'Ohh . . .' Tanya sighed. 'She weren't too bad. It were holy Joe I couldn't stand. Always touching you. Accidentally on purpose – know what I mean? Hands like damp dishcloths.'

'So where did you get out of the river?'

'Same place I got in. Terry had floated an old tyre days before. Tied with a rope to a hook under the bridge. I grabbed it, hung on till she'd run away then climbed out.'

I knew about the tyre. Barnaby flashed back to the river-bank search report. A patch of scrub – crisp packets, a pushchair frame, an old tyre. Used as a swing, the description had said, because it still had the rope round it. And I passed on that. Perhaps Joyce was right. Maybe it was time to pack it in.

'Then where did you go?' Sergeant Troy was picturing her, despite himself, cold, shivering and soaking wet in the late dark.

'Nipped back to the house. Hid in the garden till Terry come home. Spent the night in his flat. Next day hitched to Causton and took a train to the Smoke.'

Barnaby controlled his breathing, kept the rising anger in its place. Put aside his thoughts on hours, days even, of wasted time (not least his own), shifting seas of paper detailing useless interviews regarding the night in question, extensive inquiries with wide-ranging health and police authorities about a possible drowning. In short, a massive waste of desperately stretched police resources.

'So what went wrong?' asked Sergeant Troy. He had noted the savage set of the chief's mouth and the angry flush on his cheeks and felt the next question might be better coming from him.

'That cross-eyed git, Charlie Leathers. He's what went wrong. Terry'd done his blackmail letter, addressed to her, marked Personal. I posted it, first class, main office in Causton. Being that close you nearly always get twenty-four-hour delivery. He watches for the van then makes up some excuse to get into the house to see she's got it all right.'

'How was he supposed to know that?' asked Sergeant Troy.

'Do me a favour,' said Tanya. 'She ain't going to be tripping around singin' oh what a perfect day, I wanna spend it with you, with that burning a hole in her pocket, is she?'

'I suppose not,' said Barnaby. He was thinking of Ann Lawrence. Kind, ineffectual, innocent. Going quietly about her daily business. Opening her post.

'Anyway, she'd got it all right. He found her half dead with fright and the letter on the floor. Trouble is, it weren't his letter. It had stuck-on writing just the same but there was less words. And arranged different. You can imagine how he felt.'

'Must have been quite a blow,' said Barnaby.

'Yeah. But he's at his best, Terry, with his back against the wall. So, figuring a blackmail letter means payment, he watches her all the time. He thought she'd probably have to deliver at night and that's what happened. So he tails her, planning to pick up the money hisself. After all, we're the ones who earned it. *But it weren't his intention to kill nobody.*'

Barnaby, tempted to say, 'Oh, that's all right then,' restrained the impulse. He would do nothing to interfere with this, so far, wonderfully simple unravelling.

'But Charlie got there first. He was actually taking the money when Terry spotted him.'

'Some people,' muttered Sergeant Troy.

'Just as well Terry happened to have a length of wire in his pocket,' said Barnaby.

'You gotta carry something for protection in this dee and ay,' Tanya explained, less patient by now. Her attitude seemed to be that Barnaby, of all people, should appreciate what a wicked world was out there. 'And just as well he did, the way things went.'

'How do you mean?'

'Charlie drew a knife on him. They had a terrible struggle.'

The two policemen looked at each other. Both remembered the orderly neatness of the murder scene.

'So it was definitely self-defence.' Tanya, having noticed and read the look, became quite vehement.

'And what about the dog?' asked Sergeant Troy. 'Was that "self-defence"?'

'What you on about? What dog?'

Barnaby put his hand quickly on his sergeant's arm to stop any passionate denunciation of Jackson's cruelty to the animal. The last thing he wanted was an emotional diversion.

'So what happened to Terry's letter, Tanya?'

'It come the next day. He caught the mail van, offered to take the post up to the house and got it back. Then he sent another, by hand this time, like Charlie, asking for five.'

351

'And no doubt it would have been more the third time?'

'Why not? Terry reckoned that place must have been worth a quarter of a million. Anyway, he said we should give her a breather – a false sense of security, like. Maybe for a month. We was going to Paris for a few days. He'd got the five grand—'

'And you've got it now, Tanya. Right?'

'No. He never brought it with him.'

'You expect us to believe that?' said Troy.

'It's true. He hid it 'cause he thought you might be round the flat with a warrant. Then he couldn't pick it up 'cause that filthy poof was spying on him. With binoculars.'

Barnaby thought that certainly tied in with what Bennet had later told him about Fainlight. The money was probably stashed with the clothes in the rucksack. Find that and you'd copped the jackpot.

'Do you know how he came by the second lot of money?' Sergeant Troy attempted ironic patience but, as always, failed to pull it off. Even to himself he sounded merely peevish.

'Same as the first time. How many ways are there to collect a drop?'

'Try following the victim, crashing her head down on the bonnet of a car and just taking it.'

Tanya stared at Barnaby who had spoken, then at Sergeant Troy and back to Barnaby again.

'You tricky bastards. You wouldn't tell such lies if he was here to defend himself. She left it in Carter's Wood just like the first time.'

'Mrs Lawrence didn't leave any money anywhere. She'd decided not to pay and was returning it to the bank.'

'Yeah, well, that might be what she says—'

'She isn't saying anything,' said Troy. 'She's been in intensive care for the last three days. It's not even certain that she'll recover.'

Barnaby looked across the table at the girl. She had begun to look pitifully uncertain and his gaze was not unsympathetic.

'He did have a record of violence, Tanya.'

'No he didn't.' She immediately contradicted herself. 'There was reasons.'

'For a knife attack on—'

'He never done that. Terry was the youngest, he took the blame so he could belong. The actual guy would've got life. On the streets you gotta be accepted. If you're not, you're finished.'

Troy wanted to ask about the old man left in the gutter but was strangely reluctant. The fact was he was fighting sympathetic feelings himself. Not for Jackson, never that, but for her. She was visibly distressed now and was struggling not to cry. Barnaby had no such qualms.

'There was another incident. An old man—'

'Billy Wiseman. He was lucky.'

'*Lucky?*'

'I know people – he'd never have got up again.'

'What do you mean, Tanya?'

'I were ten when they fostered me, him and his wife. What he done – I couldn't even say it in words. Over and over. Sometimes in the middle of the night I'd wake up and he'd be . . . Then, when I were fourteen, I were down by Limehouse Walk with Terry. I just started talking and it all came out. He never said nothing. But his face was terrible.' Tanya gave a single cry then. A wild sound, like a frightened bird.

Barnaby said, 'I'm sorry.'

And Troy thought, Christ, I've had enough of this.

'I hadn't seen him for ages. He'd been in two or three places, then Barnardo's. I'd been moved about – once we lost touch entirely. Not knowing where each other was. And that was the worst. Like everything in the world closing down at once.' Tears poured down like rain. 'He was the only person who ever loved me.'

Troy clumsily attempted comfort. 'You'll meet someone else, Tanya.'

'What?' She gazed at him blankly.

'You're young. Pretty—'

'You stupid fuck.' She drew away from them then, staring from one to the other with fastidious contempt. 'Terry wasn't my boy friend. He was my brother.'

They would have solved the crime anyway in a couple of days as things turned out. When the prints in Tanya's room in Stepney turned out to be a perfect match with the ones in the Old Rectory attic.

Or when Barnaby remembered that Vivienne Calthrop had described Carlotta as far too short to be a model so how come she had to duck her head not to bang it on the Old Rectory door frame? Or when the bicycle on which Jackson had ridden back from Causton was found propped against the wall of Fainlight's garage under half a dozen others. And the money, still in the saddle bag. The rucksack and clothes were never found. Received opinion in the incident room had it that Jackson had buried them under the other rubbish in the Fainlights' wheelie-bin the day before it was emptied.

Valentine Fainlight, when questioned further, admitted that he had shown Jackson round the house and garden on one occasion when his sister was out. And that the man could have taken the garden key away while he was looking elsewhere but what the hell did it matter now anyway and, Jesus, when in hell were they going to leave him alone?

'So how do you see it being worked, chief?' asked Sergeant Troy as he and Barnaby walked away from the ravishing glass construction for the last time.

'Presumably he biked over that back field, through the gate into the garden, down the side of the house and into the garage. Then he could duck down behind the Alvis, change clothes and hide his stuff to be sorted later.'

'What d'you think he'll get, Fainlight?'

'Depends. Murder's a serious charge.'

'It was an accident. You heard what he said to his sister.'

'I also heard him say he was blind with jealousy. He knew the man, Troy. They had a relationship. Which means murder is a possibility. The Met were right to charge him.'

'But he was allowed bail.' Troy was getting quite worked up. 'That must mean something.'

'It means he's not regarded as a danger to the public. Not that he hasn't committed any crime.'

'So he might be found guilty?'

'Depends.'

'On what?'

'Whether anti-homosexual bias can be weeded out in the jury. How impressed they are by Fainlight's standing as a well-known author. How appalled they are when Jackson's record is read out. How they respond to Tanya Walker's testimony, which will be hostile to say the least.'

Tanya's interview had concluded with her description of the fight that led to her brother's death. According to her, Valentine had burst in, attacked Terry, dragged him over the landing and forced him back through the stair rail. Afraid for her own life, she had run away down the fire escape.

'The Crown have a witness as well, chief. DS Bennet.'

'He only saw Jackson fall. She can say what led up to it.'

'And lie.'

'Probably. The girl's heart is broken, she'll want revenge. And who could prove perjury?'

'Do for his books, this, won't it?'

'As he writes for children, I would say so.'

Barnaby had been shocked at Fainlight's appearance. He looked like a zombie. In his eyes the death of all life and hope. There was not even the colour of despair. His frame, now much less stocky, folded in on itself with utter weariness. He seemed inches shorter, pounds lighter.

Barnaby didn't envy Louise. He was sure she could tough it out, nurse Fainlight through his dark night of the soul. She had the love and the patience and, certainly at present, the energy. Everything about her had shone. Her eyes, her skin and hair. Her cheeks were rosy, not with the usual skilfully applied cosmetics but with health and happiness.

And she had time on her side. The man who had caused her brother so much agony no longer existed.

At least in the flesh. But in Fainlight's heart – that was something else. And in his mind, where all troubles start and end, what of that? Eaten up by guilt and loneliness, starved of the only company his unhappy soul craved, how would he survive, in or out of prison?

'If only,' murmured Barnaby to himself. 'Sometimes I think they're the saddest words in the English language.'

'I'd say pointless more,' said Sergeant Troy.

'You would,' replied the chief inspector. He was used to his sergeant's phlegmatic attitude and occasionally even welcomed it as a sensible corrective to his own rather free-ranging imagination.

'What's done's done,' pursued Troy. Then, just to make sure there had been no misunderstanding, 'Junna regret ay reean.'

They were making their way now across the Green, passing the village sign with its robustly priapic badger, stooks of wheat, cricket bats and lime-green chrysanthemum.

Barnaby noticed several pale furry dogs hurling themselves about in a transport of delight, happily too far away to make even the most brief exchange of courtesies with their owner feasible. A small terrier attempted to join in, not making too bad a fist of it. The owners of the dogs walked arm in arm, heads close together, talking.

'Look who's over there,' said Sergeant Troy.

'I've seen who's over there,' replied the chief inspector, quickening his step. 'Thanks very much.'

A few moments later they came to the river. Barnaby stopped by the low bridge to look into the swiftly flowing water. He wondered how it had looked in the moonlight on the night Tanya ran away. There must have been a moon for Charlie Leathers to see the faces of the two women as they swayed on the bridge locked together in a struggle which ended with an almighty splash. And he thought what he saw was for real, as we all do. Who questions the evidence of their own eyes?

'I was thinking, sir. That Tanya—'

'Poor lass,' said Barnaby, somewhat to his own surprise.

'Exactly,' Troy responded eagerly. 'If anyone needed a friend—'

'Don't even think about it.'

'There wouldn't be anything in it—'

'Yes there would. Eventually.'

'But what'll happen to her?'

'She'll survive,' said Barnaby, with a confidence he didn't really feel. 'After all, she managed to fool us.'

'I suppose.'

'Not drowning, Troy, but waving.'

'Pardon?'

'Never mind.'

Troy bit back a tsk of irritation. It was always happening, this sort of thing. The chief'd say something a little bit difficult, a bit obscure. Some quote or other from something nobody in their right mind had ever heard of. Then, when he tried for an explanation, he was brushed off.

Fair enough, you might say. But then don't go on at this person for not knowing about opera and theatre and heavy music and books and stuff. Troy had looked up Philistine in Talisa Leanne's dictionary when he had got home the other night and was not best pleased. Was it any wonder he was 'a person deficient in liberal culture' when every time he asked a question some know-all not a stone's throw away was for ever shutting him up.

'How about some lunch in the Red Lion?'

'Sounds good, chief.'

'What do you fancy? My treat.'

'Pie and chips'd be nice. And some of that raspberry Pavlova.'

'Excellent,' said Barnaby as they strode across the forecourt. 'That should keep you on your toes.'

As thing turned out, Louise did not personally nurse her brother back to health. When Valentine returned to Fainlights, it was simply for the few days it took to organise the packing of his clothes, computer and personal files, and a few books. He planned to rent somewhere in London until the trial which he was told would probably not be for several months.

While he was looking for somewhere to stay he was offered the attic flat in his publisher's house in Hampstead. The usual tenant, the publisher's son, was now in his third year at Oxford and rarely at home. Though it was rather cramped, Valentine settled there and gradually gave up the idea of looking for another place until the future became more clear. Not that he would have used such a phrase. He rarely thought beyond the present day or even the present moment, simply drifting through the hours in a state of stupefied loneliness.

Louise rang constantly. In the end he used to pull the plug, sometimes for days at a time. Once or twice, at her insistent persuasion, they met for lunch but it was not a success. Val was not hungry and her worried urging that he must eat got on his nerves. The second time they parted, Louise was struggling not to cry and Val was guiltily assuring her that it was all his fault before hugging her in a stiffly formal way and saying, 'Keep in touch.'

In the train returning to Great Missenden, Louise's natural resilience reasserted itself. It followed that these things took time. She just hadn't appreciated quite how much time. Everything would be all right, eventually. Still, she was rather glad, getting into her little yellow car at the station, that she would not be going home to an empty house.

When Ann was finally ready to leave hospital for what she had been warned might be quite a lengthy period of convalescence, she was unsure where to go. Her soul revolted at the idea of returning to the Old Rectory. The image of her childhood home had become so abhorrent she almost felt she never wanted even to see it again. But her only relative was an elderly aunt in Northumberland whom Ann had not seen for almost twenty years, during which their correspondence had been perfunctory to say the least. There was also the necessity, as a post-operative outpatient, to be near the hospital. Then, as the day of her release drew near, Louise suggested to Ann that she stay at Fainlights.

Louise had visited Stoke Mandeville almost every day and though very little was said on either side, the long silences were never uncomfortable. Both women, having grown confident in each other's company, felt the arrangement would suit them.

Inevitably there was a certain awkwardness when Ann first arrived. They had to get used to living together. Ann wanted to do more than she was able out of gratitude. Louise refused all help, convinced she could manage by herself, though for years she'd never tried. (On hearing of Valentine's crime and subsequent arrest, the domestic agency promptly struck the name Fainlight from their books.)

Eventually it was Hetty, calling in frequently anyway to see Ann, who started helping out. This suited everyone. Louise because she didn't have to do house-work, which she loathed. Ann because she loved seeing Hetty, almost the only constant in her life from its very beginning. And Hetty because she needed the money for removal expenses. She had managed to get a council exchange for a house nearer Pauline and the family. True, Alan and his mates were sorting out the move so she only needed enough for the hire of a van plus the cost of a crate of beer and fish and chips all round, but Hetty liked to pay her way.

Once the news got around that Mrs Lawrence was well enough to see people, the village began to arrive with small gifts: books or flowers or homemade cakes and sweets. Someone brought a handkerchief exqui-sitely embroidered with her name. Ann was frequently moved to tears by such kindness. Louise, a bit put out at first at the never-ending stream of well-wishers, eventually got to quite enjoy the company. She would put the kettle on, get a cake out and make people welcome. Assorted dogs also came and went. Louise, never previously interested in animals, got so fond of Candy she seriously thought of getting a pet herself.

But all of this was daytime business. After dark things were more difficult. This was the most painful time for the two women. The time when their friendship, which was to endure for the rest of their lives, was truly forged.

Louise had asked advice from the hospital almoner before collecting her friend. She had been told to expect possible sleepless nights and instructed on how to cope with nightmares as well as what was described as post-traumatic stress. But, to her immense relief, Ann remembered nothing of the attack or even of driving into Causton. The last thing she said she could recall was knocking on the door of Lionel's study to tell him lunch was ready. The one thing Louise had not been prepared for and found hard to cope with was Ann's overwhelming sense of guilt and remorse.

Ann simply could not rid herself of the conviction that she could have prevented the whole tragic business if only she had had the strength of mind to stand up to her husband in the matter of Terry Jackson. She had known from the first that there was something danger-ous about him. This fear had made her refuse to have the man in the house yet she had not had the courage to demand that he be banished entirely. If only she had . . . So Ann had wept and blamed herself and Louise had comforted her and assured her she was blameless.

This wretched scenario was repeated day after day. Louise listened sympathetically at first even though she considered such protestations of guilt to be quite unfounded. Then they began to seem to her neurotic. Eventually, when her endless assurances seemed hardly to be listened to, she had got angry. Concealed her anger then couldn't conceal it. Showed it and Ann got even more upset. Then Ann got angry.

Between them, helped by an awful lot of wine, they gradually washed with their tears, and hung out to dry, their deepest and most secret fears and longings. Ann wept for her years of loneliness and out of a passionate regret for a sterile half-life, Louise for the failure of a marriage she had thought made in heaven, for the loss of the brother she had known and for the sad, shambling counterfeit that had taken his place. For both of them, Louise so austere, aloof and cynical, and Ann so repressed, shy and anxious, this emotional exposure was a new and rather alarming experience.

Afterwards they were reserved, even a bit cool with each other. Several days were spent like this but the memory of their previous closeness was always there, a subterranean warmth, and gradually they relaxed again into comfortable familiarity.

They talked about money. Neither woman would have any serious worries although Louise would be by far the better off. Goshawk Freres had finally agreed on the amount for her golden handshake. Although somewhat depleted by litigation fees, it was still handsome. Her share of the Holland Park house, now sold, was over two hundred thousand pounds. And, sooner rather than later, she would be working again.

Ann was unsure that she would ever be working. The vivid longings for a new life, the daydreams which had seemed so exciting and realisable when she had been driving along in the sunshine towards Causton singing 'Penny Lane' had been wiped from her mind by the blow she had received. But the memory of her husband's scathing remarks had not. Didn't she know that these days people were made to retire at forty? As she had never had to cope with real life, how on earth could she possibly ever expect to do a real job?

Louise was furious when she heard all this. Ann was

barely middle-aged, very intelligent, a pleasure to look at (or would be when Louise had finished with her), and she could do anything in the world she wanted to do. So there. Ann smiled and said she would have to see how things went.

The Old Rectory, the estate agent promised, would make a very good price especially as it had what he called 'a granny flat'. The income from her trust fund, which now supported one person instead of two adults plus a steady stream of hangers-on and an old, infirm car would be more than adequate for her simple needs.

Largely because of the terrible disaster Lionel's actions had brought upon both herself and Louise, Ann was weaned without too much difficulty from her plan to buy him somewhere to live and to offer financial support. At first she had protested, saying she couldn't give him nothing. But, as Louise pointed out, even if she gave him nothing it was still ten times more than he had ever given her. And when Louise heard that Ann was also determined to set up a proper, inflation-proof pension for Hetty, she explained that accomplishing both and getting another house for herself was out of the question.

Ann visited the Old Rectory only once in the company of her solicitor. She selected the few pieces of furniture and personal things that she wished to keep and he arranged for them to be stored and for everything else to be sold. The whole transaction took less than an hour and she could not wait to get away. They also briefly discussed her will which was kept at his office. She intended to make a new one and they made an appointment for early the next month.

As things fell out, Ann never saw Lionel again. By

the time he got round to visiting the hospital she had recovered enough to tell her doctor she could not cope with even a moment of his company and admission was refused. He did not show up a second time.

A letter from Lucy and Breakbean, Causton's only legal aid solicitors, suggesting he was entitled to half a share of the Old Rectory was answered by Ann's solicitor, Taylor Reading, in no uncertain terms. A threat of further action on Lionel's part came to nothing. The following December Ann had rather a pathetic Christmas card giving an address in Slough, to which she did not respond. And that was that, really.

A few years later someone who knew Lionel told Ann they had seen him as they were leaving the National Theatre after an evening performance. Once more wearing his dog collar, he was helping to give out soup and sandwiches to the homeless on the Embankment. But it was only a glimpse and they admitted later they could easily have been mistaken.

CHAPTER THIRTEEN

The actual date of Tom and Joyce Barnaby's silver wedding fell on Sunday, 12th September. But as, like most people, they had married on Saturday they decided they would rather celebrate the day itself. And anyway, as Cully pointed out, any merrymaking worth its salt would surely stretch to cover both.

The day dawned, rather chilly and with only a small amount of watery sunshine. It was a funny morning and an awkward afternoon. The time dragged. After breakfast Barnaby put the crockery in the dishwasher and Joyce went to have her hair done. When she came back they had coffee and ploughed through the Saturday papers and it still wasn't time for lunch.

'Do you like my hair like this?'

'It's fine.'

'I thought, as it was such a special day, I should have something different.'

'It looks lovely.'

'I don't like it.'

'It's fine.'

'I liked it the old way.' Joyce gave a sort of moan. Kicked the papers off the sofa and put her feet up. Then put them down again.

'I wish it was eight o'clock,' said Barnaby.

'Well, it isn't eight o'clock. It's twenty to twelve.'

'When are we going to have our presents, again?'

'Seven, when the kids come and we open the champagne.'

'Can I have mine now?'

'No.'

Barnaby sighed, folded the arts section of the *Independent*, went into the hall, put on his scarf and old jacket and went outside. He got a border fork from the garden shed and started loosening the earth around the herbaceous perennials. Then he got his comfrey bucket and poured the foul-smelling liquid around the roots.

The trouble with today was, he decided, that it had been invested with a weight of romantic and sentimental relevance that it was just not equipped to carry. It *was* a special day, granted, but it was also an ordinary day to be lived in a comfortable, ordinary manner.

Breakfast in bed, which he could hardly remember having in his life, was not a success. Joyce brought him a tray with a lovely rose in a crystal vase and he sat wedged bolt upright with pillows against the headboard, trying to Flora his croissant without spilling the coffee.

Joyce sat next to him with her tray, eating grapefruit, shielding the side of it with her hand so the juice would not squirt all over the place and saying, more than once, 'Isn't this nice?' Reaching across the bed to turn the radio on, she knocked the rose over.

And so it had continued. Barnaby suddenly realised how his daughter felt during the days when she was coming up to a first night. Cully had described it to him once. Trying to sleep as late as you could, dawdling through breakfast, drifting down to the theatre at midday even though there was nothing to do and you would only be in the way. Finding someone to have lunch with, maybe taking in a movie then coming out with three more hours to kill. Trying to rest, going over your lines. The last hour rushing past you like the wind.

He and Joyce had slipped into the same sort of limbo. It was ridiculous. Why couldn't it be just like any normal Saturday? Barnaby saw his wife looking through the kitchen window. He waved and she responded with a rather taut smile, touching her hair. He started to sing as he returned the bucket to the comfrey patch, 'What a difference a day makes . . .'

The crate in the garage had disappeared. He had been getting quite excited about that. When he pointed out it was no longer there, Joyce told him it was a chair belonging to a member of her drama group who was moving house and didn't have room for it. Yesterday the man he had given it to had come and picked it up. So that was that.

Barnaby packed his bucket with more comfrey, filled it with water and started cutting back a huge cotoneaster that was getting vastly above itself. The rest of the morning passed so pleasantly it seemed no time at all before Joyce was calling him in for lunch.

Afterwards she said she had to go out so Barnaby dozed, watched some sport on the box, dozed some more and made himself a cup of tea at tea time. Joyce didn't come back till nearly six. She had been to the movies, she said, *Wag the Dog*, which was so brilliant they must get the video.

Barnaby did not ask why he hadn't been invited to the movies. They were each getting through this odd, unfamiliar sort of day in their own manner, himself by doing what he usually did on his day off but sighing rather more, Joyce filling in time by going out and about.

By six o'clock both were in their bedroom getting dressed. Barnaby had on a rather stiffly starched white shirt and dark blue suit plus waistcoat. As he was pulling on his shiny black Oxfords, he watched Joyce putting on her make-up in front of a magnifying mirror, brightly illuminated by an Anglepoise. She was wearing a coffee-coloured petticoat trimmed with Viennese lace which Cully had long ago christened Mum's Freudian slip.

It suddenly struck her husband that his anniversary gift, so carefully thought of, beautifully designed and lavishly wrapped, was nothing but a frivol. Luxurious but of no real use whatsoever. Where in the world, apart from illustrations in old books of fairy tales and thirties movies, did women sit holding a mirror in front of their face with one hand and combing their hair with the other? They needed both hands and an excellent light. He sighed.

'For heaven's sake,' said Joyce.

She had bought a new suit for the occasion. Cyclamen with black braid. Chanel-ish. The colour looked harder than it had in the shop and her lipstick didn't match. Her earrings were already pinching but they were the only ones that looked right. Bearing in mind that make-up had to last the evening through, she had put on rather more than usual and now wondered if she should take it off and start again. Everyone said the older you were, the less you needed. She only just stopped herself sighing as well. That's all the evening needed. Two of them at it.

Barnaby, who had been looking out of the window on and off for the past twenty minutes, said, 'They're here.'

The first bottle of Mumm Cordon Rouge '90 was opened and they all had a glass. Cully and Nicolas cried, 'Congratulations!' and handed their presents over. Joyce received a silver locket, engraved on the back with the date of her wedding and a tiny picture of herself and Tom inside. It was quite unfamiliar and must have been cut out of a holiday snap that Cully had taken years ago. Barnaby had some plain square silver cufflinks, likewise engraved, in a blue leather box.

Joyce gave her husband a leather Filofax with a thin silver plate screwed into a specially reinforced front cover. It showed his name, inscribed in beautiful copperplate, and the dates 1973–1998. Barnaby said it was very handsome and at last he could get organised. Cully said it was about time. They drained their glasses, had them re-filled and Joyce opened her present.

She gasped with surprise and pleasure, her indrawn breath an 'ahhh' of happiness.

'Tom! It's the most . . . beautiful thing . . . I ever . . . ever . . .'

She kissed him. Barnaby smiled and gave his wife a hug. Watched her hold up the mirror at arm's length, just as he had pictured her doing in his imagination. But the kitchen's harsh fluorescent light was not flattering. A shadow passed over Joyce's face. She had too much make-up on. She did not look in the mirror as she did in her mind. She looked older and rather hard. Haggard even. She turned to her daughter.

'I don't think this lipstick suits me.'

'Mum, nothing suits anybody in this dreadful light. I look at least a hundred.'

'And I,' said Nicolas gallantly, 'look like the creature from the black lagoon.'

'Speaking of lights, shouldn't we turn the ones in the garden on, Dad? Safety and all?'

'I suppose.' He had rigged up a series of seven lamps concealed in the greenery. They were connected to a dimmer switch which he turned slowly on to full. The effect was magically theatrical. He could have been looking at a wood outside Athens, with Oberon and Titania waiting in the wings. As he got back to the kitchen, the doorbell rang and Cully chose that moment to make a quick phone call.

They were taking a cab to Uxbridge Tube, going into town by Underground and back by taxi. The nearest station to Monmouth Street was Tottenham Court Road and at eight o'clock Saturday night both the place and the pavements outside were jam packed with rowdy people all determined to have a good time. It was only ten minutes' walk to Mon Plaisir but seemed longer.

They were welcomed warmly, shown to their table and given a menu. Barnaby looked around him. He hadn't expected the place to look the same – that would have been foolish after twenty-five years – but he was surprised at how small it seemed. He couldn't remember where they had sat before though he did recall looking out of the window occasionally and being sorry for the people walking by because they could never, ever, if they lived to be a hundred be as happy as he was.

He looked across at Joyce but she was reading the menu. He studied his own and saw that neither boeuf bourguignon nor raspberry tart was available. Barnaby began to feel rather resentful. They were both classic French dishes. In a French bistro you'd think they'd be on offer.

'They don't have steak au poivre, Tom.' Joyce was smiling at him across the table. She had slipped her high heels off and was rubbing the soles of her feet against her calves to warm them up.

'Sorry?'

'It's what we had before,' Joyce explained to the others. 'And apricot tart.'

'They still have that,' said Cully.

Barnaby said nothing. He was realising that this whole idea, put forward by Nicolas and leapt at so enthusiastically by himself, had been a mistake. Joyce had been right to hesitate, himself wrong to dissuade her. The past was indeed another country where they did things differently.

He ordered onion and cream tart with green salad, red mullet wrapped in fennel and served with tiny potatoes and mange tout, and apples with Calvados. Joyce had the same. Cully and Nicolas had mushrooms à la Grecque, pork trotters with mustard sauce, haricots verts and pommes frites followed by pears with crème Chantilly. They drank Muscadet and Sandeman claret.

It wasn't until they were halfway through the main course and conversation had almost petered out that Barnaby realised why. Cully and Nicolas were not talking about themselves. Apart from pleasantries about the food, assurances about what a nice time they were having and some polite inquiries from Cully to her dad as to how the garden was keeping, they had said next to nothing. Barnaby decided to gee things up a bit.

'So, Nicolas. Have you heard anything about casting yet?'

'Yes!' cried Nicolas. 'I'm playing Dolabella in *Antony and Cleo*. Cough and a spit. I'm not even on till—'

'Nico.' Cully glared at him.

'Mm? Oh, yes – sorry.'

'What?' said Barnaby, looking from one to the other. 'What's going on?'

'We're not talking about ourselves,' said Cully.

'Why on earth not?' Joyce stared at her daughter, amazed.

'Because it's your special evening. Yours and Dad's.'

'That's right,' said Nicolas, rather less firmly.

'Don't be so silly,' said Joyce. 'If all I was going to do was sit and talk to your father all night we might as well have stayed at home.'

'You got that, Nicolas?' asked Barnaby. 'So let's hear it for Dolabella.'

'He's also understudying Lepidus.' Enthusiasm warmed Cully's voice. 'A much bigger part with some great lines.'

'My favourite, Tom – very apropos, actually – is "'Tis not a time for private stomaching".'

This rather contrived witticism went down a treat. Cully laughed, Nicolas laughed. Joyce, well into her third large glass of Muscadet, laughed so much she got hiccups. Barnaby, under cover of his nicely ironed napkin, looked at his watch.

Going home in the cab, more than a little what Jax would have called 'swacked', Barnaby reflected on the disappointing dullness of the day. Not that it was the day's fault. Poor old day. What was it after all but an ordinary common or garden stretch of time that had had totally unrealistic expectations placed on it? No wonder it couldn't come up to scratch.

Barnaby sighed and heard the wife of his bosom growl softly. Ran his finger round his tight collar to loosen it and noticed Joyce had taken her shoes off. He wished he could take his shoes off. And everything else come to that. Get into his old gardening trousers and a comfortable sweater. Still, look on the bright side – it would soon be Sunday morning. He was allowed bacon and egg on Sunday.

The other three were still chatting away. Barnaby was pleased but surprised when Joyce had explained that Cully and Nicolas were coming home with them and sleeping over. They had not done that for a couple of years – the last time being when they were between flats with their stuff in storage and a six-week wait for their new place to become empty.

It was gone midnight when the cab pulled up at 17 Arbury Crescent. Twelve fifteen on Sunday, 13 September. The actual date. A second chance, as it were, to transform the ordinary into the extraordinary. Perhaps because of the wine, perhaps because of a sudden rush of memory, a concentrated longing to turn the moment round and maybe even transform it, possessed Barnaby. He reached out and touched his wife's arm.

'I just wanted to say—'

But she was talking to Nicolas. He was paying for the cab and needed extra change for the tip. Barnaby fumbled in his pocket saying, 'I've got that.'

'All done, darling.'

Joyce had handed five pounds over and was getting out of the cab. Around them, silence. Barnaby's neighbours had retired, the other five houses that made up the crescent were dark.

As he put his key in the front door, Barnaby came to a decision. He would let the day go. He would let the whole idea of celebration go. He was a 58-year-old man, not a child to expect magic and fireworks just because he was living through a specially significant twenty-four hours. Anyway, wasn't all of his life significant in some way or other? The very ordinariness of it was in itself cause for celebration. He had everything a person could possibly want. Cultivate your garden, he told himself sternly. Grow up. Count your blessings.

In the kitchen the dirty glasses and champagne bottles were still on the table. Everybody took off their coats. Joyce asked if anyone wanted a cup of tea. Cully yawned and said if she didn't lie down soon she'd fall down and Nicolas said the evening had been great and thanked Tom and Joyce for a wonderful time. Barnaby gravitated to the kitchen window and gazed out at his garden. Enjoyed the beautiful illumined plants, was impressed by the magnetic pull of dark shadows.

He blinked, looked and looked again. Something was standing in the middle of the lawn. A very large thing, glowing with a pure dazzling radiance. He shifted his face closer to the glass, squinting. Became vaguely aware that someone was opening the kitchen door and wandered outside.

It was a lawn mower. A silver lawn mower. Every bit of it had been painted silver. Handle, wheels, grass box

– the lot. Attached to the crosspiece of the handle by shining satin ribbons were lots and lots and lots of silver balloons.

Barnaby tilted back his head and looked at them, bobbing and moving gently against a dark sky, soft with stars. The heart shapes had writing on them which for some reason, just at this minute, he couldn't quite read.

And there was music flooding from the open windows of his sitting room from which his daughter and her husband leaned out, smiling. The Hollies, 'The Air That I Breathe'.

'I think I'm coming down with a cold,' said Barnaby to his wife who was walking slowly across the grass in his direction. He produced a large white hanky and trumpeted into it.

Joyce took his hand and murmured softly, 'If I could make a wish, I think I'd pass . . . can't think of anything I need . . . no cigarettes, no sleep, no . . . Oh, Tom! I've forgotten.'

'No light . . .'

'That's it. No light, no sound, nothing to eat, no books to read . . .'

'Making love with you . . .'

He put his arms round her then and she leaned into him, resting her head on his shoulder. They stood quietly as more and more stars gathered, holding fast against the relentless movement of time that changes all things. And then they began to dance.

Now you can buy any of these other bestselling
Headline books from your bookshop or
direct from the publisher.

FREE P&P AND UK DELIVERY
(Overseas and Ireland £3.50 per book)

A Place of Safety	Caroline Graham	£6.99
Running Scared	Ann Granger	£5.99
Shades of Murder	Ann Granger	£5.99
Biting the Moon	Martha Grimes	£5.99
The Lamorna Wink	Martha Grimes	£5.99
Tip Off	John Francome	£6.99
The Cat Who Robbed a Bank	Lilian Jackson Braun	£5.99
Screen Savers	Quintin Jardine	£5.99
Thursday Legends	Quintin Jardine	£5.99
A Chemical Prison	Barbara Nadel	£5.99
Stronger Than Death	Manda Scott	£5.99
Oxford Shift	Veronica Stallwood	£5.99
Fleeced	Georgina Wroe	£6.99

TO ORDER SIMPLY CALL THIS NUMBER

01235 400 414

or e-mail orders@bookpoint.co.uk

Prices and availability subject to change without notice.